BALTIMORE

The Curse Bells

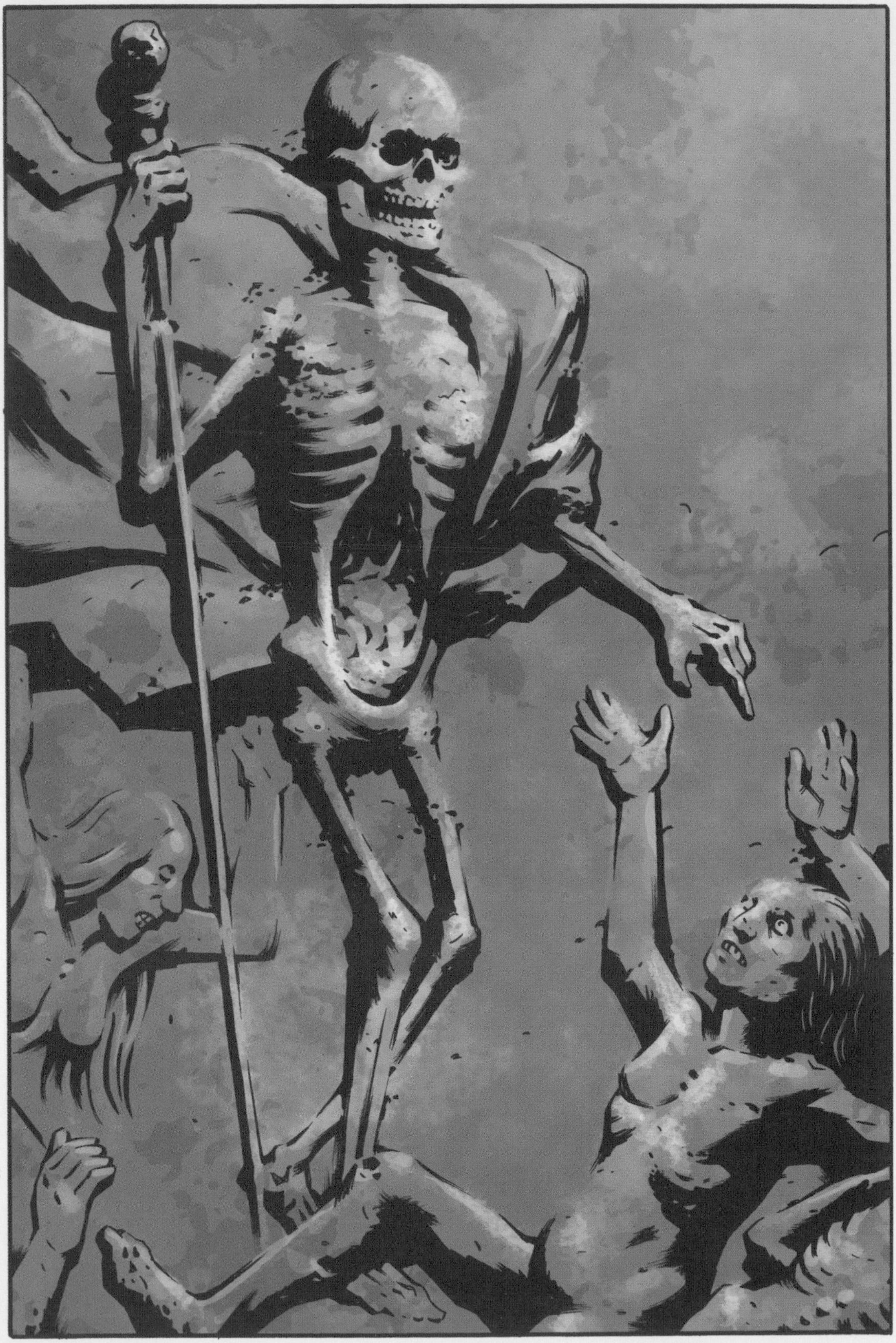

BALTIMORE™
THE CURSE BELLS

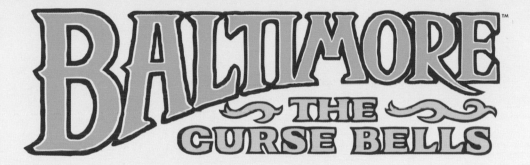

VOLUME TWO

Story by
MIKE MIGNOLA
CHRISTOPHER GOLDEN

Art by
BEN STENBECK

Colors by
DAVE STEWART

Letters by
CLEM ROBINS

Cover Art by
MIKE MIGNOLA with **DAVE STEWART**

Editor **SCOTT ALLIE**
Assistant Editor **DANIEL CHABON**
Collection Designer **AMY ARENDTS**
Publisher **MIKE RICHARDSON**

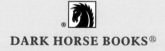

DARK HORSE BOOKS®

*For the great Peter Cushing, whose hollow-cheeked spirit
certainly lives in (or haunts) these pages.*
—Mike Mignola

*For my brother, Jamie, who kept me company during
hundreds of Creature Double Features.*
—Christopher Golden

For Bernie Wrightson.
—Ben Stenbeck

Neil Hankerson *Executive Vice President* • Tom Weddle *Chief Financial Officer* • Randy Stradley *Vice President of Publishing* • Michael Martens *Vice President of Book Trade Sales* • Anita Nelson *Vice President of Business Affairs* • David Scroggy *Vice President of Product Development* • Dale LaFountain *Vice President of Information Technology* • Darlene Vogel *Senior Director of Print, Design, and Production* • Ken Lizzi *General Counsel* • Matt Parkinson *Senior Director of Marketing* • Davey Estrada *Editorial Director* • Scott Allie *Senior Managing Editor* • Chris Warner *Senior Books Editor* • Diana Schutz *Executive Editor* • Cary Grazzini *Director of Print and Development* • Lia Ribacchi *Art Director* • Cara Niece *Director of Scheduling*

Special thanks to Jason Hvam

DarkHorse.com

Published by Dark Horse Books
A division of Dark Horse Comics, Inc.
10956 SE Main Street
Milwaukie, OR 97222

First edition: June 2012
ISBN 978-1-59582-674-9

3   5   7   9   10   8   6   4   2

Printed in China

This volume collects the *Baltimore: The Curse Bells* comic-book series,
issues #1–#5, published by Dark Horse Comics.

A WORLD OF CHILLED SHADOWS

by

JOE R. LANSDALE

THERE'S NOT A LOT THESE DAYS creepier than politics, but here's something that is, and the good thing about it is when it's over you can enjoy it again without it messing with your life, unlike politics.

But that's not entirely true if it hits you the way it hit me. *The Curse Bells* will continue to mess with my life, my head, but the messing is of a darkly entertaining kind: hot-flash visuals like someone pulling an old strip of film through the brain, flossing into it eerie images so deep they leave scar tissue. What we have here is a perfect dark wedding of word and picture with the shade of Bram Stoker as best man, for the feelings I had while reading *The Curse Bells* were akin to the feelings I had when I first read Stoker's *Dracula* on a wet day in Austin, Texas, in the early seventies. I was living in a co-op then, a few months away from a collapsing marriage—thank goodness, or I wouldn't have met my current, wonderful wife. The co-op was a kind of shared housing where we had our own rooms but did chores to keep the place up. I remember I was alone that day and I also remember being sick of school and sick of the fact I was going to the University of Texas instead of writing, which is what I knew I was born to do, and sick of washing other people's dishes who didn't wash mine, so I skipped class and hid out in my

room, settled into bed with *Dracula* (the book, not the creature of the night) on a wet day with the air conditioner turned up so high it was as cold as a polar bear's nose. I cocooned myself beneath the blankets, my head and book and hands barely poking out, opened the book, and was instantly invited into Bram Stoker's gothic world through the aid of what Tarzan called little bugs—meaning words, of course.

This series, *The Curse Bells*, puts me in the exact same frame of mind as *Dracula* did on that fine and wonderful day so long ago, though it uses both words and visuals.

I don't mean the story reminds me of *Dracula* altogether, though they are kissing cousins, and may in fact be more intimate than that. But like *Dracula*, *The Curse Bells* is the kind of narrative that grabs and pulls you into the tale, pulls you down deep and dark as a child that has fallen into a well.

Reading it also brought to mind the Universal horror films of old, with their wonderfully gothic sets and shifty-eyed peasants and shambling monsters and fluttering bats. This film on paper, this comic, goes where your mind went when you saw those films as a kid, goes where the film didn't, but you think it did, because at that age your mind is fresh and open and full of light and shadow, all of it moving about in savage flickers, having not yet settled and found its civilized position. For everything you see with your eyes at that age, your mind's eye sees a hundred times more. Our personalities and imaginations are forming then; there are open doors through which light and shadow come. None of those doors have closed due to age and experience.

When we get older it's said that nothing is as fresh and bold and enticing as it once was, but I beg to differ. Not all of us closed those doors. The creators involved with this beautifully tantalizing creep of an adventure certainly did not close theirs. And frankly, though my imaginative doors are still wide open, if they weren't, this beautifully strange work would kick them wide open again. Isn't that the job of all great art, to kick open doors to light and shadow and let us view something that otherwise we might not see?

I think it is.

And this fine piece of work sure does it. I was absorbed by the story written by Mike Mignola and Christopher Golden, entranced by the art of Ben Stenbeck, the setups, the simple use of color. No cute and weird angles and a story you can't follow because you don't know which panel you're supposed to be reading. No real tricks are used or are needed here. You don't have to distract from your limitations when you have pure storytelling in your grasp.

There's a lot of cool characterization and attention to detail, and I want to point that out, but this is one of those magic things. Somewhat inexplicable and wonderful and strange: a beast from within. The best thing I can say is the appeal of this kind of story is primal. It's tapping into something that comes not from purely conscious consideration, but from the depths of the subconscious. A lot of internal human fears are here, made into story without obvious intent of sculpture. No chip marks are on the statue.

My only dislike of this series is how swiftly it ended. I was so caught up in it I breezed through the first four issues breathless; then realized, my goodness, they forgot to send me the fifth. I wrote Chris Golden a hasty e-mail, and he was able to supply me with the last issue via return e-mail, and I promptly read it, sitting at the computer.

Man, what a finale.

Okay. I'm starting to sound like a child that has discovered his first piece of candy.

So, enough. I dislike discussing a story too much, mine or anyone else's. I think it's like handling something beautiful, freshly painted, and having the paint come off in your hands. You don't want to do that. You want it to stay clean and bright, or in this case, dark in your mind.

Mike Mignola. Christopher Golden. You have a beautiful story. Ben Stenbeck. Dave Stewart. You have made simple sublime. Clem Robins, you cool letterer, you. Listen up, you guys. I just want to say one thing to you: You done good.

Oh hell, make it two things. The other: More, please.

Joe R. Lansdale
Nacogdoches, Texas
December 2011

CHAPTER ONE

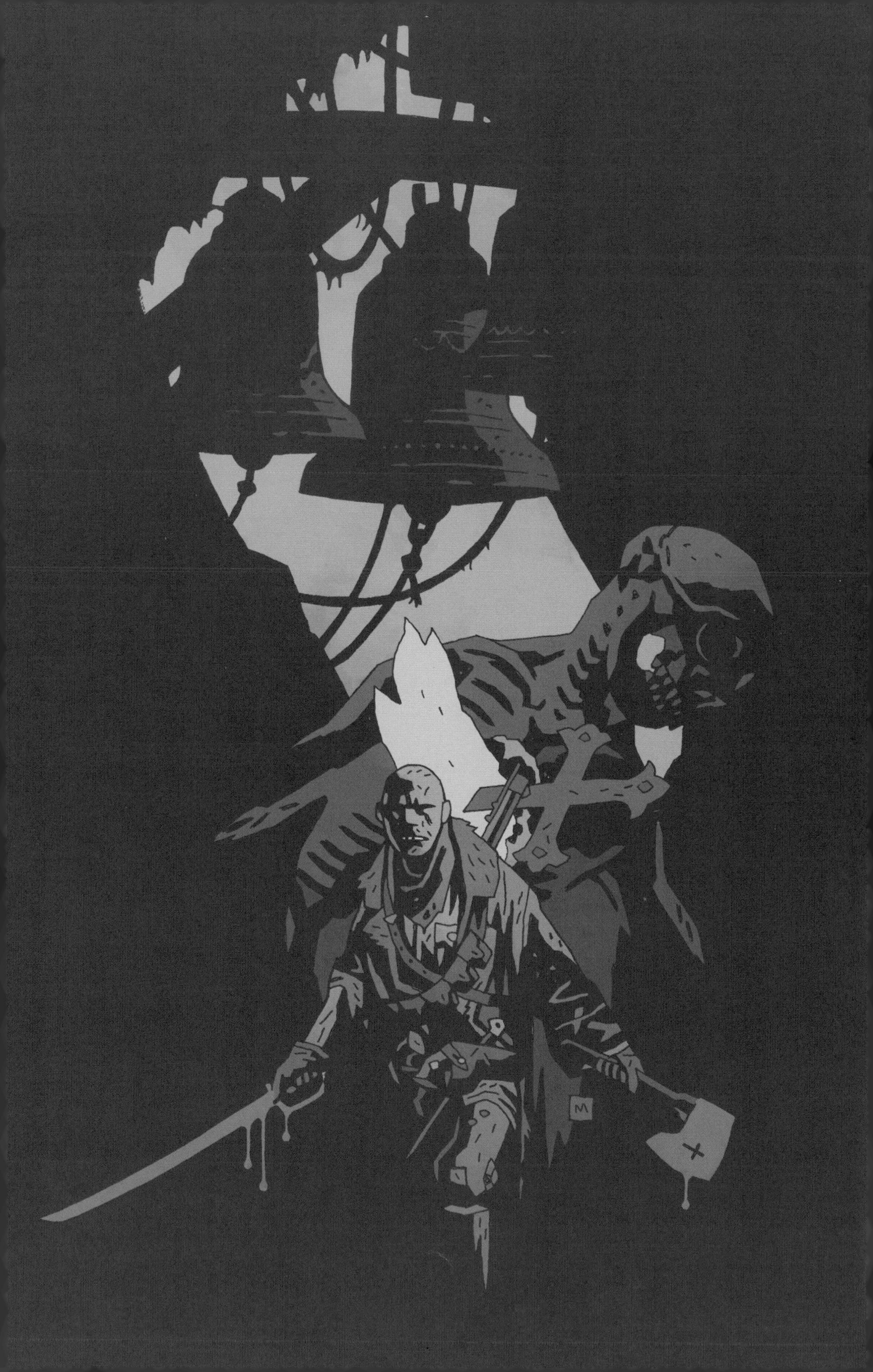

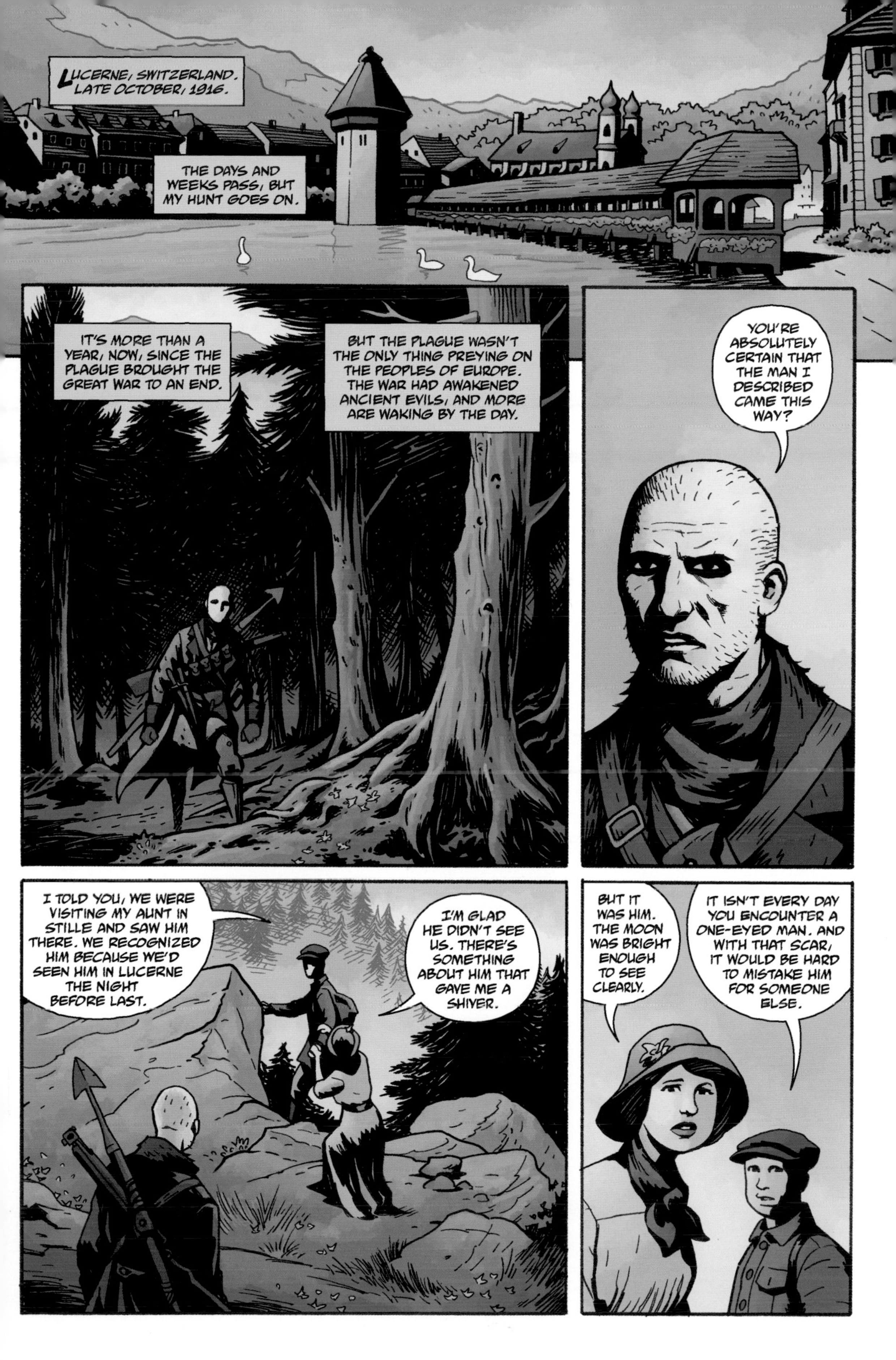
LUCERNE, SWITZERLAND. LATE OCTOBER, 1916.
THE DAYS AND WEEKS PASS, BUT MY HUNT GOES ON.
IT'S MORE THAN A YEAR, NOW, SINCE THE PLAGUE BROUGHT THE GREAT WAR TO AN END.
BUT THE PLAGUE WASN'T THE ONLY THING PREYING ON THE PEOPLES OF EUROPE. THE WAR HAD AWAKENED ANCIENT EVILS, AND MORE ARE WAKING BY THE DAY.
YOU'RE ABSOLUTELY CERTAIN THAT THE MAN I DESCRIBED CAME THIS WAY?
I TOLD YOU, WE WERE VISITING MY AUNT IN STILLE AND SAW HIM THERE. WE RECOGNIZED HIM BECAUSE WE'D SEEN HIM IN LUCERNE THE NIGHT BEFORE LAST.
I'M GLAD HE DIDN'T SEE US. THERE'S SOMETHING ABOUT HIM THAT GAVE ME A SHIVER.
BUT IT WAS HIM. THE MOON WAS BRIGHT ENOUGH TO SEE CLEARLY.
IT ISN'T EVERY DAY YOU ENCOUNTER A ONE-EYED MAN. AND WITH THAT SCAR, IT WOULD BE HARD TO MISTAKE HIM FOR SOMEONE ELSE.

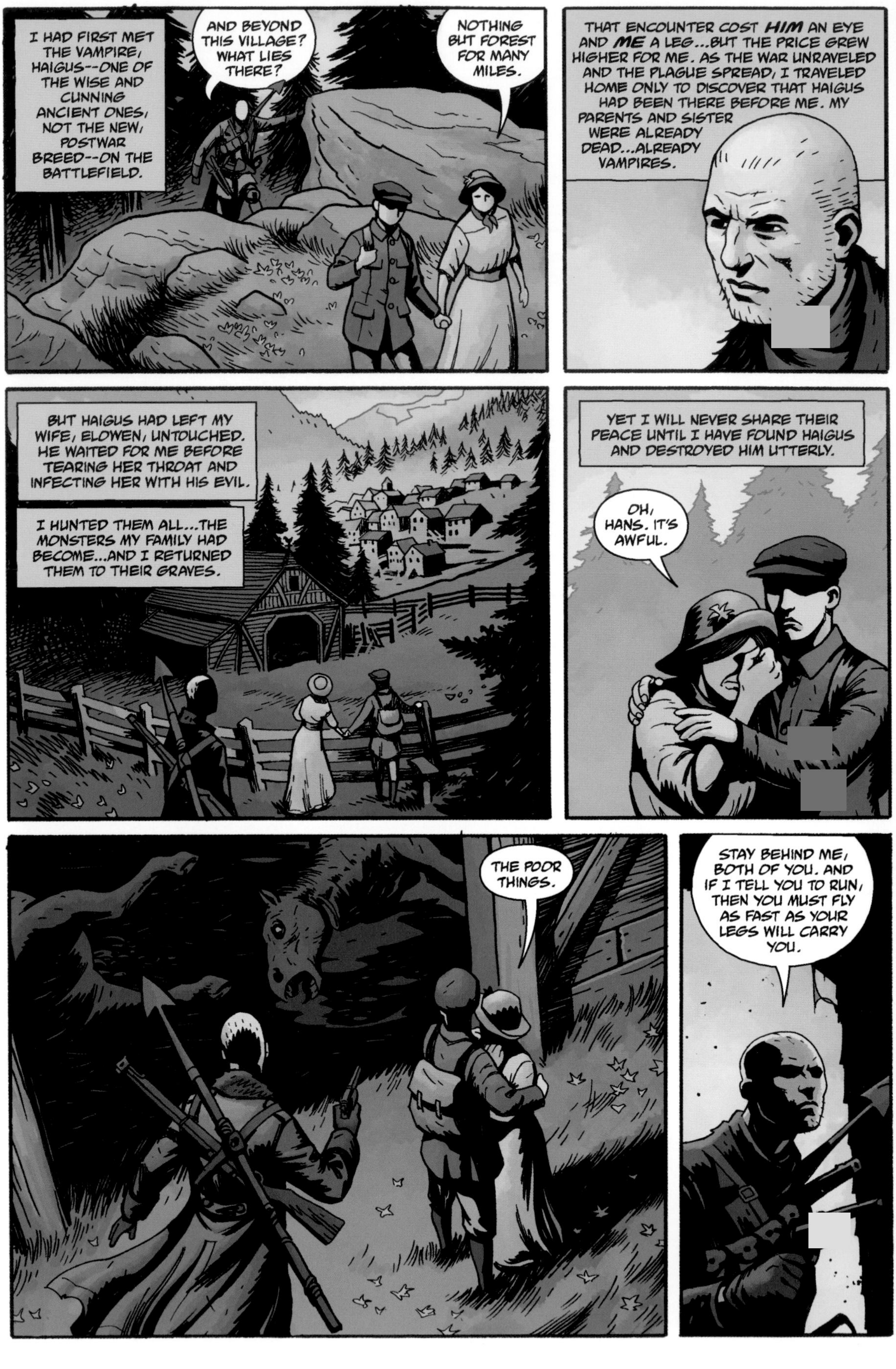
I HAD FIRST MET THE VAMPIRE, HAIGUS--ONE OF THE WISE AND CUNNING ANCIENT ONES, NOT THE NEW, POSTWAR BREED--ON THE BATTLEFIELD.
AND BEYOND THIS VILLAGE? WHAT LIES THERE?
NOTHING BUT FOREST FOR MANY MILES.
THAT ENCOUNTER COST HIM AN EYE AND ME A LEG...BUT THE PRICE GREW HIGHER FOR ME. AS THE WAR UNRAVELED AND THE PLAGUE SPREAD, I TRAVELED HOME ONLY TO DISCOVER THAT HAIGUS HAD BEEN THERE BEFORE ME. MY PARENTS AND SISTER WERE ALREADY DEAD...ALREADY VAMPIRES.
BUT HAIGUS HAD LEFT MY WIFE, ELOWEN, UNTOUCHED. HE WAITED FOR ME BEFORE TEARING HER THROAT AND INFECTING HER WITH HIS EVIL.
I HUNTED THEM ALL...THE MONSTERS MY FAMILY HAD BECOME...AND I RETURNED THEM TO THEIR GRAVES.
YET I WILL NEVER SHARE THEIR PEACE UNTIL I HAVE FOUND HAIGUS AND DESTROYED HIM UTTERLY.
OH, HANS. IT'S AWFUL.
THE POOR THINGS.
STAY BEHIND ME, BOTH OF YOU. AND IF I TELL YOU TO RUN, THEN YOU MUST FLY AS FAST AS YOUR LEGS WILL CARRY YOU.

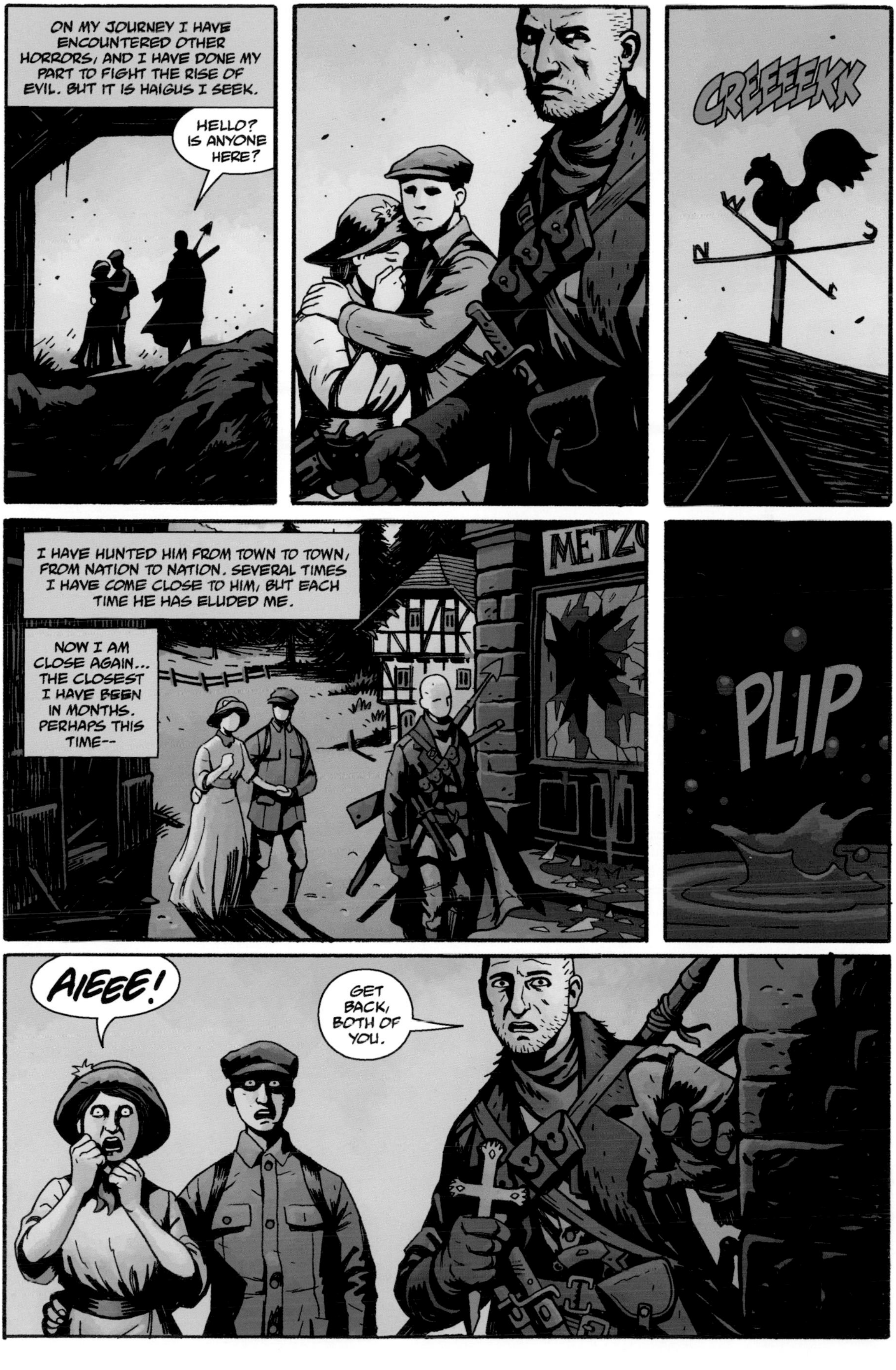
ON MY JOURNEY I HAVE ENCOUNTERED OTHER HORRORS, AND I HAVE DONE MY PART TO FIGHT THE RISE OF EVIL. BUT IT IS HAIGUS I SEEK.
HELLO? IS ANYONE HERE?
CREEEEKK
N
I HAVE HUNTED HIM FROM TOWN TO TOWN, FROM NATION TO NATION. SEVERAL TIMES I HAVE COME CLOSE TO HIM, BUT EACH TIME HE HAS ELUDED ME.
NOW I AM CLOSE AGAIN... THE CLOSEST I HAVE BEEN IN MONTHS. PERHAPS THIS TIME--
METZ
PLIP
AIEEE!
GET BACK, BOTH OF YOU.

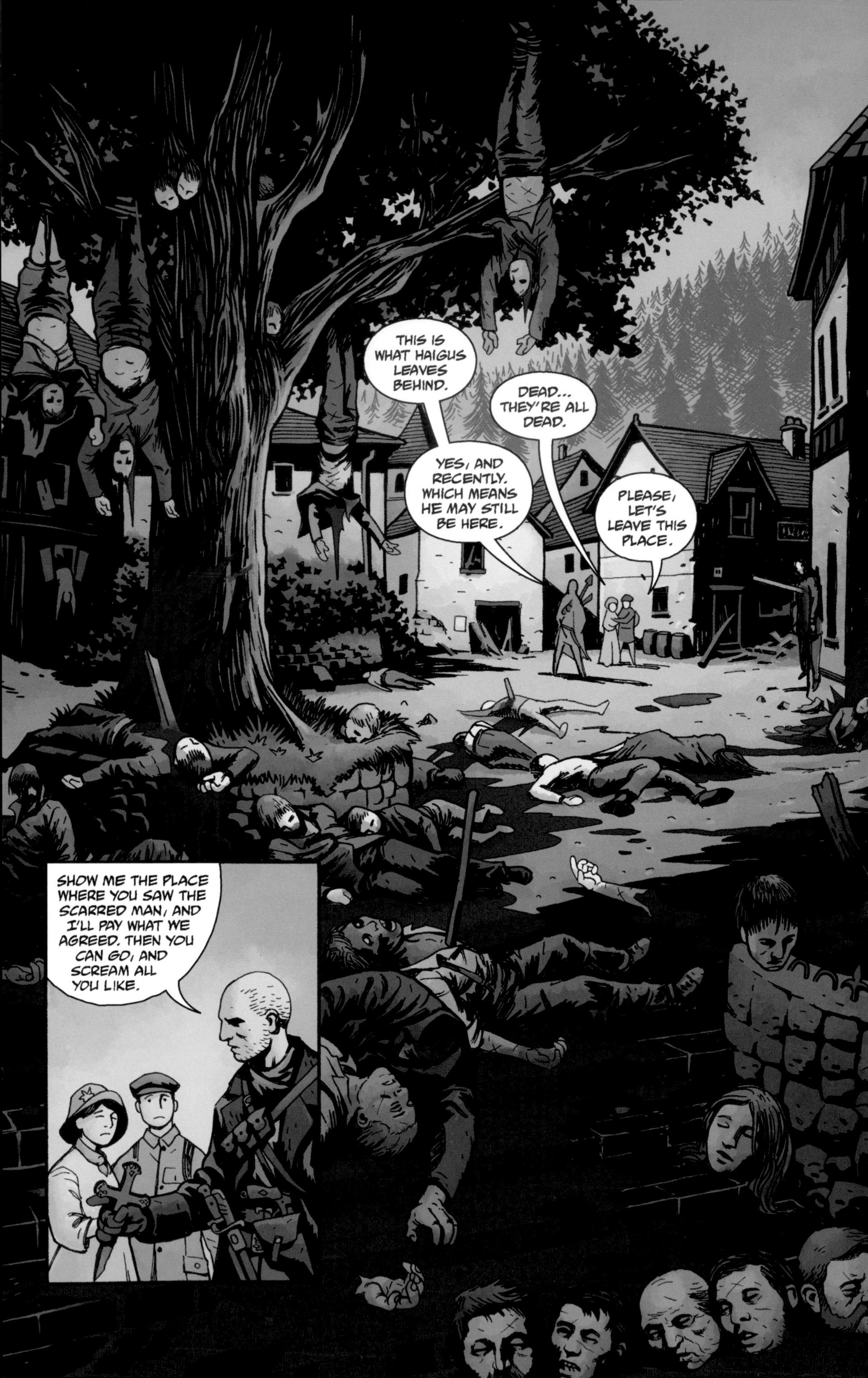
THIS IS WHAT HAIGUS LEAVES BEHIND.
DEAD... THEY'RE ALL DEAD.
YES, AND RECENTLY. WHICH MEANS HE MAY STILL BE HERE.
PLEASE, LET'S LEAVE THIS PLACE.
SHOW ME THE PLACE WHERE YOU SAW THE SCARRED MAN, AND I'LL PAY WHAT WE AGREED. THEN YOU CAN GO, AND SCREAM ALL YOU LIKE.

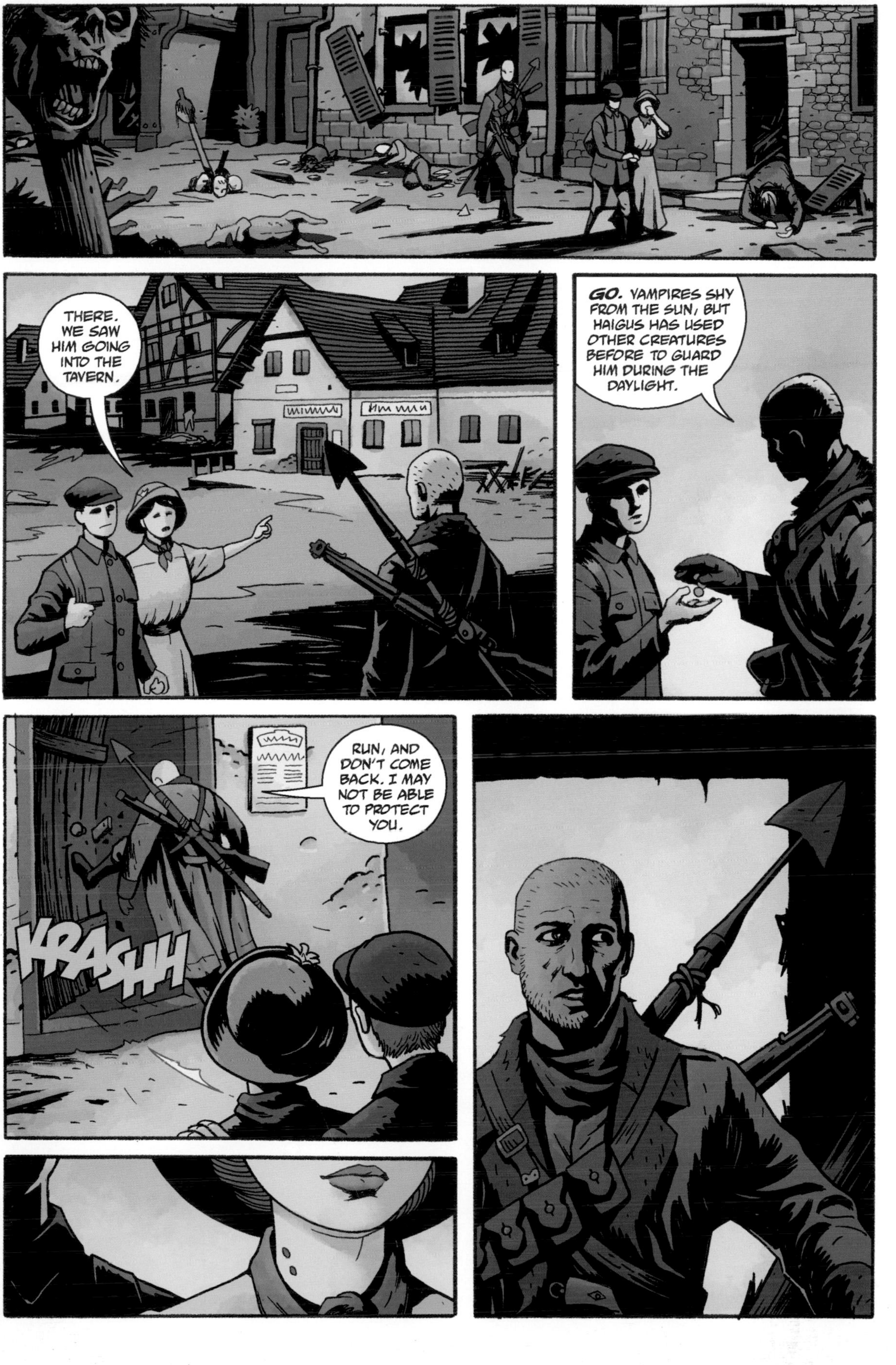

THERE. WE SAW HIM GOING INTO THE TAVERN.
GO. VAMPIRES SHY FROM THE SUN, BUT HAIGUS HAS USED OTHER CREATURES BEFORE TO GUARD HIM DURING THE DAYLIGHT.
RUN, AND DON'T COME BACK. I MAY NOT BE ABLE TO PROTECT YOU.
KRASHH

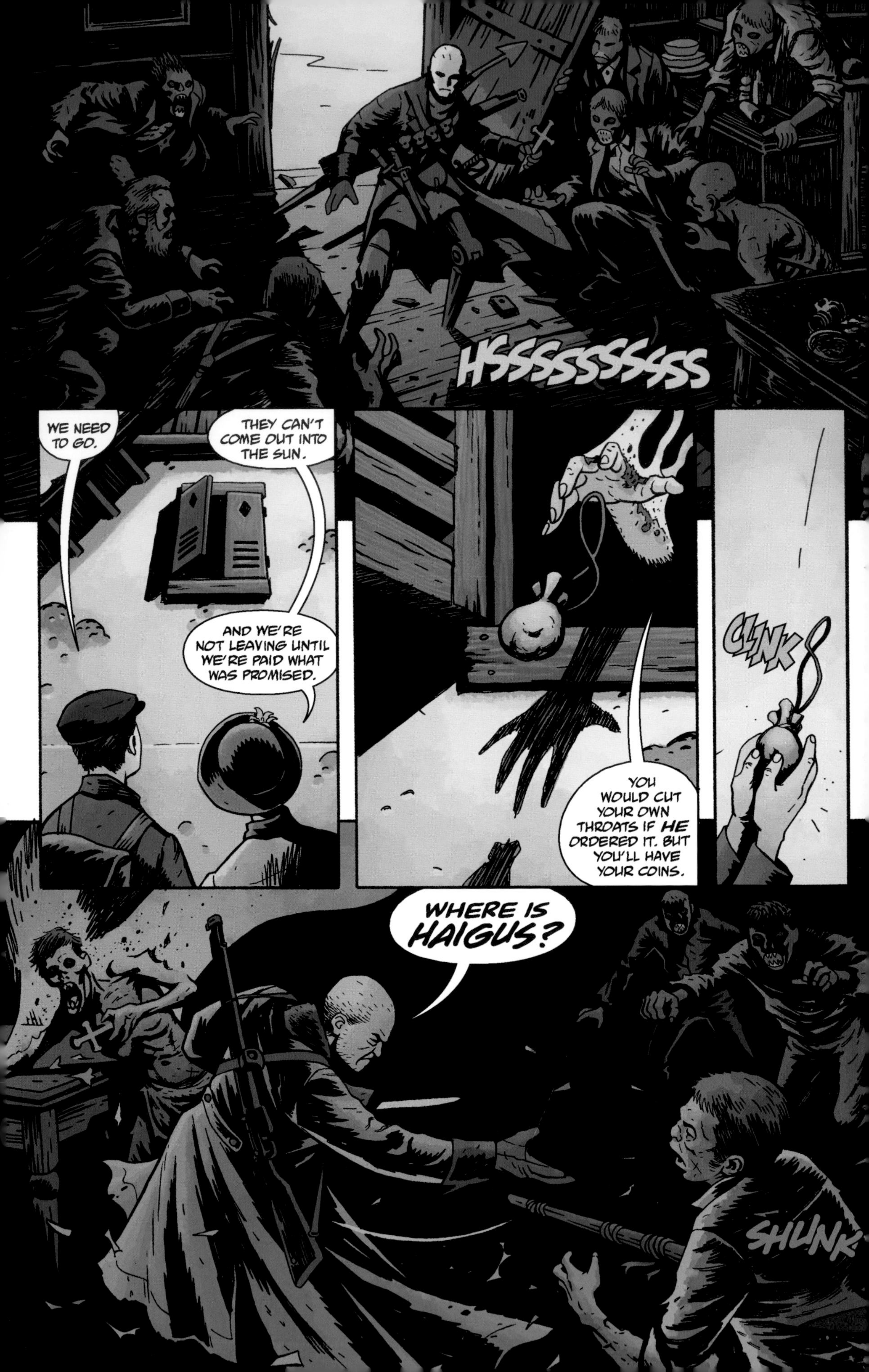
HSSSSSSSSS
WE NEED TO GO.
THEY CAN'T COME OUT INTO THE SUN.
AND WE'RE NOT LEAVING UNTIL WE'RE PAID WHAT WAS PROMISED.
YOU WOULD CUT YOUR OWN THROATS IF HE ORDERED IT. BUT YOU'LL HAVE YOUR COINS.
CLINK
WHERE IS HAIGUS?
SHUNK

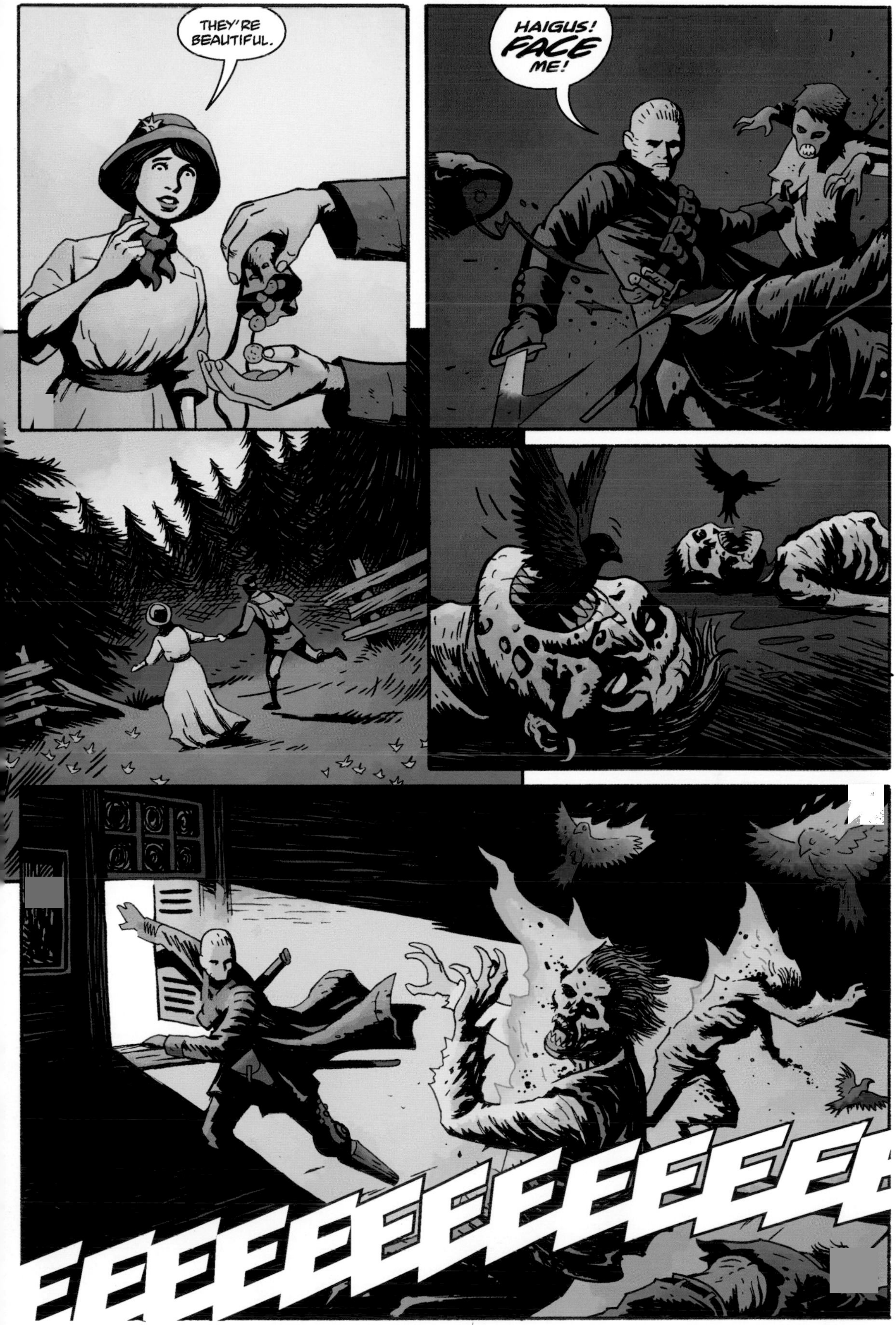
THEY'RE BEAUTIFUL.
HAIGUS! FACE ME!
EEEEEEEEEEEEEEEEE

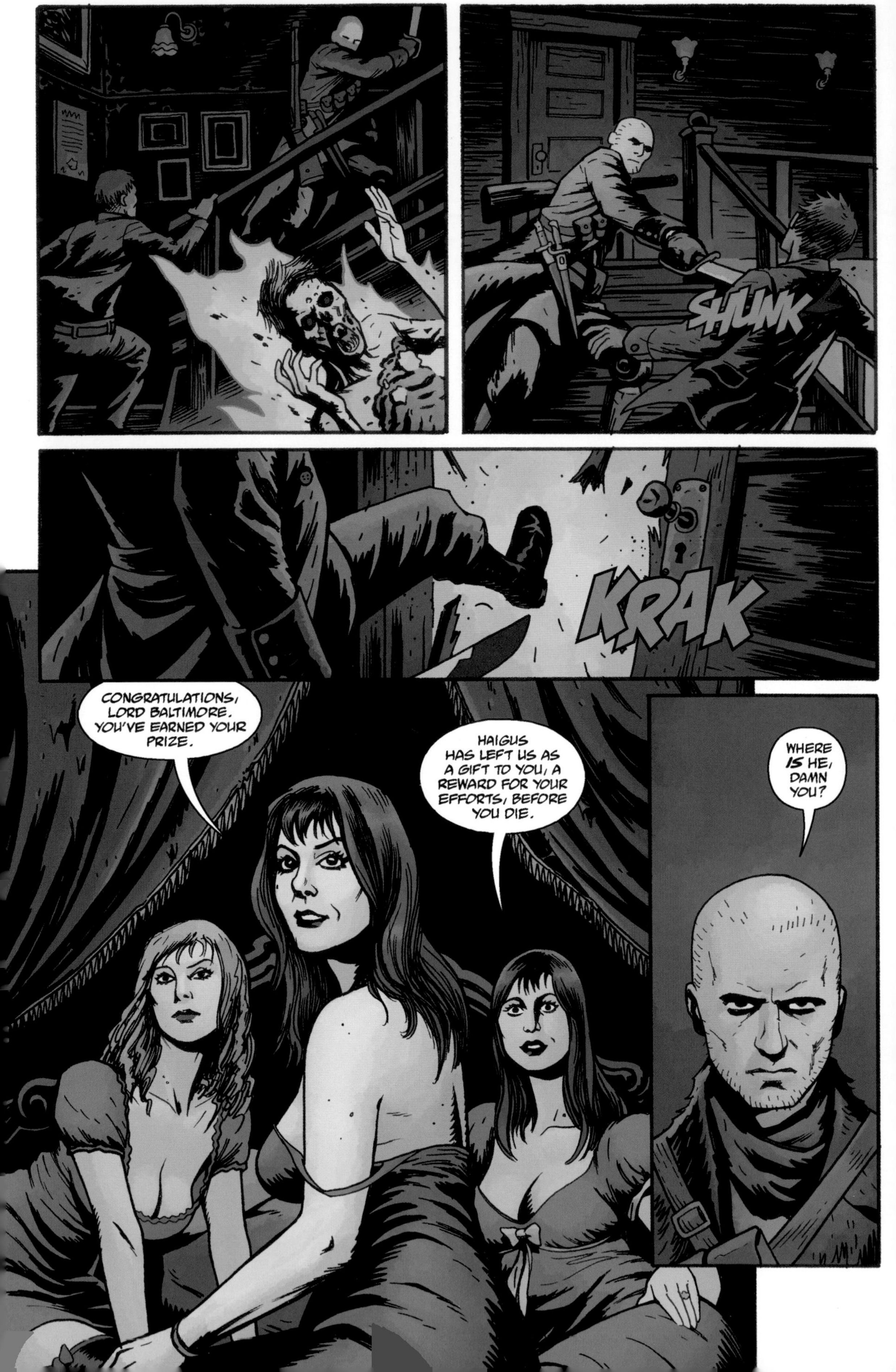
SHUNK
KRAK
CONGRATULATIONS, LORD BALTIMORE. YOU'VE EARNED YOUR PRIZE.
HAIGUS HAS LEFT US AS A GIFT TO YOU, A REWARD FOR YOUR EFFORTS, BEFORE YOU DIE.
WHERE IS HE, DAMN YOU?

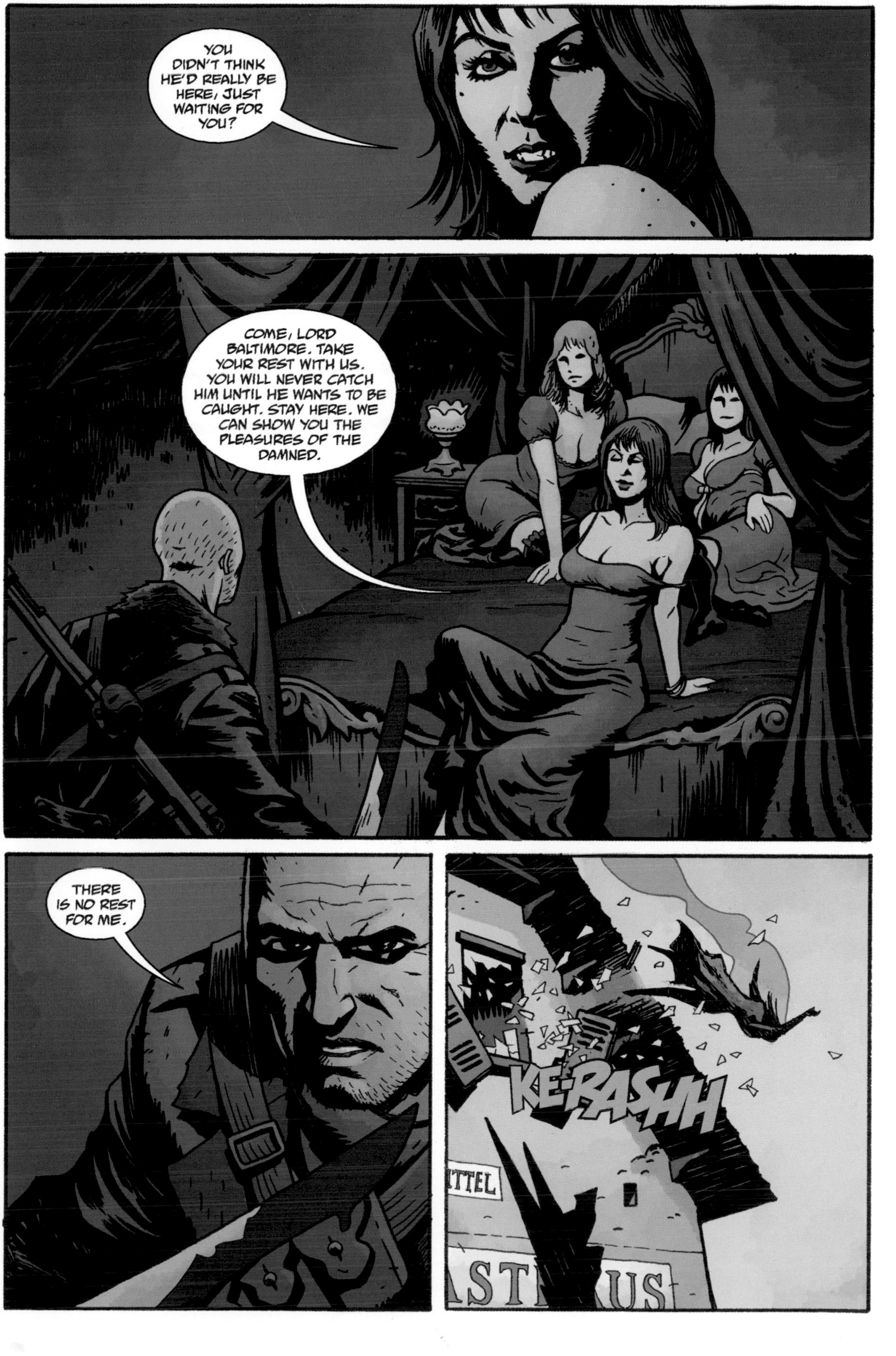
YOU DIDN'T THINK HE'D REALLY BE HERE, JUST WAITING FOR YOU?
COME, LORD BALTIMORE. TAKE YOUR REST WITH US. YOU WILL NEVER CATCH HIM UNTIL HE WANTS TO BE CAUGHT. STAY HERE. WE CAN SHOW YOU THE PLEASURES OF THE DAMNED.
THERE IS NO REST FOR ME.
KE-RASHH
ITTEL
ASTE US

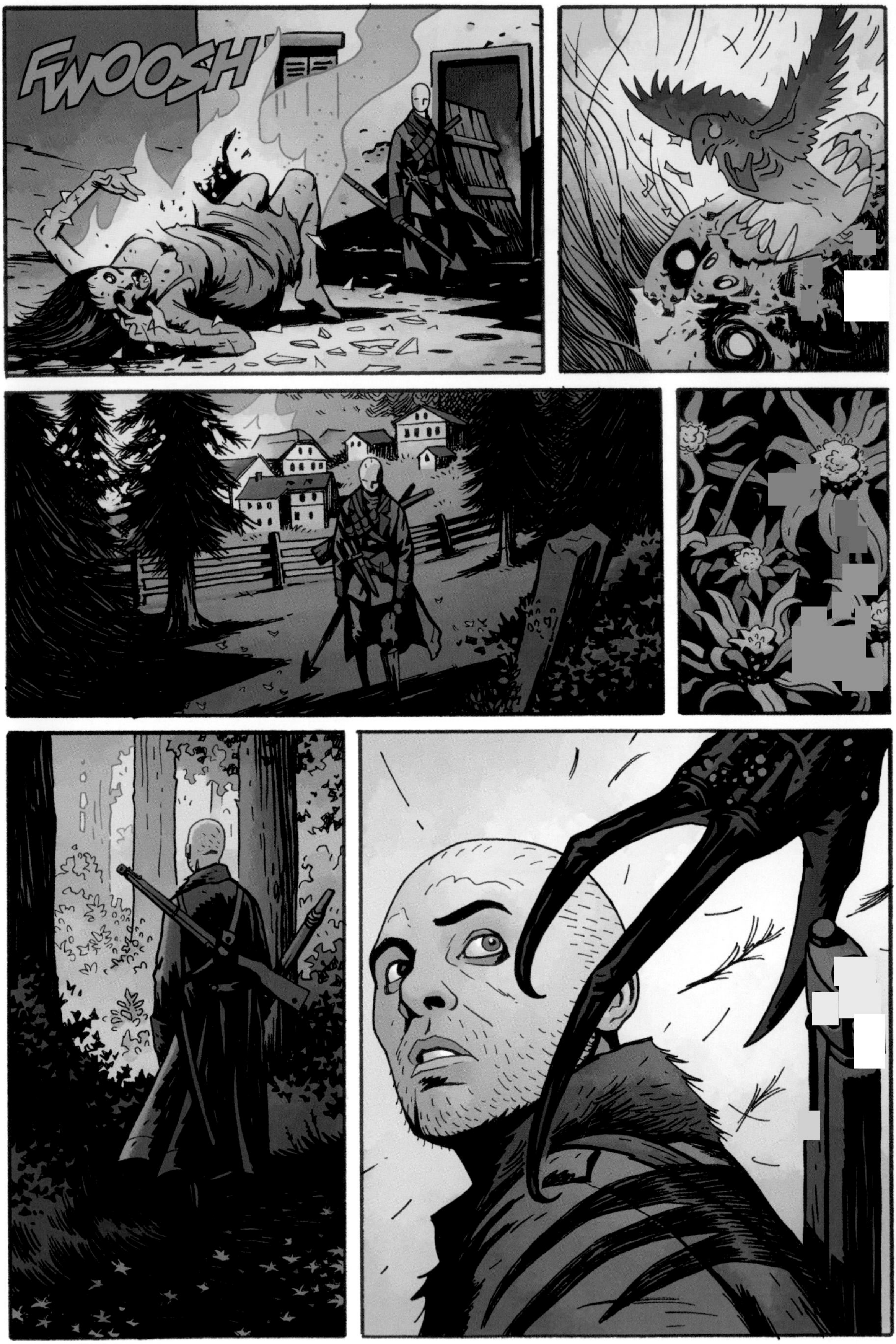
FWOOSH

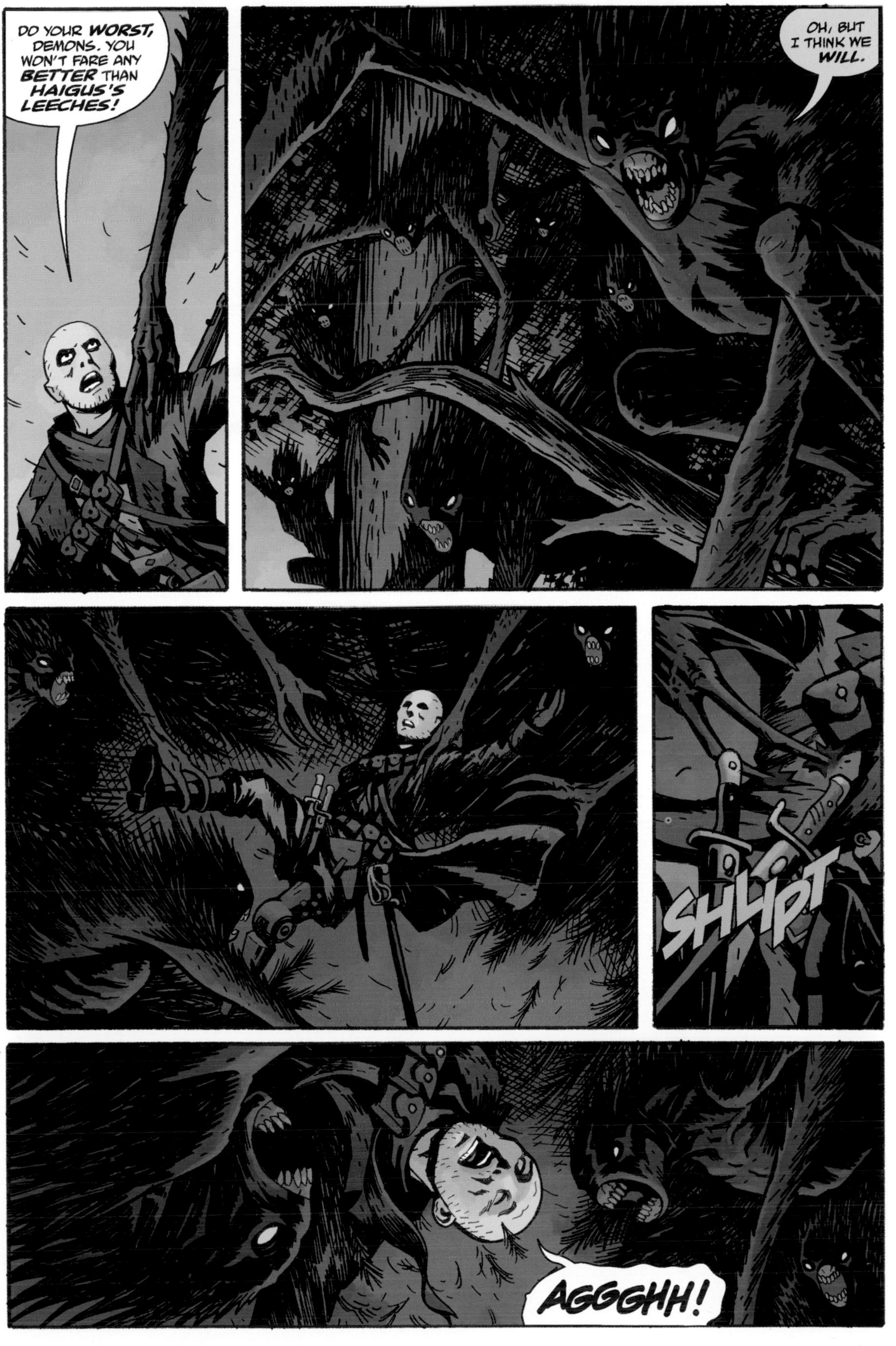
DO YOUR WORST, DEMONS. YOU WON'T FARE ANY BETTER THAN HAIGUS'S LEECHES!
OH, BUT I THINK WE WILL.
SHLIPT
AGGGHH!

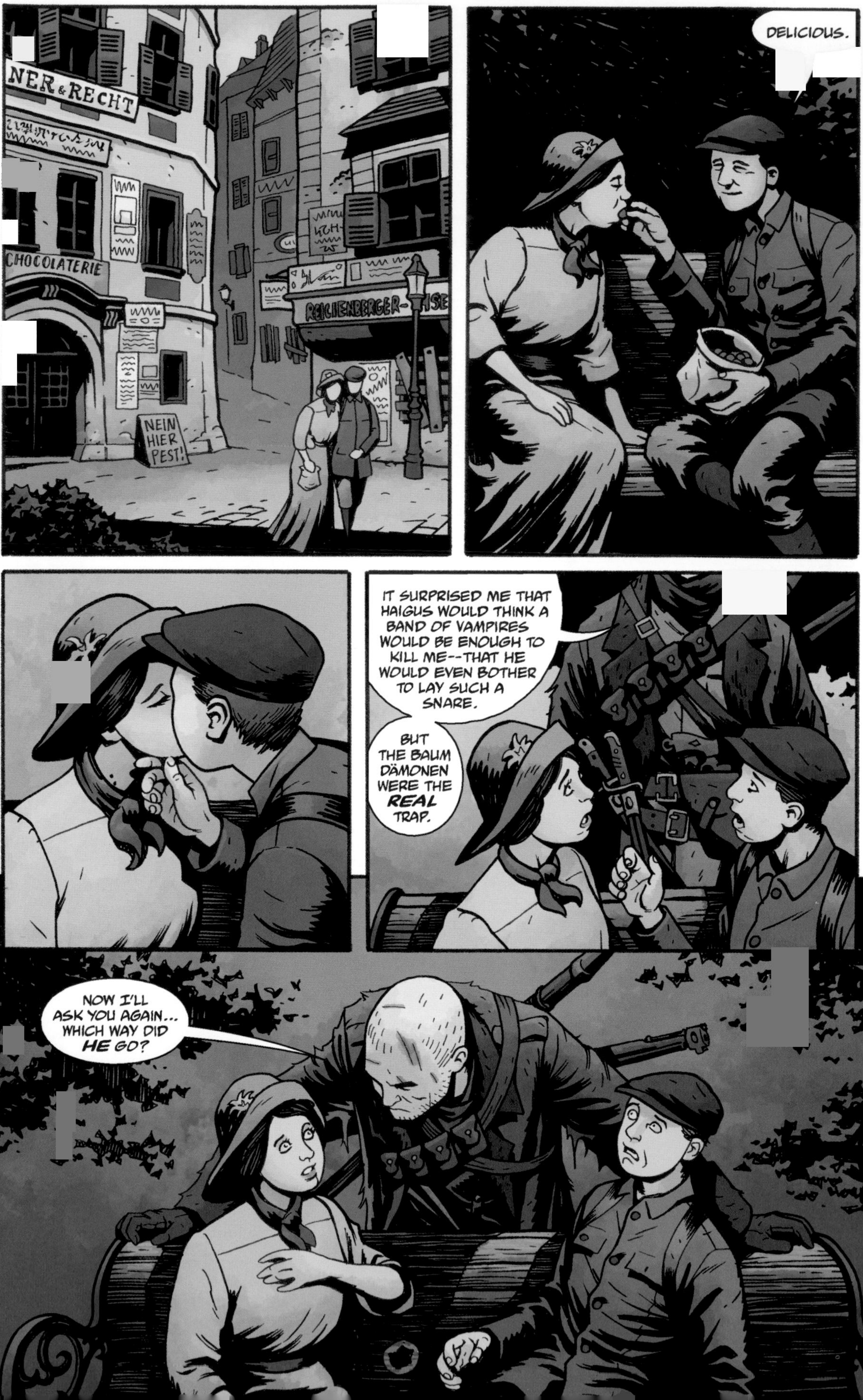

NER & RECHT
CHOCOLATERIE
NEIN HIER PEST!
REICHENBERGER
DELICIOUS.
IT SURPRISED ME THAT HAIGUS WOULD THINK A BAND OF VAMPIRES WOULD BE ENOUGH TO KILL ME--THAT HE WOULD EVEN BOTHER TO LAY SUCH A SNARE.
BUT THE BAUM DÄMONEN WERE THE REAL TRAP.
NOW I'LL ASK YOU AGAIN... WHICH WAY DID HE GO?

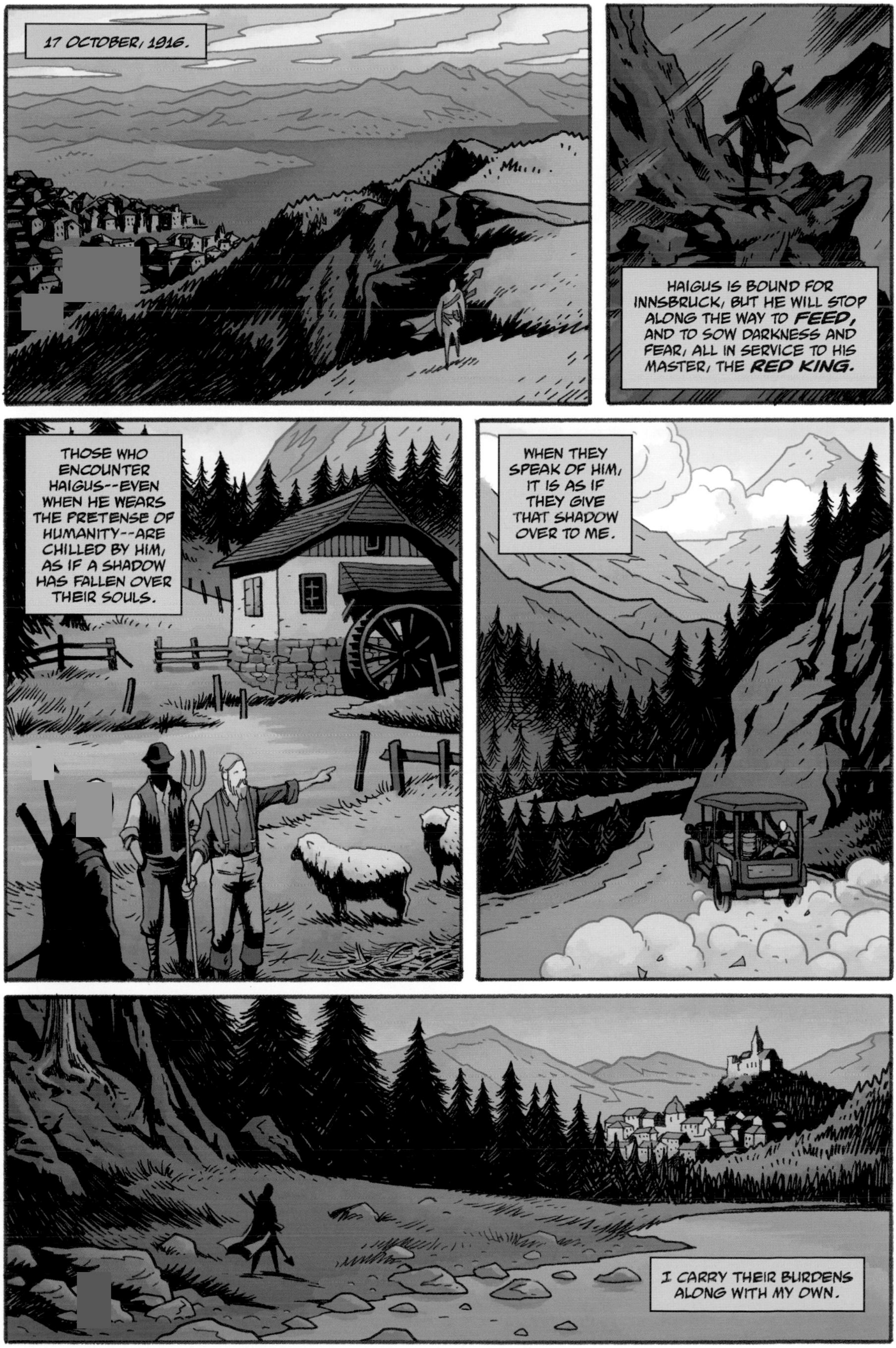
17 OCTOBER, 1916.
HAIGUS IS BOUND FOR INNSBRUCK, BUT HE WILL STOP ALONG THE WAY TO FEED, AND TO SOW DARKNESS AND FEAR, ALL IN SERVICE TO HIS MASTER, THE RED KING.
THOSE WHO ENCOUNTER HAIGUS--EVEN WHEN HE WEARS THE PRETENSE OF HUMANITY--ARE CHILLED BY HIM, AS IF A SHADOW HAS FALLEN OVER THEIR SOULS.
WHEN THEY SPEAK OF HIM, IT IS AS IF THEY GIVE THAT SHADOW OVER TO ME.
I CARRY THEIR BURDENS ALONG WITH MY OWN.

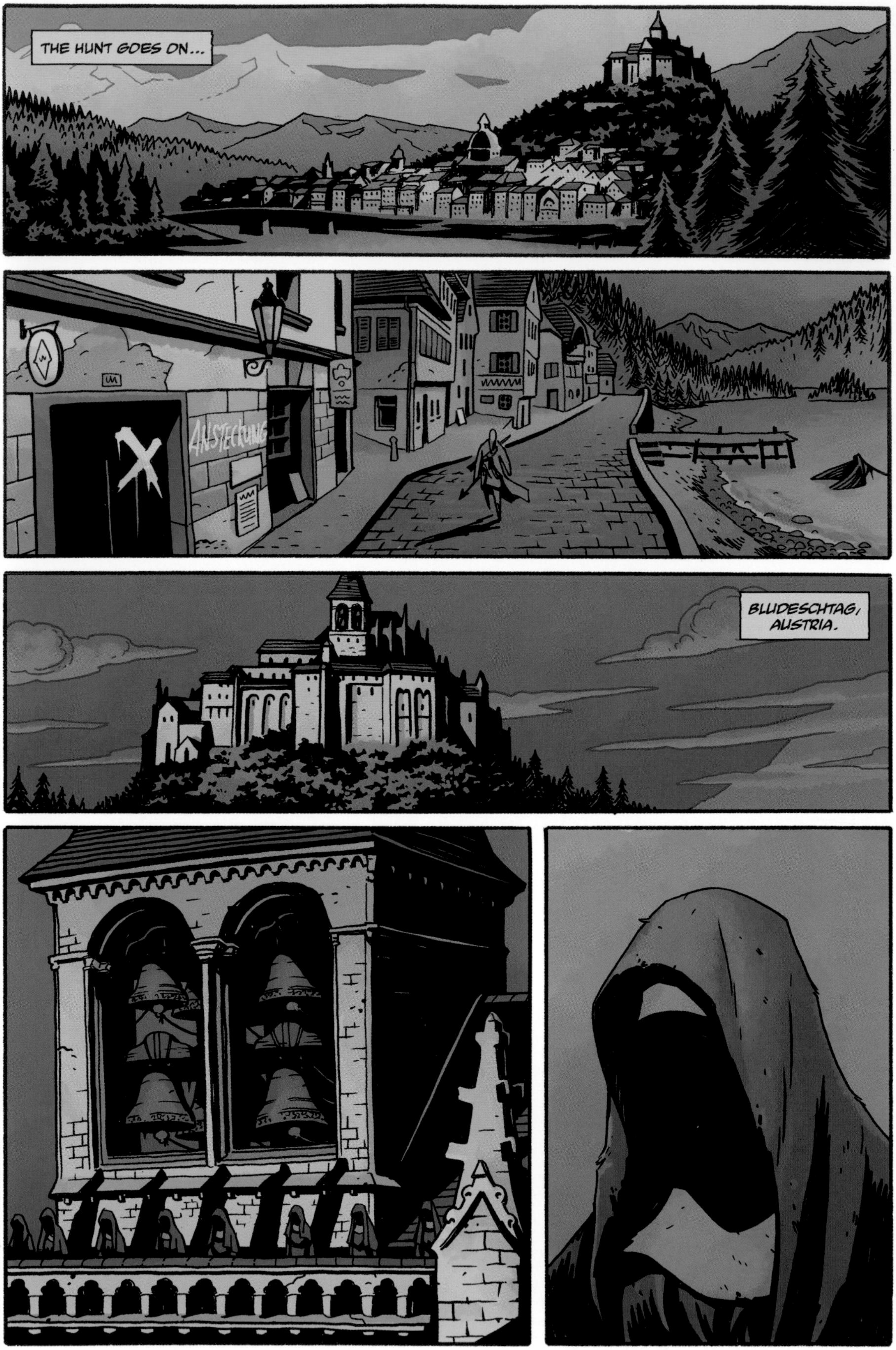
THE HUNT GOES ON...
ANSTECKUNG
BLUDESCHTAG, AUSTRIA.

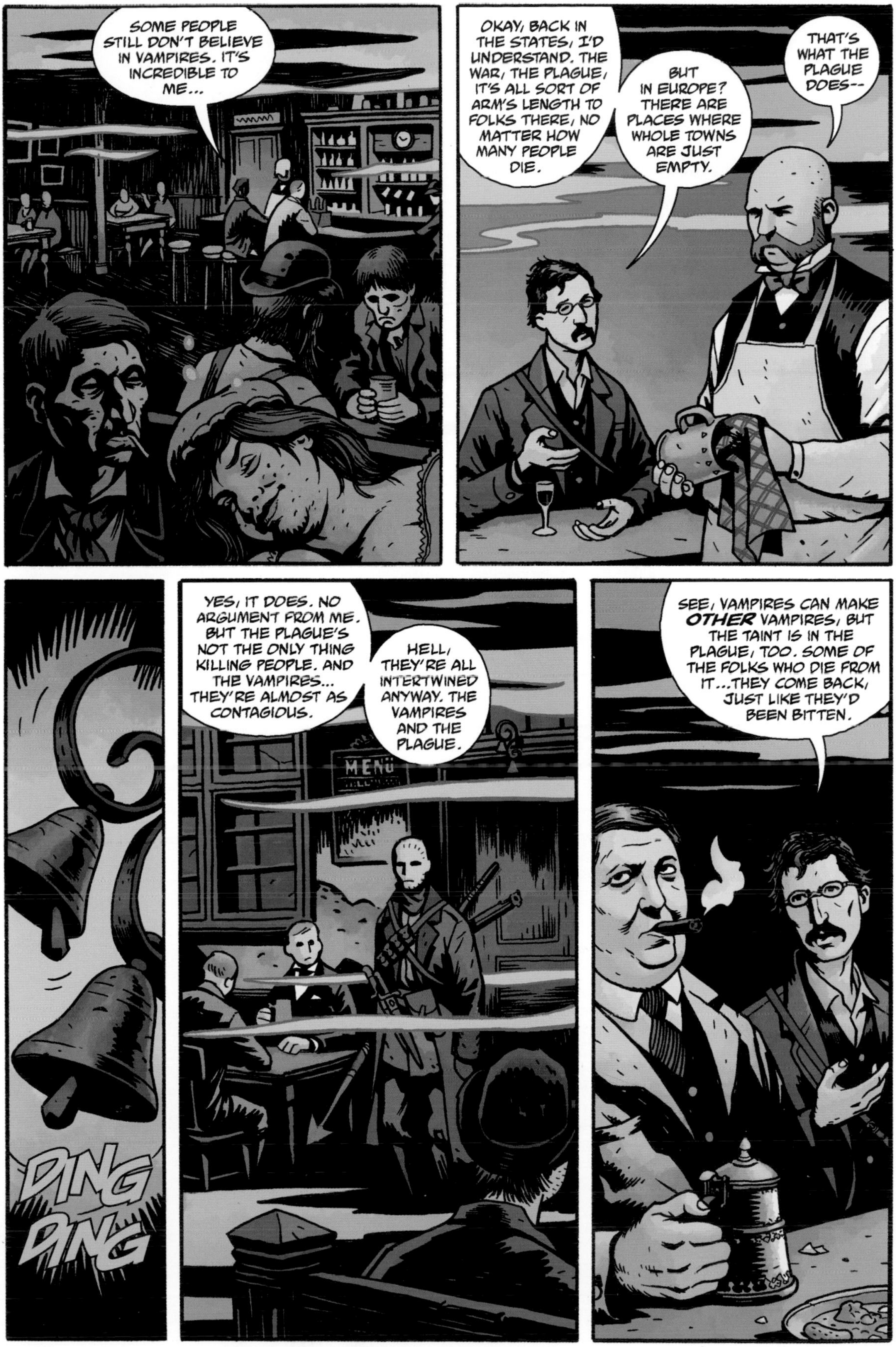
SOME PEOPLE STILL DON'T BELIEVE IN VAMPIRES. IT'S INCREDIBLE TO ME...
OKAY, BACK IN THE STATES, I'D UNDERSTAND. THE WAR, THE PLAGUE, IT'S ALL SORT OF ARM'S LENGTH TO FOLKS THERE, NO MATTER HOW MANY PEOPLE DIE.
BUT IN EUROPE? THERE ARE PLACES WHERE WHOLE TOWNS ARE JUST EMPTY.
THAT'S WHAT THE PLAGUE DOES--
DING DING
YES, IT DOES. NO ARGUMENT FROM ME. BUT THE PLAGUE'S NOT THE ONLY THING KILLING PEOPLE. AND THE VAMPIRES... THEY'RE ALMOST AS CONTAGIOUS.
HELL, THEY'RE ALL INTERTWINED ANYWAY. THE VAMPIRES AND THE PLAGUE.
MENÜ
SEE, VAMPIRES CAN MAKE OTHER VAMPIRES, BUT THE TAINT IS IN THE PLAGUE, TOO. SOME OF THE FOLKS WHO DIE FROM IT...THEY COME BACK, JUST LIKE THEY'D BEEN BITTEN.

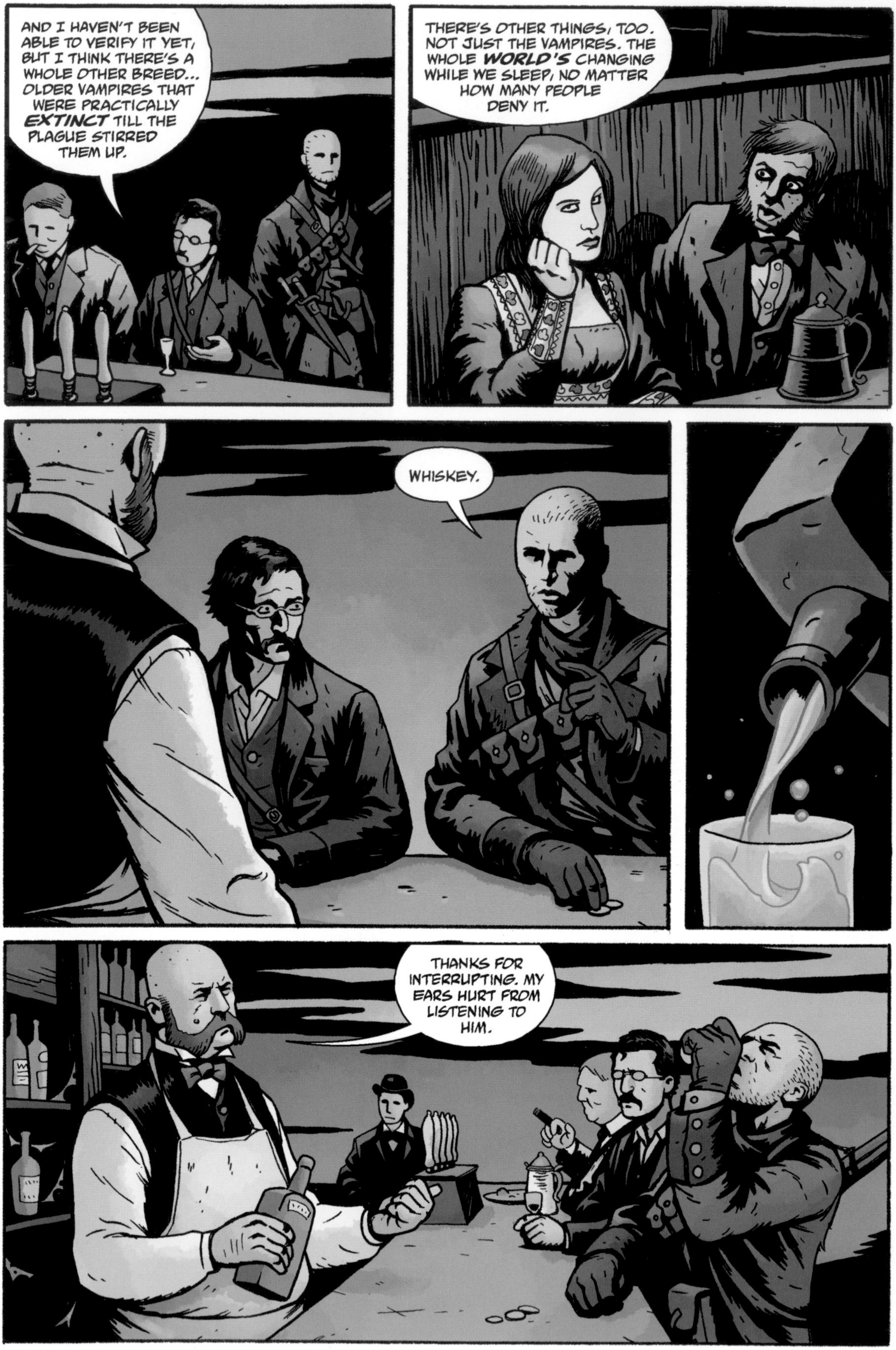
AND I HAVEN'T BEEN ABLE TO VERIFY IT YET, BUT I THINK THERE'S A WHOLE OTHER BREED... OLDER VAMPIRES THAT WERE PRACTICALLY EXTINCT TILL THE PLAGUE STIRRED THEM UP.
THERE'S OTHER THINGS, TOO. NOT JUST THE VAMPIRES. THE WHOLE WORLD'S CHANGING WHILE WE SLEEP, NO MATTER HOW MANY PEOPLE DENY IT.
WHISKEY.
THANKS FOR INTERRUPTING. MY EARS HURT FROM LISTENING TO HIM.

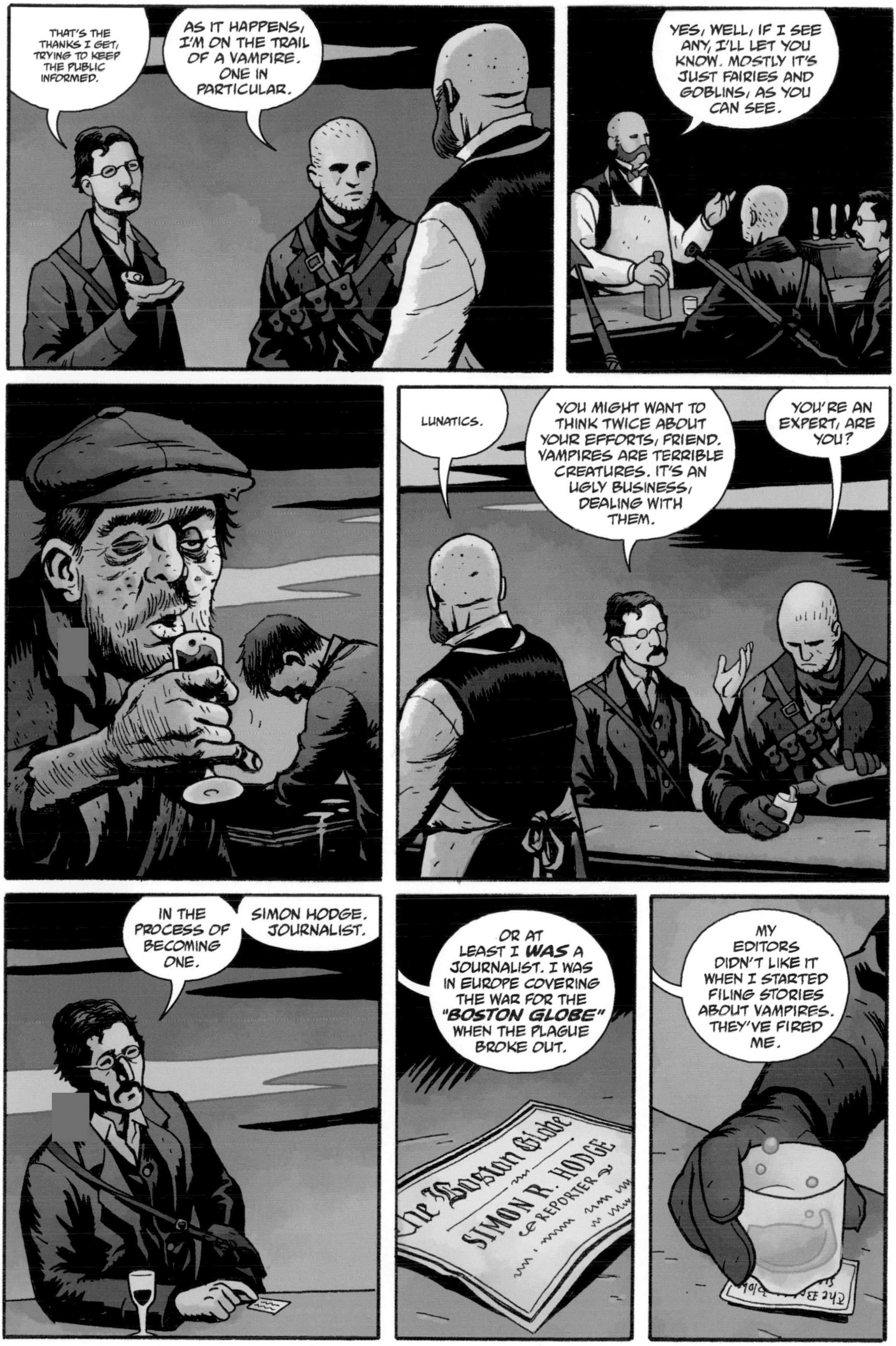
THAT'S THE THANKS I GET, TRYING TO KEEP THE PUBLIC INFORMED.
AS IT HAPPENS, I'M ON THE TRAIL OF A VAMPIRE. ONE IN PARTICULAR.
YES, WELL, IF I SEE ANY, I'LL LET YOU KNOW. MOSTLY IT'S JUST FAIRIES AND GOBLINS, AS YOU CAN SEE.
LUNATICS.
YOU MIGHT WANT TO THINK TWICE ABOUT YOUR EFFORTS, FRIEND. VAMPIRES ARE TERRIBLE CREATURES. IT'S AN UGLY BUSINESS, DEALING WITH THEM.
YOU'RE AN EXPERT, ARE YOU?
IN THE PROCESS OF BECOMING ONE.
SIMON HODGE. JOURNALIST.
OR AT LEAST I **WAS** A JOURNALIST. I WAS IN EUROPE COVERING THE WAR FOR THE "**BOSTON GLOBE**" WHEN THE PLAGUE BROKE OUT.
The Boston Globe
SIMON R. HODGE
REPORTER
MY EDITORS DIDN'T LIKE IT WHEN I STARTED FILING STORIES ABOUT VAMPIRES. THEY'VE FIRED ME.

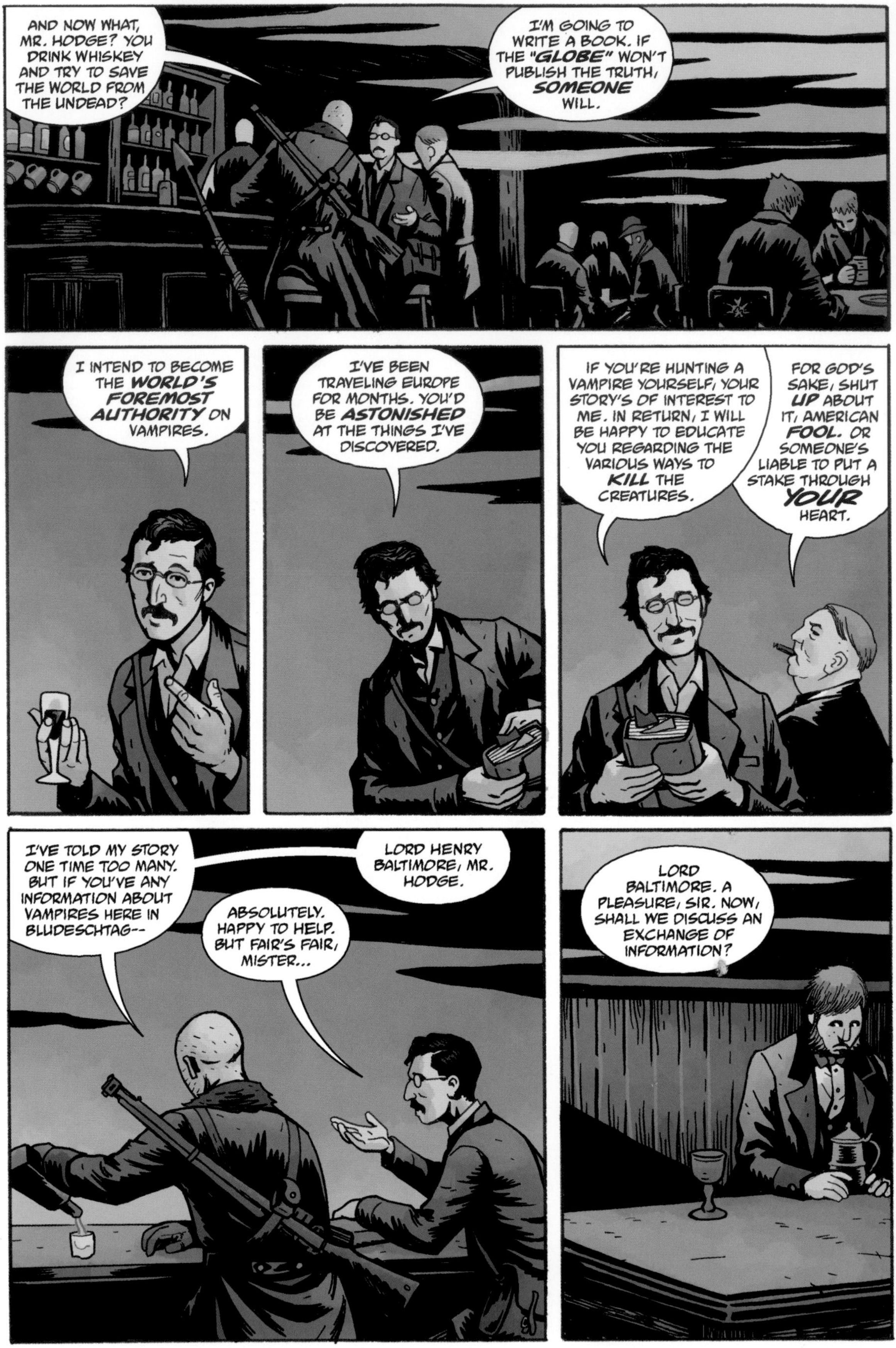
AND NOW WHAT, MR. HODGE? YOU DRINK WHISKEY AND TRY TO SAVE THE WORLD FROM THE UNDEAD?
I'M GOING TO WRITE A BOOK. IF THE "GLOBE" WON'T PUBLISH THE TRUTH, SOMEONE WILL.
I INTEND TO BECOME THE WORLD'S FOREMOST AUTHORITY ON VAMPIRES.
I'VE BEEN TRAVELING EUROPE FOR MONTHS. YOU'D BE ASTONISHED AT THE THINGS I'VE DISCOVERED.
IF YOU'RE HUNTING A VAMPIRE YOURSELF, YOUR STORY'S OF INTEREST TO ME. IN RETURN, I WILL BE HAPPY TO EDUCATE YOU REGARDING THE VARIOUS WAYS TO KILL THE CREATURES.
FOR GOD'S SAKE, SHUT UP ABOUT IT, AMERICAN FOOL. OR SOMEONE'S LIABLE TO PUT A STAKE THROUGH YOUR HEART.
I'VE TOLD MY STORY ONE TIME TOO MANY. BUT IF YOU'VE ANY INFORMATION ABOUT VAMPIRES HERE IN BLUDESCHTAG--
ABSOLUTELY. HAPPY TO HELP. BUT FAIR'S FAIR, MISTER...
LORD HENRY BALTIMORE, MR. HODGE.
LORD BALTIMORE. A PLEASURE, SIR. NOW, SHALL WE DISCUSS AN EXCHANGE OF INFORMATION?

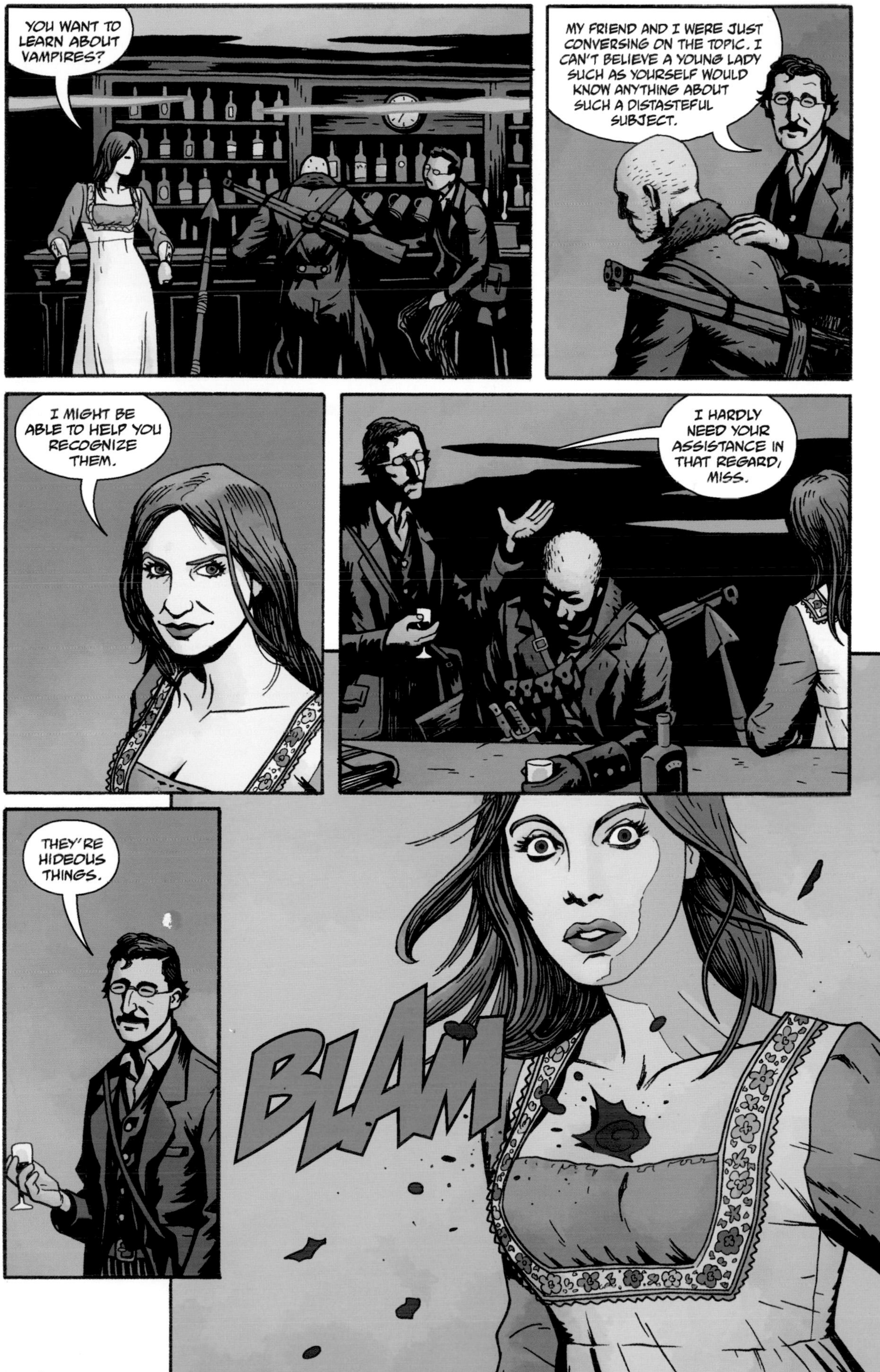
YOU WANT TO LEARN ABOUT VAMPIRES?
MY FRIEND AND I WERE JUST CONVERSING ON THE TOPIC. I CAN'T BELIEVE A YOUNG LADY SUCH AS YOURSELF WOULD KNOW ANYTHING ABOUT SUCH A DISTASTEFUL SUBJECT.
I MIGHT BE ABLE TO HELP YOU RECOGNIZE THEM.
I HARDLY NEED YOUR ASSISTANCE IN THAT REGARD, MISS.
THEY'RE HIDEOUS THINGS.
BLAM

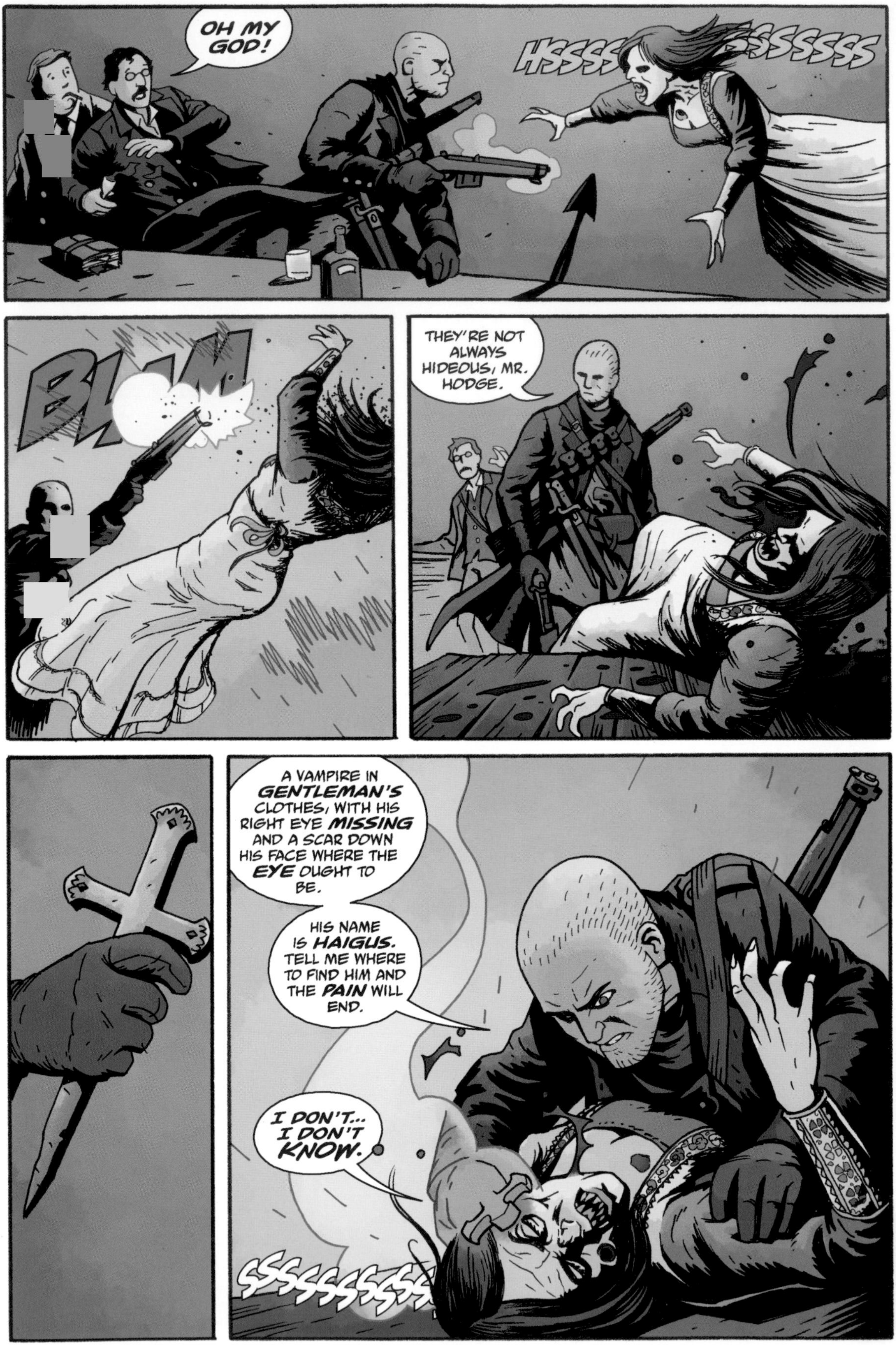
OH MY GOD!
HSSSS
SSSSSS
THEY'RE NOT ALWAYS HIDEOUS, MR. HODGE.
A VAMPIRE IN GENTLEMAN'S CLOTHES, WITH HIS RIGHT EYE MISSING AND A SCAR DOWN HIS FACE WHERE THE EYE OUGHT TO BE.
HIS NAME IS HAIGUS. TELL ME WHERE TO FIND HIM AND THE PAIN WILL END.
I DON'T... I DON'T KNOW.
SSSSSSSSSS

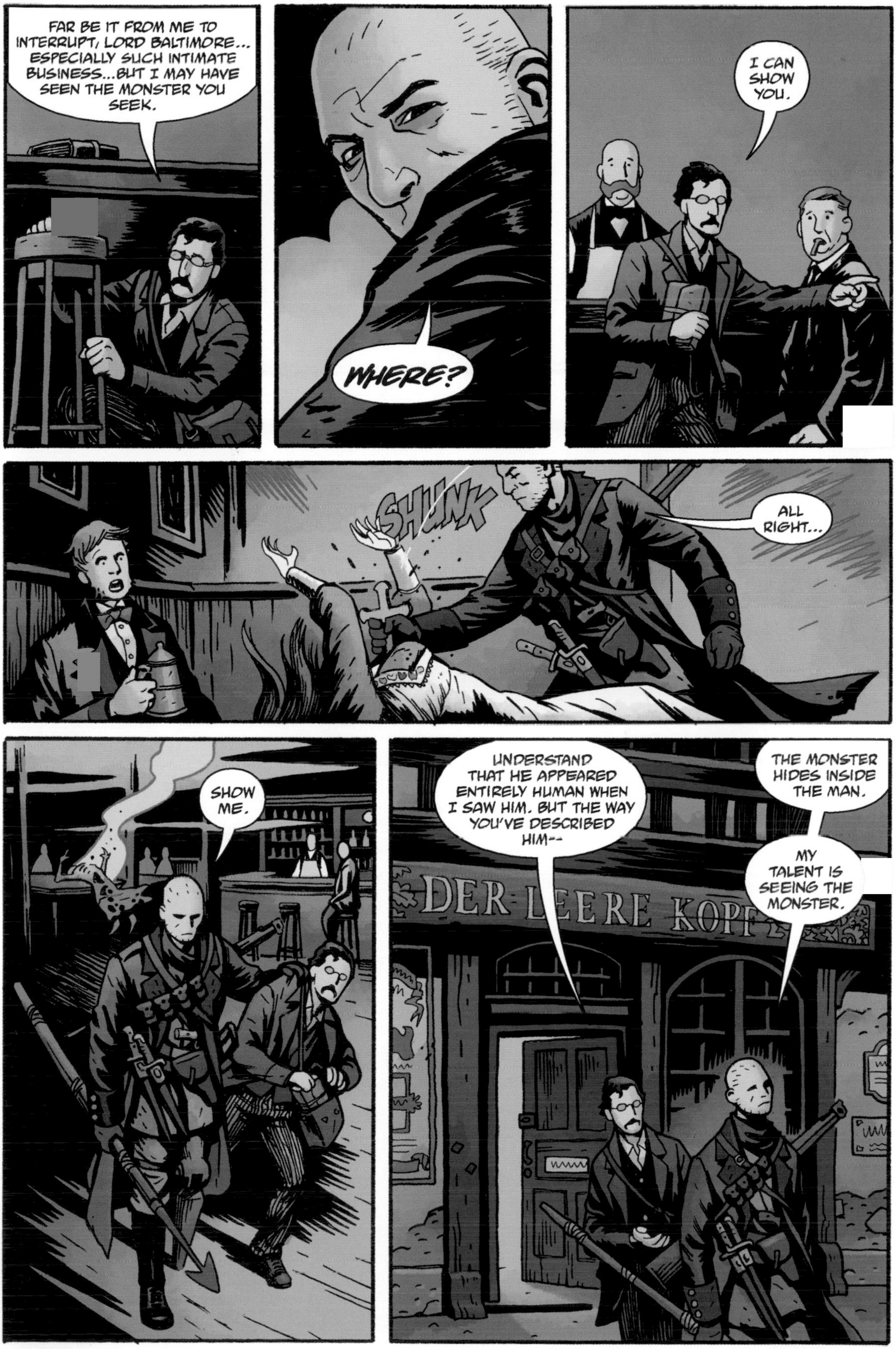
FAR BE IT FROM ME TO INTERRUPT, LORD BALTIMORE... ESPECIALLY SUCH INTIMATE BUSINESS...BUT I MAY HAVE SEEN THE MONSTER YOU SEEK.
WHERE?
I CAN SHOW YOU.
SHUNK
ALL RIGHT...
SHOW ME.
UNDERSTAND THAT HE APPEARED ENTIRELY HUMAN WHEN I SAW HIM. BUT THE WAY YOU'VE DESCRIBED HIM--
THE MONSTER HIDES INSIDE THE MAN.
MY TALENT IS SEEING THE MONSTER.
DER LEERE KOPF

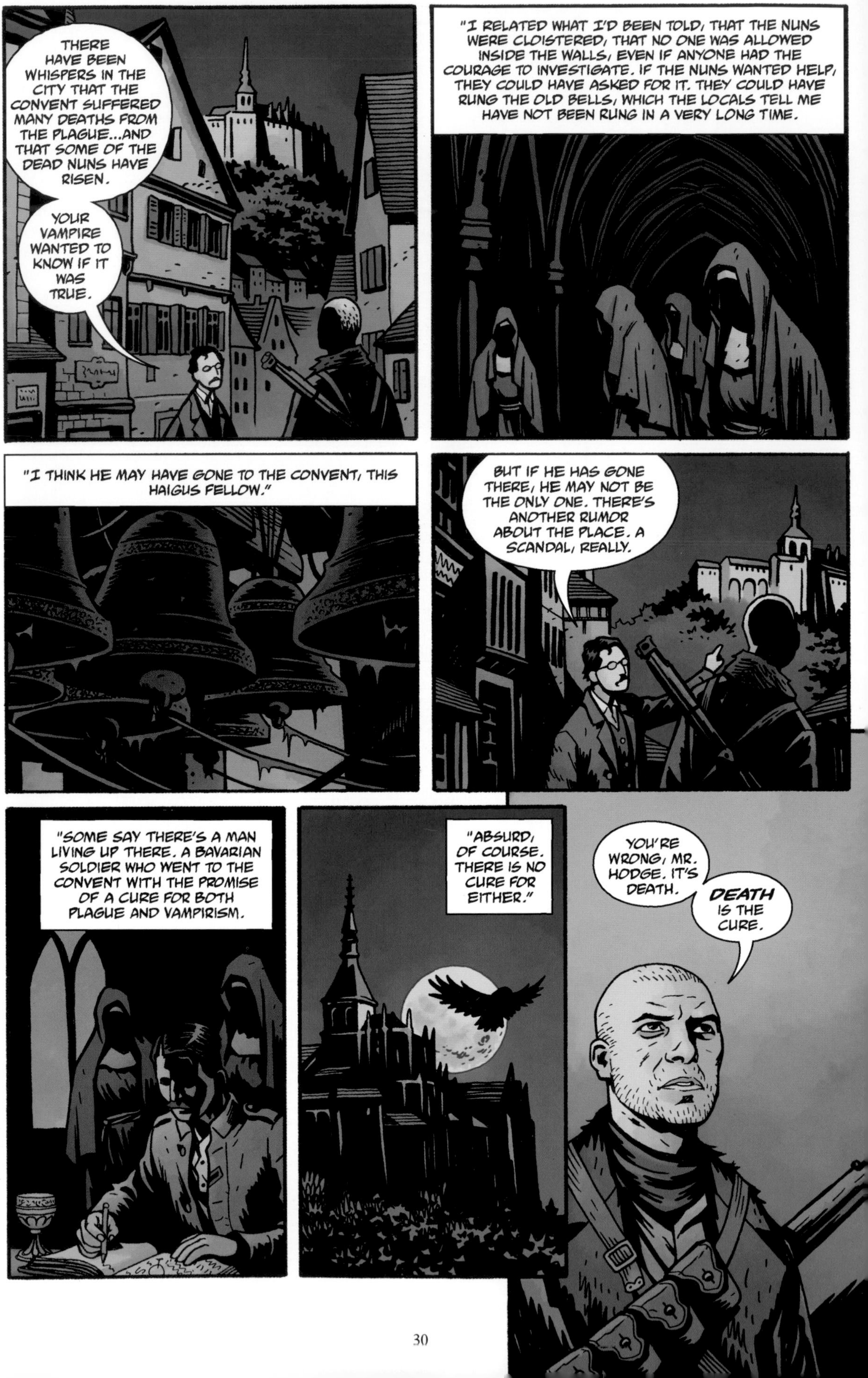
THERE HAVE BEEN WHISPERS IN THE CITY THAT THE CONVENT SUFFERED MANY DEATHS FROM THE PLAGUE...AND THAT SOME OF THE DEAD NUNS HAVE RISEN.
YOUR VAMPIRE WANTED TO KNOW IF IT WAS TRUE.
"I RELATED WHAT I'D BEEN TOLD, THAT THE NUNS WERE CLOISTERED, THAT NO ONE WAS ALLOWED INSIDE THE WALLS, EVEN IF ANYONE HAD THE COURAGE TO INVESTIGATE. IF THE NUNS WANTED HELP, THEY COULD HAVE ASKED FOR IT. THEY COULD HAVE RUNG THE OLD BELLS, WHICH THE LOCALS TELL ME HAVE NOT BEEN RUNG IN A VERY LONG TIME.
"I THINK HE MAY HAVE GONE TO THE CONVENT, THIS HAIGUS FELLOW."
BUT IF HE HAS GONE THERE, HE MAY NOT BE THE ONLY ONE. THERE'S ANOTHER RUMOR ABOUT THE PLACE. A SCANDAL, REALLY.
"SOME SAY THERE'S A MAN LIVING UP THERE. A BAVARIAN SOLDIER WHO WENT TO THE CONVENT WITH THE PROMISE OF A CURE FOR BOTH PLAGUE AND VAMPIRISM.
"ABSURD, OF COURSE. THERE IS NO CURE FOR EITHER."
YOU'RE WRONG, MR. HODGE. IT'S DEATH.
DEATH IS THE CURE.

CHAPTER TWO

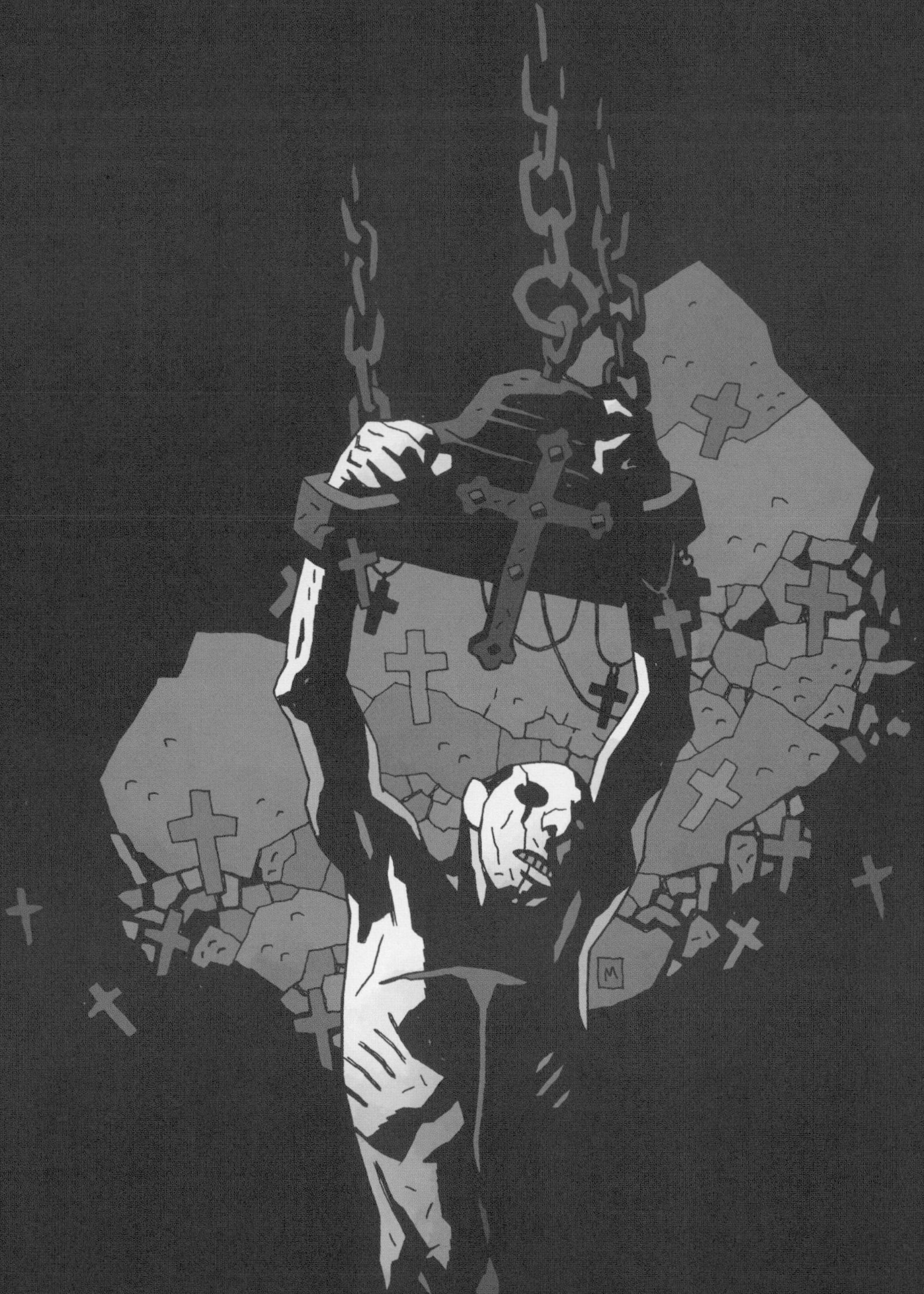

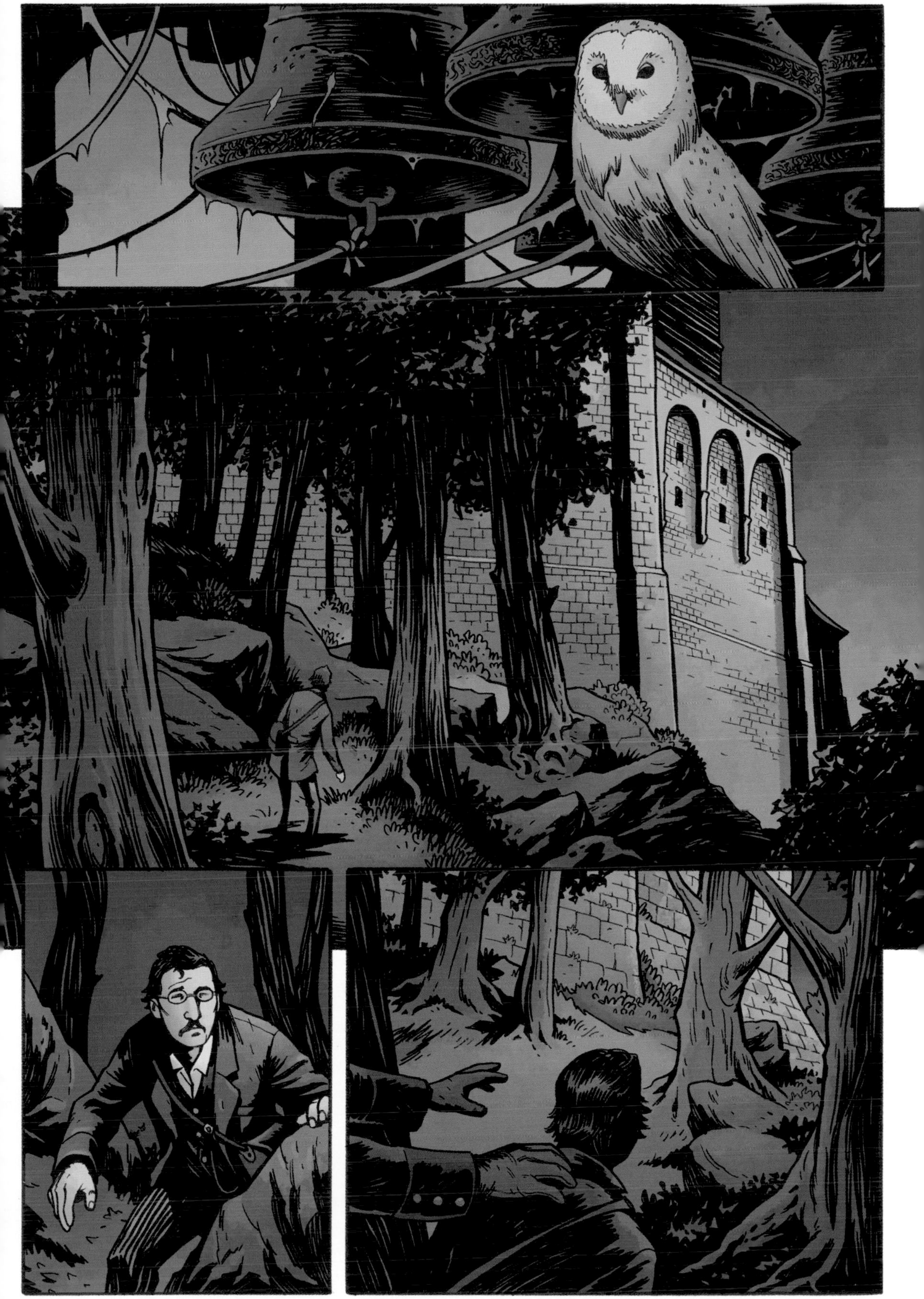

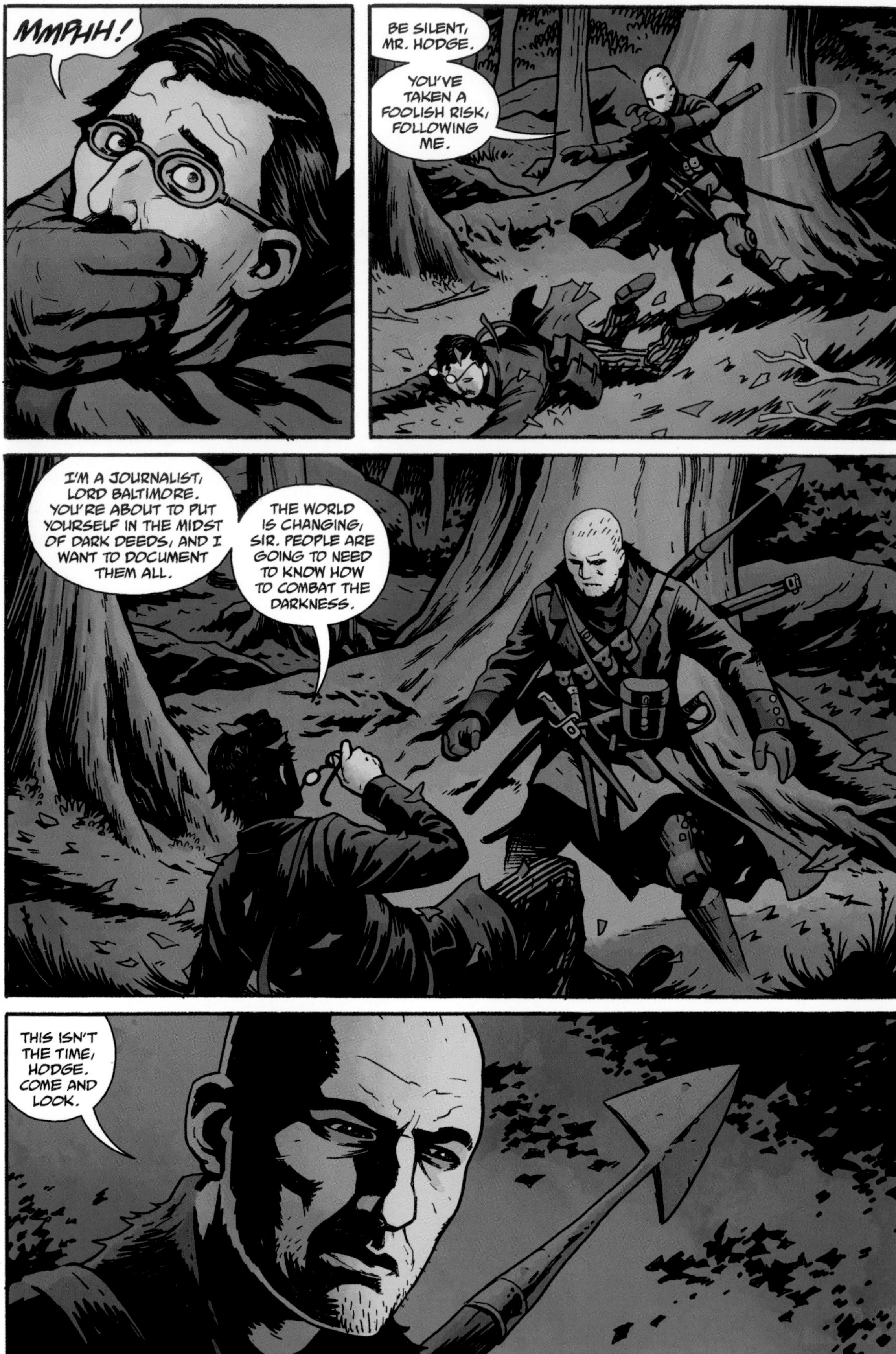
MMPHH!
BE SILENT, MR. HODGE.
YOU'VE TAKEN A FOOLISH RISK, FOLLOWING ME.
I'M A JOURNALIST, LORD BALTIMORE. YOU'RE ABOUT TO PUT YOURSELF IN THE MIDST OF DARK DEEDS, AND I WANT TO DOCUMENT THEM ALL.
THE WORLD IS CHANGING, SIR. PEOPLE ARE GOING TO NEED TO KNOW HOW TO COMBAT THE DARKNESS.
THIS ISN'T THE TIME, HODGE. COME AND LOOK.

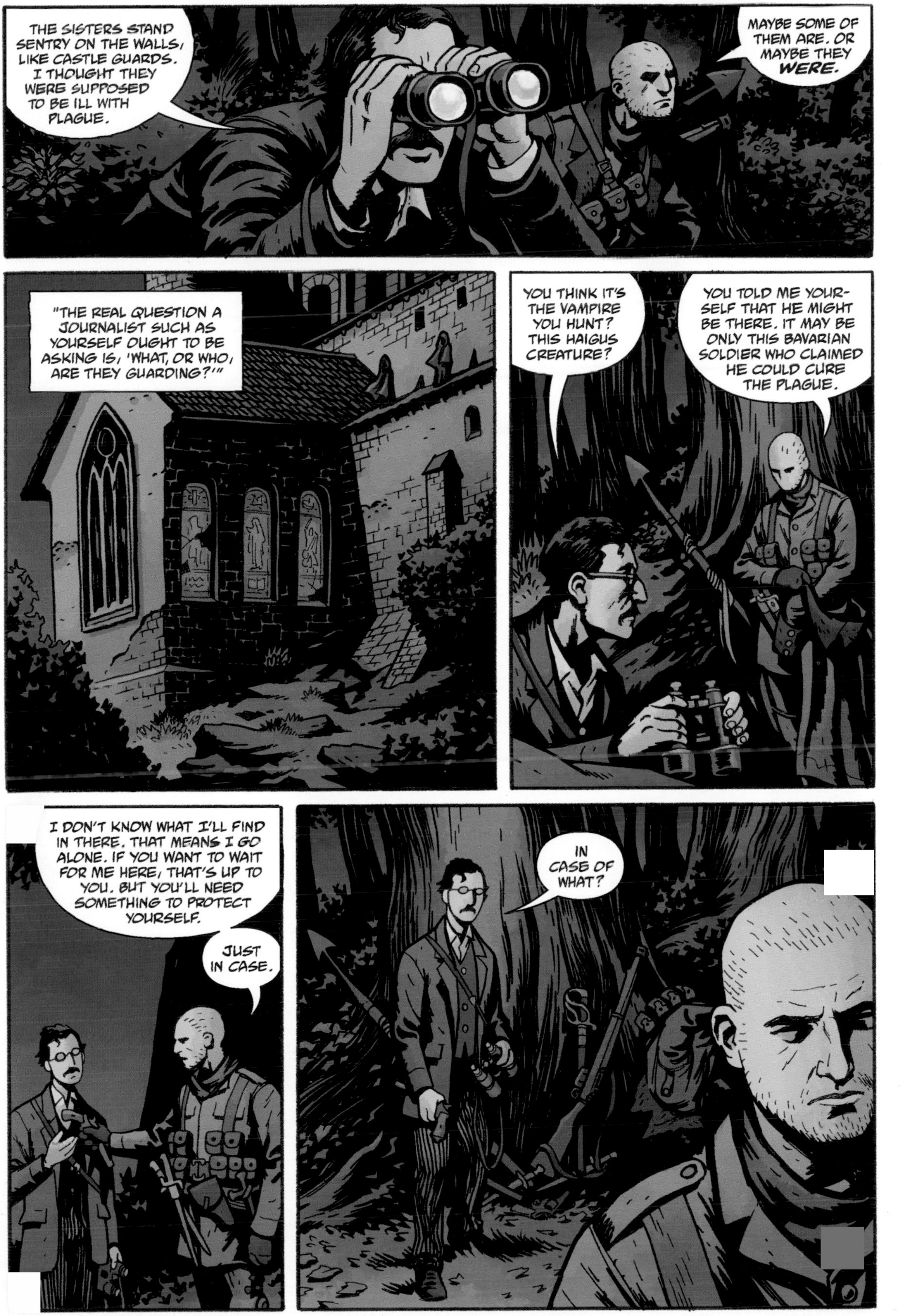
THE SISTERS STAND SENTRY ON THE WALLS, LIKE CASTLE GUARDS. I THOUGHT THEY WERE SUPPOSED TO BE ILL WITH PLAGUE.
MAYBE SOME OF THEM ARE. OR MAYBE THEY *WERE.*
"THE REAL QUESTION A JOURNALIST SUCH AS YOURSELF OUGHT TO BE ASKING IS, 'WHAT, OR WHO, ARE THEY GUARDING?'"
YOU THINK IT'S THE VAMPIRE YOU HUNT? THIS HAIGUS CREATURE?
YOU TOLD ME YOURSELF THAT HE MIGHT BE THERE. IT MAY BE ONLY THIS BAVARIAN SOLDIER WHO CLAIMED HE COULD CURE THE PLAGUE.
I DON'T KNOW WHAT I'LL FIND IN THERE. THAT MEANS I GO ALONE. IF YOU WANT TO WAIT FOR ME HERE, THAT'S UP TO YOU. BUT YOU'LL NEED SOMETHING TO PROTECT YOURSELF.
JUST IN CASE.
IN CASE OF WHAT?

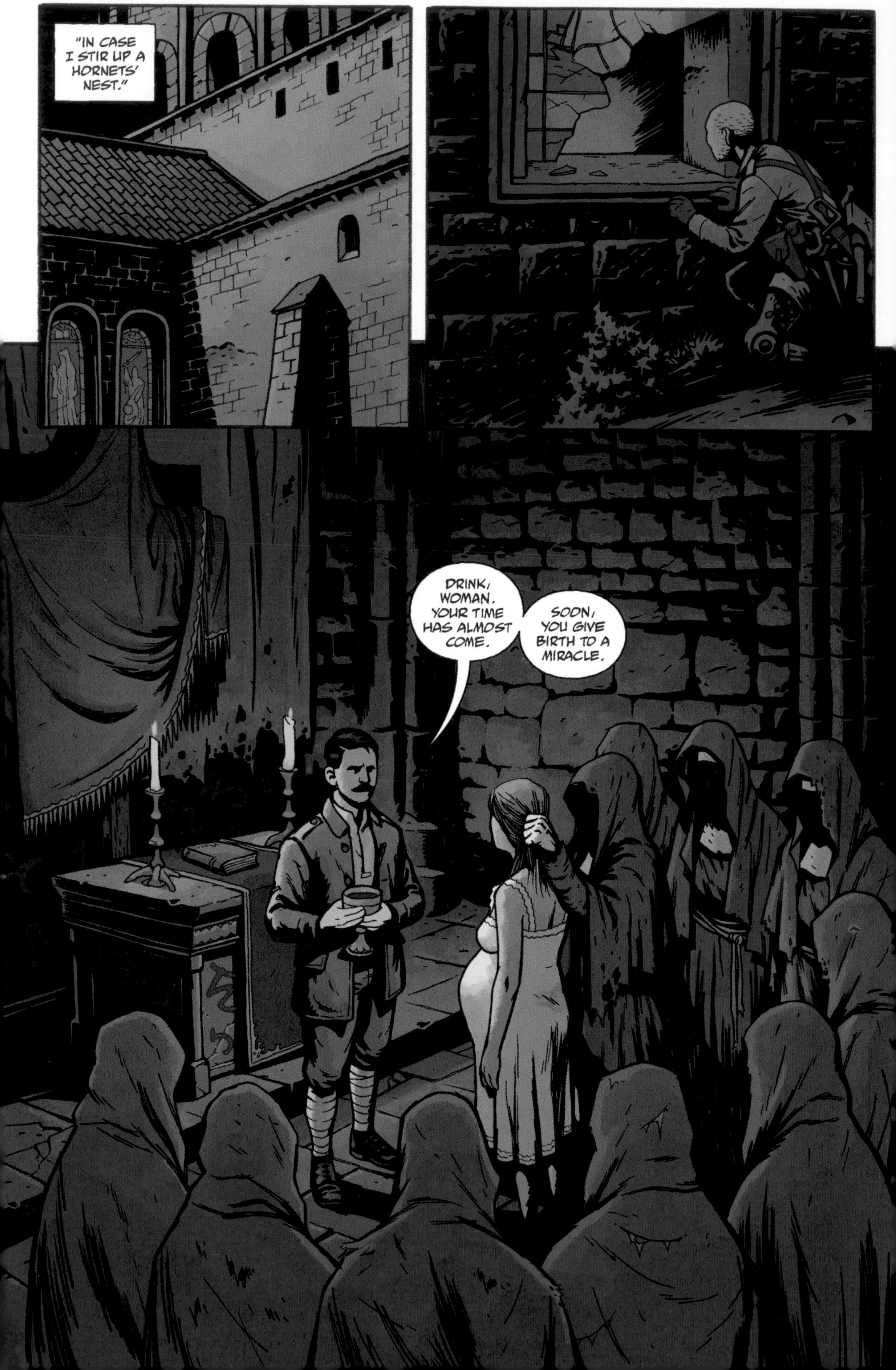
"IN CASE I STIR UP A HORNETS' NEST."
DRINK, WOMAN. YOUR TIME HAS ALMOST COME.
SOON, YOU GIVE BIRTH TO A MIRACLE.

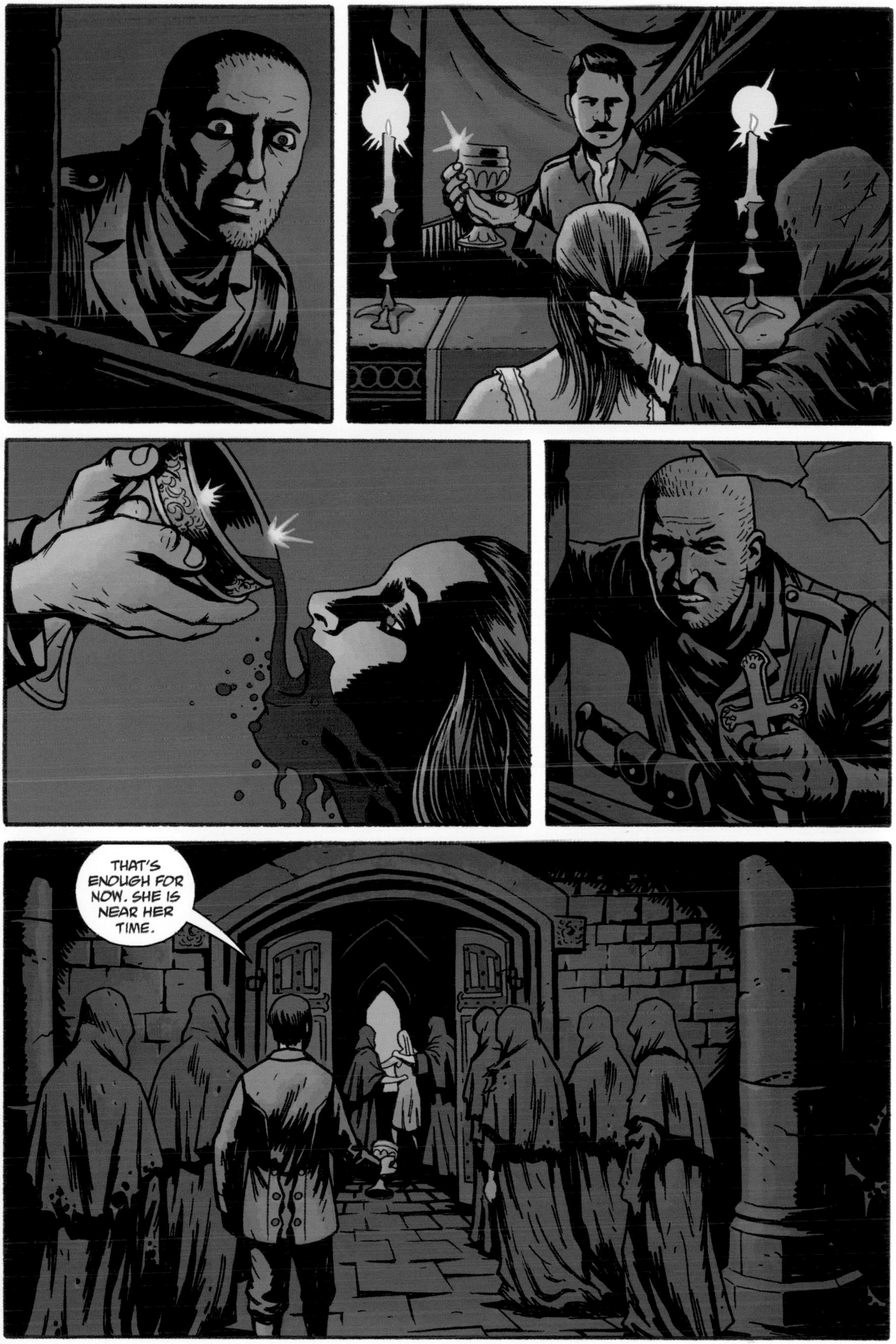
THAT'S ENOUGH FOR NOW. SHE IS NEAR HER TIME.

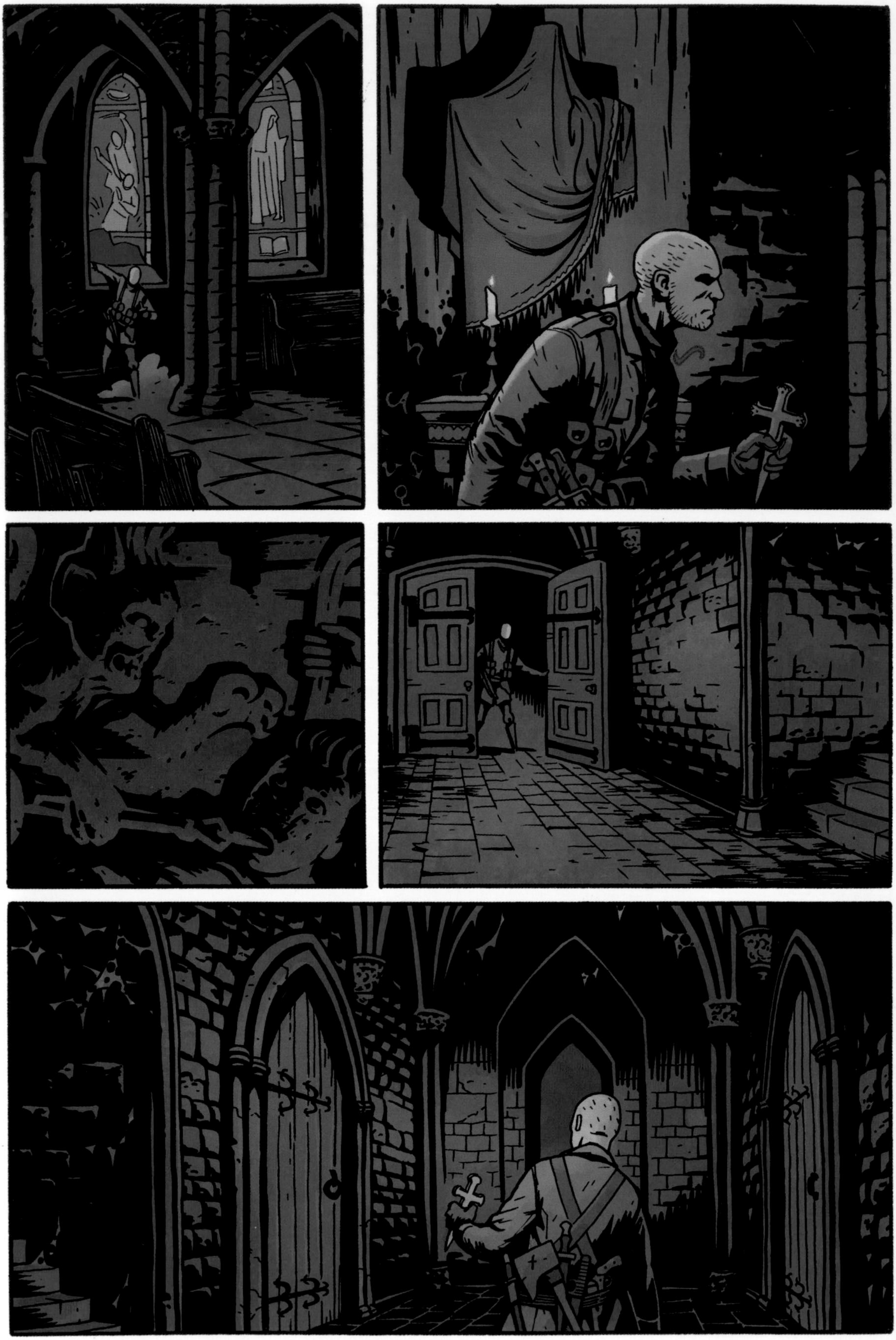

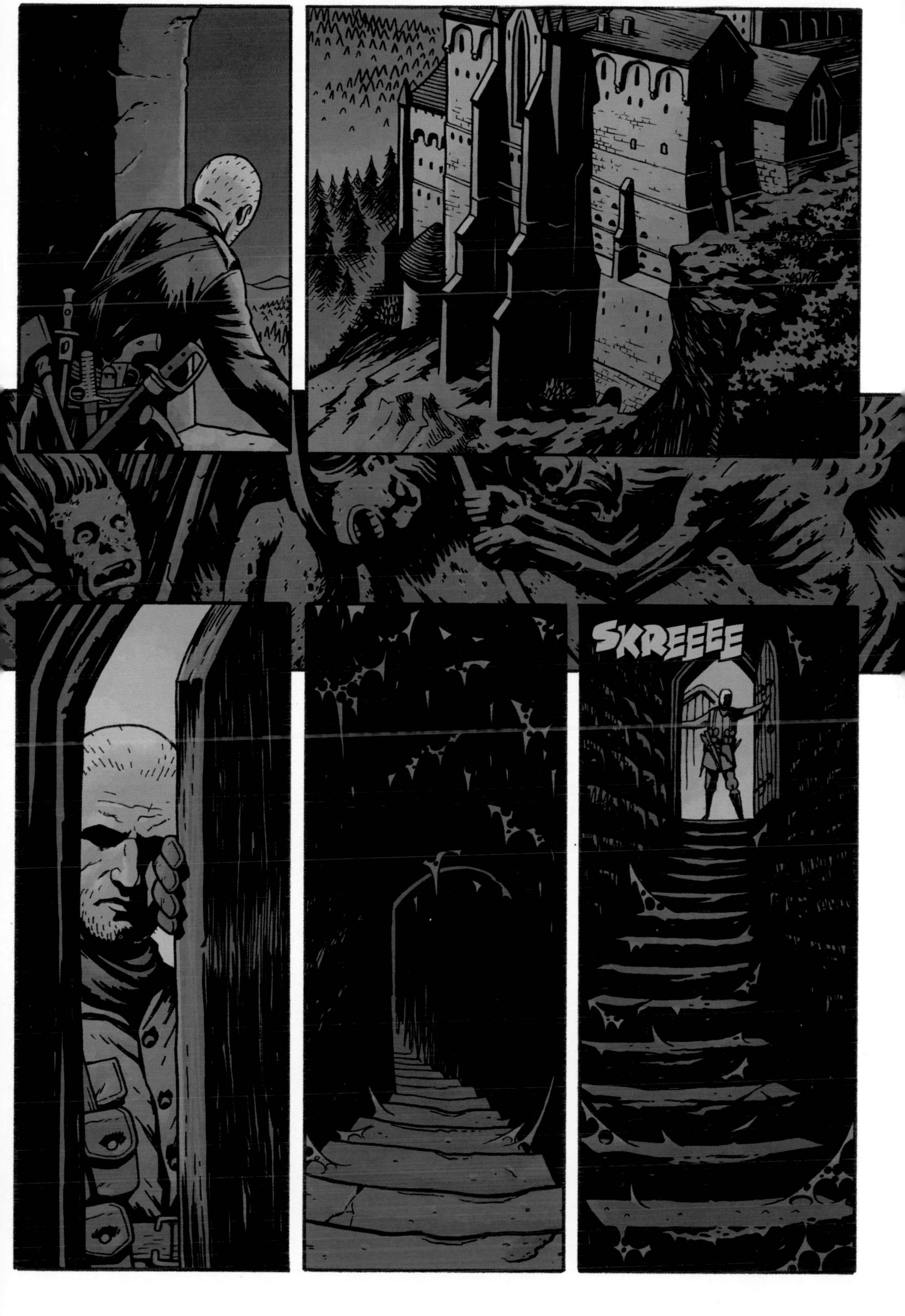
SKREEEE

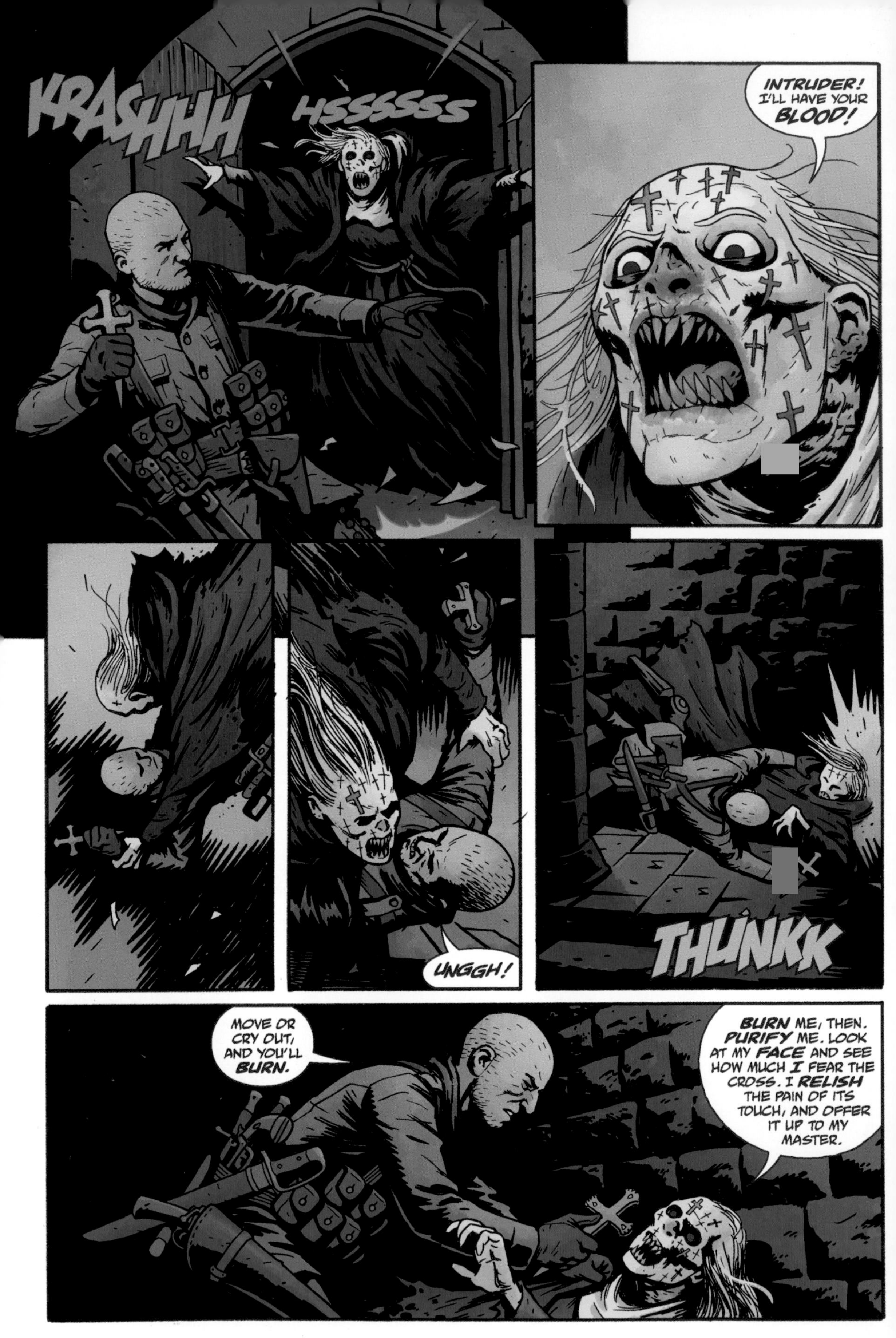
KRASHHH
HSSSSSS
INTRUDER! I'LL HAVE YOUR BLOOD!
UNGGH!
THUNKK
MOVE OR CRY OUT, AND YOU'LL BURN.
BURN ME, THEN. PURIFY ME. LOOK AT MY FACE AND SEE HOW MUCH I FEAR THE CROSS. I RELISH THE PAIN OF ITS TOUCH, AND OFFER IT UP TO MY MASTER.

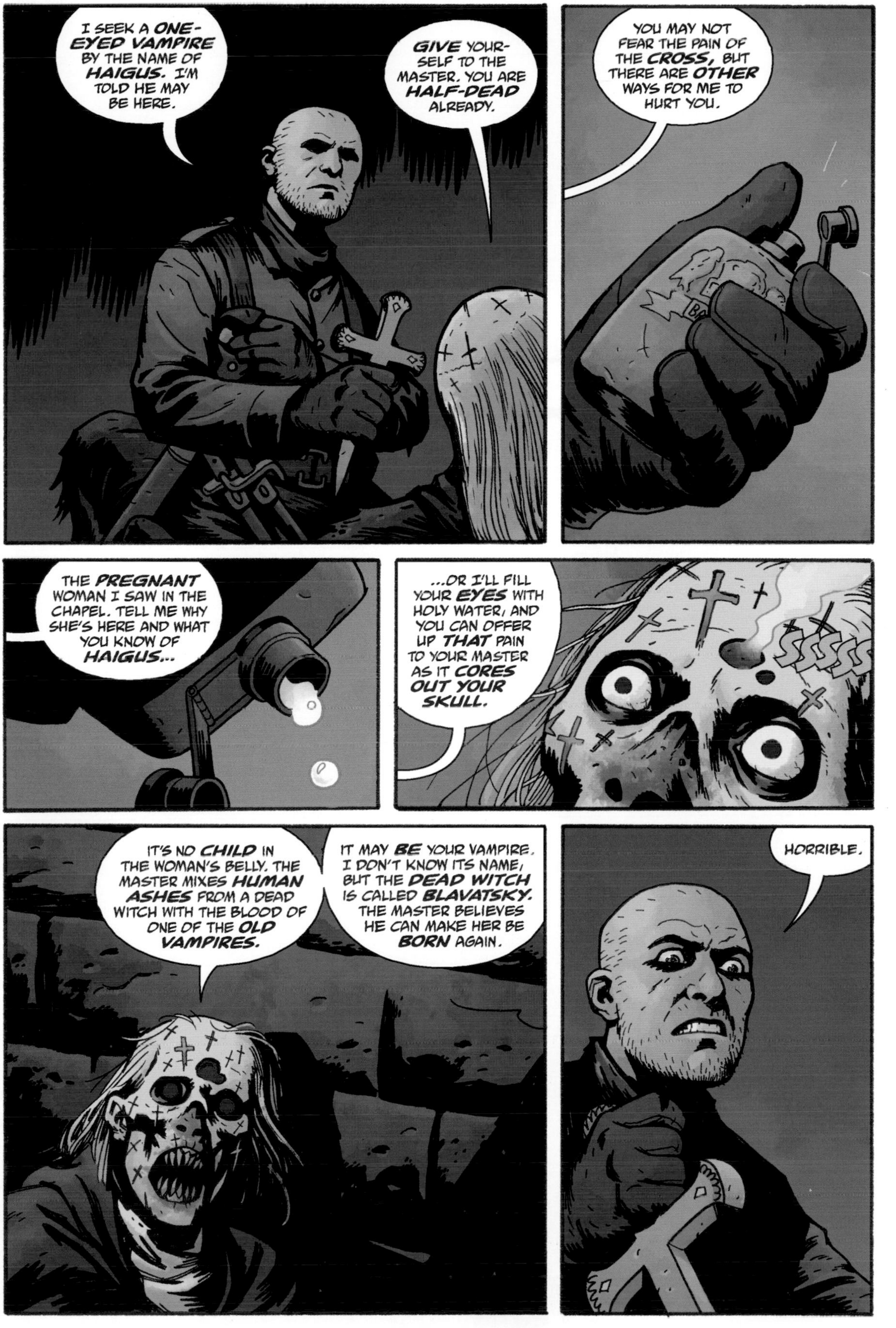
I SEEK A ONE-EYED VAMPIRE BY THE NAME OF HAIGUS. I'M TOLD HE MAY BE HERE.
GIVE YOURSELF TO THE MASTER. YOU ARE HALF-DEAD ALREADY.
YOU MAY NOT FEAR THE PAIN OF THE CROSS, BUT THERE ARE OTHER WAYS FOR ME TO HURT YOU.
THE PREGNANT WOMAN I SAW IN THE CHAPEL. TELL ME WHY SHE'S HERE AND WHAT YOU KNOW OF HAIGUS...
...OR I'LL FILL YOUR EYES WITH HOLY WATER, AND YOU CAN OFFER UP THAT PAIN TO YOUR MASTER AS IT CORES OUT YOUR SKULL.
SSSSS
IT'S NO CHILD IN THE WOMAN'S BELLY. THE MASTER MIXES HUMAN ASHES FROM A DEAD WITCH WITH THE BLOOD OF ONE OF THE OLD VAMPIRES.
IT MAY BE YOUR VAMPIRE. I DON'T KNOW ITS NAME, BUT THE DEAD WITCH IS CALLED BLAVATSKY. THE MASTER BELIEVES HE CAN MAKE HER BE BORN AGAIN.
HORRIBLE.

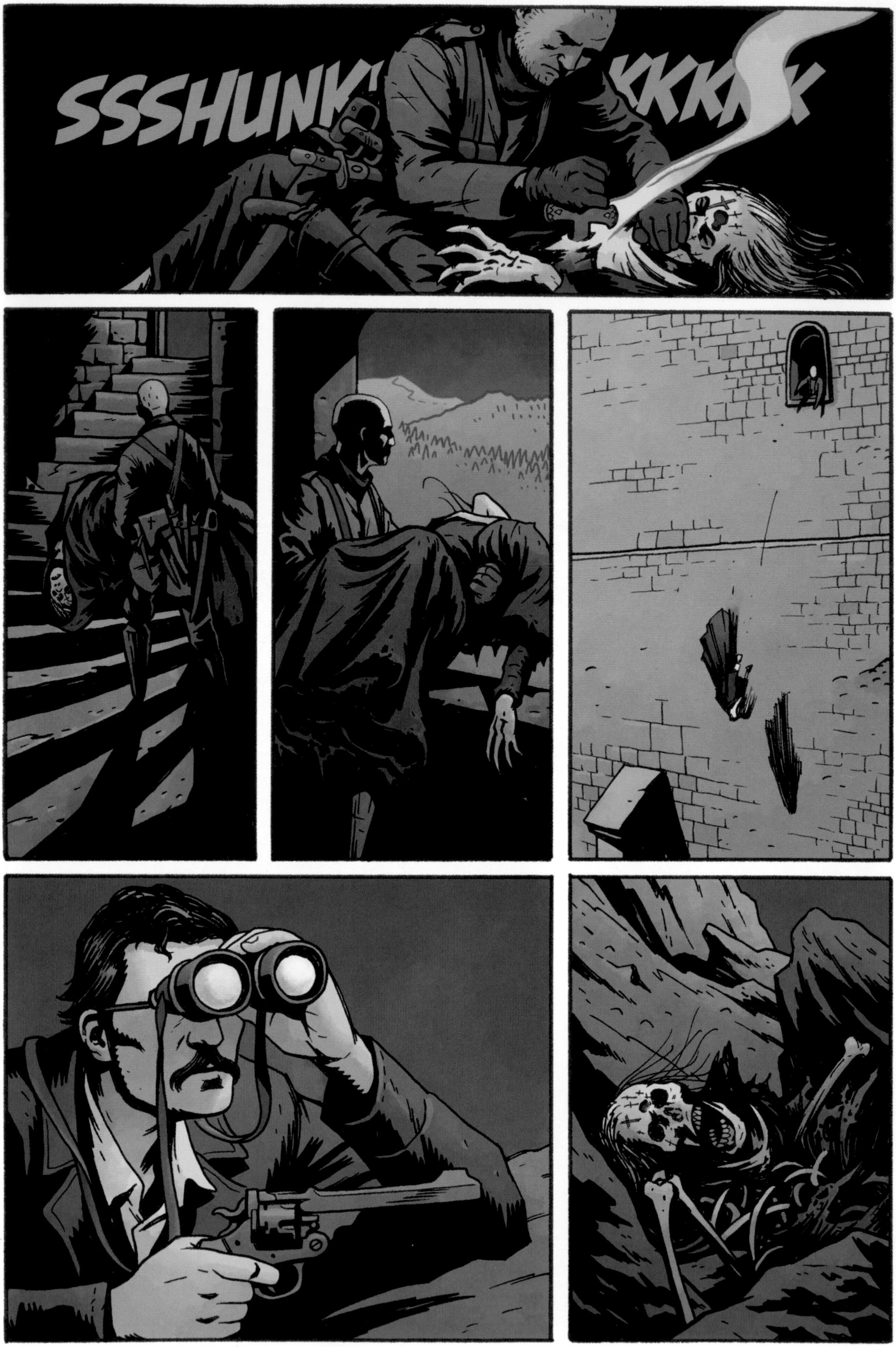
SSSHUNK KKKK

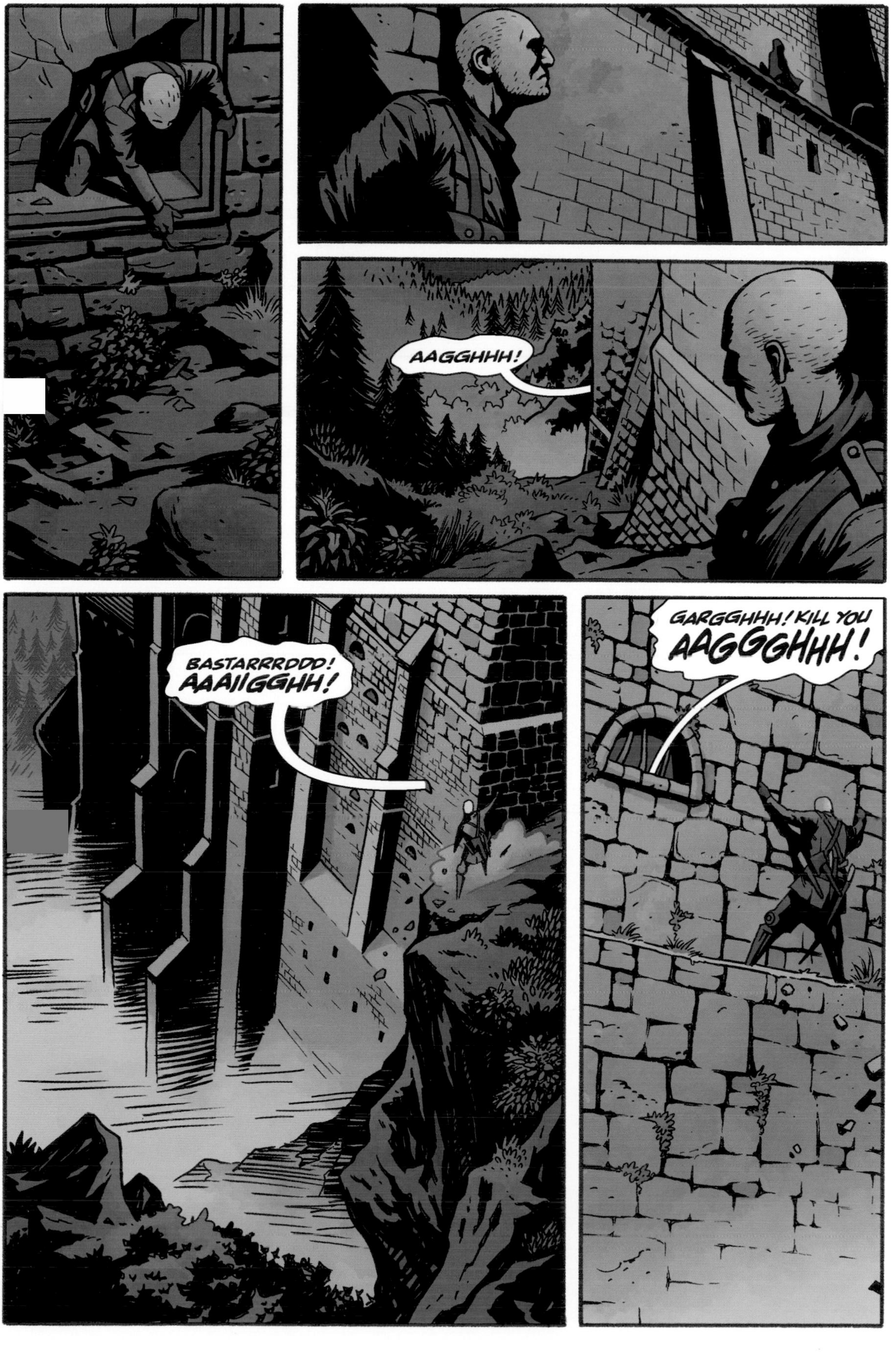
AAGGHHH!
BASTARRRDDD! AAAIIGGHH!
GARGGHHH! KILL YOU AAGGGHHH!

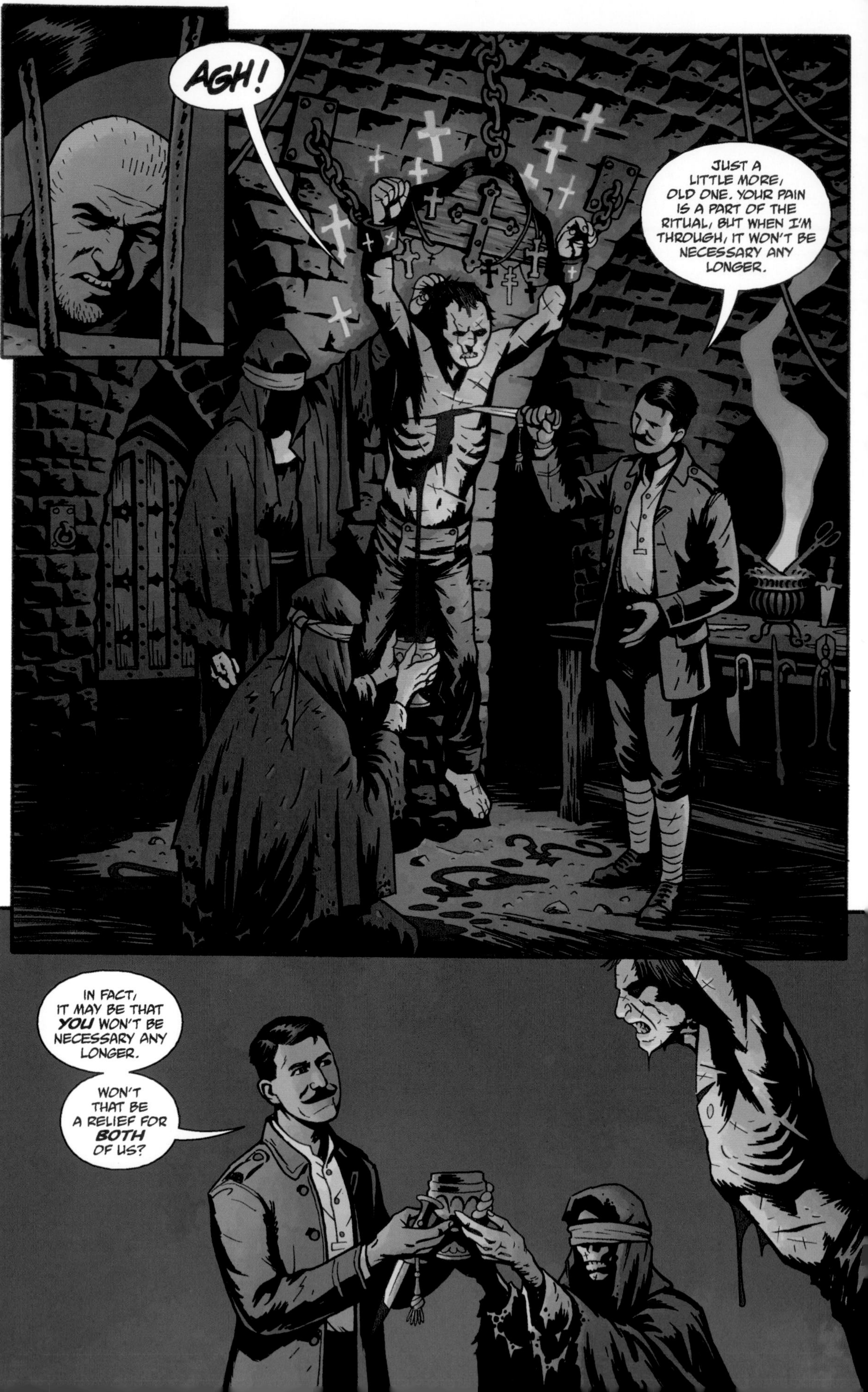
AGH!
JUST A LITTLE MORE, OLD ONE. YOUR PAIN IS A PART OF THE RITUAL, BUT WHEN I'M THROUGH, IT WON'T BE NECESSARY ANY LONGER.
IN FACT, IT MAY BE THAT YOU WON'T BE NECESSARY ANY LONGER.
WON'T THAT BE A RELIEF FOR BOTH OF US?

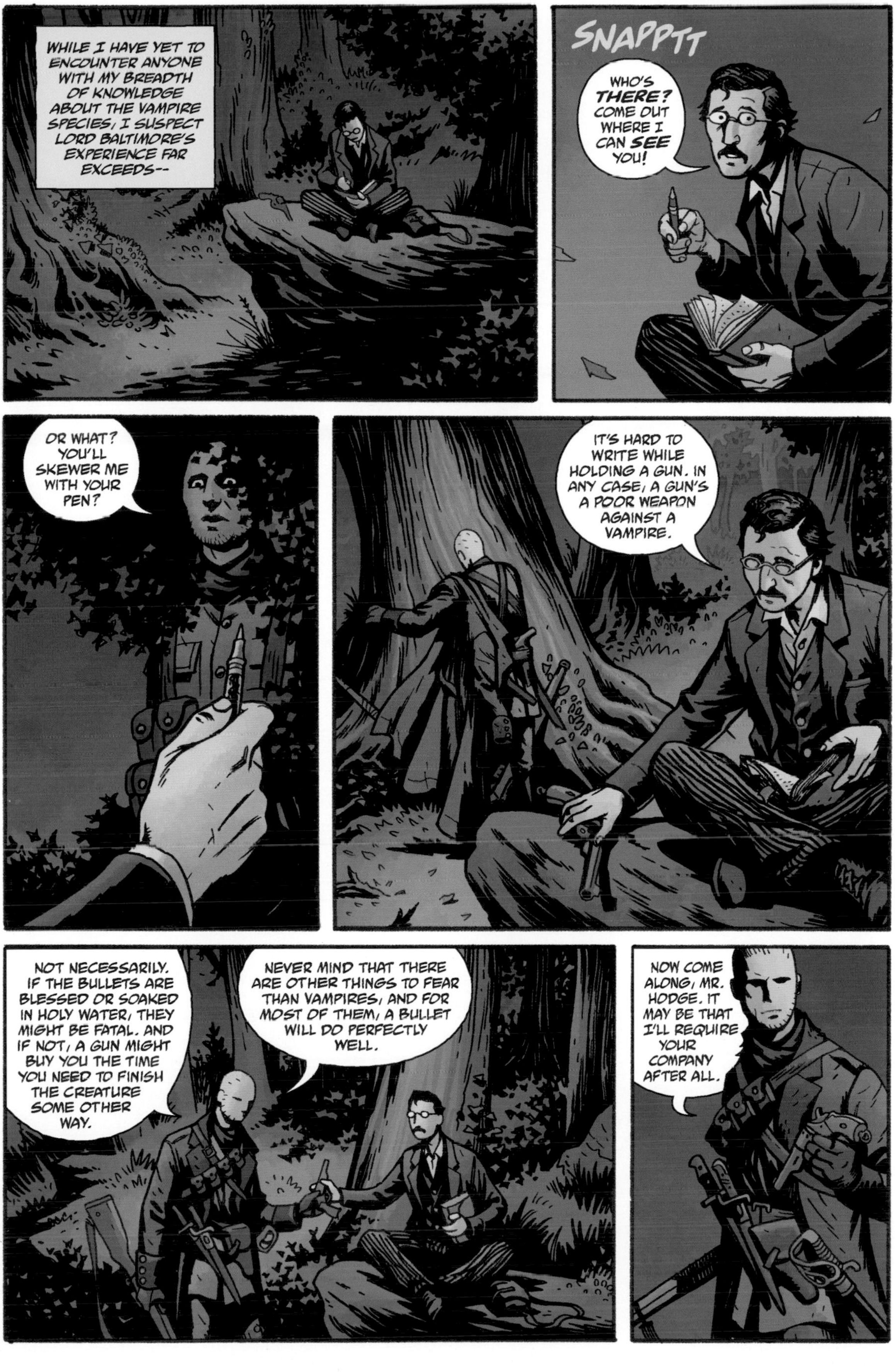
WHILE I HAVE YET TO ENCOUNTER ANYONE WITH MY BREADTH OF KNOWLEDGE ABOUT THE VAMPIRE SPECIES, I SUSPECT LORD BALTIMORE'S EXPERIENCE FAR EXCEEDS--
SNAPPTT
WHO'S THERE? COME OUT WHERE I CAN SEE YOU!
OR WHAT? YOU'LL SKEWER ME WITH YOUR PEN?
IT'S HARD TO WRITE WHILE HOLDING A GUN. IN ANY CASE, A GUN'S A POOR WEAPON AGAINST A VAMPIRE.
NOT NECESSARILY. IF THE BULLETS ARE BLESSED OR SOAKED IN HOLY WATER, THEY MIGHT BE FATAL. AND IF NOT, A GUN MIGHT BUY YOU THE TIME YOU NEED TO FINISH THE CREATURE SOME OTHER WAY.
NEVER MIND THAT THERE ARE OTHER THINGS TO FEAR THAN VAMPIRES, AND FOR MOST OF THEM, A BULLET WILL DO PERFECTLY WELL.
NOW COME ALONG, MR. HODGE. IT MAY BE THAT I'LL REQUIRE YOUR COMPANY AFTER ALL.

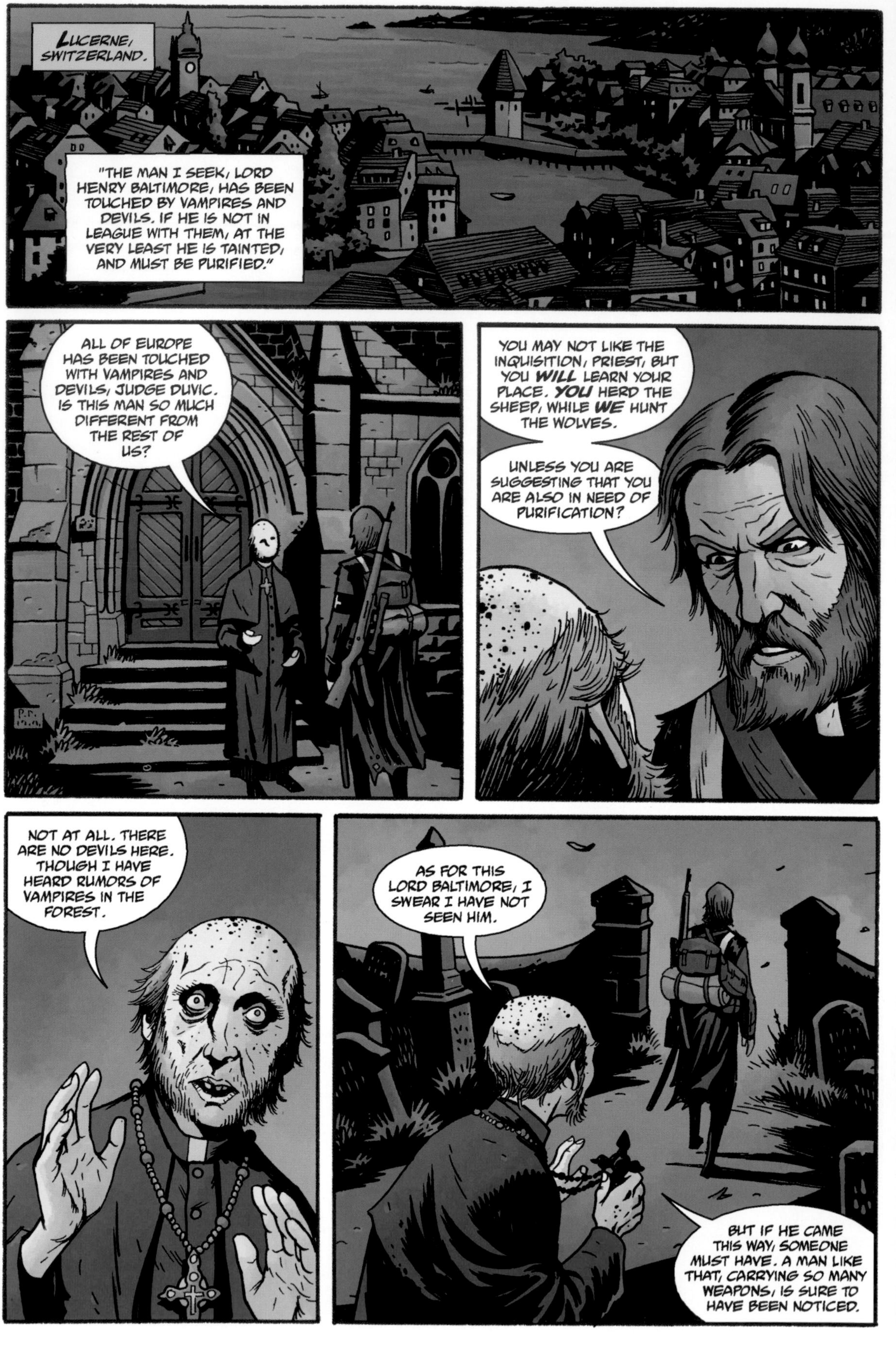
LUCERNE, SWITZERLAND.
"THE MAN I SEEK, LORD HENRY BALTIMORE, HAS BEEN TOUCHED BY VAMPIRES AND DEVILS. IF HE IS NOT IN LEAGUE WITH THEM, AT THE VERY LEAST HE IS TAINTED, AND MUST BE PURIFIED."
ALL OF EUROPE HAS BEEN TOUCHED WITH VAMPIRES AND DEVILS, JUDGE DUVIC. IS THIS MAN SO MUCH DIFFERENT FROM THE REST OF US?
YOU MAY NOT LIKE THE INQUISITION, PRIEST, BUT YOU WILL LEARN YOUR PLACE. YOU HERD THE SHEEP, WHILE WE HUNT THE WOLVES.
UNLESS YOU ARE SUGGESTING THAT YOU ARE ALSO IN NEED OF PURIFICATION?
NOT AT ALL. THERE ARE NO DEVILS HERE. THOUGH I HAVE HEARD RUMORS OF VAMPIRES IN THE FOREST.
AS FOR THIS LORD BALTIMORE, I SWEAR I HAVE NOT SEEN HIM.
BUT IF HE CAME THIS WAY, SOMEONE MUST HAVE. A MAN LIKE THAT, CARRYING SO MANY WEAPONS, IS SURE TO HAVE BEEN NOTICED.

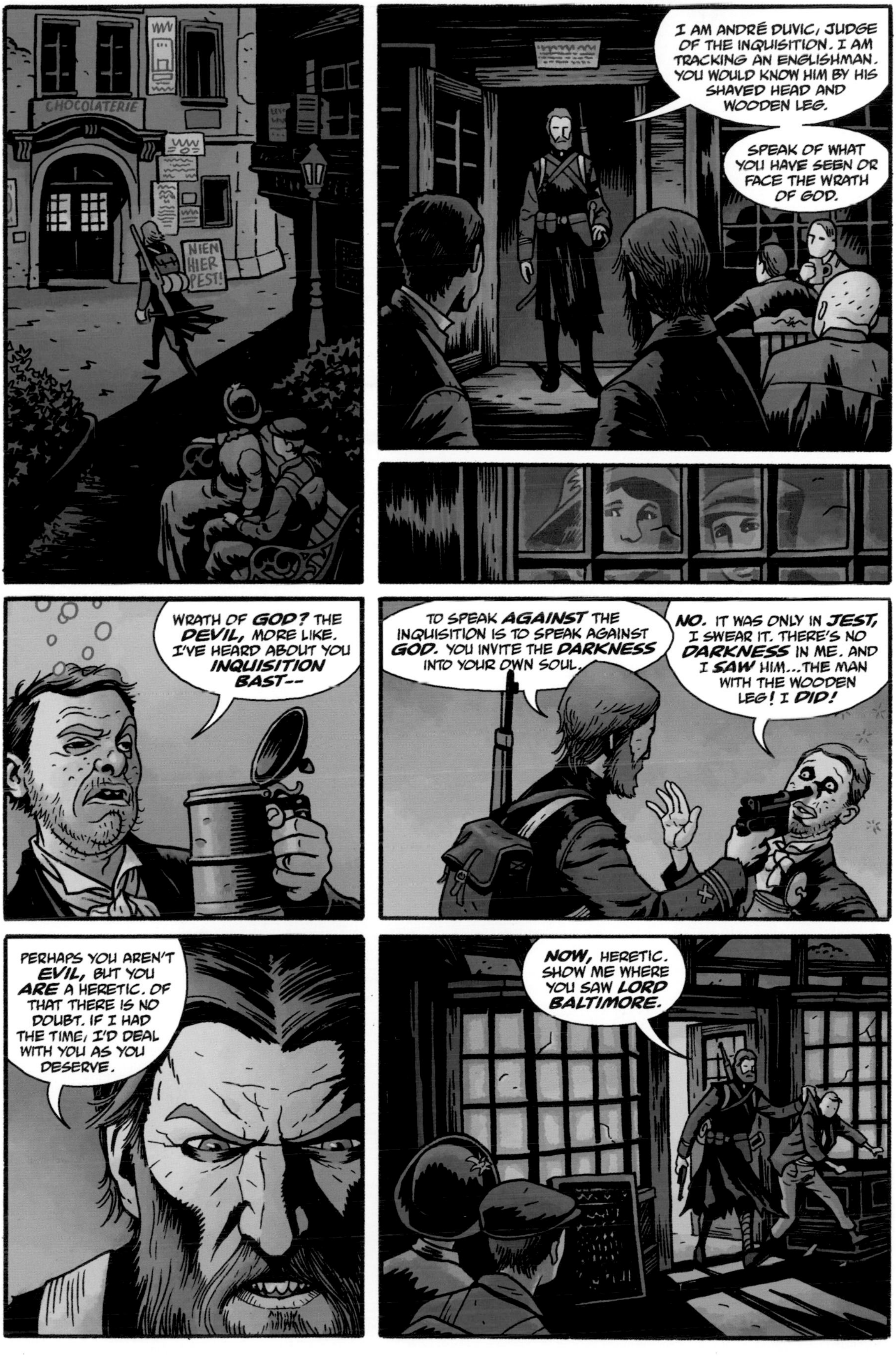
CHOCOLATERIE
NIEN HIER PEST!
I AM ANDRÉ DUVIC, JUDGE OF THE INQUISITION. I AM TRACKING AN ENGLISHMAN. YOU WOULD KNOW HIM BY HIS SHAVED HEAD AND WOODEN LEG.
SPEAK OF WHAT YOU HAVE SEEN OR FACE THE WRATH OF GOD.
WRATH OF GOD? THE DEVIL, MORE LIKE. I'VE HEARD ABOUT YOU INQUISITION BAST--
TO SPEAK AGAINST THE INQUISITION IS TO SPEAK AGAINST GOD. YOU INVITE THE DARKNESS INTO YOUR OWN SOUL.
NO. IT WAS ONLY IN JEST, I SWEAR IT. THERE'S NO DARKNESS IN ME. AND I SAW HIM... THE MAN WITH THE WOODEN LEG! I DID!
PERHAPS YOU AREN'T EVIL, BUT YOU ARE A HERETIC. OF THAT THERE IS NO DOUBT. IF I HAD THE TIME, I'D DEAL WITH YOU AS YOU DESERVE.
NOW, HERETIC. SHOW ME WHERE YOU SAW LORD BALTIMORE.

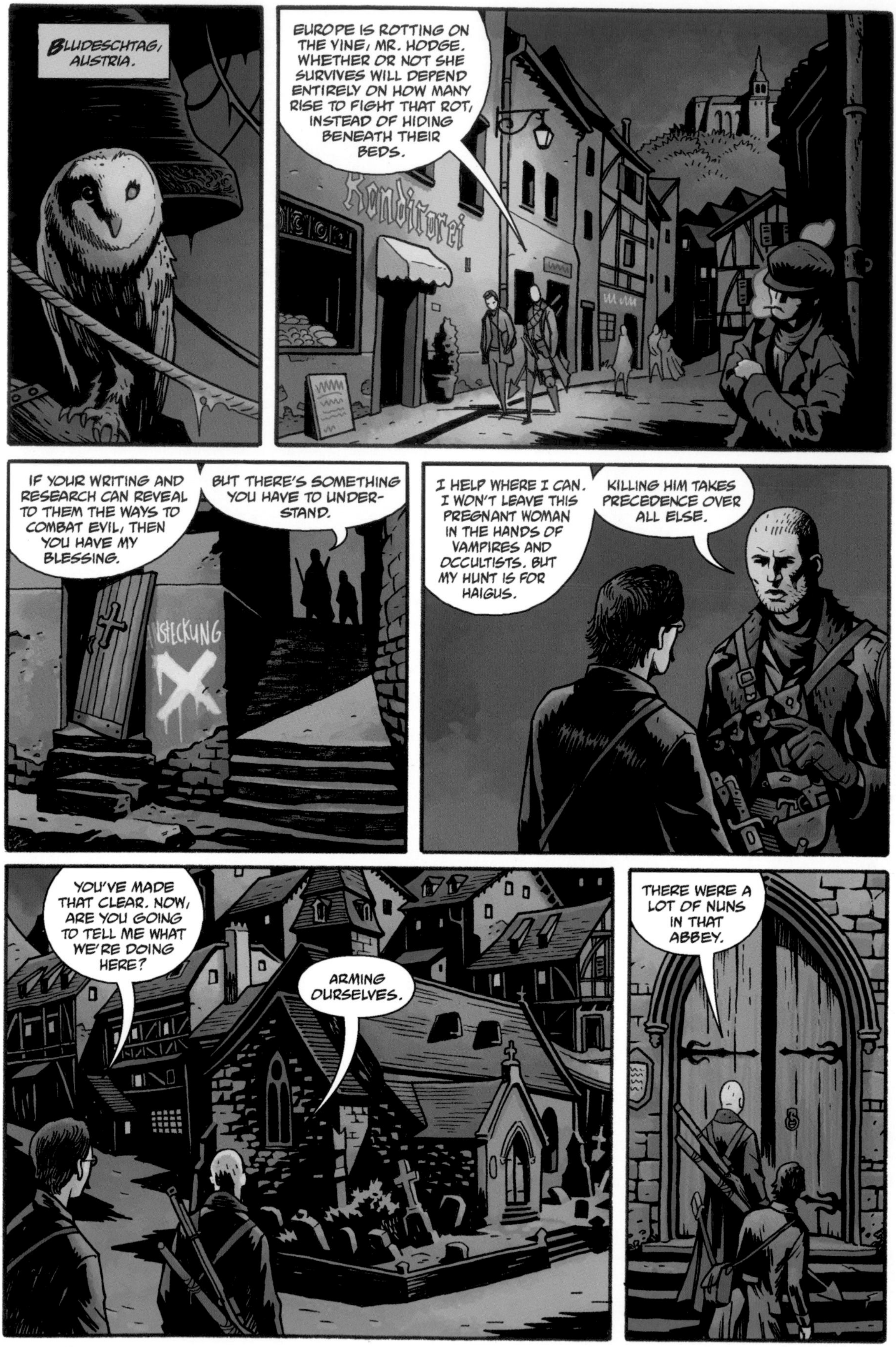
BLUDESCHTAG, AUSTRIA.
EUROPE IS ROTTING ON THE VINE, MR. HODGE. WHETHER OR NOT SHE SURVIVES WILL DEPEND ENTIRELY ON HOW MANY RISE TO FIGHT THAT ROT, INSTEAD OF HIDING BENEATH THEIR BEDS.
Konditorei
IF YOUR WRITING AND RESEARCH CAN REVEAL TO THEM THE WAYS TO COMBAT EVIL, THEN YOU HAVE MY BLESSING.
BUT THERE'S SOMETHING YOU HAVE TO UNDERSTAND.
ANSTECKUNG
I HELP WHERE I CAN. I WON'T LEAVE THIS PREGNANT WOMAN IN THE HANDS OF VAMPIRES AND OCCULTISTS. BUT MY HUNT IS FOR HAIGUS.
KILLING HIM TAKES PRECEDENCE OVER ALL ELSE.
YOU'VE MADE THAT CLEAR. NOW, ARE YOU GOING TO TELL ME WHAT WE'RE DOING HERE?
ARMING OURSELVES.
THERE WERE A LOT OF NUNS IN THAT ABBEY.

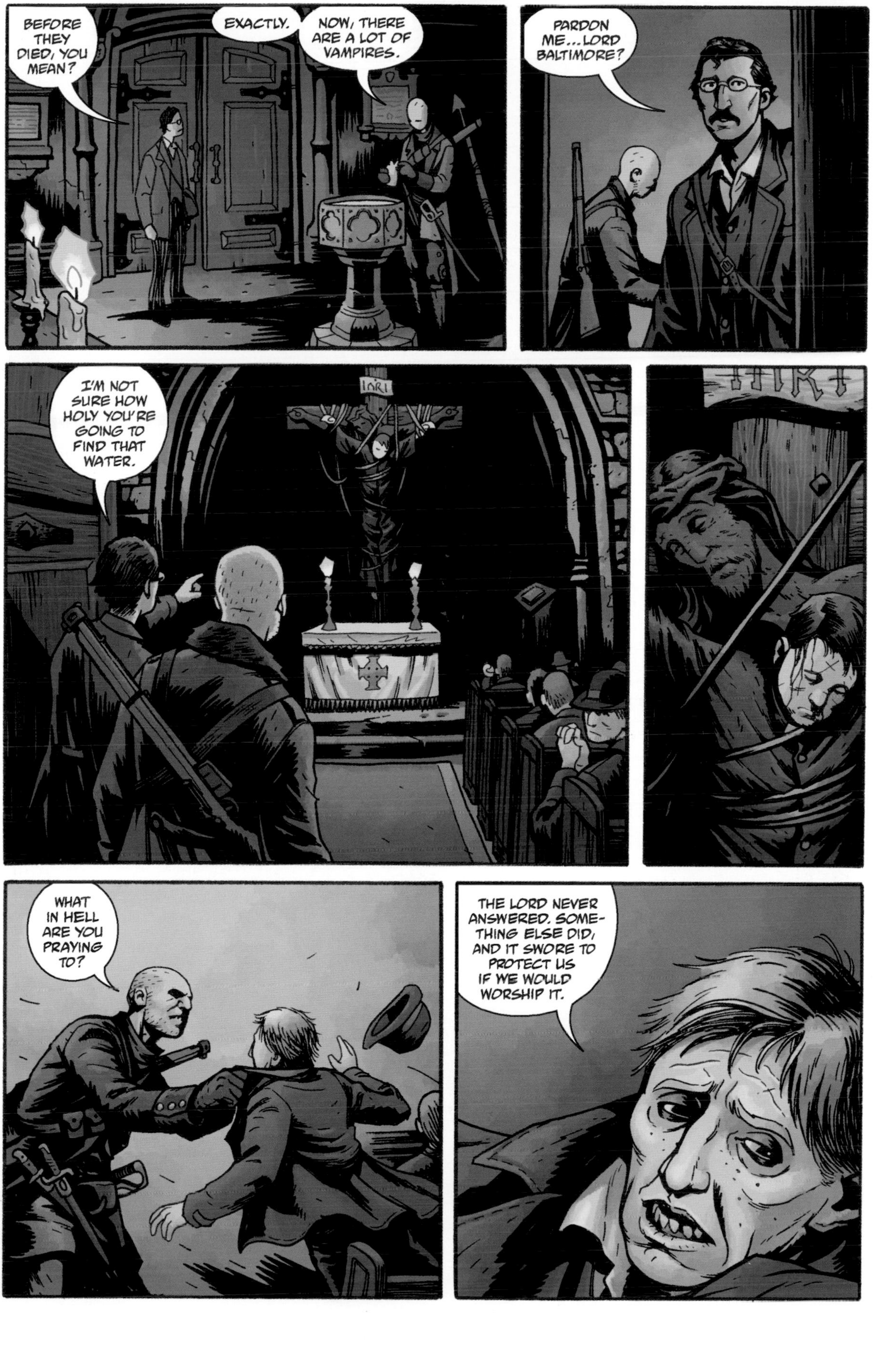
BEFORE THEY DIED, YOU MEAN?
EXACTLY.
NOW, THERE ARE A LOT OF VAMPIRES.
PARDON ME...LORD BALTIMORE?
I'M NOT SURE HOW HOLY YOU'RE GOING TO FIND THAT WATER.
INRI
WHAT IN HELL ARE YOU PRAYING TO?
THE LORD NEVER ANSWERED. SOMETHING ELSE DID, AND IT SWORE TO PROTECT US IF WE WOULD WORSHIP IT.

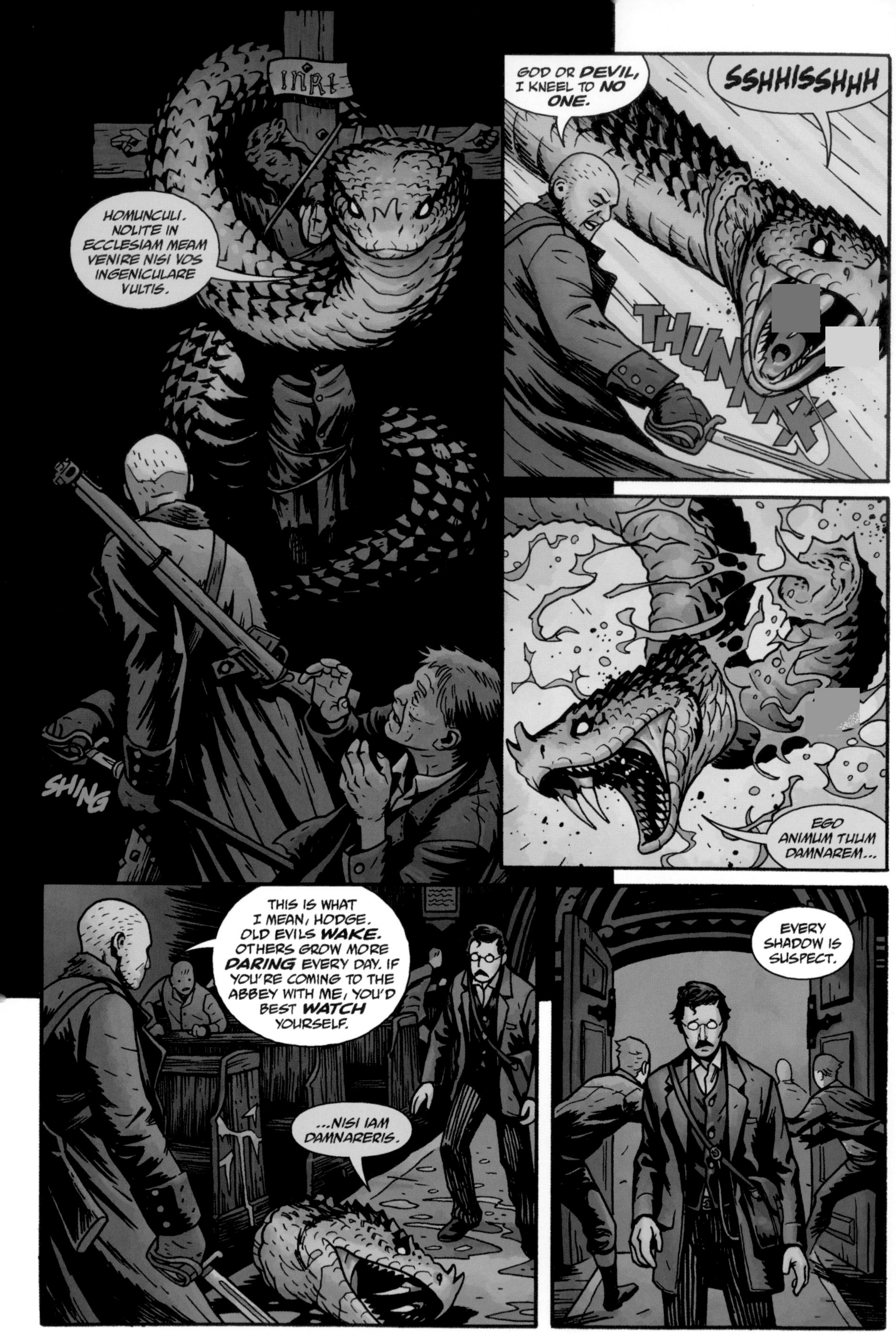
INRI
HOMUNCULI. NOLITE IN ECCLESIAM MEAM VENIRE NISI VOS INGENICULARE VULTIS.
SHING
GOD OR DEVIL, I KNEEL TO NO ONE.
SSHHISSHHH
THUNNKK
EGO ANIMUM TUUM DAMNAREM...
THIS IS WHAT I MEAN, HODGE. OLD EVILS WAKE. OTHERS GROW MORE DARING EVERY DAY. IF YOU'RE COMING TO THE ABBEY WITH ME, YOU'D BEST WATCH YOURSELF.
...NISI IAM DAMNARERIS.
EVERY SHADOW IS SUSPECT.

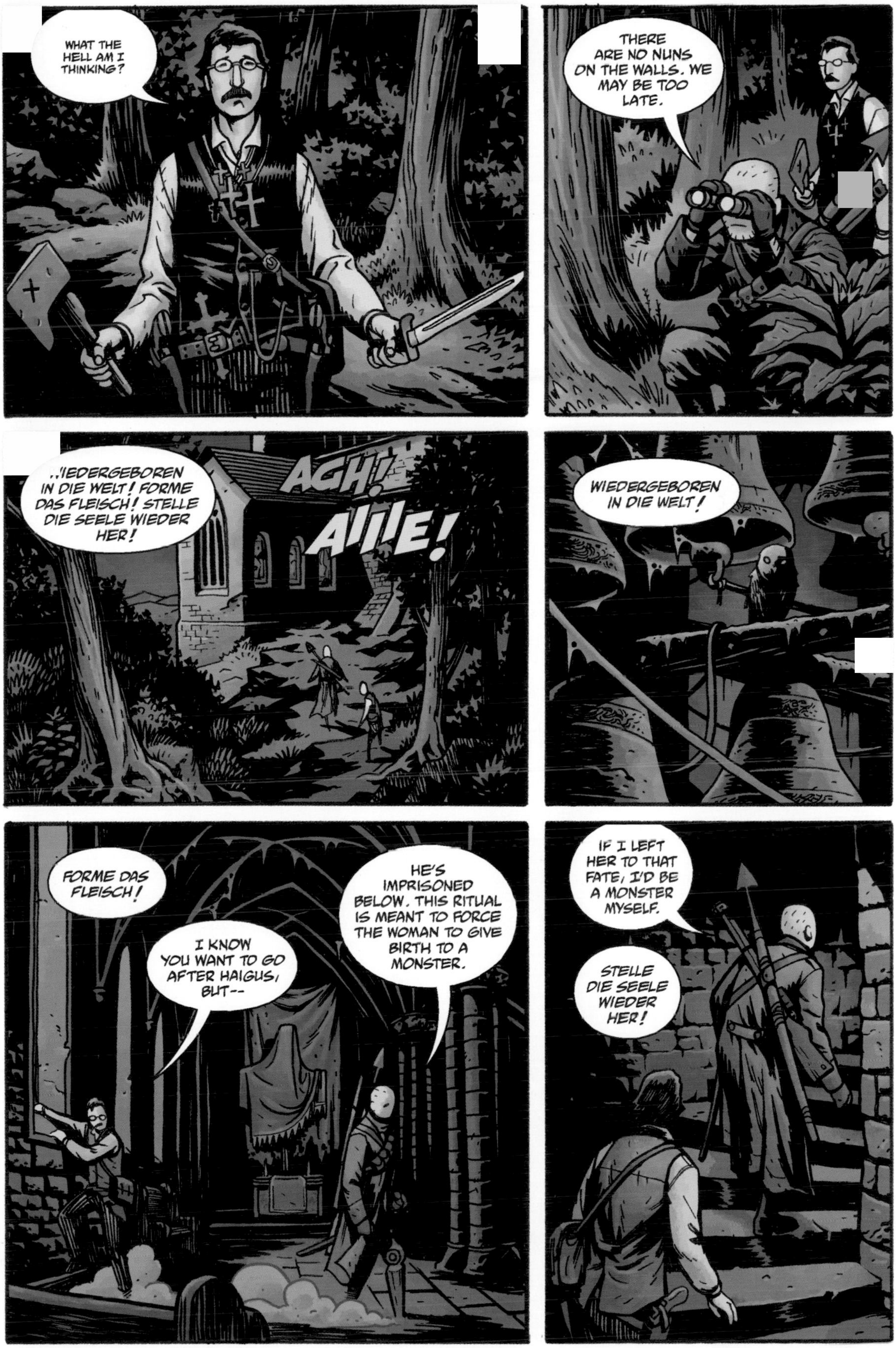
WHAT THE HELL AM I THINKING?
THERE ARE NO NUNS ON THE WALLS. WE MAY BE TOO LATE.
..IEDERGEBOREN IN DIE WELT! FORME DAS FLEISCH! STELLE DIE SEELE WIEDER HER!
AGH!
AIIIE!
WIEDERGEBOREN IN DIE WELT!
FORME DAS FLEISCH!
I KNOW YOU WANT TO GO AFTER HAIGUS, BUT--
HE'S IMPRISONED BELOW. THIS RITUAL IS MEANT TO FORCE THE WOMAN TO GIVE BIRTH TO A MONSTER.
IF I LEFT HER TO THAT FATE, I'D BE A MONSTER MYSELF.
STELLE DIE SEELE WIEDER HER!

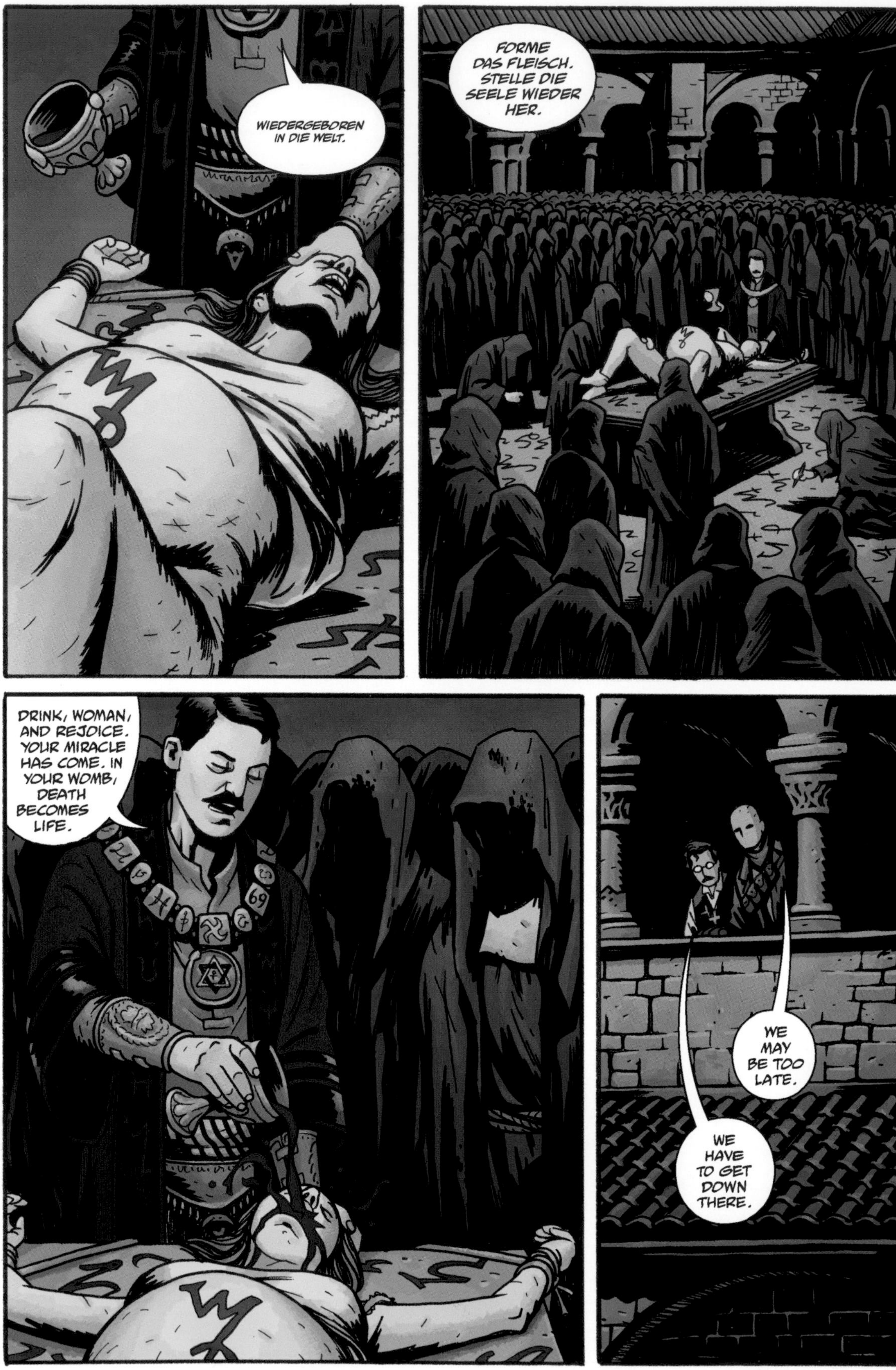
WIEDERGEBOREN IN DIE WELT.
FORME DAS FLEISCH. STELLE DIE SEELE WIEDER HER.
DRINK, WOMAN, AND REJOICE. YOUR MIRACLE HAS COME. IN YOUR WOMB, DEATH BECOMES LIFE.
WE MAY BE TOO LATE.
WE HAVE TO GET DOWN THERE.

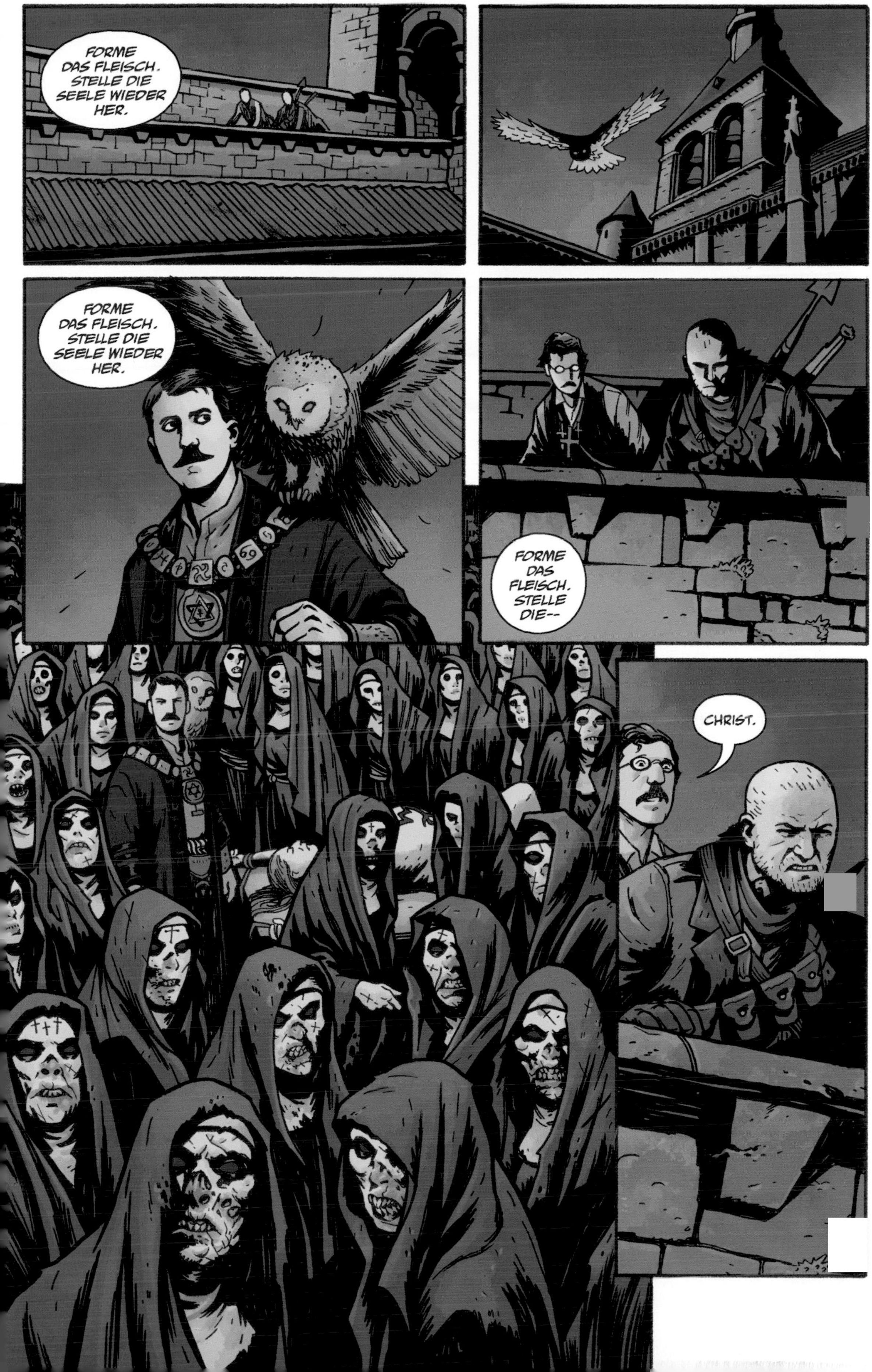
FORME DAS FLEISCH. STELLE DIE SEELE WIEDER HER.
FORME DAS FLEISCH. STELLE DIE SEELE WIEDER HER.
FORME DAS FLEISCH. STELLE DIE--
CHRIST.

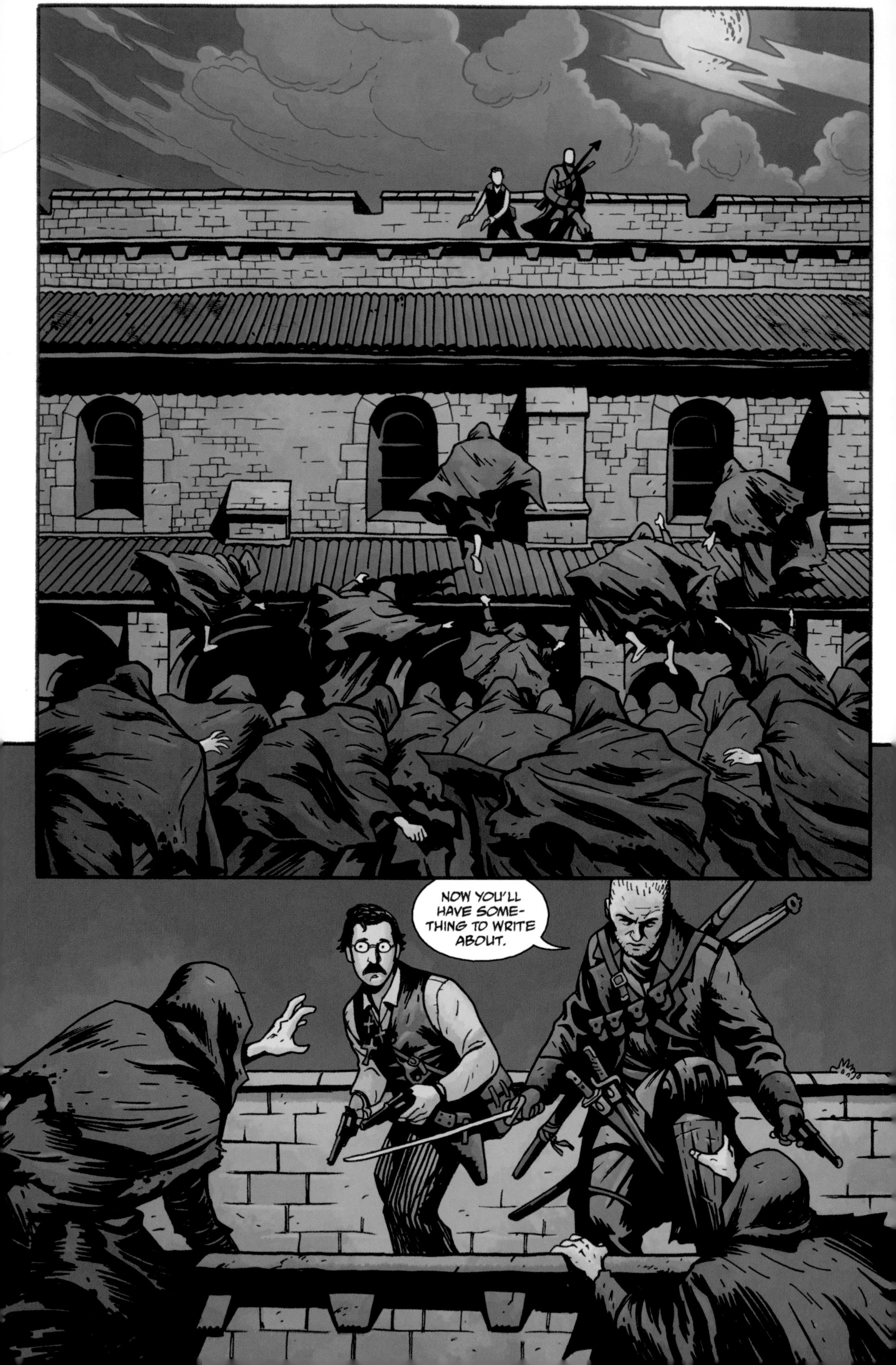
NOW YOU'LL HAVE SOME-THING TO WRITE ABOUT.

CHAPTER THREE

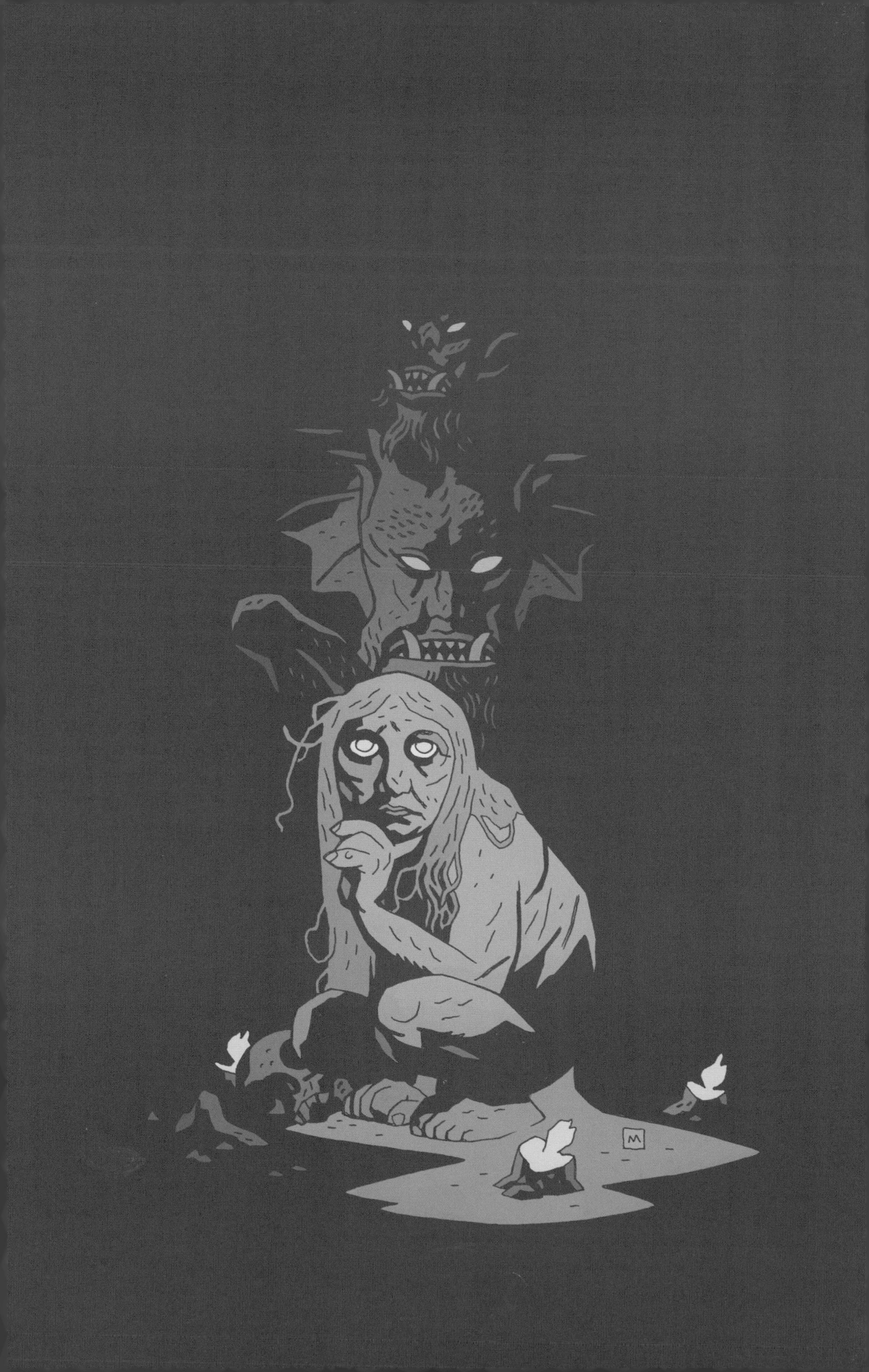

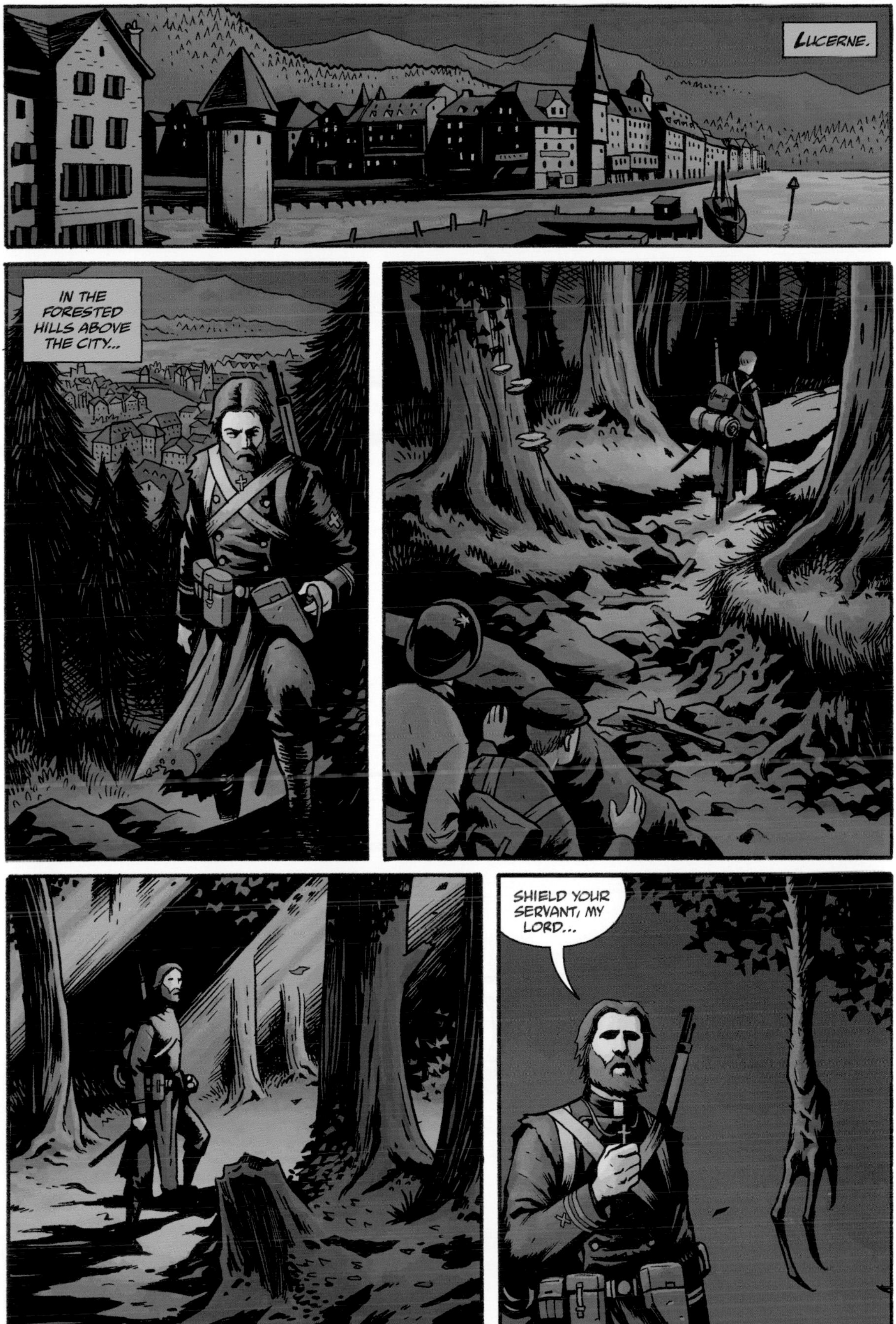
LUCERNE.
IN THE FORESTED HILLS ABOVE THE CITY...
SHIELD YOUR SERVANT, MY LORD...

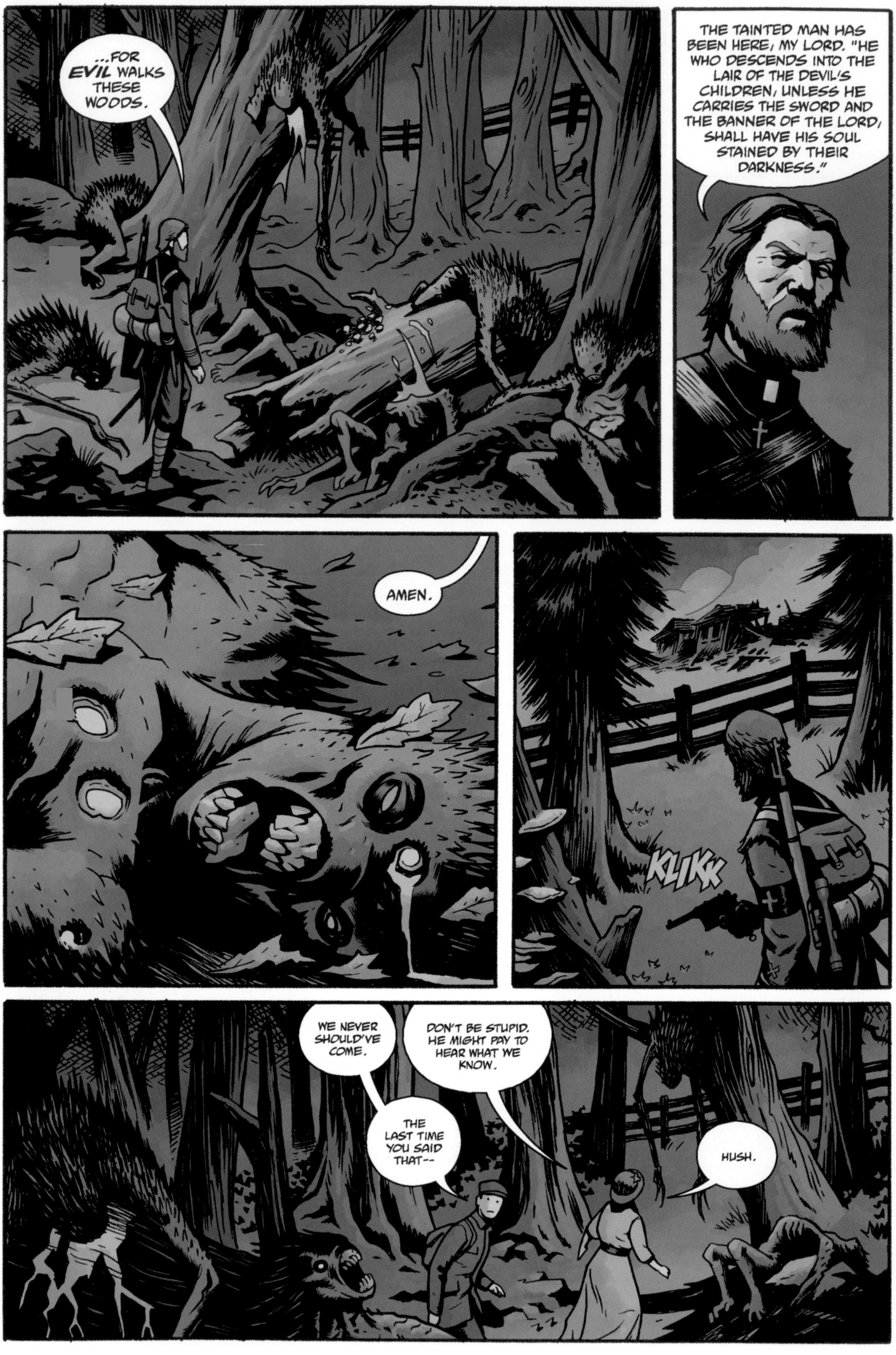
...FOR EVIL WALKS THESE WOODS.
THE TAINTED MAN HAS BEEN HERE, MY LORD. "HE WHO DESCENDS INTO THE LAIR OF THE DEVIL'S CHILDREN, UNLESS HE CARRIES THE SWORD AND THE BANNER OF THE LORD, SHALL HAVE HIS SOUL STAINED BY THEIR DARKNESS."
AMEN.
KLIKK
WE NEVER SHOULD'VE COME.
DON'T BE STUPID. HE MIGHT PAY TO HEAR WHAT WE KNOW.
THE LAST TIME YOU SAID THAT--
HUSH.

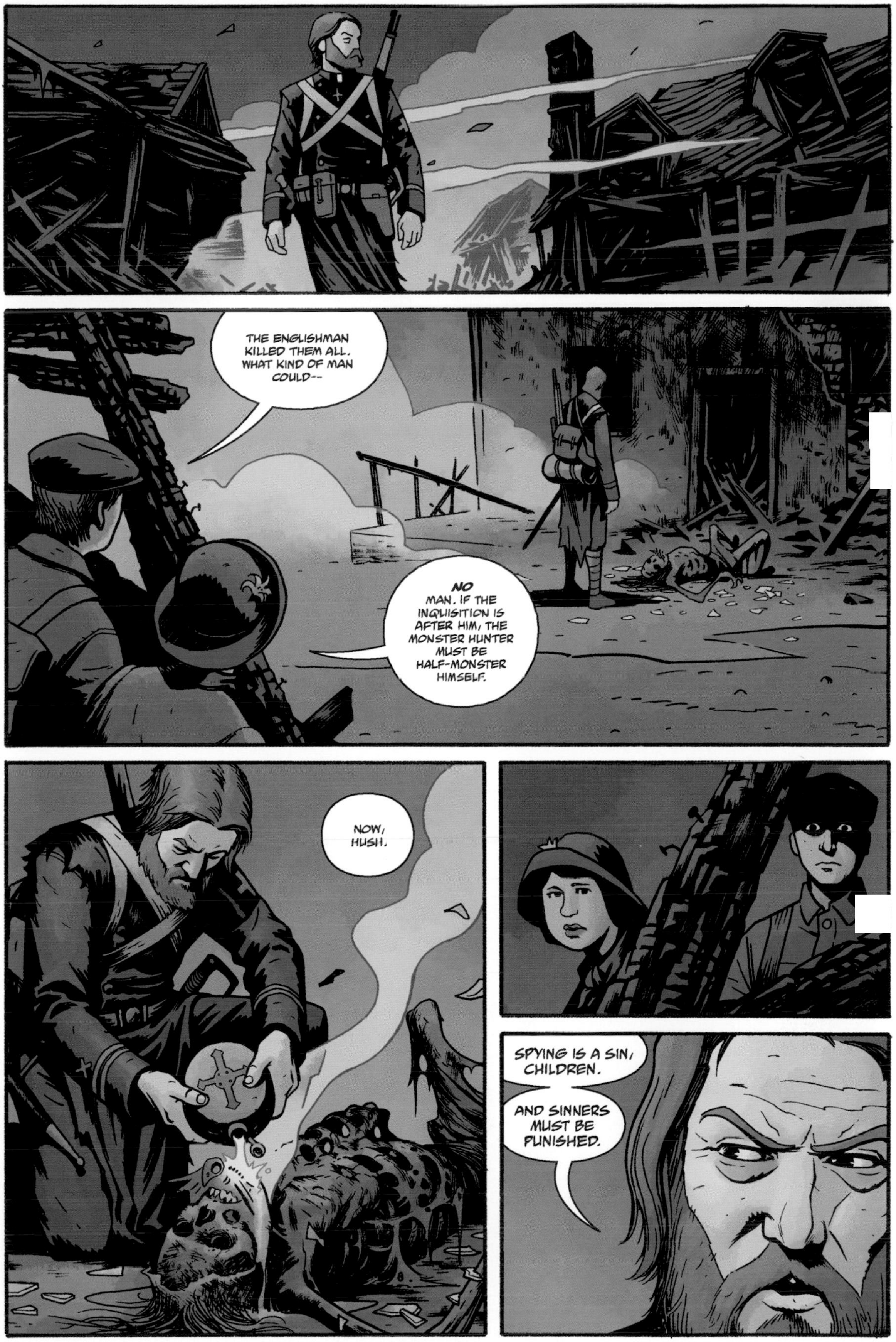
THE ENGLISHMAN KILLED THEM ALL. WHAT KIND OF MAN COULD--
NO MAN. IF THE INQUISITION IS AFTER HIM, THE MONSTER HUNTER MUST BE HALF-MONSTER HIMSELF.
NOW, HUSH.
SPYING IS A SIN, CHILDREN.
AND SINNERS MUST BE PUNISHED.

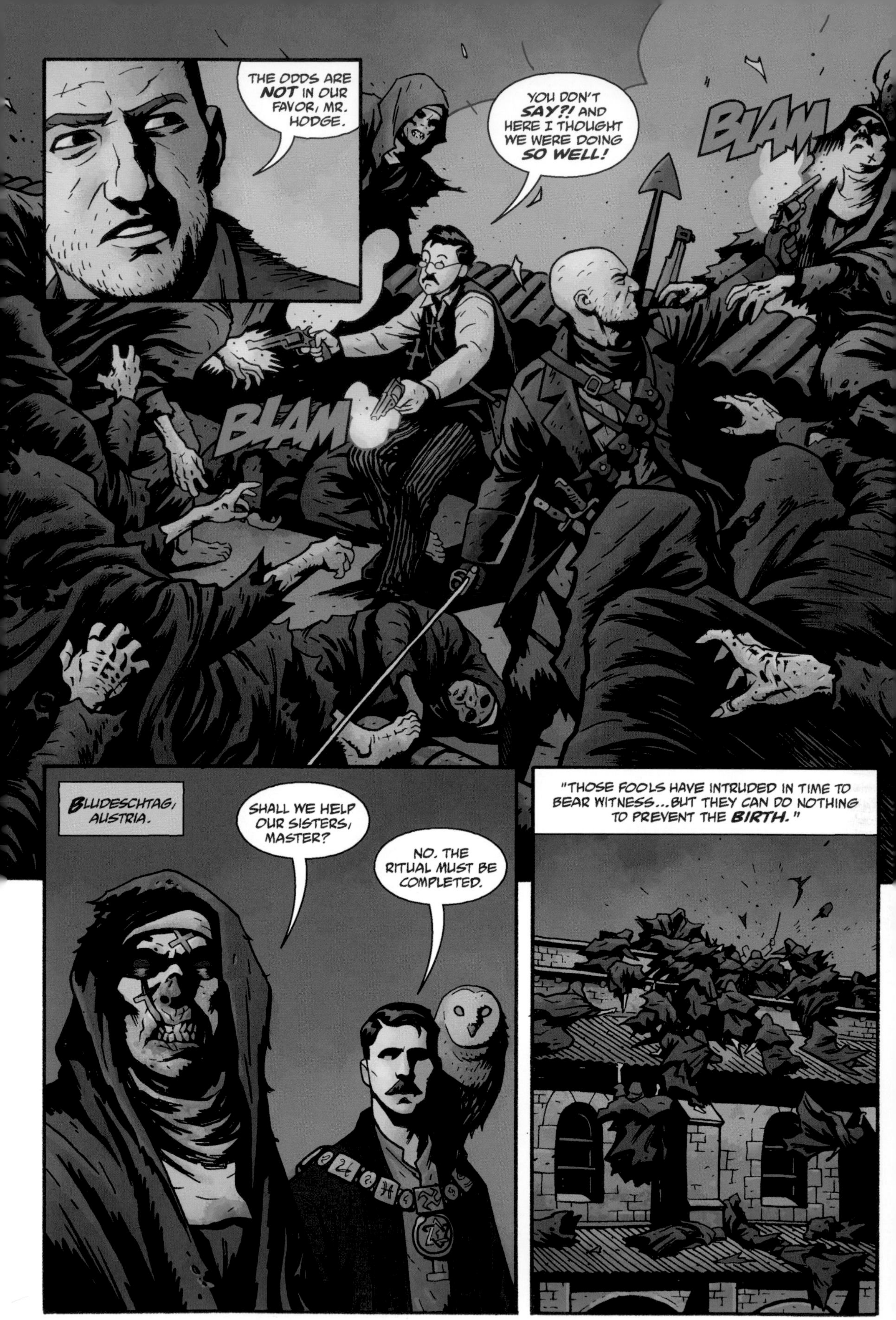
THE ODDS ARE NOT IN OUR FAVOR, MR. HODGE.
YOU DON'T SAY?! AND HERE I THOUGHT WE WERE DOING SO WELL!
BLAM
BLAM
BLUDESCHTAG, AUSTRIA.
SHALL WE HELP OUR SISTERS, MASTER?
NO. THE RITUAL MUST BE COMPLETED.
"THOSE FOOLS HAVE INTRUDED IN TIME TO BEAR WITNESS...BUT THEY CAN DO NOTHING TO PREVENT THE BIRTH."

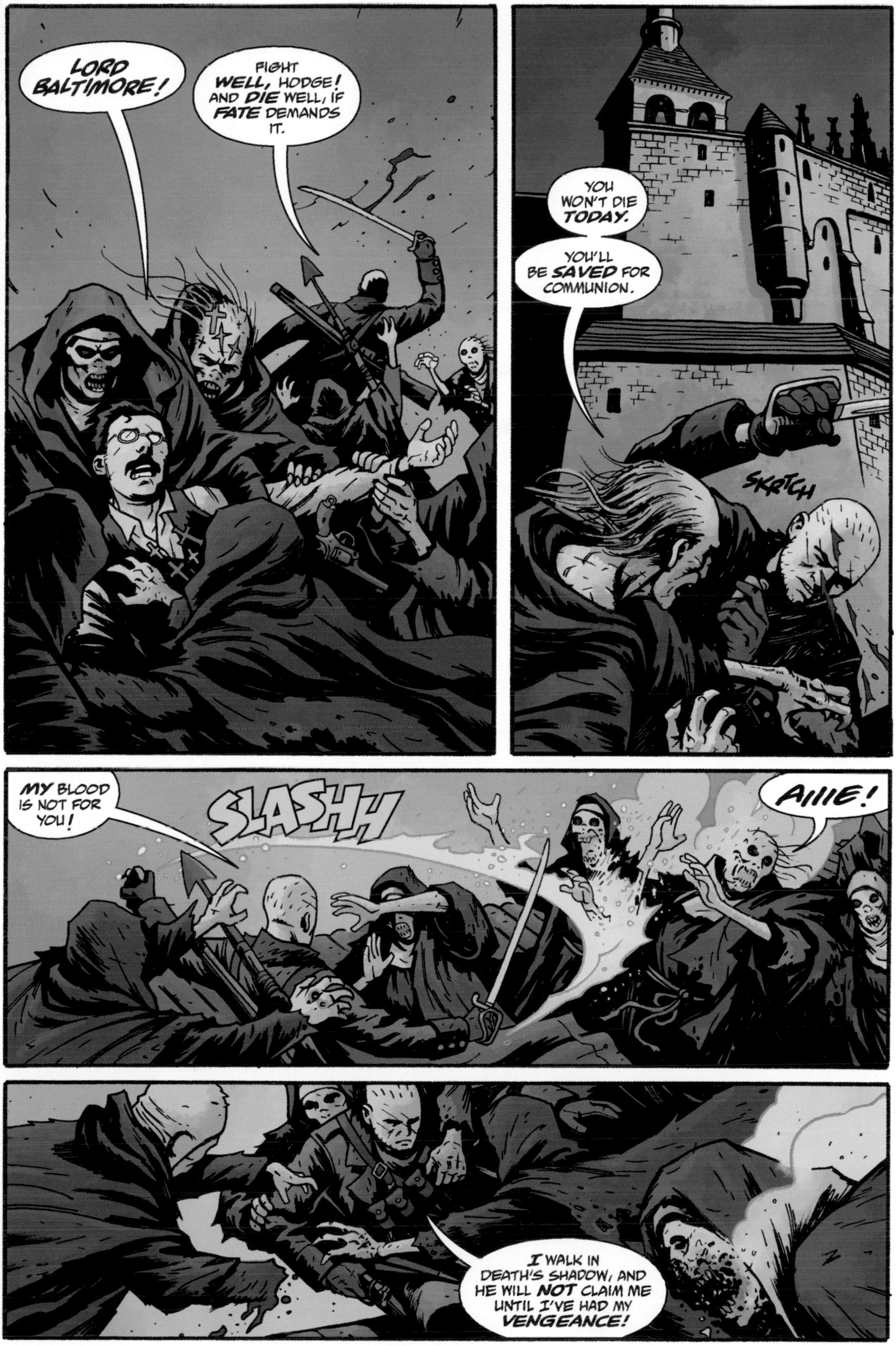
LORD BALTIMORE!
FIGHT WELL, HODGE! AND DIE WELL, IF FATE DEMANDS IT.
YOU WON'T DIE TODAY.
YOU'LL BE SAVED FOR COMMUNION.
SKRTCH
MY BLOOD IS NOT FOR YOU!
SLASHH
AIIIE!
I WALK IN DEATH'S SHADOW, AND HE WILL NOT CLAIM ME UNTIL I'VE HAD MY VENGEANCE!

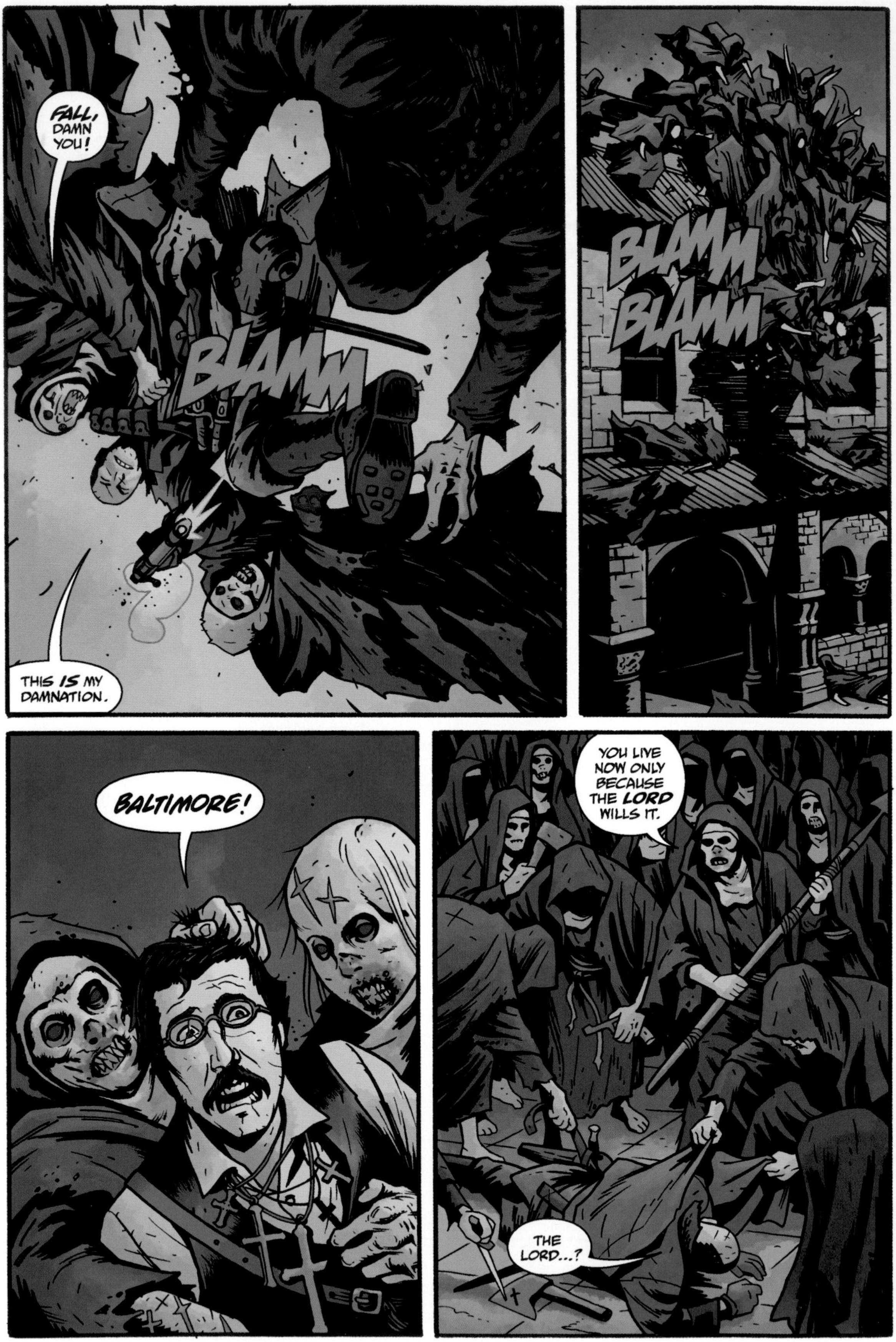
FALL, DAMN YOU!
BLAMM
THIS IS MY DAMNATION.
BLAMM
BLAMM
BALTIMORE!
YOU LIVE NOW ONLY BECAUSE THE LORD WILLS IT.
THE LORD...?

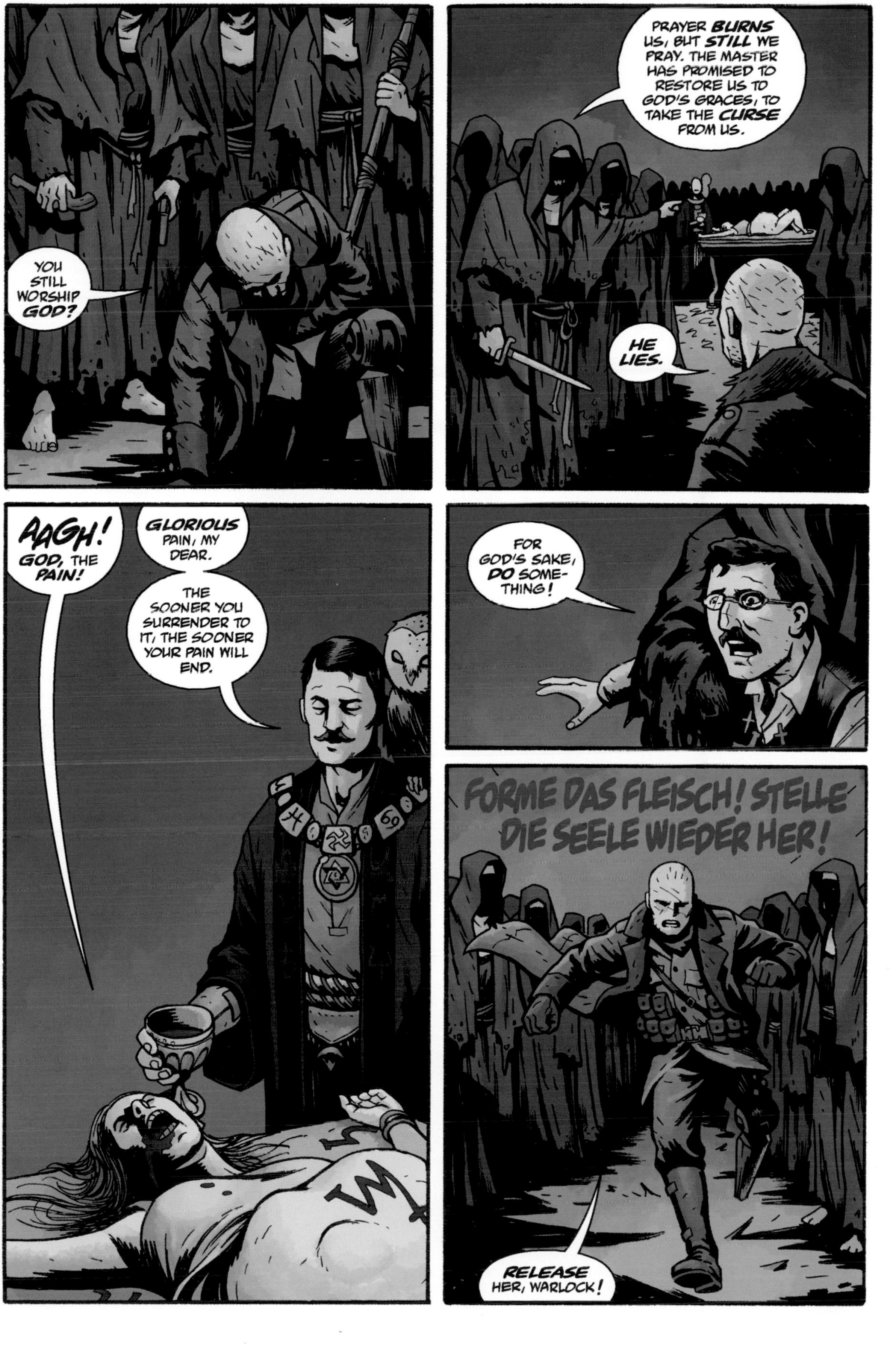
YOU STILL WORSHIP GOD?
PRAYER BURNS US, BUT STILL WE PRAY. THE MASTER HAS PROMISED TO RESTORE US TO GOD'S GRACES, TO TAKE THE CURSE FROM US.
HE LIES.
AAGH! GOD, THE PAIN!
GLORIOUS PAIN, MY DEAR.
THE SOONER YOU SURRENDER TO IT, THE SOONER YOUR PAIN WILL END.
FOR GOD'S SAKE, DO SOME-THING!
FORME DAS FLEISCH! STELLE DIE SEELE WIEDER HER!
RELEASE HER, WARLOCK!

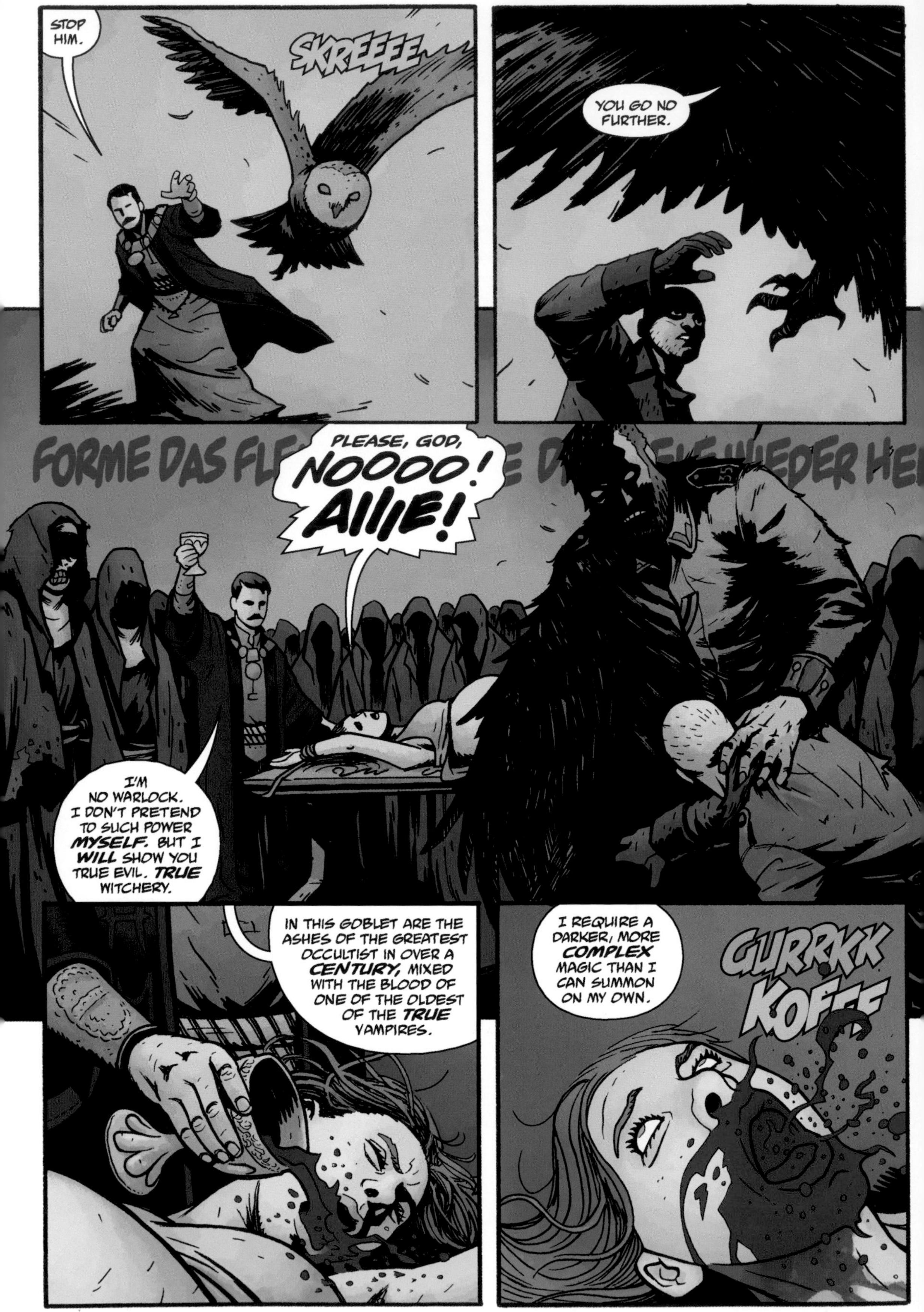

STOP HIM.
SKREEEEE
YOU GO NO FURTHER.
FORME DAS FLE
E D
EDER HE
PLEASE, GOD, NOOOO! ALLIE!
I'M NO WARLOCK. I DON'T PRETEND TO SUCH POWER MYSELF. BUT I WILL SHOW YOU TRUE EVIL. TRUE WITCHERY.
IN THIS GOBLET ARE THE ASHES OF THE GREATEST OCCULTIST IN OVER A CENTURY, MIXED WITH THE BLOOD OF ONE OF THE OLDEST OF THE TRUE VAMPIRES.
I REQUIRE A DARKER, MORE COMPLEX MAGIC THAN I CAN SUMMON ON MY OWN.
GURRKK KOFFF

STOP HIM, BALTIMORE. WE'VE **GOT** TO--

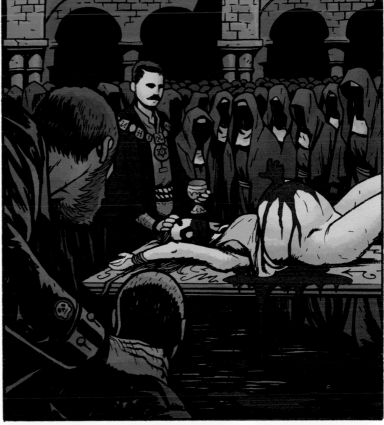

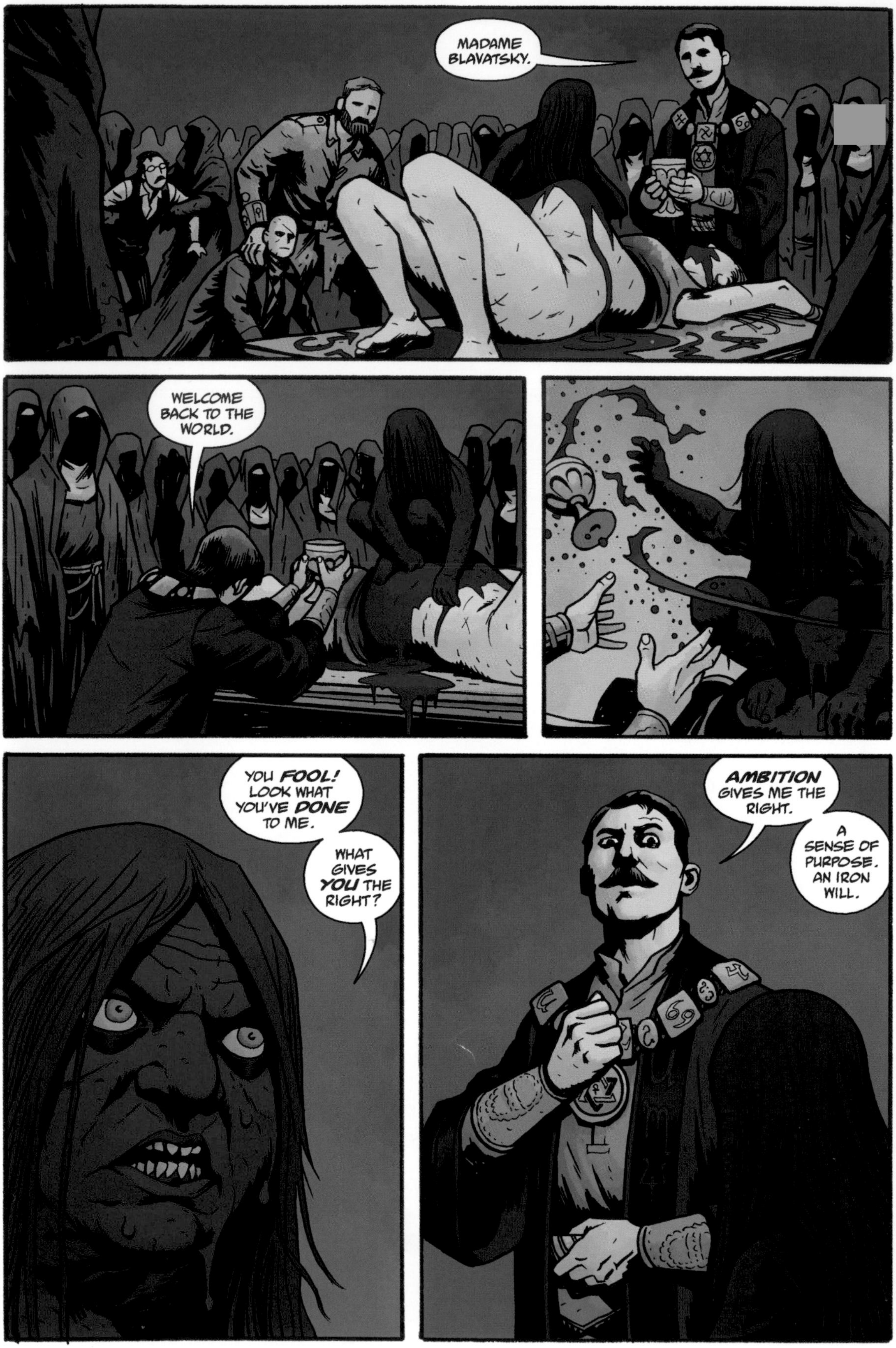

MADAME BLAVATSKY.
WELCOME BACK TO THE WORLD.
YOU FOOL! LOOK WHAT YOU'VE DONE TO ME.
WHAT GIVES YOU THE RIGHT?
AMBITION GIVES ME THE RIGHT.
A SENSE OF PURPOSE. AN IRON WILL.

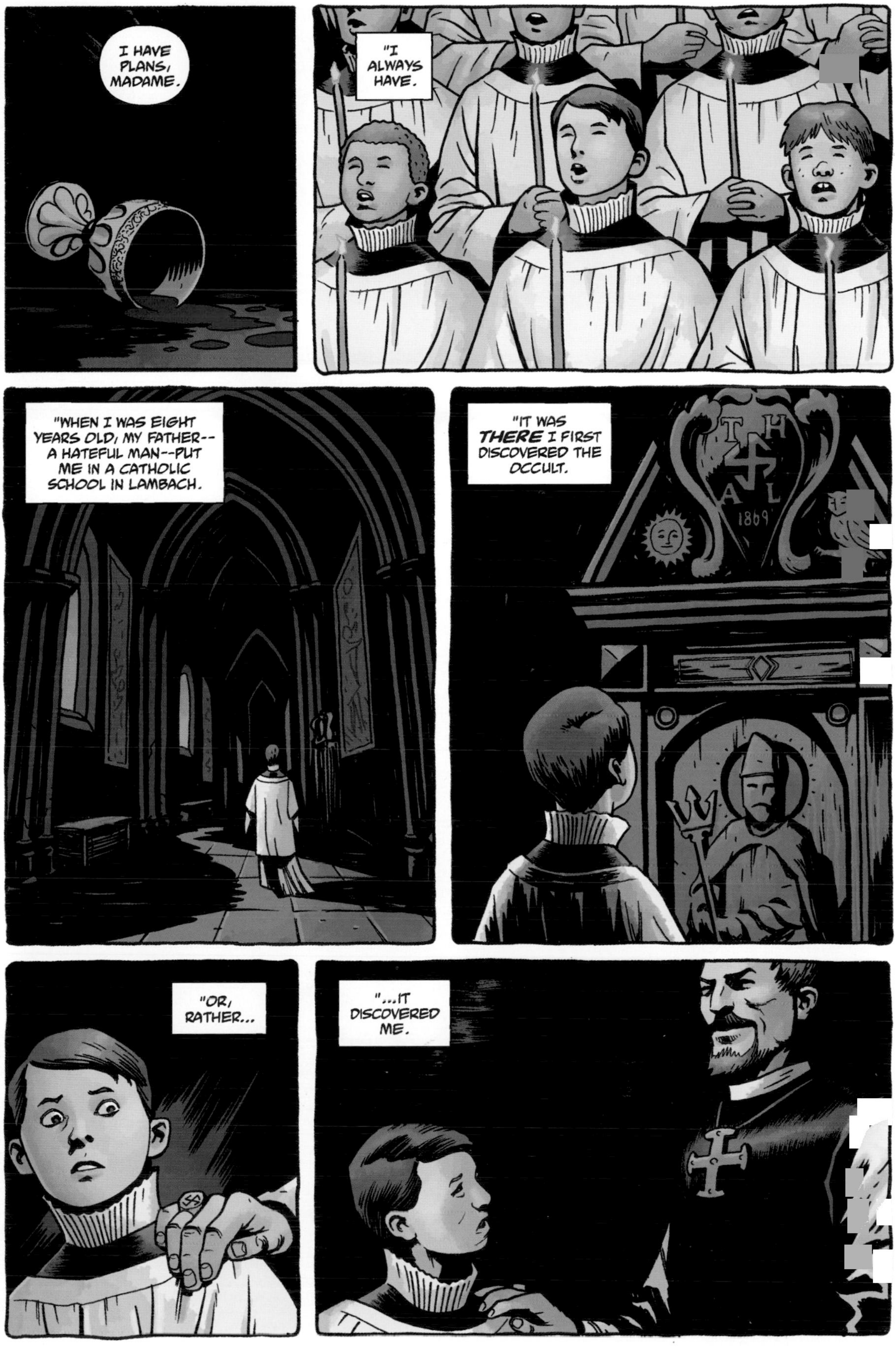
I HAVE PLANS, MADAME.
"I ALWAYS HAVE.
"WHEN I WAS EIGHT YEARS OLD, MY FATHER-- A HATEFUL MAN--PUT ME IN A CATHOLIC SCHOOL IN LAMBACH.
"IT WAS THERE I FIRST DISCOVERED THE OCCULT.
T H A L 1869
"OR, RATHER...
"...IT DISCOVERED ME.

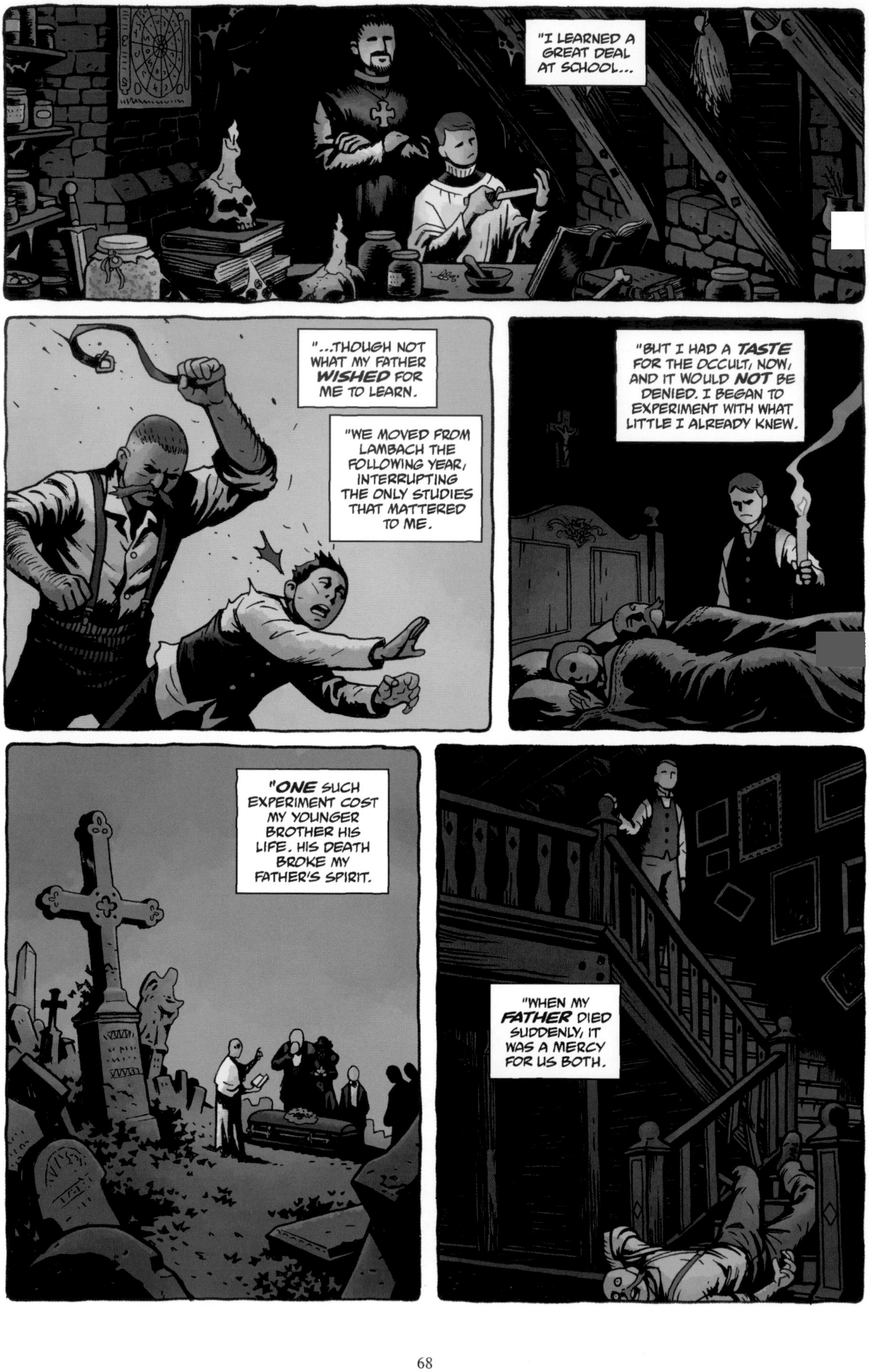
"I LEARNED A GREAT DEAL AT SCHOOL...
"...THOUGH NOT WHAT MY FATHER WISHED FOR ME TO LEARN.
"WE MOVED FROM LAMBACH THE FOLLOWING YEAR, INTERRUPTING THE ONLY STUDIES THAT MATTERED TO ME.
"BUT I HAD A TASTE FOR THE OCCULT, NOW, AND IT WOULD NOT BE DENIED. I BEGAN TO EXPERIMENT WITH WHAT LITTLE I ALREADY KNEW.
"ONE SUCH EXPERIMENT COST MY YOUNGER BROTHER HIS LIFE. HIS DEATH BROKE MY FATHER'S SPIRIT.
"WHEN MY FATHER DIED SUDDENLY, IT WAS A MERCY FOR US BOTH.

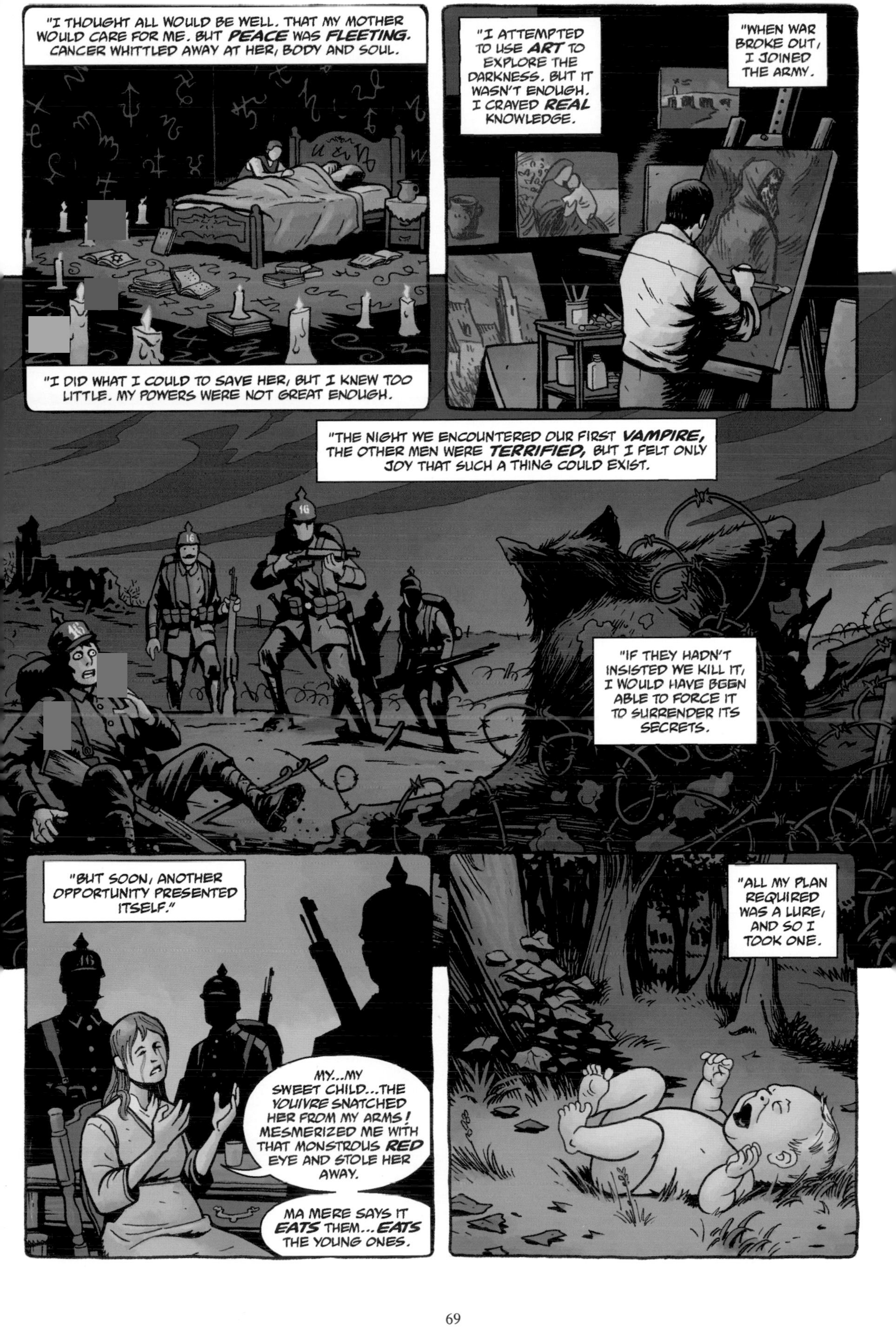
"I THOUGHT ALL WOULD BE WELL. THAT MY MOTHER WOULD CARE FOR ME. BUT PEACE WAS FLEETING. CANCER WHITTLED AWAY AT HER, BODY AND SOUL.
"I DID WHAT I COULD TO SAVE HER, BUT I KNEW TOO LITTLE. MY POWERS WERE NOT GREAT ENOUGH.
"I ATTEMPTED TO USE ART TO EXPLORE THE DARKNESS. BUT IT WASN'T ENOUGH. I CRAVED REAL KNOWLEDGE.
"WHEN WAR BROKE OUT, I JOINED THE ARMY.
"THE NIGHT WE ENCOUNTERED OUR FIRST VAMPIRE, THE OTHER MEN WERE TERRIFIED, BUT I FELT ONLY JOY THAT SUCH A THING COULD EXIST.
"IF THEY HADN'T INSISTED WE KILL IT, I WOULD HAVE BEEN ABLE TO FORCE IT TO SURRENDER ITS SECRETS.
"BUT SOON, ANOTHER OPPORTUNITY PRESENTED ITSELF."
MY...MY SWEET CHILD...THE VOUIVRE SNATCHED HER FROM MY ARMS! MESMERIZED ME WITH THAT MONSTROUS RED EYE AND STOLE HER AWAY.
MA MERE SAYS IT EATS THEM... EATS THE YOUNG ONES.
"ALL MY PLAN REQUIRED WAS A LURE, AND SO I TOOK ONE.

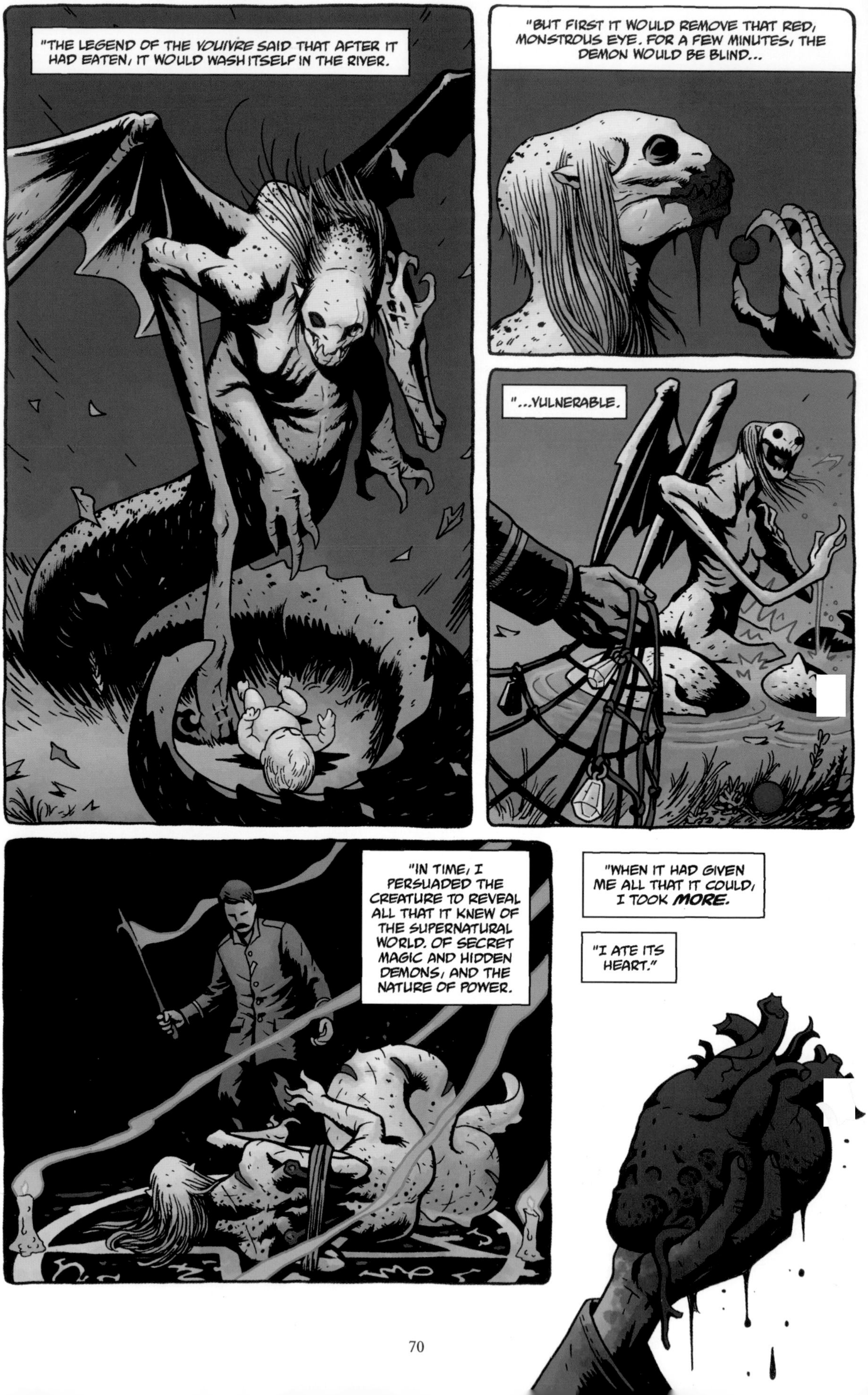
"THE LEGEND OF THE *VOUIVRE* SAID THAT AFTER IT HAD EATEN, IT WOULD WASH ITSELF IN THE RIVER.
"BUT FIRST IT WOULD REMOVE THAT RED, MONSTROUS EYE. FOR A FEW MINUTES, THE DEMON WOULD BE BLIND...
"...VULNERABLE.
"IN TIME, I PERSUADED THE CREATURE TO REVEAL ALL THAT IT KNEW OF THE SUPERNATURAL WORLD. OF SECRET MAGIC AND HIDDEN DEMONS, AND THE NATURE OF POWER.
"WHEN IT HAD GIVEN ME ALL THAT IT COULD, I TOOK ***MORE.***
"I ATE ITS HEART."

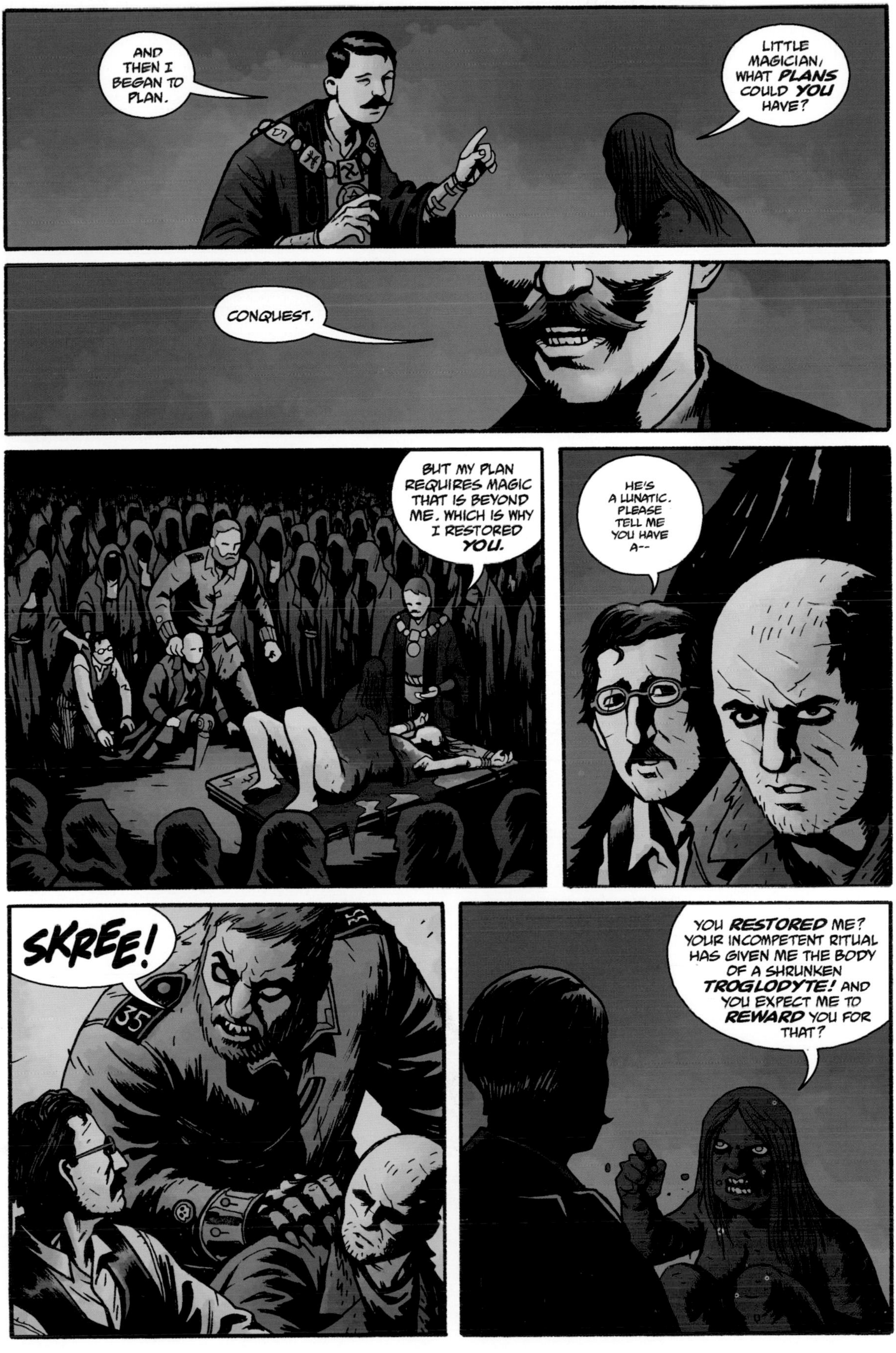
AND THEN I BEGAN TO PLAN.
LITTLE MAGICIAN, WHAT PLANS COULD YOU HAVE?
CONQUEST.
BUT MY PLAN REQUIRES MAGIC THAT IS BEYOND ME. WHICH IS WHY I RESTORED YOU.
HE'S A LUNATIC. PLEASE TELL ME YOU HAVE A--
SKREE!
YOU RESTORED ME? YOUR INCOMPETENT RITUAL HAS GIVEN ME THE BODY OF A SHRUNKEN TROGLODYTE! AND YOU EXPECT ME TO REWARD YOU FOR THAT?

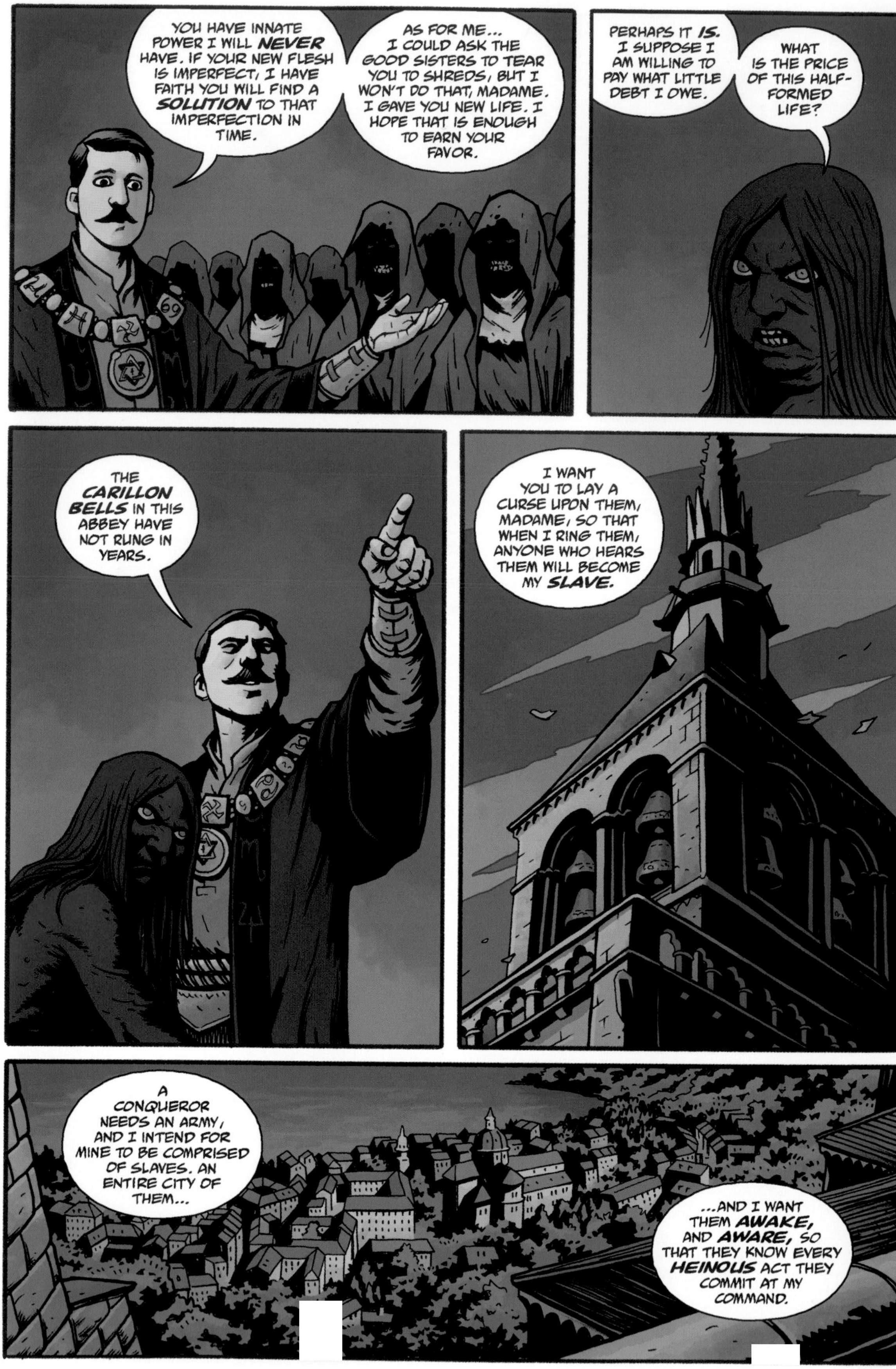
YOU HAVE INNATE POWER I WILL NEVER HAVE. IF YOUR NEW FLESH IS IMPERFECT, I HAVE FAITH YOU WILL FIND A SOLUTION TO THAT IMPERFECTION IN TIME.
AS FOR ME... I COULD ASK THE GOOD SISTERS TO TEAR YOU TO SHREDS, BUT I WON'T DO THAT, MADAME. I GAVE YOU NEW LIFE. I HOPE THAT IS ENOUGH TO EARN YOUR FAVOR.
PERHAPS IT IS. I SUPPOSE I AM WILLING TO PAY WHAT LITTLE DEBT I OWE.
WHAT IS THE PRICE OF THIS HALF-FORMED LIFE?
THE CARILLON BELLS IN THIS ABBEY HAVE NOT RUNG IN YEARS.
I WANT YOU TO LAY A CURSE UPON THEM, MADAME, SO THAT WHEN I RING THEM, ANYONE WHO HEARS THEM WILL BECOME MY SLAVE.
A CONQUEROR NEEDS AN ARMY, AND I INTEND FOR MINE TO BE COMPRISED OF SLAVES. AN ENTIRE CITY OF THEM...
...AND I WANT THEM AWAKE, AND AWARE, SO THAT THEY KNOW EVERY HEINOUS ACT THEY COMMIT AT MY COMMAND.

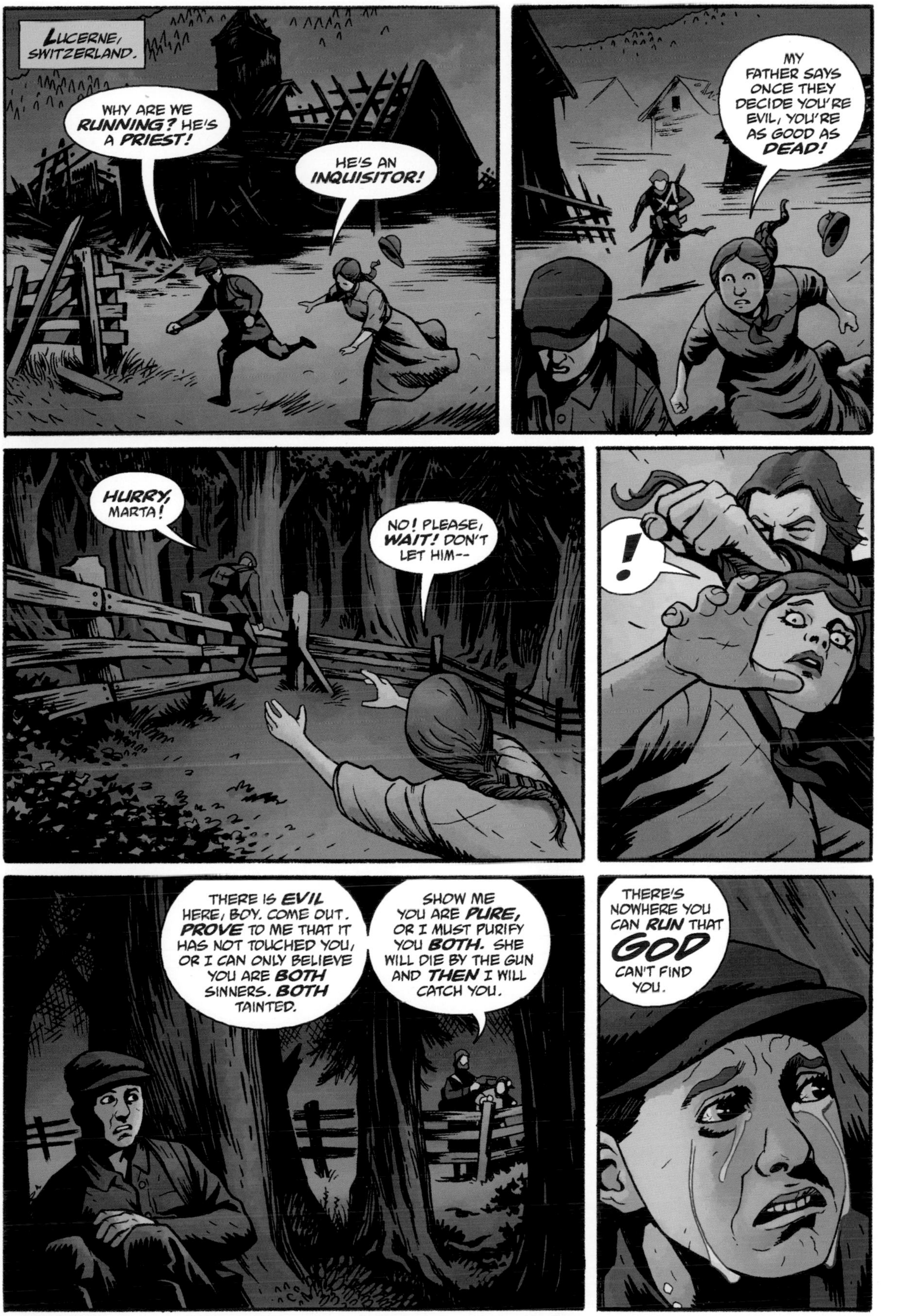

LUCERNE, SWITZERLAND.
WHY ARE WE RUNNING? HE'S A PRIEST!
HE'S AN INQUISITOR!
MY FATHER SAYS ONCE THEY DECIDE YOU'RE EVIL, YOU'RE AS GOOD AS DEAD!
HURRY, MARTA!
NO! PLEASE, WAIT! DON'T LET HIM--
!
THERE IS EVIL HERE, BOY. COME OUT. PROVE TO ME THAT IT HAS NOT TOUCHED YOU, OR I CAN ONLY BELIEVE YOU ARE BOTH SINNERS. BOTH TAINTED.
SHOW ME YOU ARE PURE, OR I MUST PURIFY YOU BOTH. SHE WILL DIE BY THE GUN AND THEN I WILL CATCH YOU.
THERE'S NOWHERE YOU CAN RUN THAT GOD CAN'T FIND YOU.

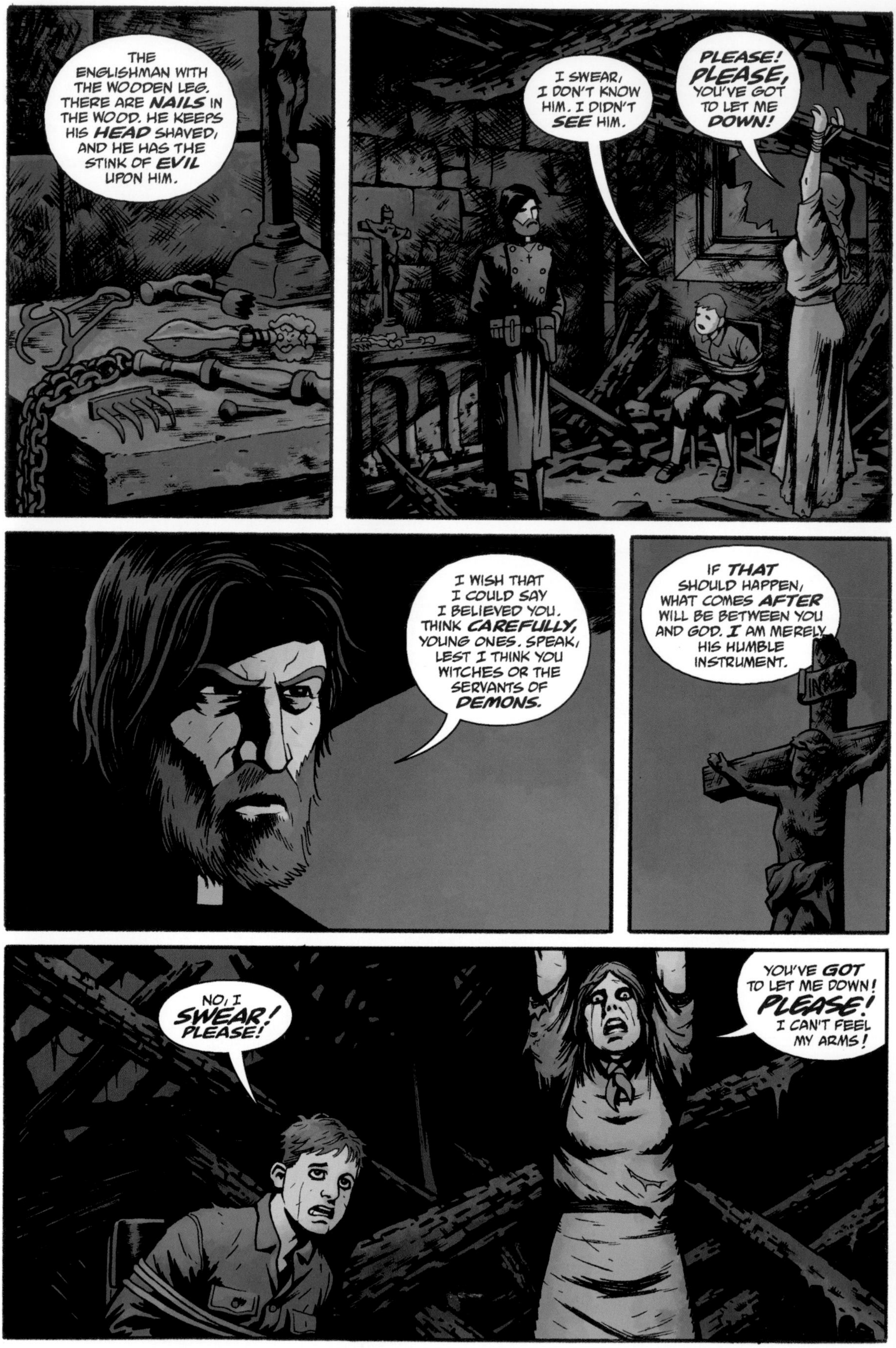
THE ENGLISHMAN WITH THE WOODEN LEG. THERE ARE NAILS IN THE WOOD. HE KEEPS HIS HEAD SHAVED, AND HE HAS THE STINK OF EVIL UPON HIM.
I SWEAR, I DON'T KNOW HIM. I DIDN'T SEE HIM.
PLEASE! PLEASE, YOU'VE GOT TO LET ME DOWN!
I WISH THAT I COULD SAY I BELIEVED YOU. THINK CAREFULLY, YOUNG ONES. SPEAK, LEST I THINK YOU WITCHES OR THE SERVANTS OF DEMONS.
IF THAT SHOULD HAPPEN, WHAT COMES AFTER WILL BE BETWEEN YOU AND GOD. I AM MERELY HIS HUMBLE INSTRUMENT.
NO, I SWEAR! PLEASE!
YOU'VE GOT TO LET ME DOWN! PLEASE! I CAN'T FEEL MY ARMS!

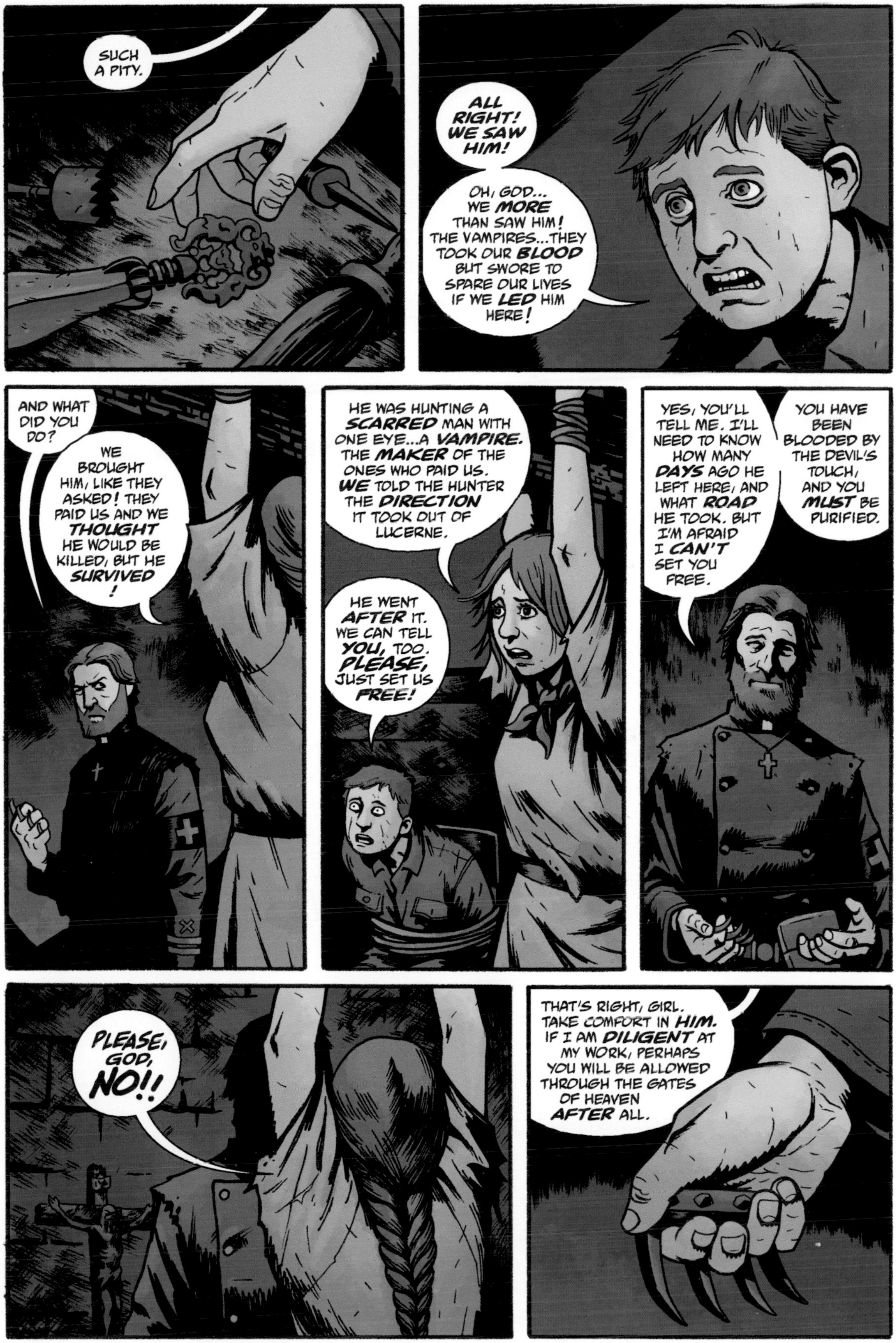
SUCH A PITY.
ALL RIGHT! WE SAW HIM!
OH, GOD... WE MORE THAN SAW HIM! THE VAMPIRES...THEY TOOK OUR BLOOD BUT SWORE TO SPARE OUR LIVES IF WE LED HIM HERE!
AND WHAT DID YOU DO?
WE BROUGHT HIM, LIKE THEY ASKED! THEY PAID US AND WE THOUGHT HE WOULD BE KILLED, BUT HE SURVIVED!
HE WAS HUNTING A SCARRED MAN WITH ONE EYE...A VAMPIRE. THE MAKER OF THE ONES WHO PAID US. WE TOLD THE HUNTER THE DIRECTION IT TOOK OUT OF LUCERNE.
HE WENT AFTER IT. WE CAN TELL YOU, TOO. PLEASE, JUST SET US FREE!
YES, YOU'LL TELL ME. I'LL NEED TO KNOW HOW MANY DAYS AGO HE LEFT HERE, AND WHAT ROAD HE TOOK. BUT I'M AFRAID I CAN'T SET YOU FREE.
YOU HAVE BEEN BLOODED BY THE DEVIL'S TOUCH, AND YOU MUST BE PURIFIED.
PLEASE, GOD, NO!!
THAT'S RIGHT, GIRL. TAKE COMFORT IN HIM. IF I AM DILIGENT AT MY WORK, PERHAPS YOU WILL BE ALLOWED THROUGH THE GATES OF HEAVEN AFTER ALL.

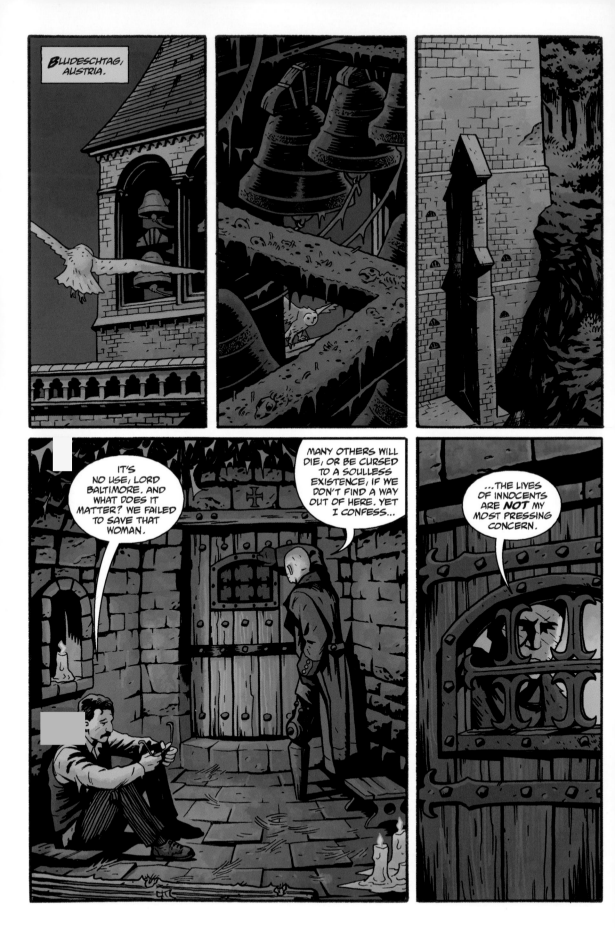

BLUDESCHTAG, AUSTRIA.

IT'S NO USE, LORD BALTIMORE. AND WHAT DOES IT MATTER? WE FAILED TO SAVE THAT WOMAN.

MANY OTHERS WILL DIE, OR BE CURSED TO A SOULLESS EXISTENCE, IF WE DON'T FIND A WAY OUT OF HERE. YET I CONFESS...

...THE LIVES OF INNOCENTS ARE **NOT** MY MOST PRESSING CONCERN.

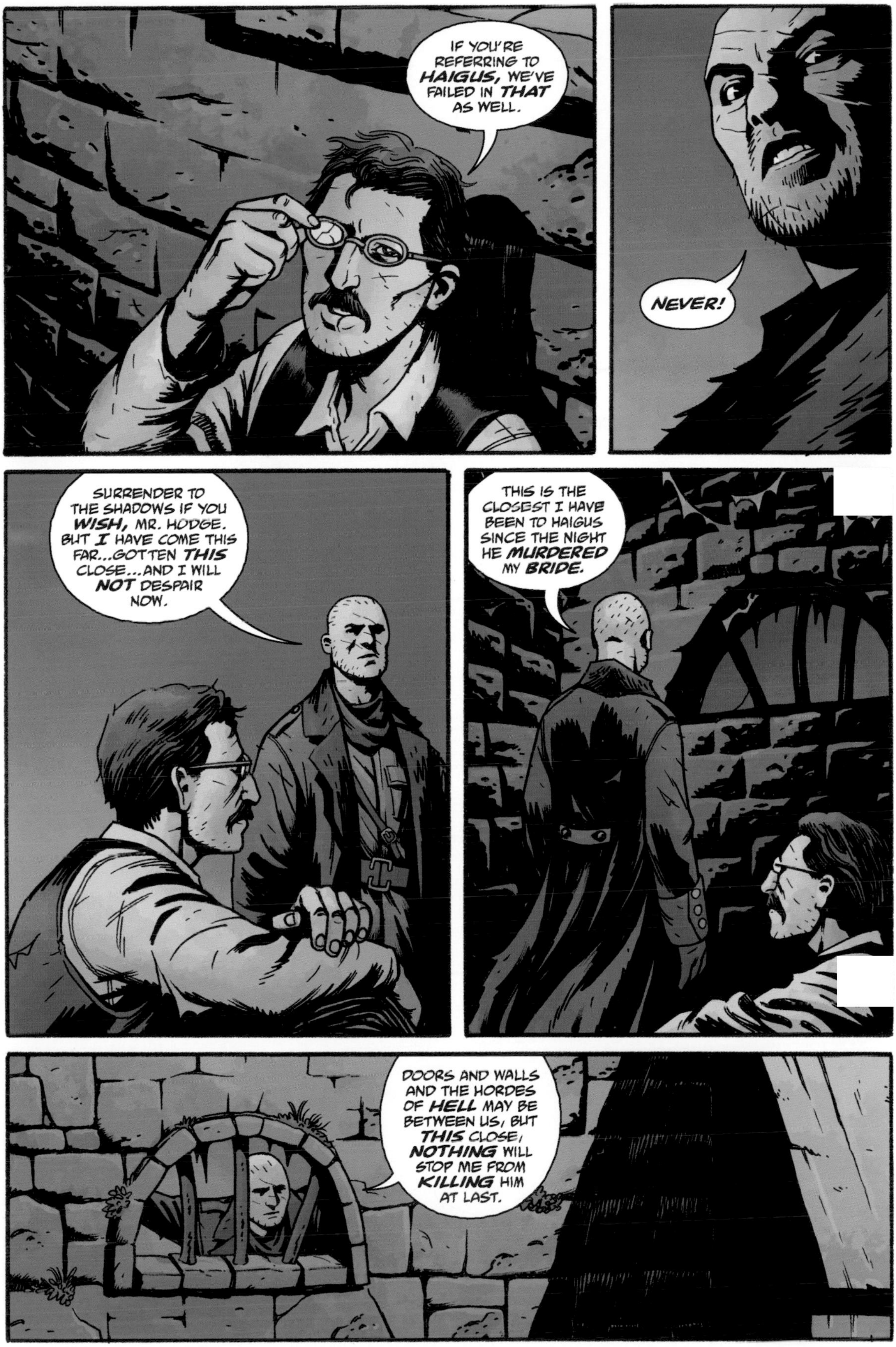
IF YOU'RE REFERRING TO HAIGUS, WE'VE FAILED IN THAT AS WELL.
NEVER!
SURRENDER TO THE SHADOWS IF YOU WISH, MR. HODGE. BUT I HAVE COME THIS FAR...GOTTEN THIS CLOSE...AND I WILL NOT DESPAIR NOW.
THIS IS THE CLOSEST I HAVE BEEN TO HAIGUS SINCE THE NIGHT HE MURDERED MY BRIDE.
DOORS AND WALLS AND THE HORDES OF HELL MAY BE BETWEEN US, BUT THIS CLOSE, NOTHING WILL STOP ME FROM KILLING HIM AT LAST.

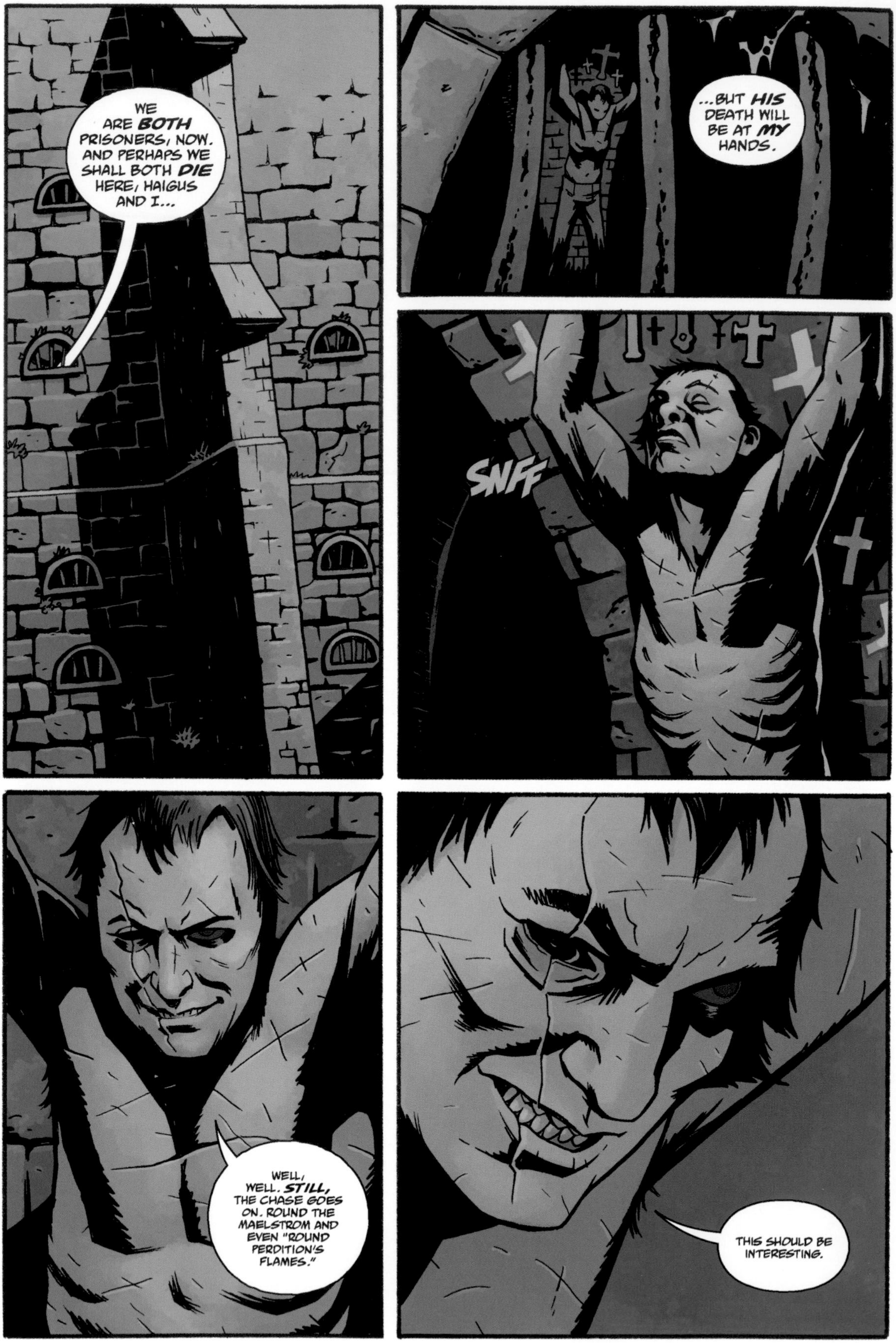
WE ARE BOTH PRISONERS, NOW. AND PERHAPS WE SHALL BOTH DIE HERE, HAIGUS AND I...
...BUT HIS DEATH WILL BE AT MY HANDS.
SNFF
WELL, WELL. STILL, THE CHASE GOES ON. ROUND THE MAELSTROM AND EVEN "ROUND PERDITION'S FLAMES."
THIS SHOULD BE INTERESTING.

CHAPTER FOUR

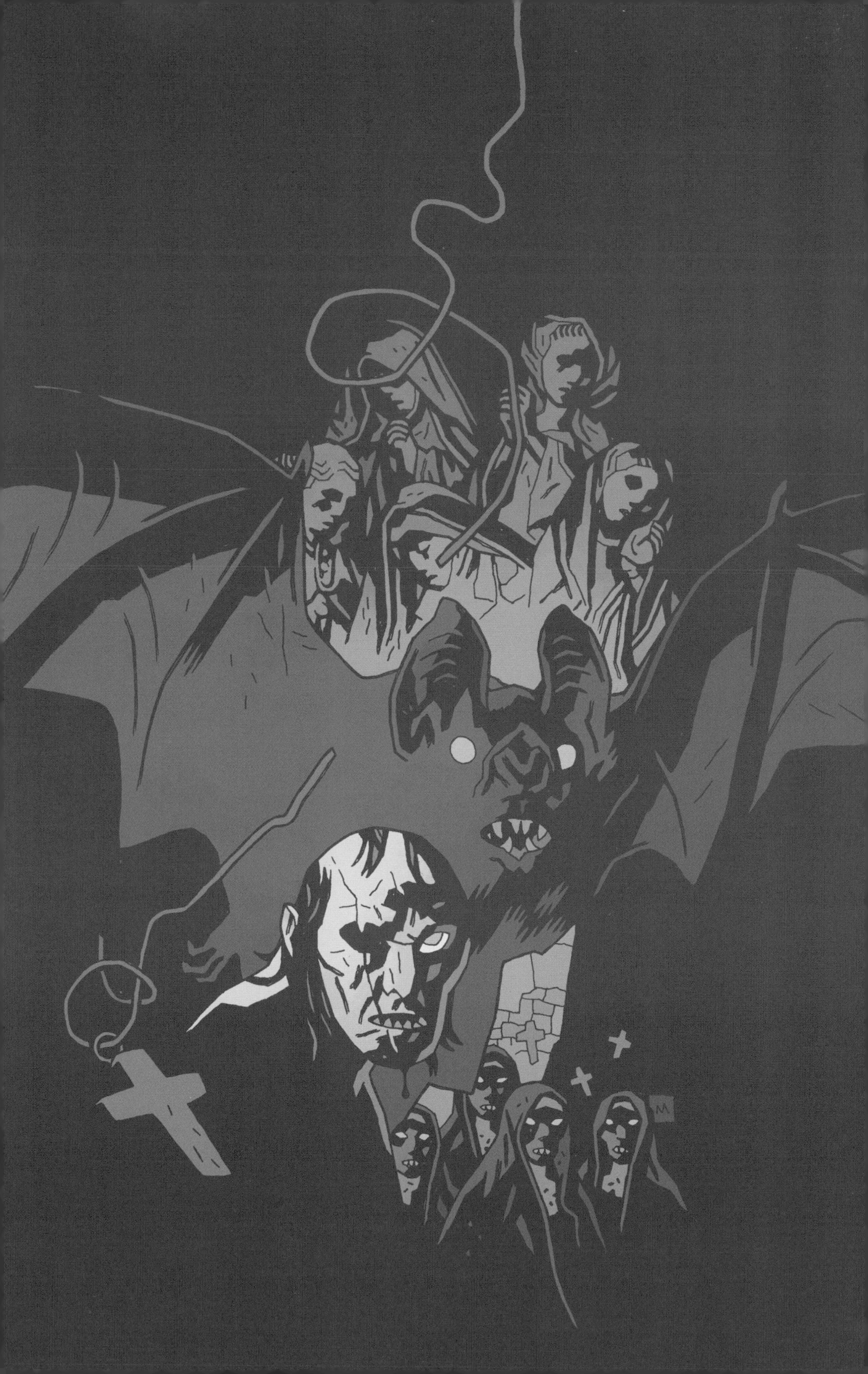

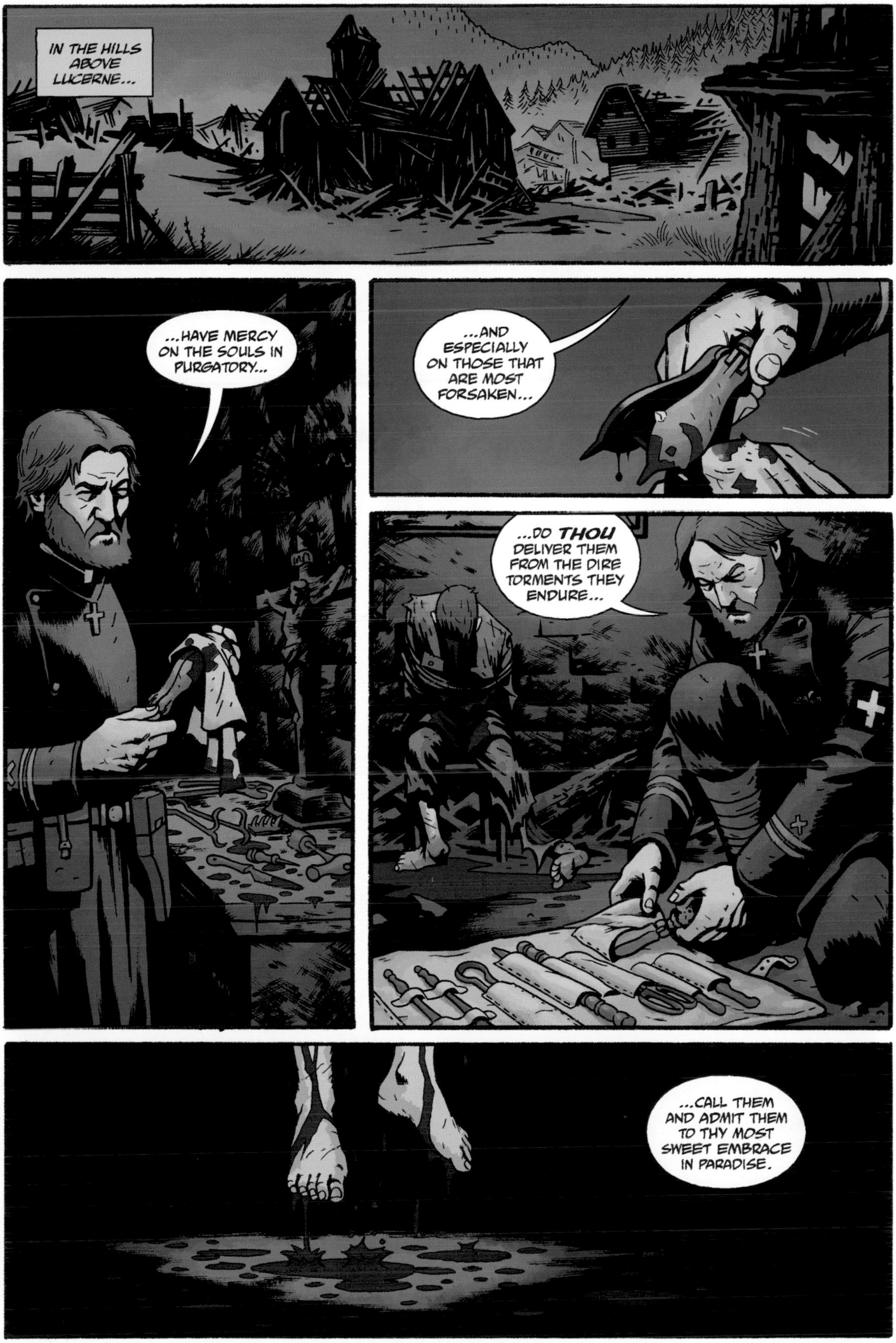
IN THE HILLS ABOVE LUCERNE...
...HAVE MERCY ON THE SOULS IN PURGATORY...
...AND ESPECIALLY ON THOSE THAT ARE MOST FORSAKEN...
...DO THOU DELIVER THEM FROM THE DIRE TORMENTS THEY ENDURE...
...CALL THEM AND ADMIT THEM TO THY MOST SWEET EMBRACE IN PARADISE.

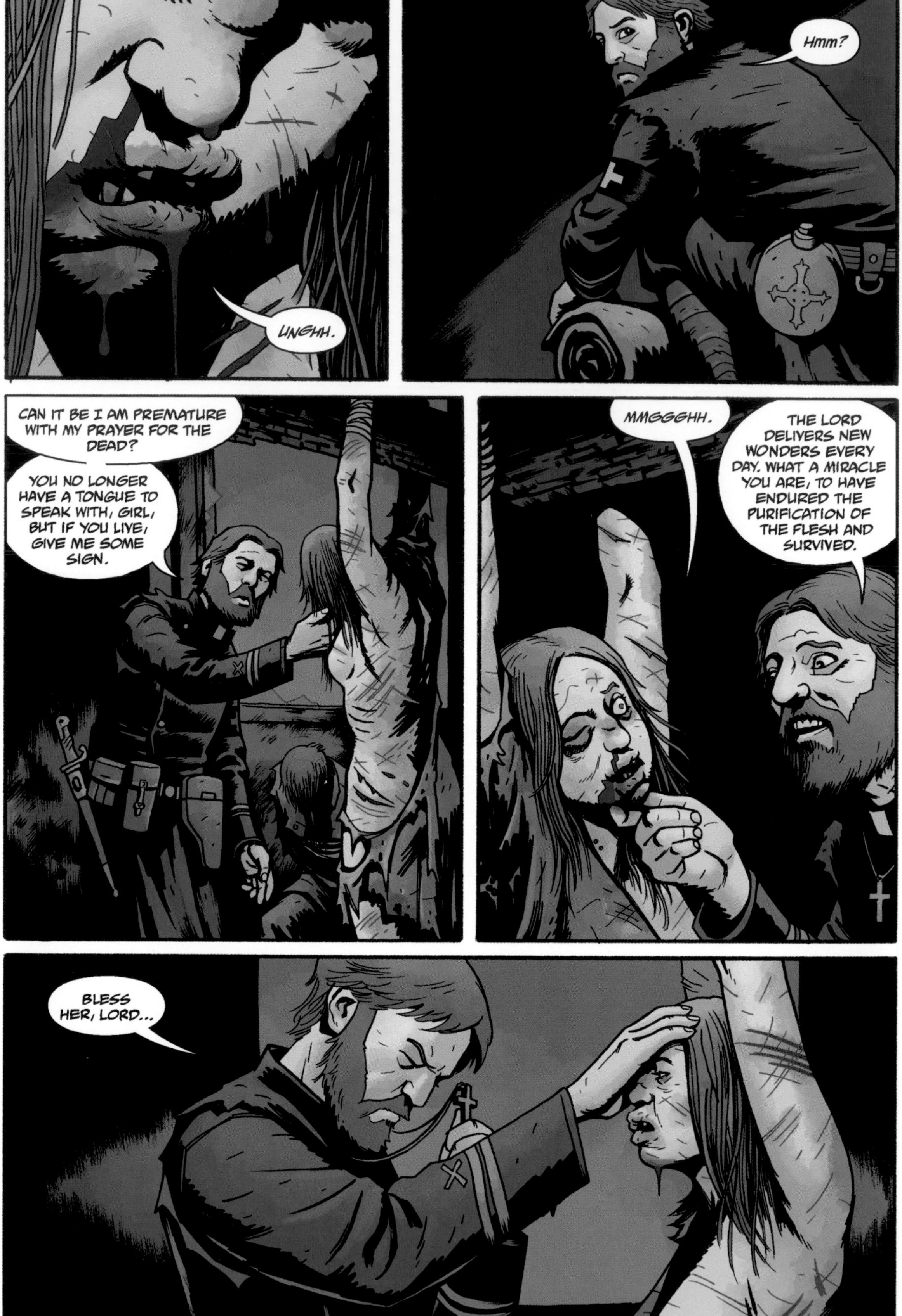
UNGHH.
Hmm?
CAN IT BE I AM PREMATURE WITH MY PRAYER FOR THE DEAD?
YOU NO LONGER HAVE A TONGUE TO SPEAK WITH, GIRL, BUT IF YOU LIVE, GIVE ME SOME SIGN.
MMGGGHH.
THE LORD DELIVERS NEW WONDERS EVERY DAY. WHAT A MIRACLE YOU ARE, TO HAVE ENDURED THE PURIFICATION OF THE FLESH AND SURVIVED.
BLESS HER, LORD...

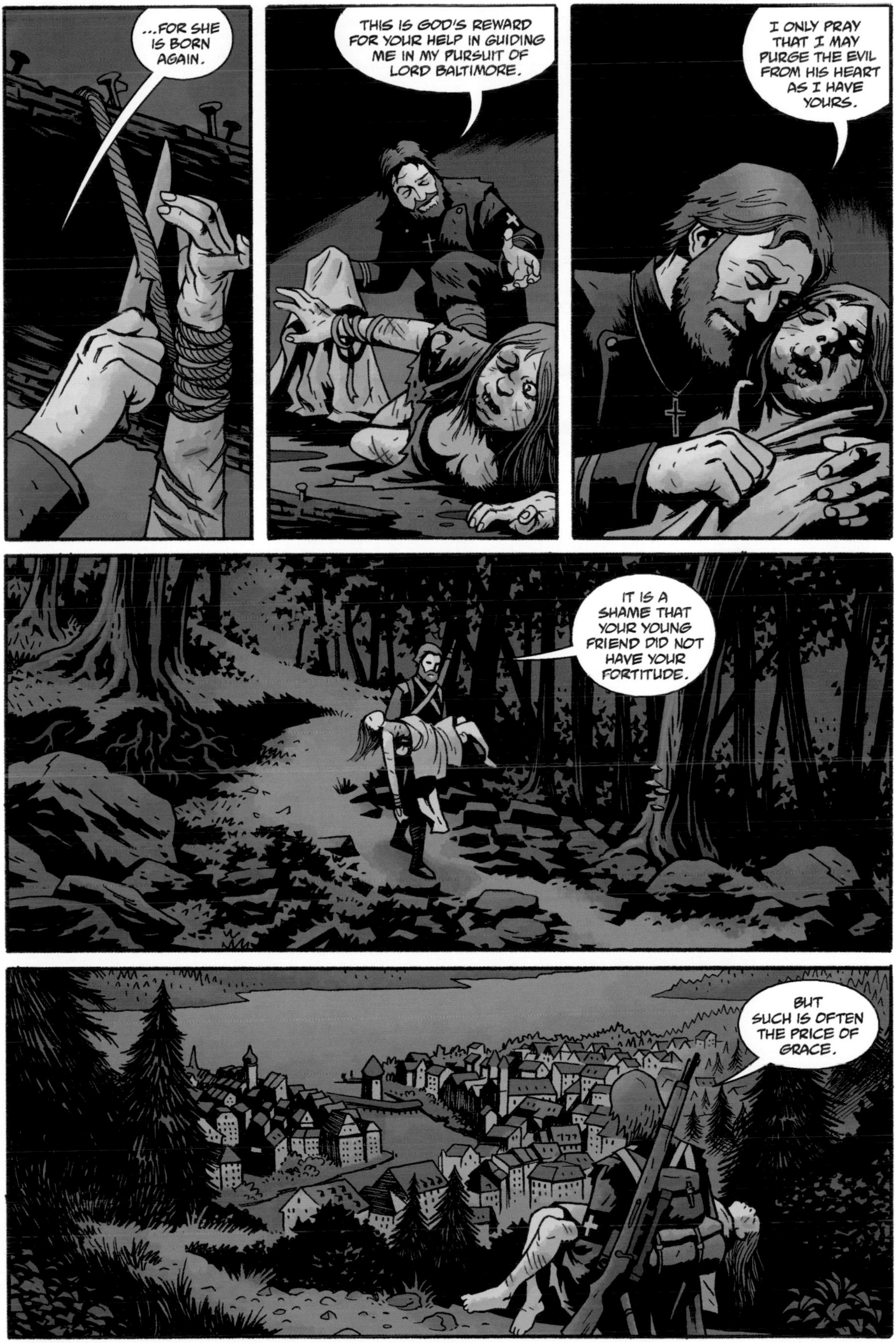
...FOR SHE IS BORN AGAIN.
THIS IS GOD'S REWARD FOR YOUR HELP IN GUIDING ME IN MY PURSUIT OF LORD BALTIMORE.
I ONLY PRAY THAT I MAY PURGE THE EVIL FROM HIS HEART AS I HAVE YOURS.
IT IS A SHAME THAT YOUR YOUNG FRIEND DID NOT HAVE YOUR FORTITUDE.
BUT SUCH IS OFTEN THE PRICE OF GRACE.

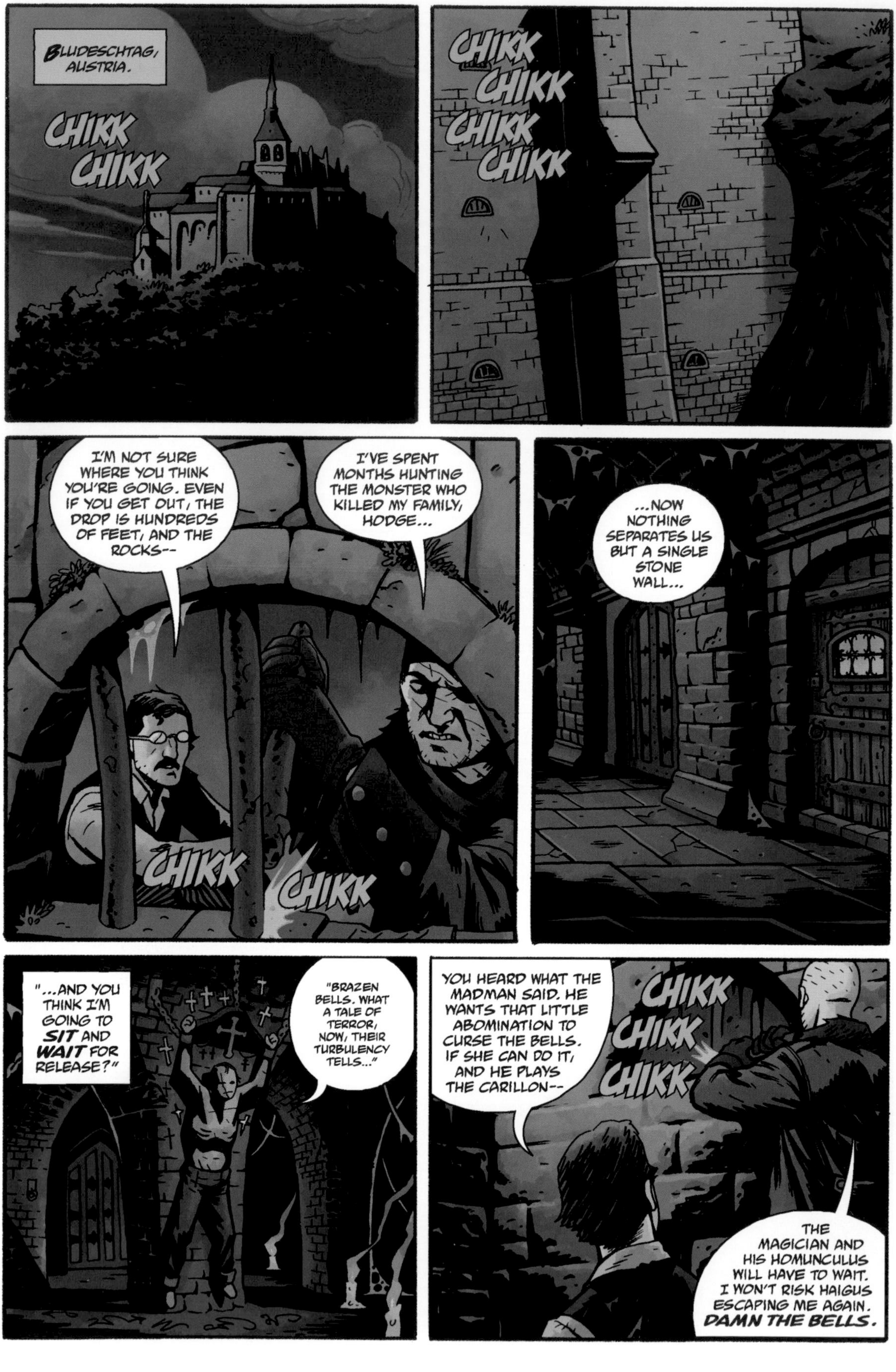
BLUDESCHTAG, AUSTRIA.
CHIKK CHIKK
CHIKK CHIKK CHIKK CHIKK
I'M NOT SURE WHERE YOU THINK YOU'RE GOING. EVEN IF YOU GET OUT, THE DROP IS HUNDREDS OF FEET, AND THE ROCKS--
I'VE SPENT MONTHS HUNTING THE MONSTER WHO KILLED MY FAMILY, HODGE...
CHIKK CHIKK
...NOW NOTHING SEPARATES US BUT A SINGLE STONE WALL...
"...AND YOU THINK I'M GOING TO SIT AND WAIT FOR RELEASE?"
"BRAZEN BELLS. WHAT A TALE OF TERROR, NOW, THEIR TURBULENCY TELLS..."
YOU HEARD WHAT THE MADMAN SAID. HE WANTS THAT LITTLE ABOMINATION TO CURSE THE BELLS. IF SHE CAN DO IT, AND HE PLAYS THE CARILLON--
CHIKK CHIKK CHIKK
THE MAGICIAN AND HIS HOMUNCULUS WILL HAVE TO WAIT. I WON'T RISK HAIGUS ESCAPING ME AGAIN. DAMN THE BELLS.

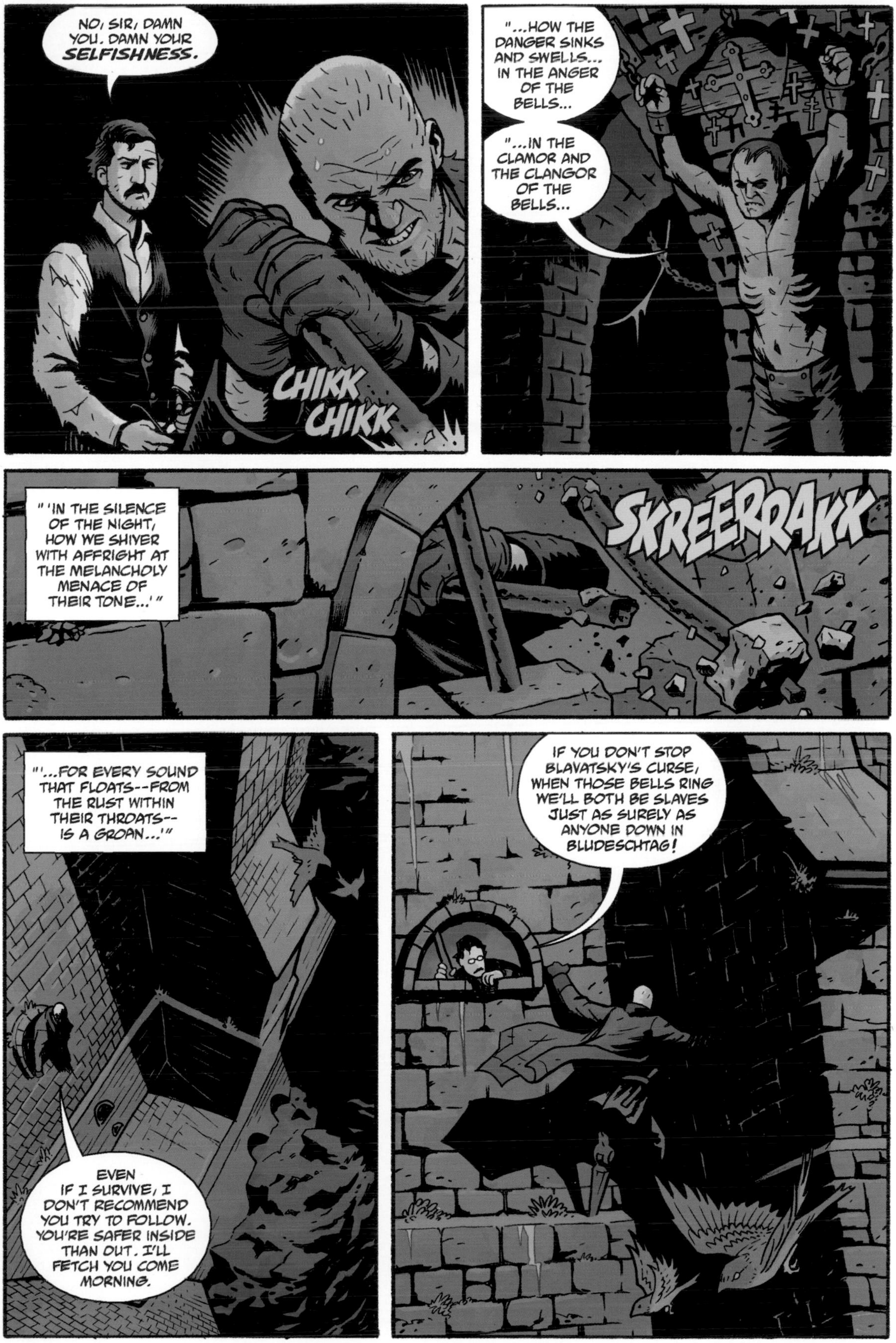
NO, SIR, DAMN YOU. DAMN YOUR *SELFISHNESS.*
CHIKK CHIKK
"...HOW THE DANGER SINKS AND SWELLS... IN THE ANGER OF THE BELLS...
"...IN THE CLAMOR AND THE CLANGOR OF THE BELLS...
"'IN THE SILENCE OF THE NIGHT, HOW WE SHIVER WITH AFFRIGHT AT THE MELANCHOLY MENACE OF THEIR TONE...'"
SKREERRAKK
"'...FOR EVERY SOUND THAT FLOATS--FROM THE RUST WITHIN THEIR THROATS-- IS A GROAN...'"
EVEN IF I SURVIVE, I DON'T RECOMMEND YOU TRY TO FOLLOW. YOU'RE SAFER INSIDE THAN OUT. I'LL FETCH YOU COME MORNING.
IF YOU DON'T STOP BLAVATSKY'S CURSE, WHEN THOSE BELLS RING WE'LL BOTH BE SLAVES JUST AS SURELY AS ANYONE DOWN IN BLUDESCHTAG!

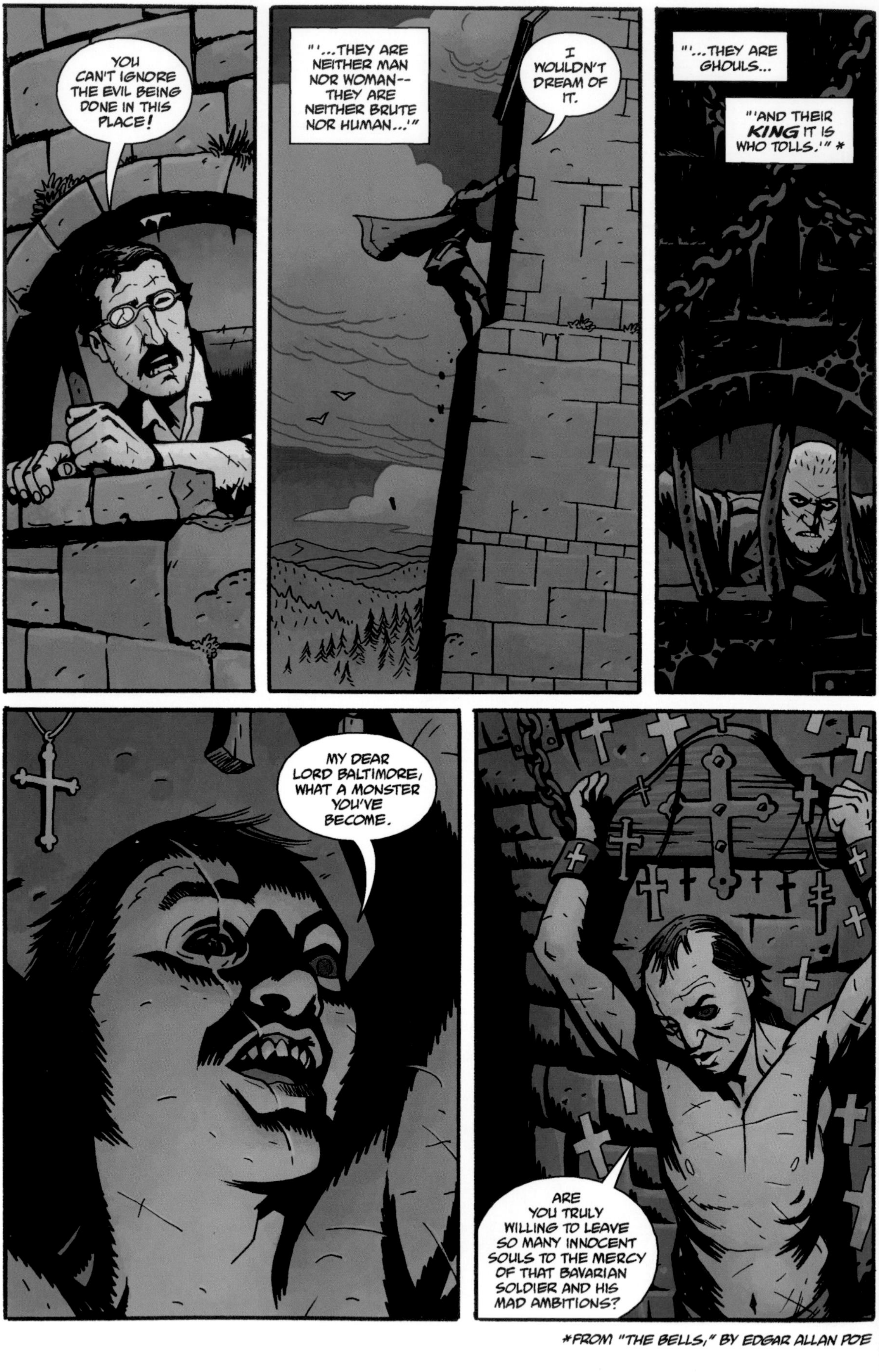
YOU CAN'T IGNORE THE EVIL BEING DONE IN THIS PLACE!
"'...THEY ARE NEITHER MAN NOR WOMAN-- THEY ARE NEITHER BRUTE NOR HUMAN...'"
I WOULDN'T DREAM OF IT.
"'...THEY ARE GHOULS...
"'AND THEIR KING IT IS WHO TOLLS.'" *
MY DEAR LORD BALTIMORE, WHAT A MONSTER YOU'VE BECOME.
ARE YOU TRULY WILLING TO LEAVE SO MANY INNOCENT SOULS TO THE MERCY OF THAT BAVARIAN SOLDIER AND HIS MAD AMBITIONS?

*FROM "THE BELLS," BY EDGAR ALLAN POE

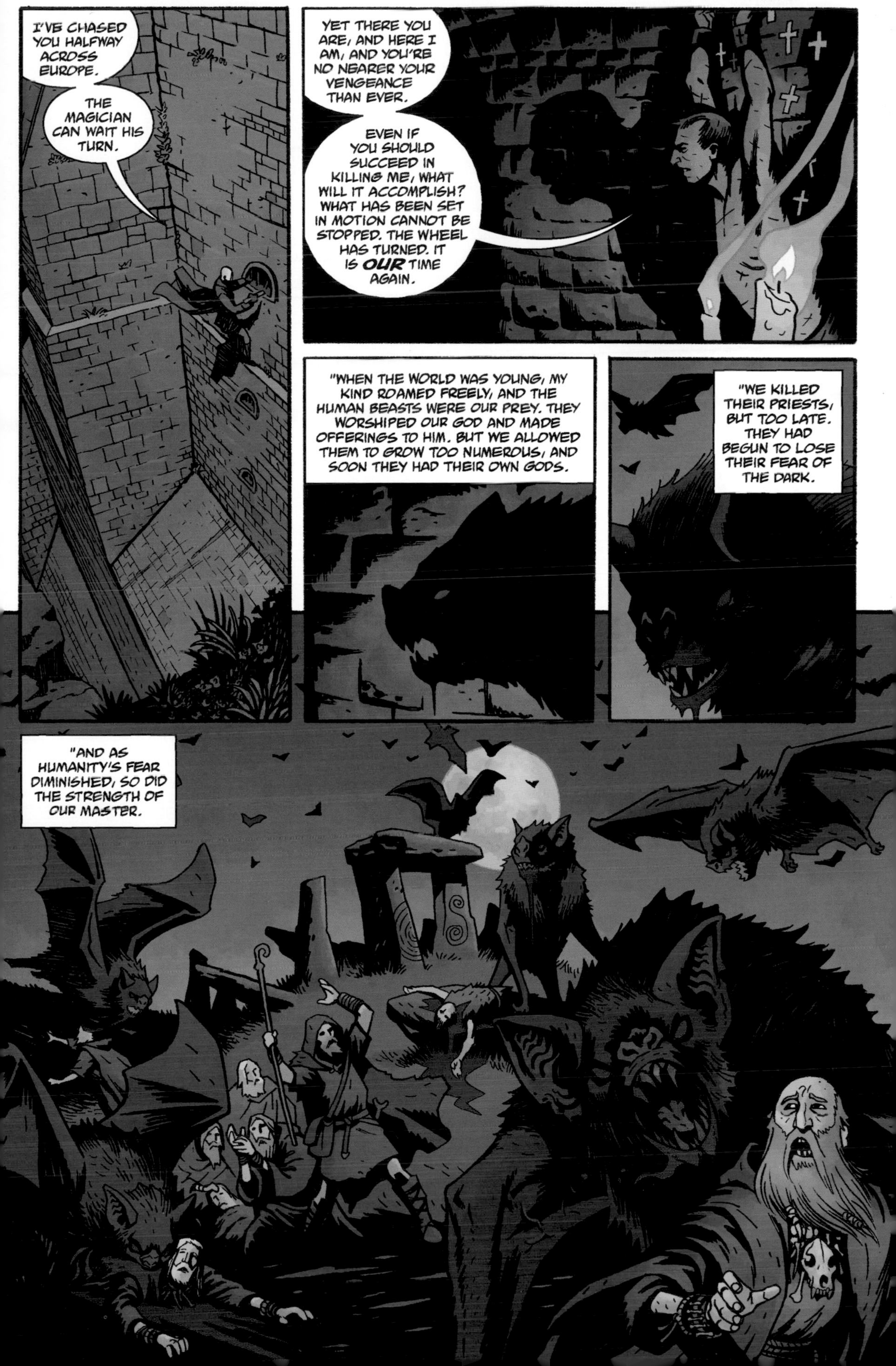
I'VE CHASED YOU HALFWAY ACROSS EUROPE.
THE MAGICIAN CAN WAIT HIS TURN.
YET THERE YOU ARE, AND HERE I AM, AND YOU'RE NO NEARER YOUR VENGEANCE THAN EVER.
EVEN IF YOU SHOULD SUCCEED IN KILLING ME, WHAT WILL IT ACCOMPLISH? WHAT HAS BEEN SET IN MOTION CANNOT BE STOPPED. THE WHEEL HAS TURNED. IT IS OUR TIME AGAIN.
"WHEN THE WORLD WAS YOUNG, MY KIND ROAMED FREELY, AND THE HUMAN BEASTS WERE OUR PREY. THEY WORSHIPED OUR GOD AND MADE OFFERINGS TO HIM. BUT WE ALLOWED THEM TO GROW TOO NUMEROUS, AND SOON THEY HAD THEIR OWN GODS.
"WE KILLED THEIR PRIESTS, BUT TOO LATE. THEY HAD BEGUN TO LOSE THEIR FEAR OF THE DARK.
"AND AS HUMANITY'S FEAR DIMINISHED, SO DID THE STRENGTH OF OUR MASTER.

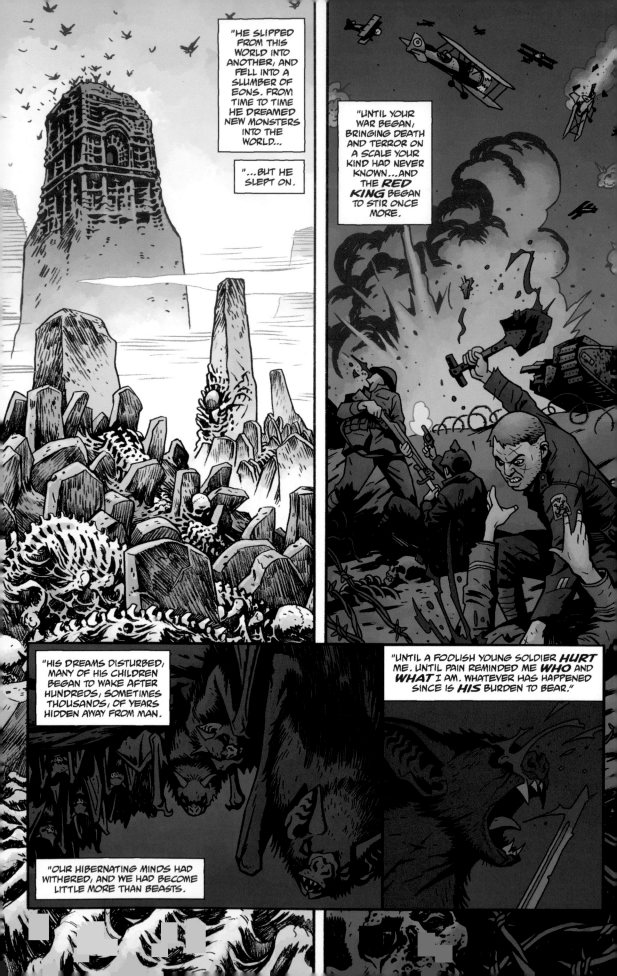

"HE SLIPPED FROM THIS WORLD INTO ANOTHER, AND FELL INTO A SLUMBER OF EONS. FROM TIME TO TIME HE DREAMED NEW MONSTERS INTO THE WORLD...

"...BUT HE SLEPT ON.

"UNTIL YOUR WAR BEGAN, BRINGING DEATH AND TERROR ON A SCALE YOUR KIND HAD NEVER KNOWN...AND THE *RED KING* BEGAN TO STIR ONCE MORE.

"HIS DREAMS DISTURBED, MANY OF HIS CHILDREN BEGAN TO WAKE AFTER HUNDREDS, SOMETIMES THOUSANDS, OF YEARS HIDDEN AWAY FROM MAN.

"UNTIL A FOOLISH YOUNG SOLDIER *HURT* ME. UNTIL PAIN REMINDED ME *WHO* AND *WHAT* I AM. WHATEVER HAS HAPPENED SINCE IS *HIS* BURDEN TO BEAR."

"OUR HIBERNATING MINDS HAD WITHERED, AND WE HAD BECOME LITTLE MORE THAN BEASTS.

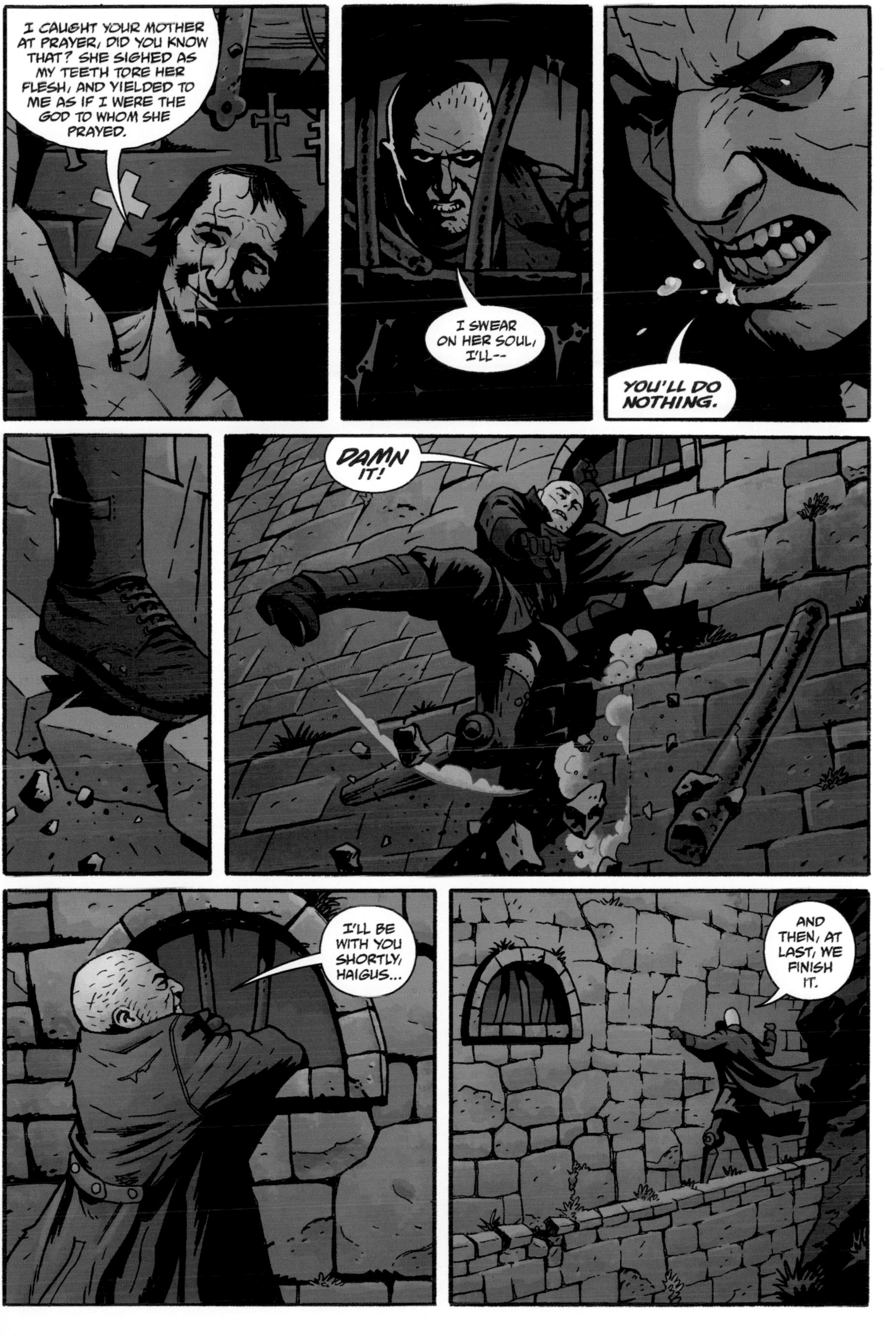
I CAUGHT YOUR MOTHER AT PRAYER, DID YOU KNOW THAT? SHE SIGHED AS MY TEETH TORE HER FLESH, AND YIELDED TO ME AS IF I WERE THE GOD TO WHOM SHE PRAYED.
I SWEAR ON HER SOUL, I'LL--
YOU'LL DO NOTHING.
DAMN IT!
I'LL BE WITH YOU SHORTLY, HAIGUS...
AND THEN, AT LAST, WE FINISH IT.

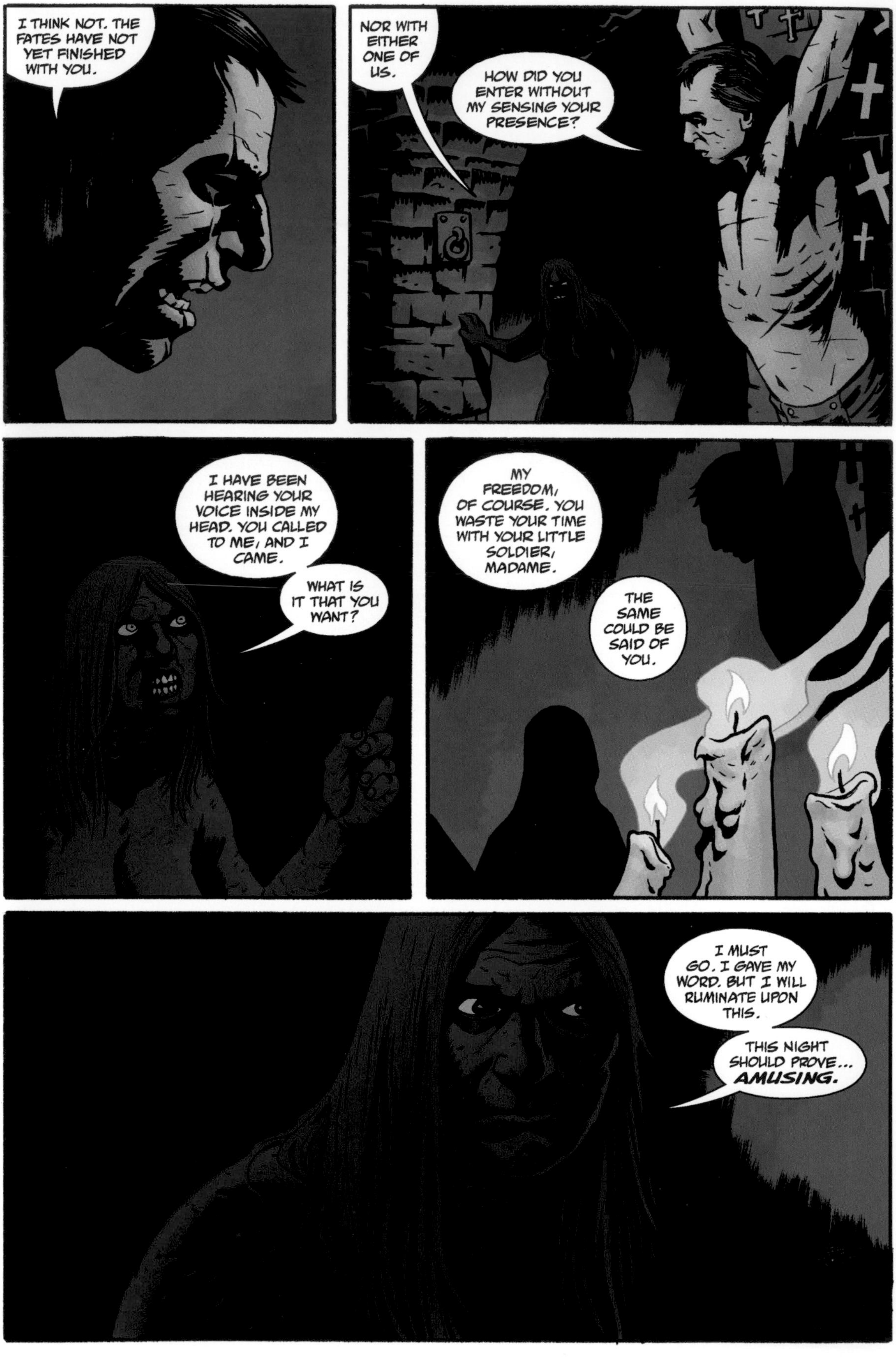
I THINK NOT. THE FATES HAVE NOT YET FINISHED WITH YOU.
NOR WITH EITHER ONE OF US.
HOW DID YOU ENTER WITHOUT MY SENSING YOUR PRESENCE?
I HAVE BEEN HEARING YOUR VOICE INSIDE MY HEAD. YOU CALLED TO ME, AND I CAME.
WHAT IS IT THAT YOU WANT?
MY FREEDOM, OF COURSE. YOU WASTE YOUR TIME WITH YOUR LITTLE SOLDIER, MADAME.
THE SAME COULD BE SAID OF YOU.
I MUST GO. I GAVE MY WORD. BUT I WILL RUMINATE UPON THIS.
THIS NIGHT SHOULD PROVE... AMUSING.

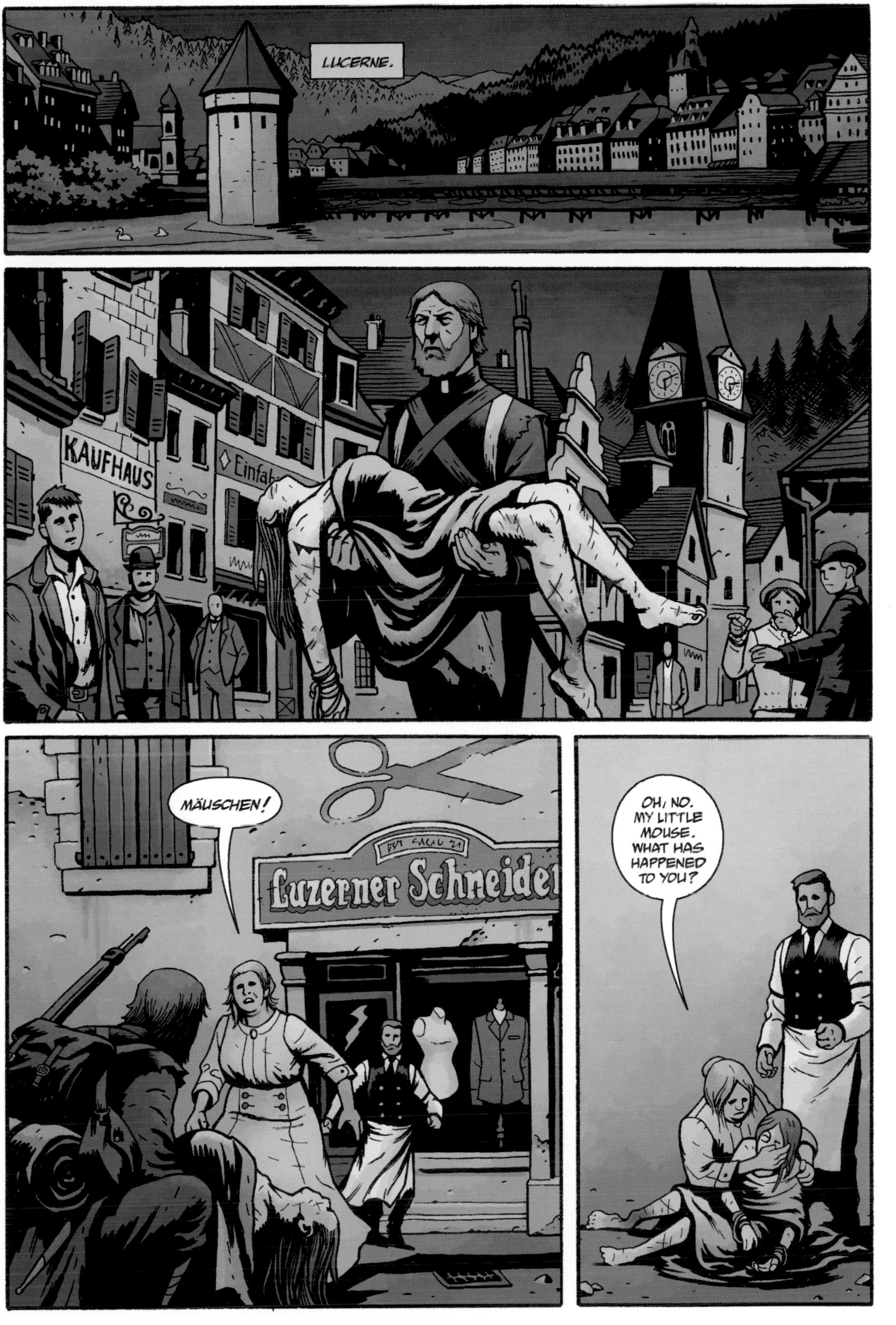
LUCERNE.
KAUFHAUS
Luzerner Schneider
MÄUSCHEN!
OH, NO. MY LITTLE MOUSE. WHAT HAS HAPPENED TO YOU?

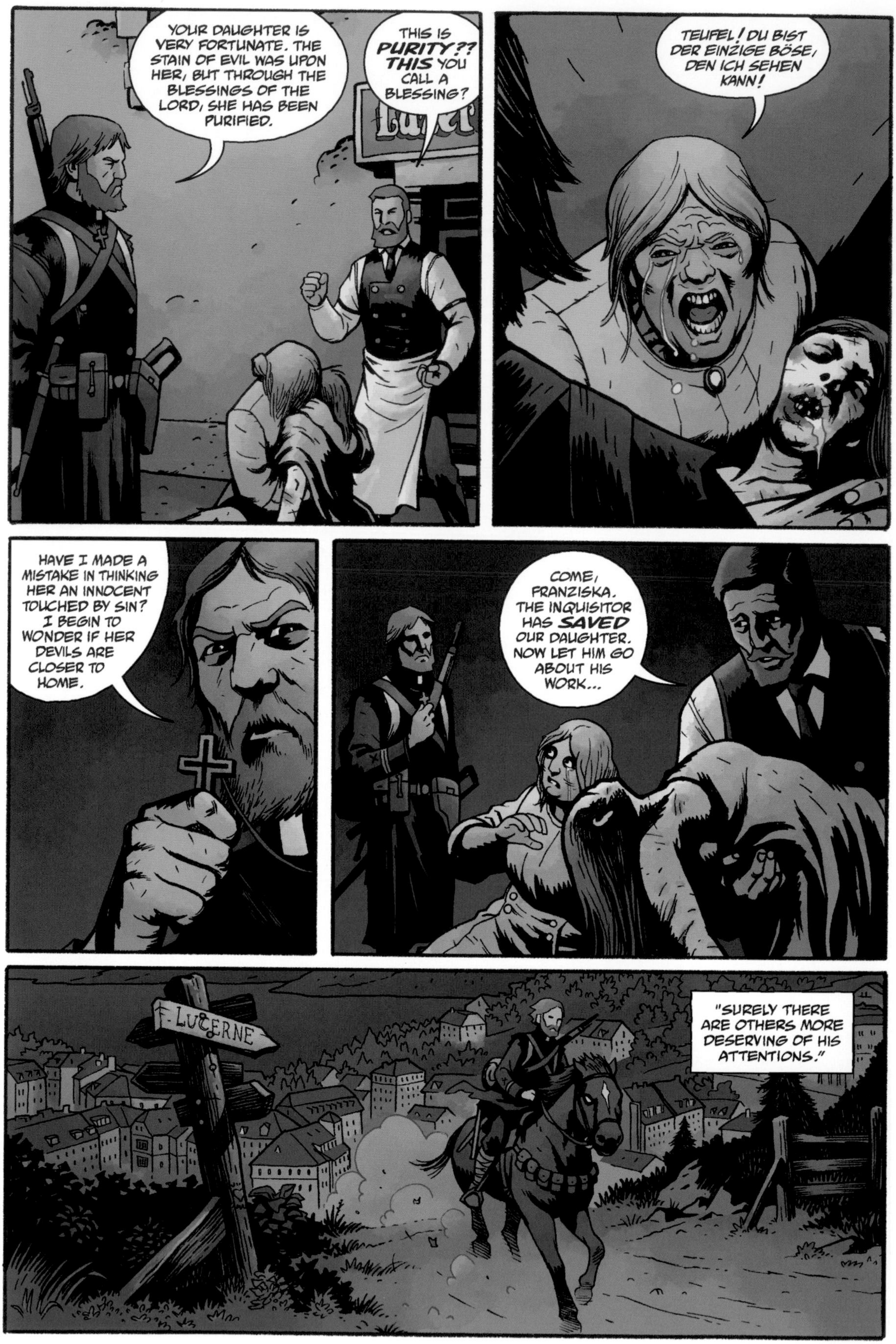
YOUR DAUGHTER IS VERY FORTUNATE. THE STAIN OF EVIL WAS UPON HER, BUT THROUGH THE BLESSINGS OF THE LORD, SHE HAS BEEN PURIFIED.
THIS IS PURITY?? THIS YOU CALL A BLESSING?
TEUFEL! DU BIST DER EINZIGE BÖSE, DEN ICH SEHEN KANN!
HAVE I MADE A MISTAKE IN THINKING HER AN INNOCENT TOUCHED BY SIN? I BEGIN TO WONDER IF HER DEVILS ARE CLOSER TO HOME.
COME, FRANZISKA. THE INQUISITOR HAS SAVED OUR DAUGHTER. NOW LET HIM GO ABOUT HIS WORK...
LUCERNE
"SURELY THERE ARE OTHERS MORE DESERVING OF HIS ATTENTIONS."

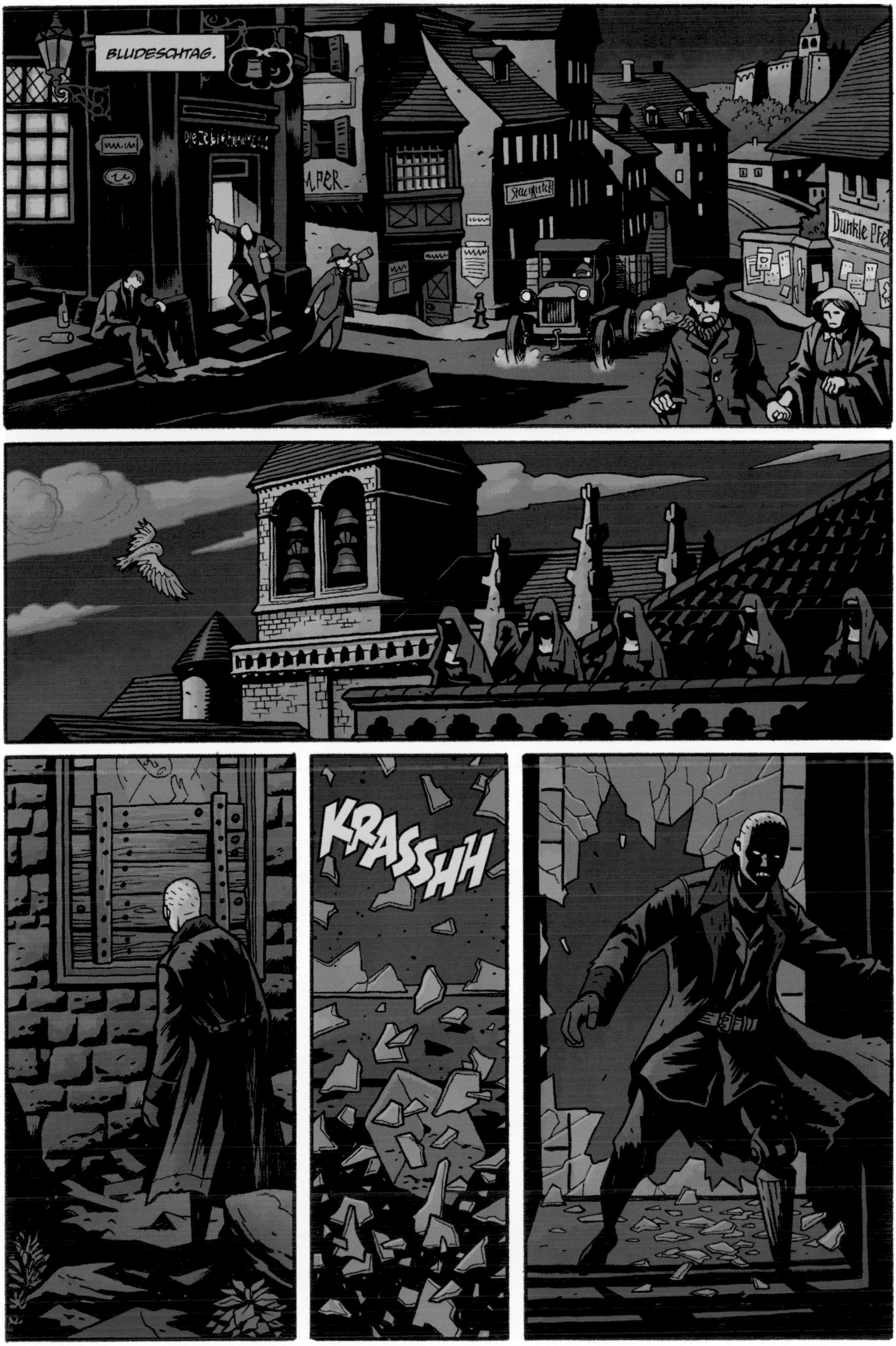
BLUDESCHTAG.
KRASSHH

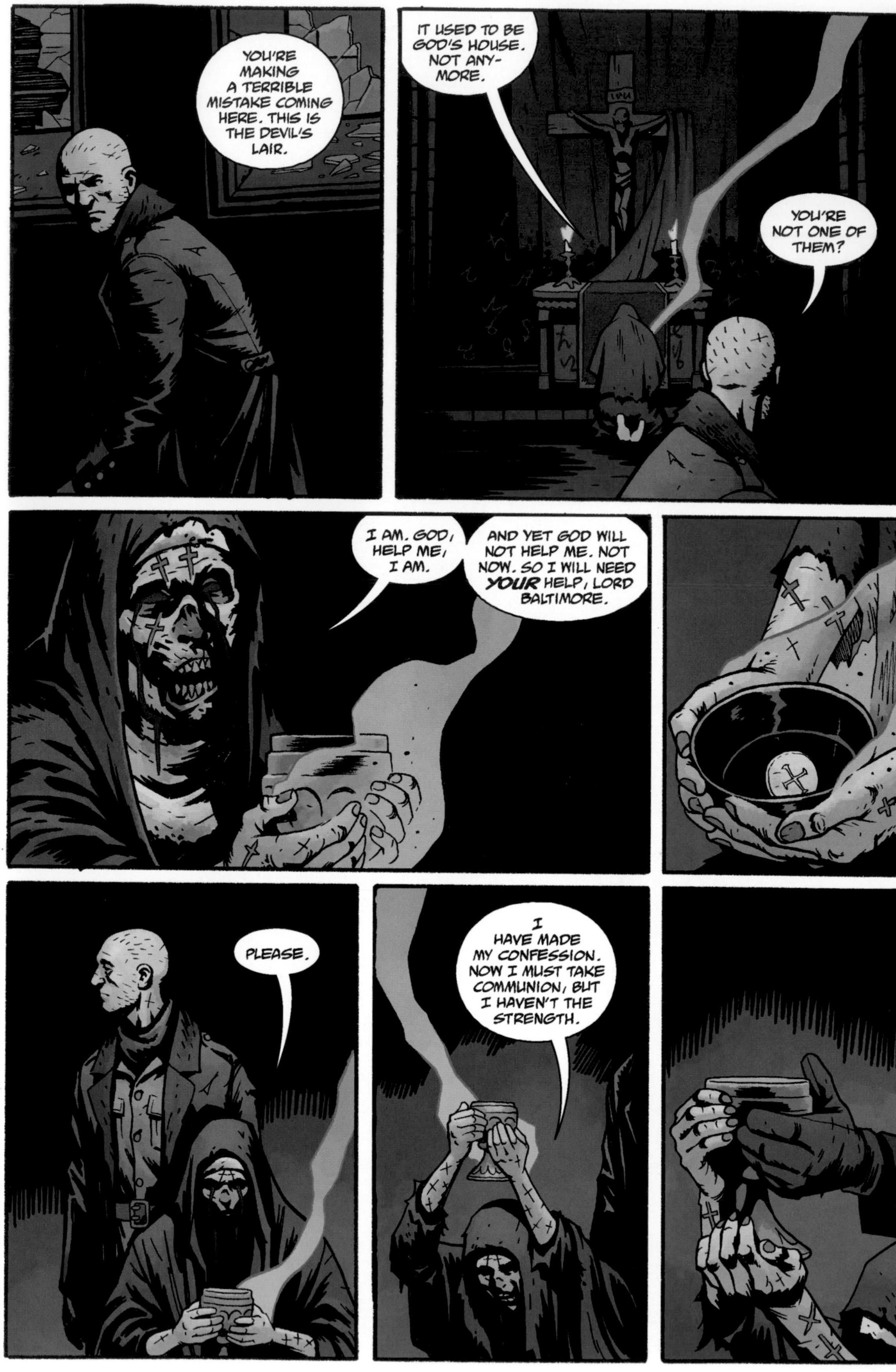
YOU'RE MAKING A TERRIBLE MISTAKE COMING HERE. THIS IS THE DEVIL'S LAIR.
IT USED TO BE GOD'S HOUSE. NOT ANYMORE.
YOU'RE NOT ONE OF THEM?
I AM. GOD, HELP ME, I AM.
AND YET GOD WILL NOT HELP ME. NOT NOW. SO I WILL NEED YOUR HELP, LORD BALTIMORE.
PLEASE.
I HAVE MADE MY CONFESSION. NOW I MUST TAKE COMMUNION, BUT I HAVEN'T THE STRENGTH.

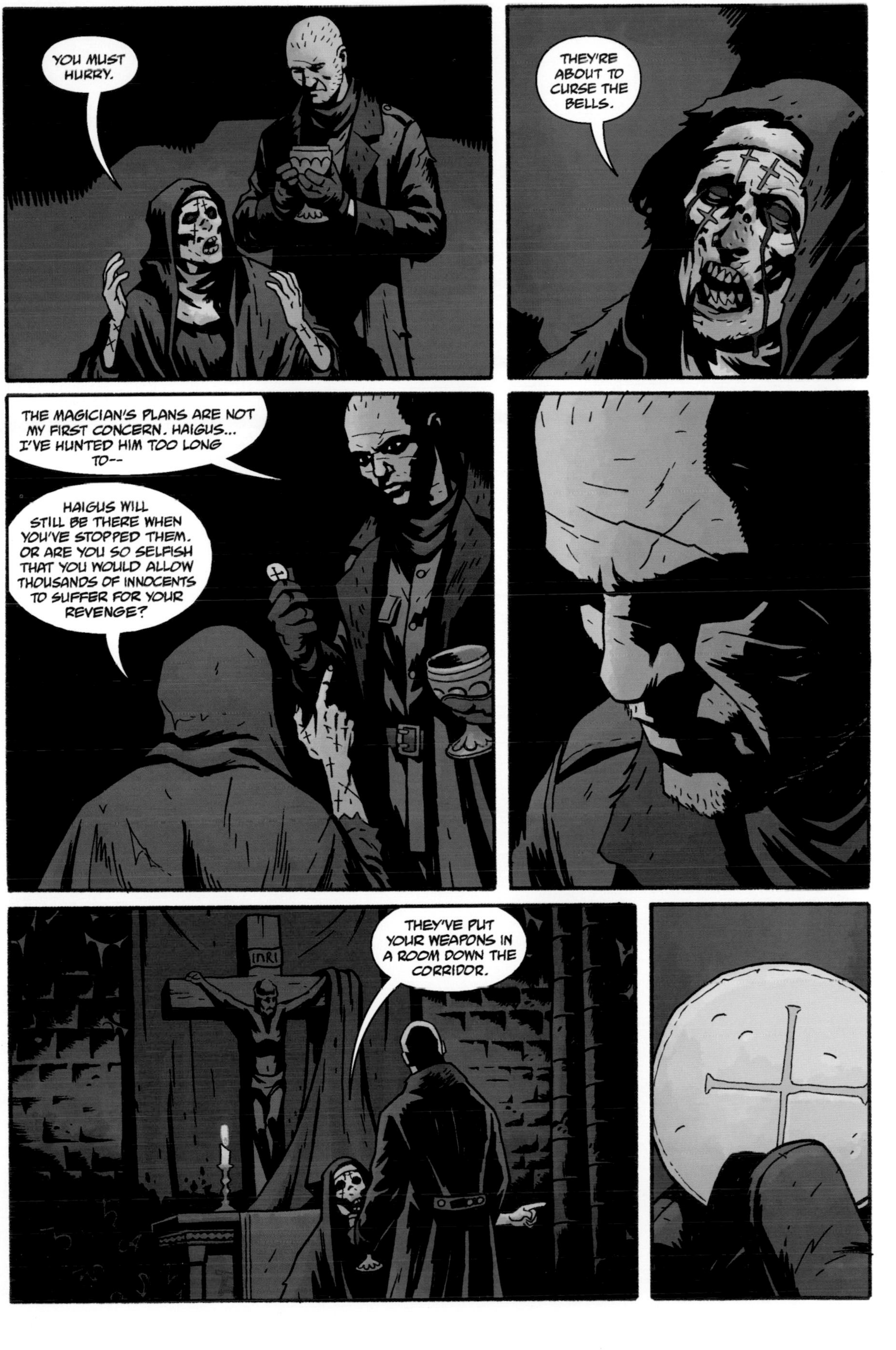
YOU MUST HURRY.
THEY'RE ABOUT TO CURSE THE BELLS.
THE MAGICIAN'S PLANS ARE NOT MY FIRST CONCERN. HAIGUS... I'VE HUNTED HIM TOO LONG TO--
HAIGUS WILL STILL BE THERE WHEN YOU'VE STOPPED THEM. OR ARE YOU SO SELFISH THAT YOU WOULD ALLOW THOUSANDS OF INNOCENTS TO SUFFER FOR YOUR REVENGE?
INRI
THEY'VE PUT YOUR WEAPONS IN A ROOM DOWN THE CORRIDOR.

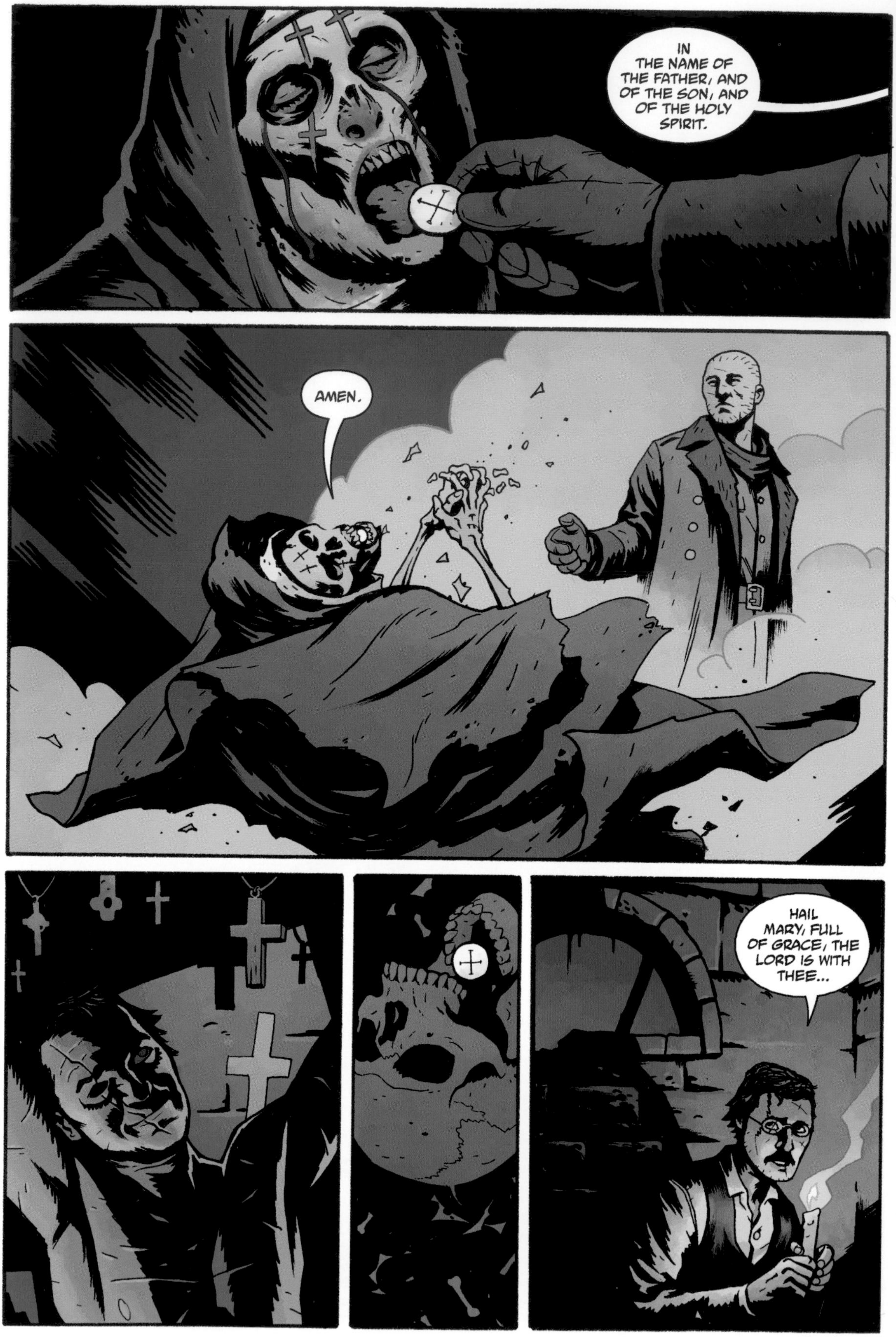
IN THE NAME OF THE FATHER, AND OF THE SON, AND OF THE HOLY SPIRIT.
AMEN.
HAIL MARY, FULL OF GRACE, THE LORD IS WITH THEE...

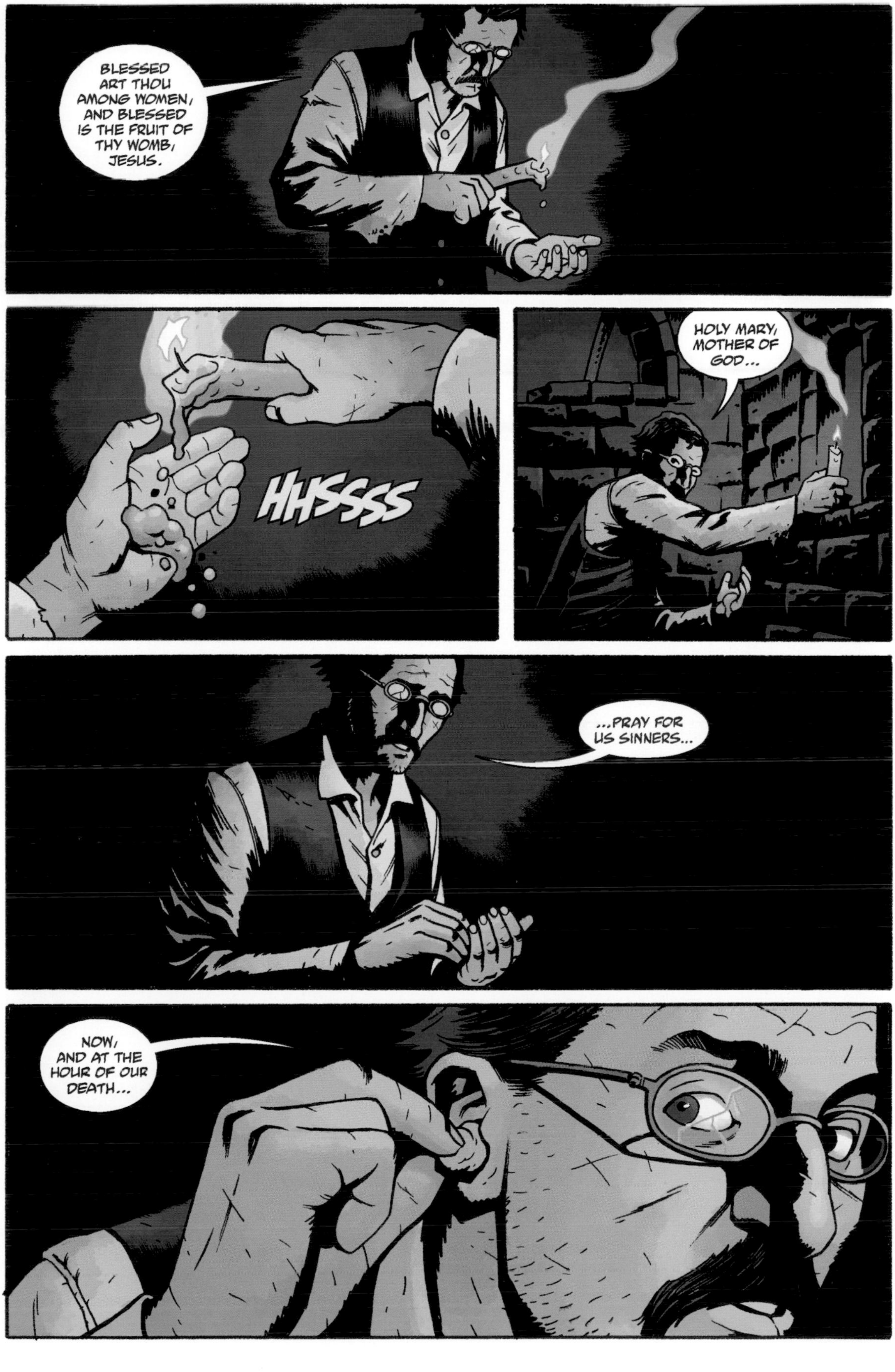
BLESSED ART THOU AMONG WOMEN, AND BLESSED IS THE FRUIT OF THY WOMB, JESUS.
HHSSSS
HOLY MARY, MOTHER OF GOD...
...PRAY FOR US SINNERS...
NOW, AND AT THE HOUR OF OUR DEATH...

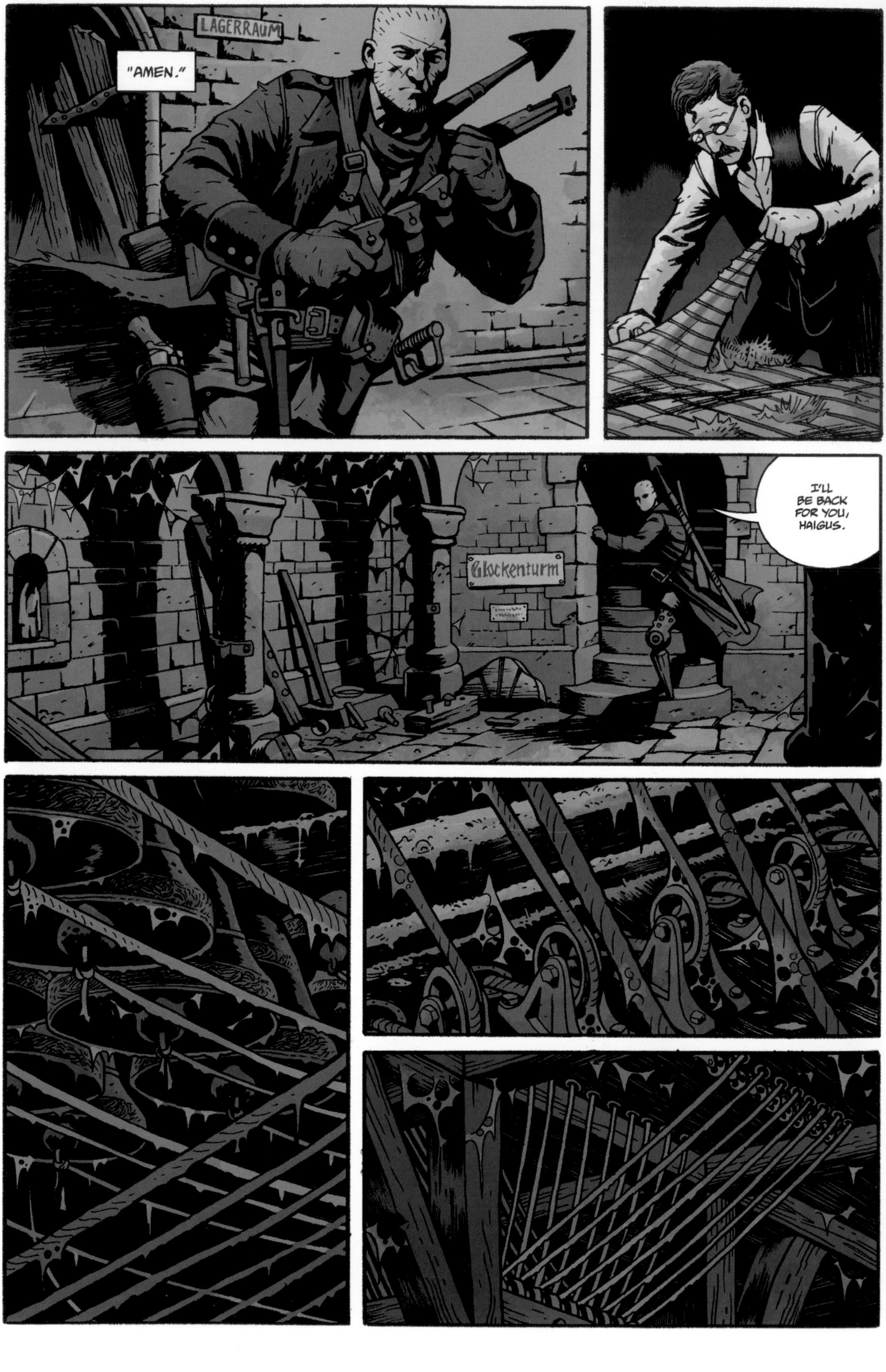
LAGERRAUM
"AMEN."
Glockenturm
I'LL BE BACK FOR YOU, HAIGUS.

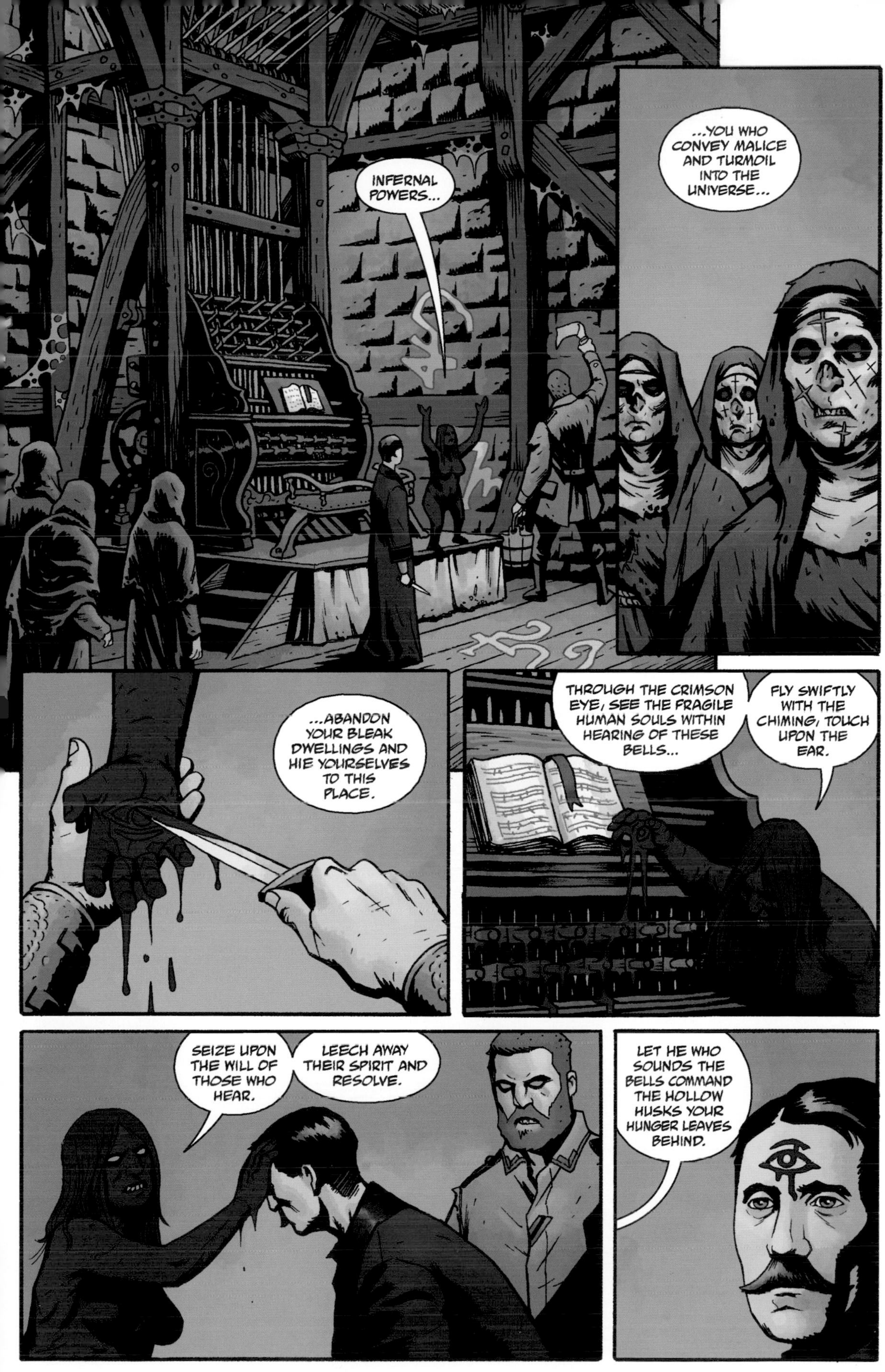
INFERNAL POWERS...
...YOU WHO CONVEY MALICE AND TURMOIL INTO THE UNIVERSE...
...ABANDON YOUR BLEAK DWELLINGS AND HIE YOURSELVES TO THIS PLACE.
THROUGH THE CRIMSON EYE, SEE THE FRAGILE HUMAN SOULS WITHIN HEARING OF THESE BELLS...
FLY SWIFTLY WITH THE CHIMING, TOUCH UPON THE EAR.
SEIZE UPON THE WILL OF THOSE WHO HEAR.
LEECH AWAY THEIR SPIRIT AND RESOLVE.
LET HE WHO SOUNDS THE BELLS COMMAND THE HOLLOW HUSKS YOUR HUNGER LEAVES BEHIND.

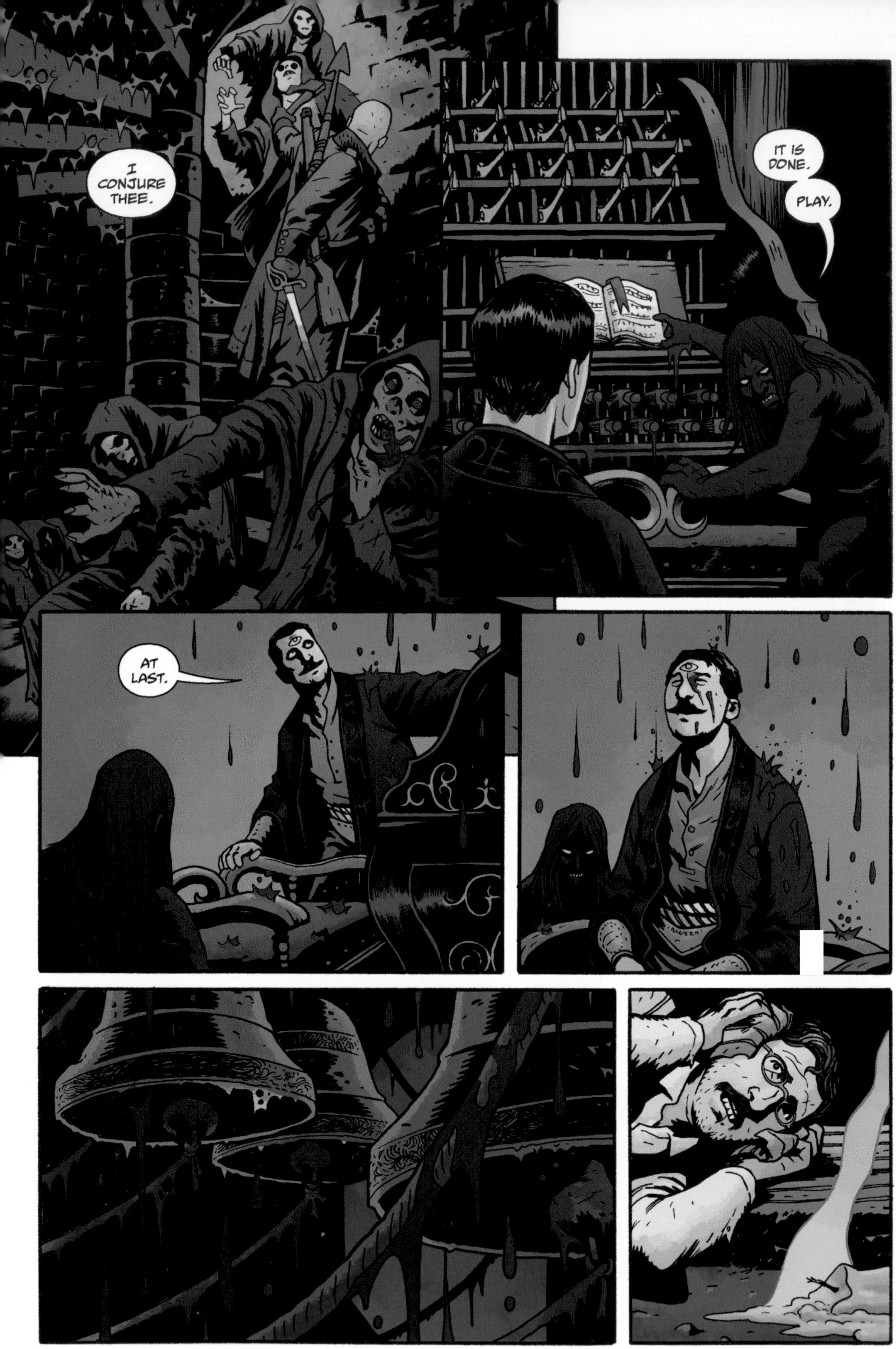
I CONJURE THEE.
IT IS DONE.
PLAY.
AT LAST.

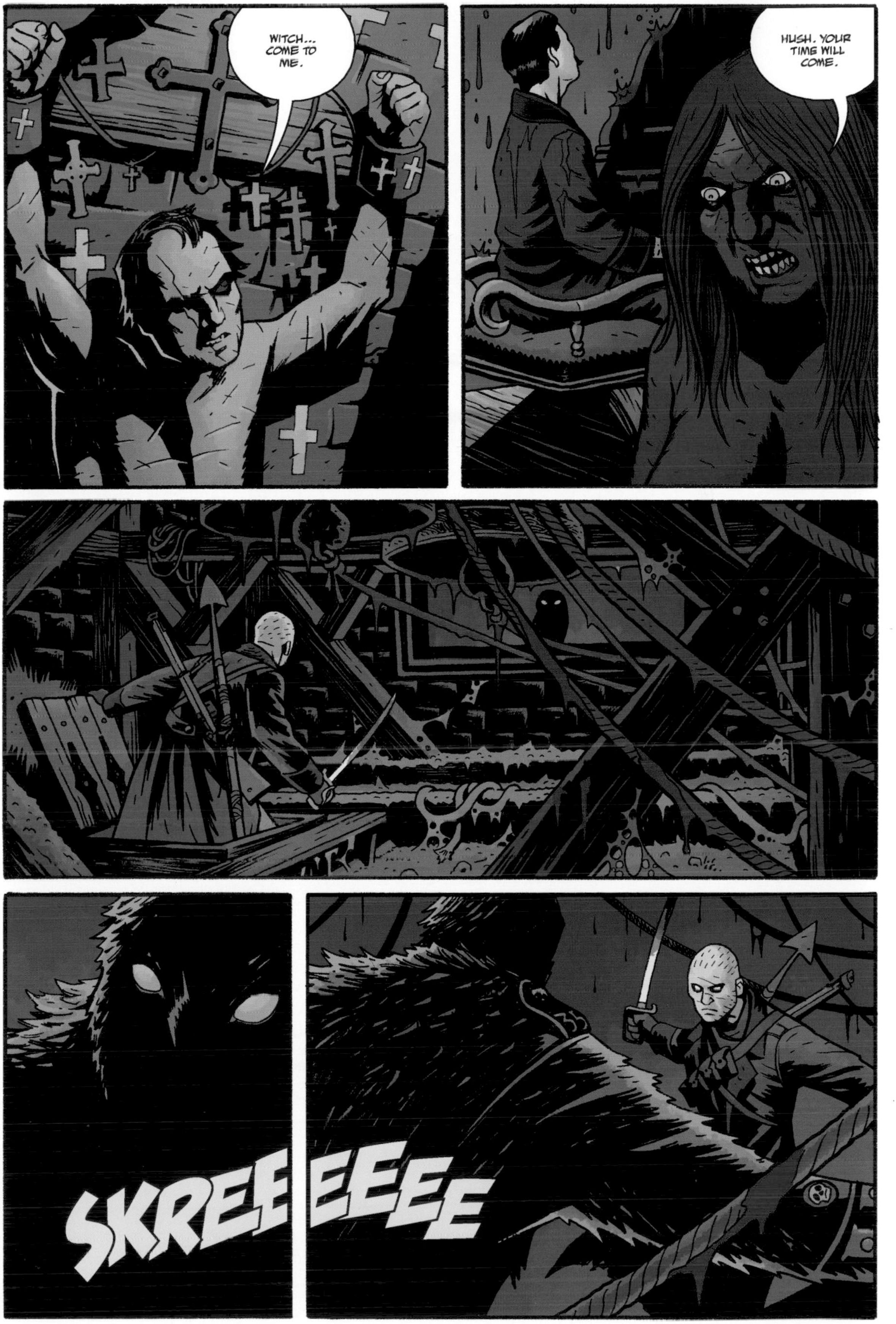
WITCH... COME TO ME.
HUSH. YOUR TIME WILL COME.
SKREEEEEEE

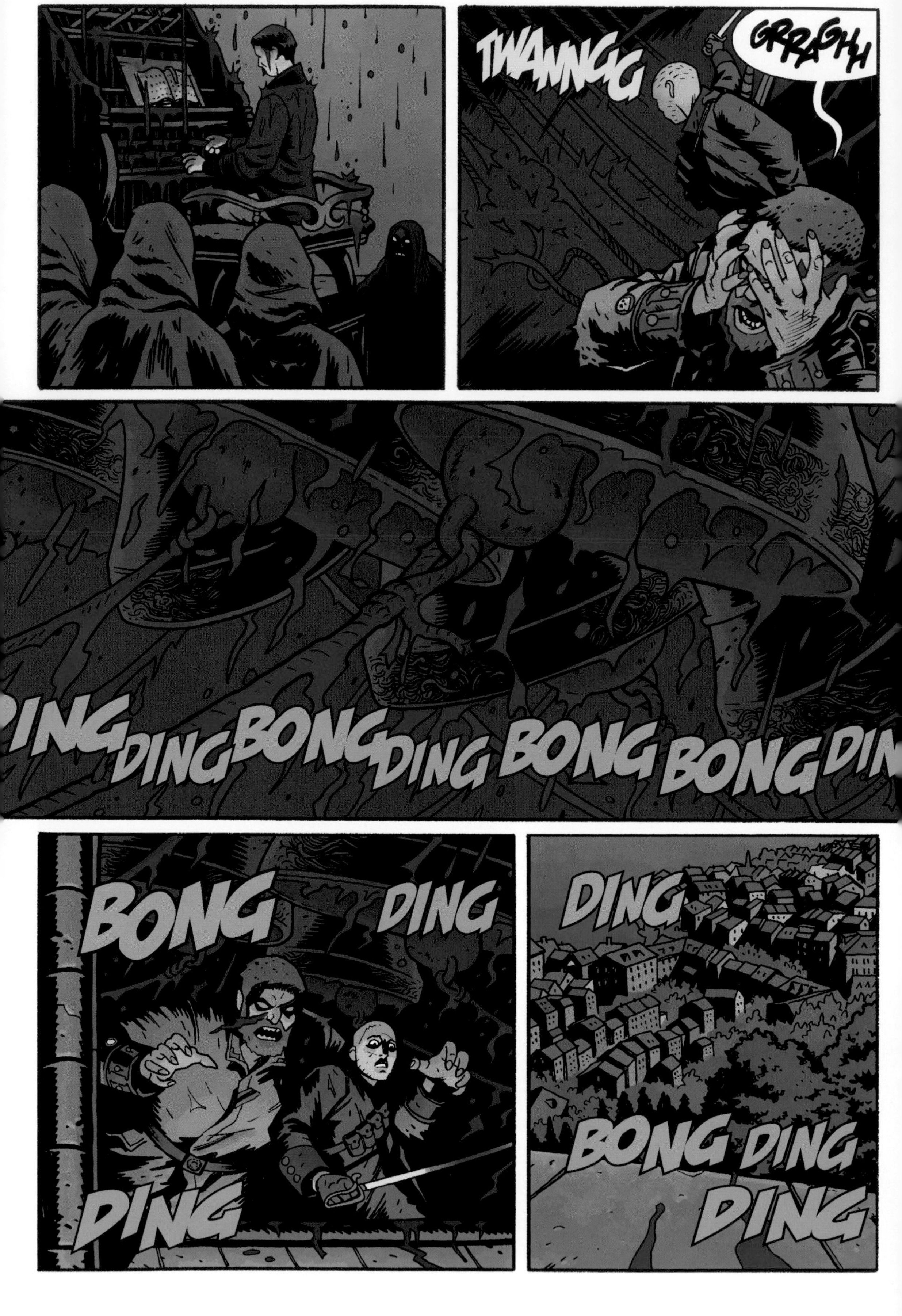
TWANNGG
GRRAGHH
ING DING BONG DING BONG BONG DIN
BONG
DING
DING
DING
BONG DING
DING

CHAPTER FIVE

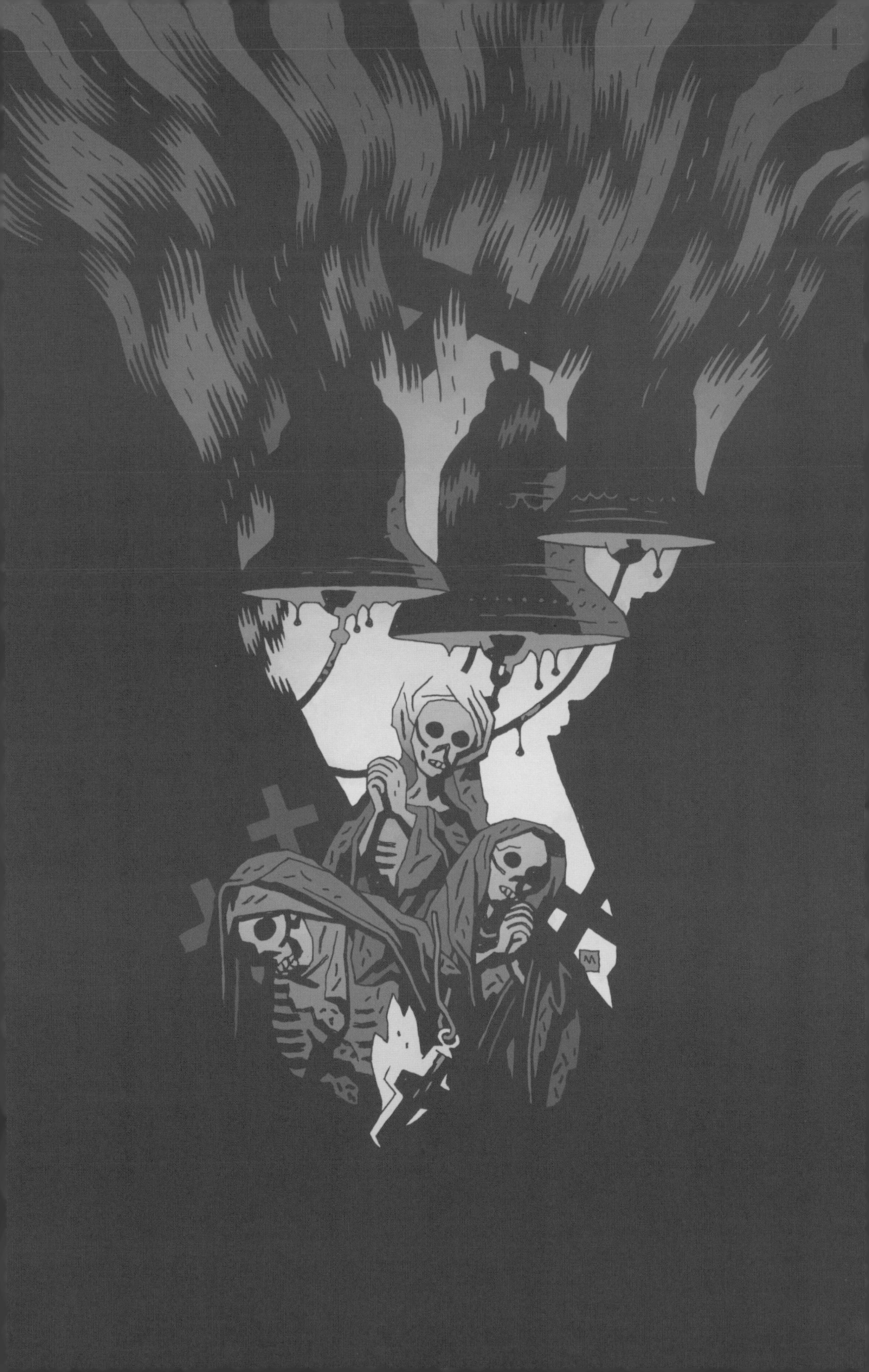

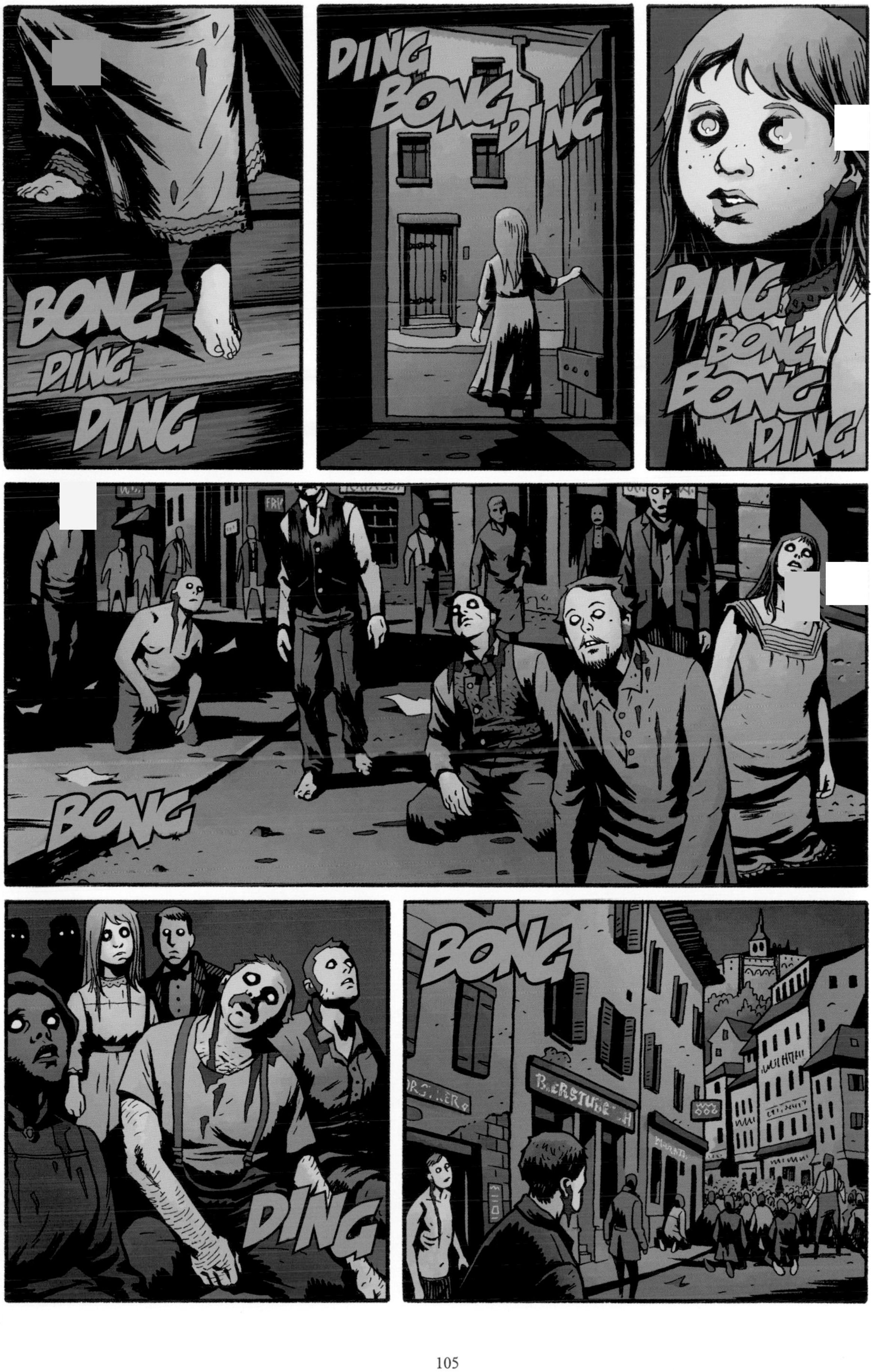
BONG
DING
DING
DING
BONG
DING
DING
BONG
BONG
DING
BONG
DING
BONG

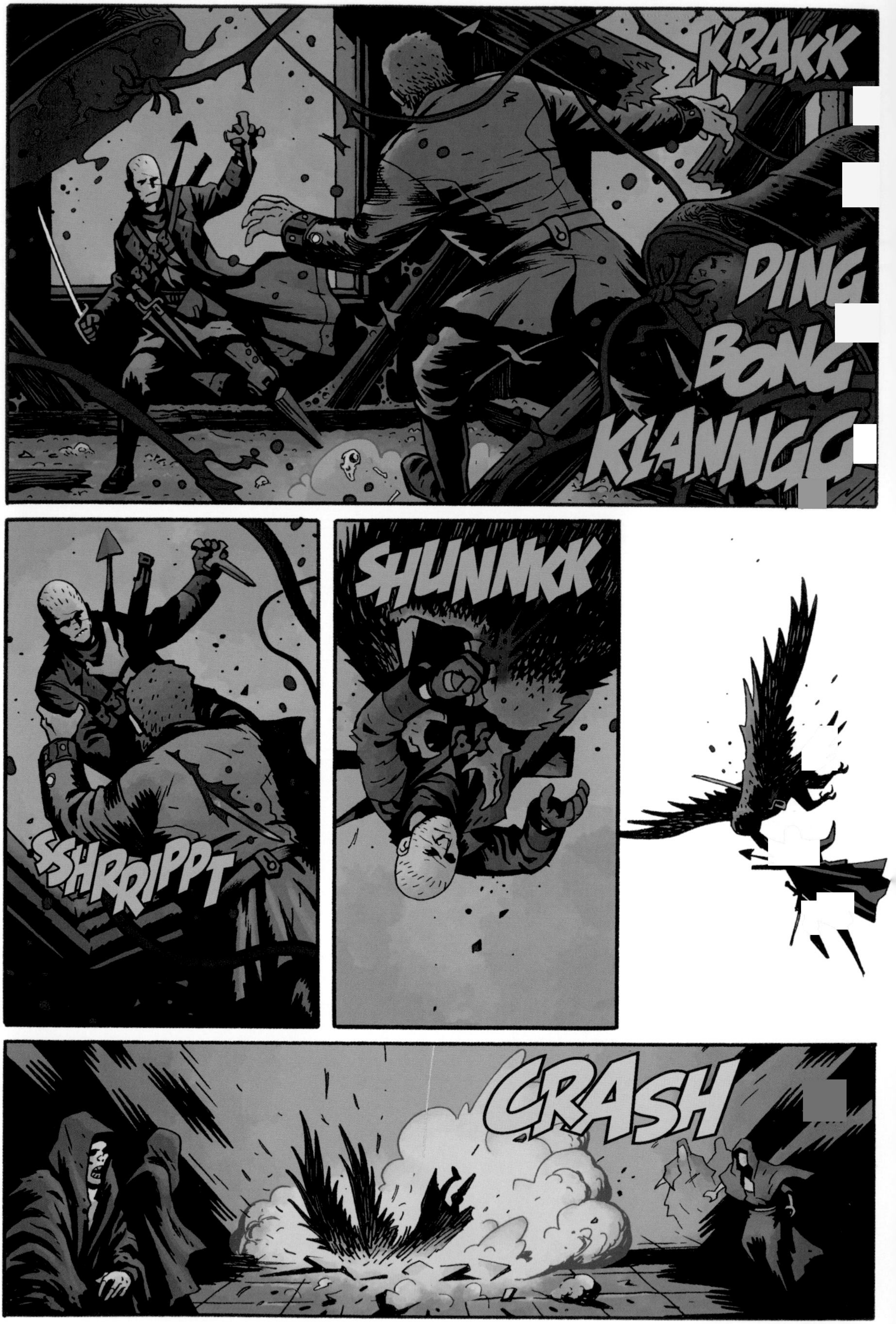
KRAKK
DING
BONG
KLANNGG
SHUNNKK
SSHRRIPPT
CRASH

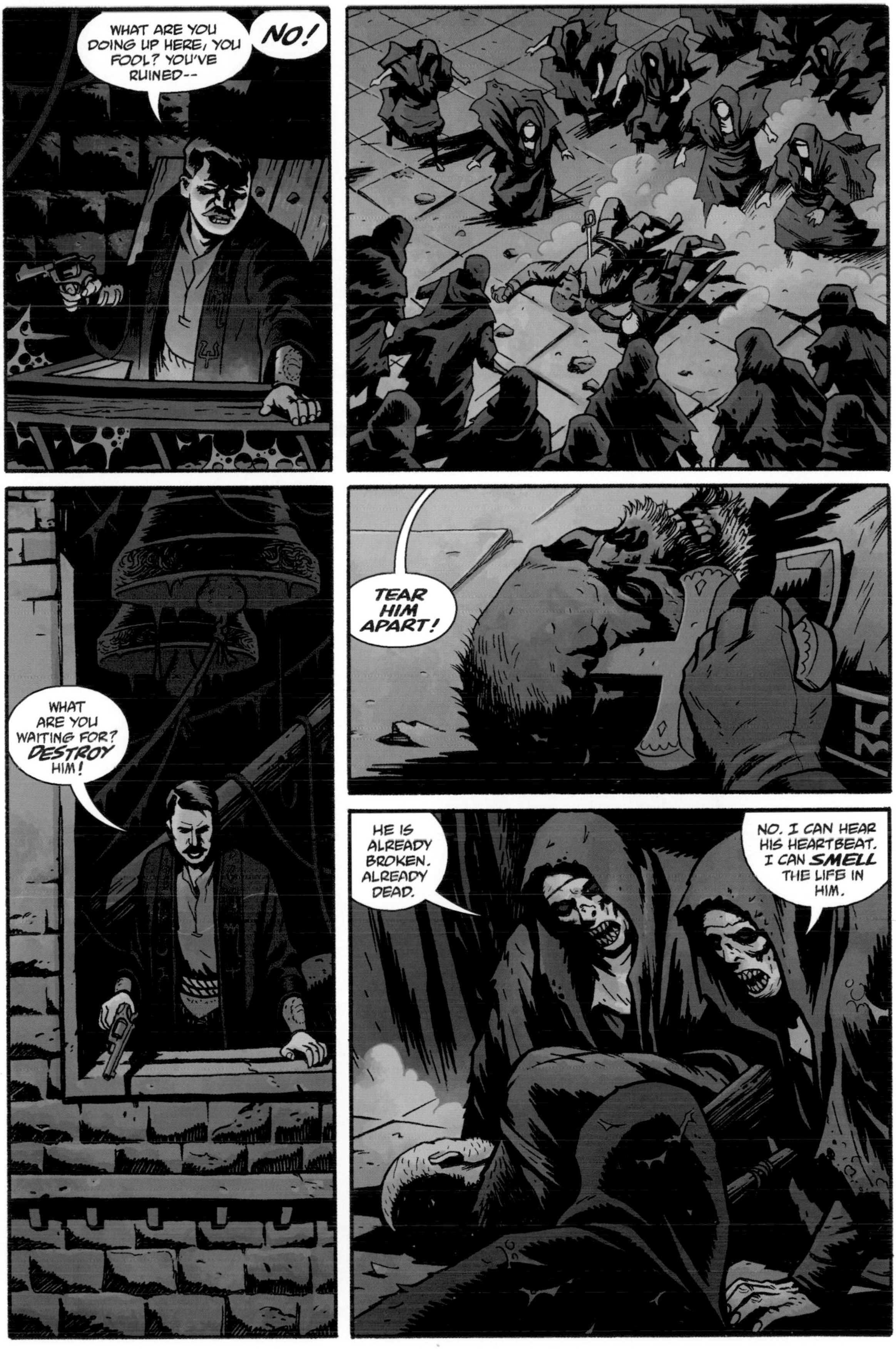
WHAT ARE YOU DOING UP HERE, YOU FOOL? YOU'VE RUINED--
NO!
WHAT ARE YOU WAITING FOR? DESTROY HIM!
TEAR HIM APART!
HE IS ALREADY BROKEN. ALREADY DEAD.
NO. I CAN HEAR HIS HEARTBEAT. I CAN SMELL THE LIFE IN HIM.

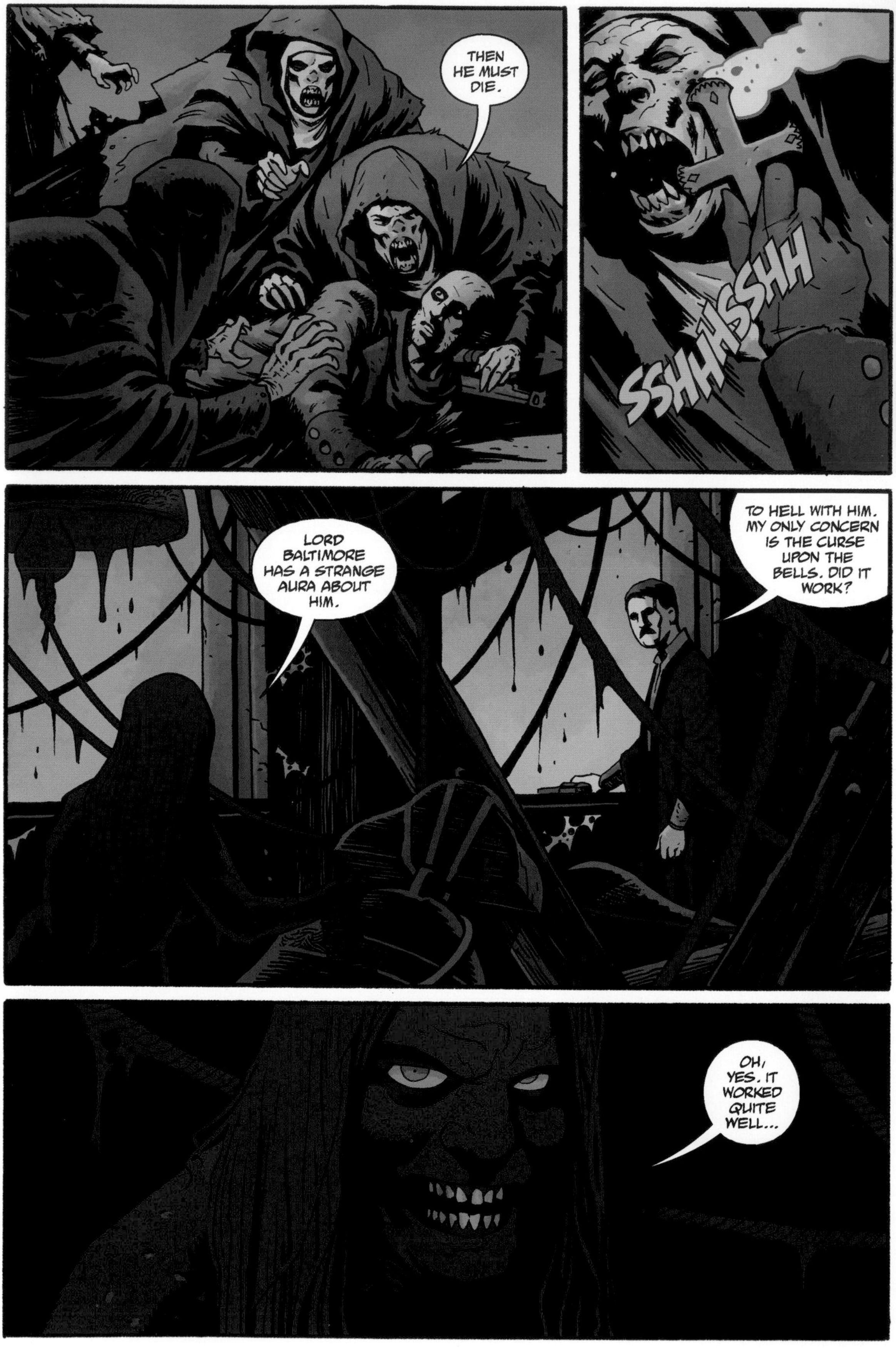
THEN HE MUST DIE.
SSHHSSHH
LORD BALTIMORE HAS A STRANGE AURA ABOUT HIM.
TO HELL WITH HIM. MY ONLY CONCERN IS THE CURSE UPON THE BELLS. DID IT WORK?
OH, YES. IT WORKED QUITE WELL...

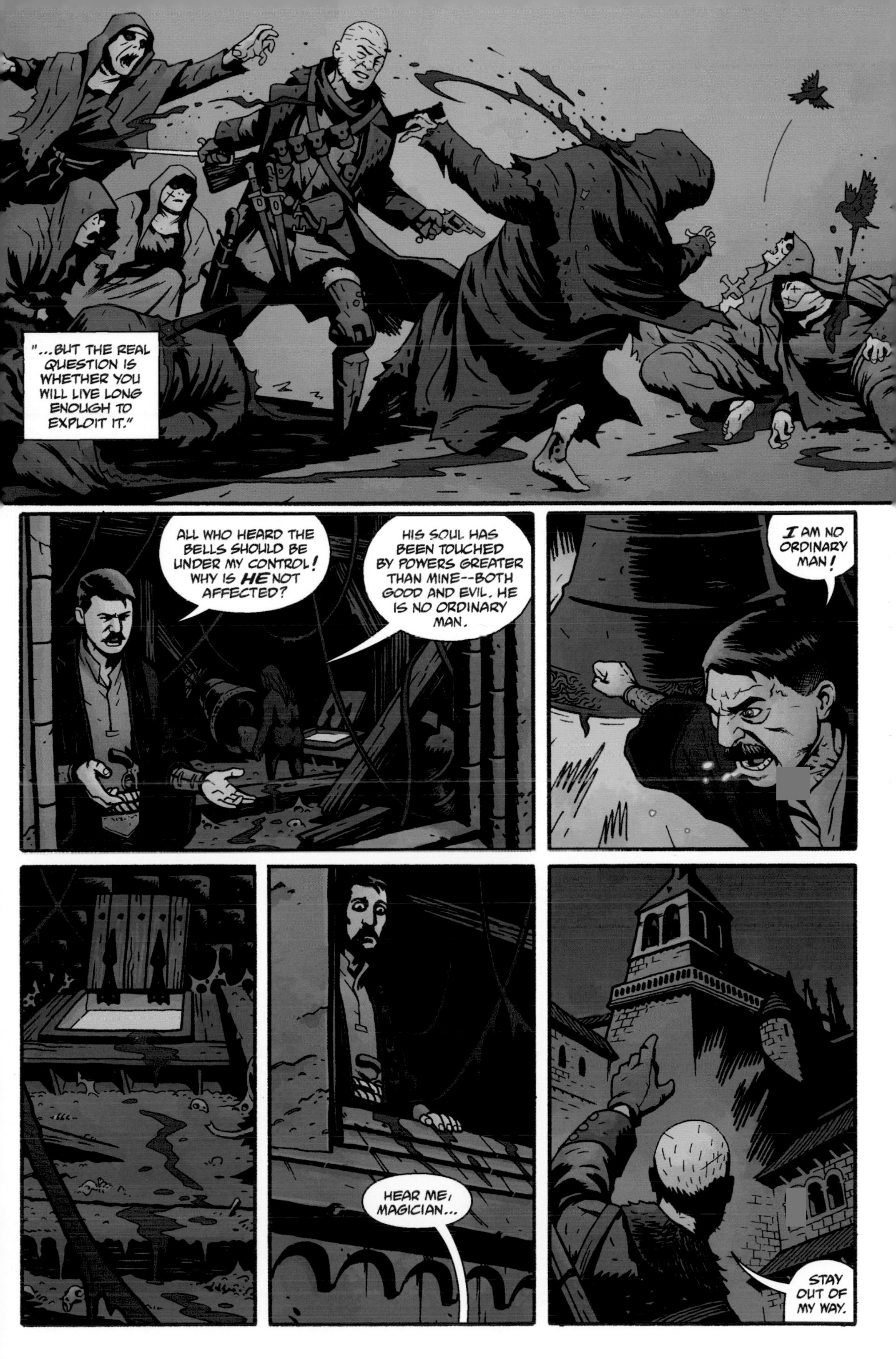
"...BUT THE REAL QUESTION IS WHETHER YOU WILL LIVE LONG ENOUGH TO EXPLOIT IT."
ALL WHO HEARD THE BELLS SHOULD BE UNDER MY CONTROL! WHY IS HE NOT AFFECTED?
HIS SOUL HAS BEEN TOUCHED BY POWERS GREATER THAN MINE--BOTH GOOD AND EVIL. HE IS NO ORDINARY MAN.
I AM NO ORDINARY MAN!
HEAR ME, MAGICIAN...
STAY OUT OF MY WAY.

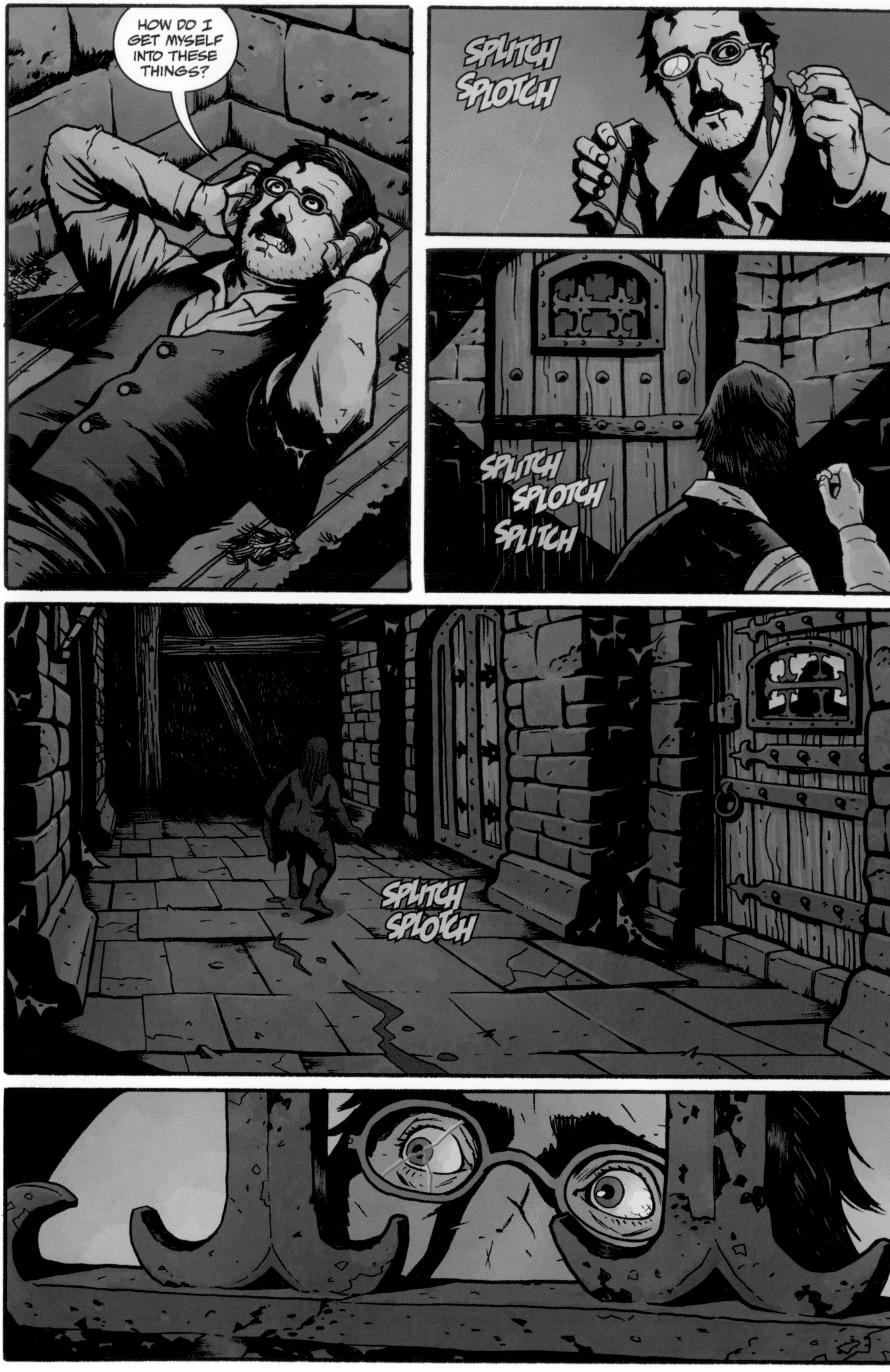
HOW DO I GET MYSELF INTO THESE THINGS?
SPLITCH
SPLOTCH
SPLITCH
SPLOTCH
SPLITCH
SPLITCH
SPLOTCH

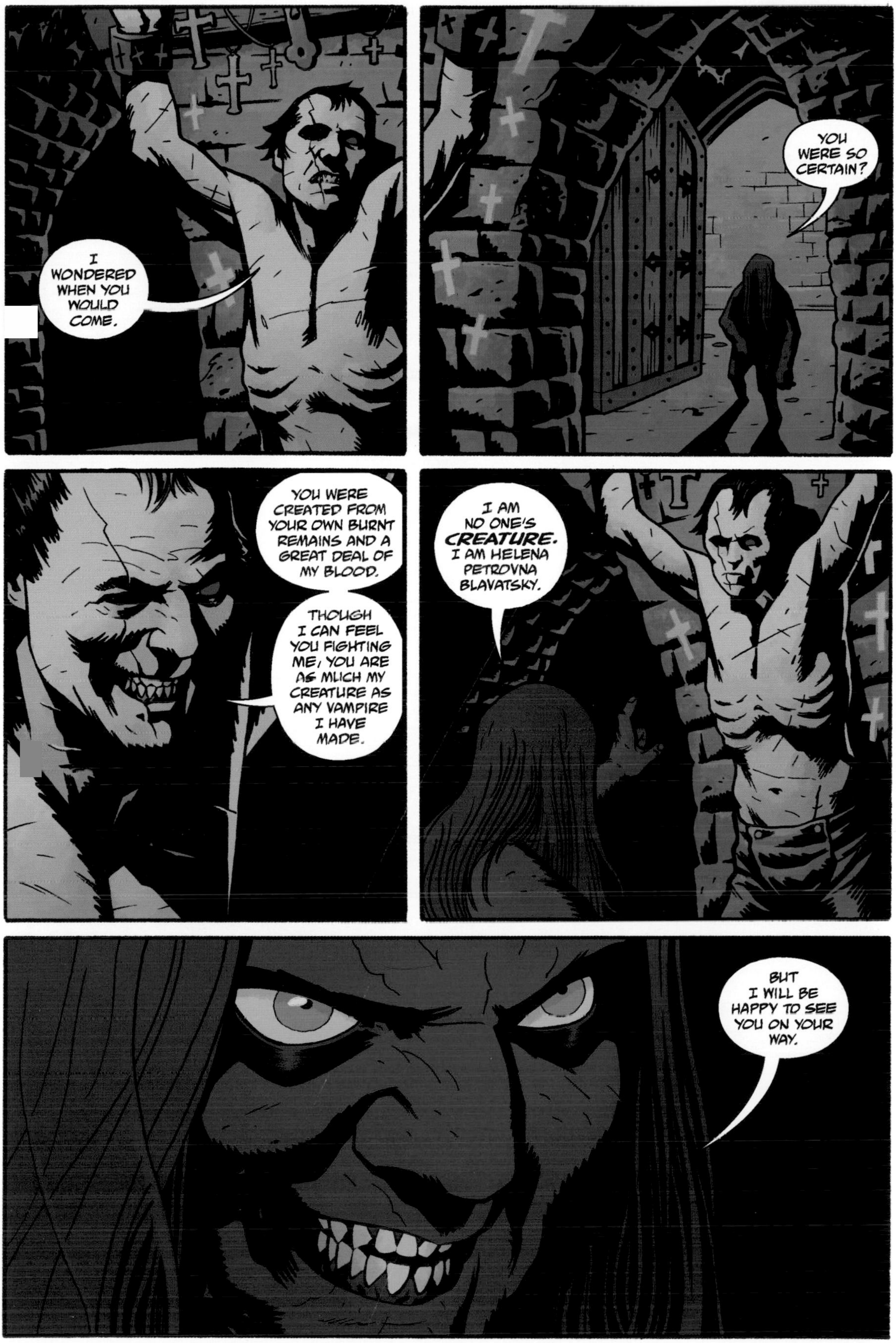
I WONDERED WHEN YOU WOULD COME.
YOU WERE SO CERTAIN?
YOU WERE CREATED FROM YOUR OWN BURNT REMAINS AND A GREAT DEAL OF MY BLOOD.
THOUGH I CAN FEEL YOU FIGHTING ME, YOU ARE AS MUCH MY CREATURE AS ANY VAMPIRE I HAVE MADE.
I AM NO ONE'S *CREATURE.* I AM HELENA PETROVNA BLAVATSKY.
BUT I WILL BE HAPPY TO SEE YOU ON YOUR WAY.

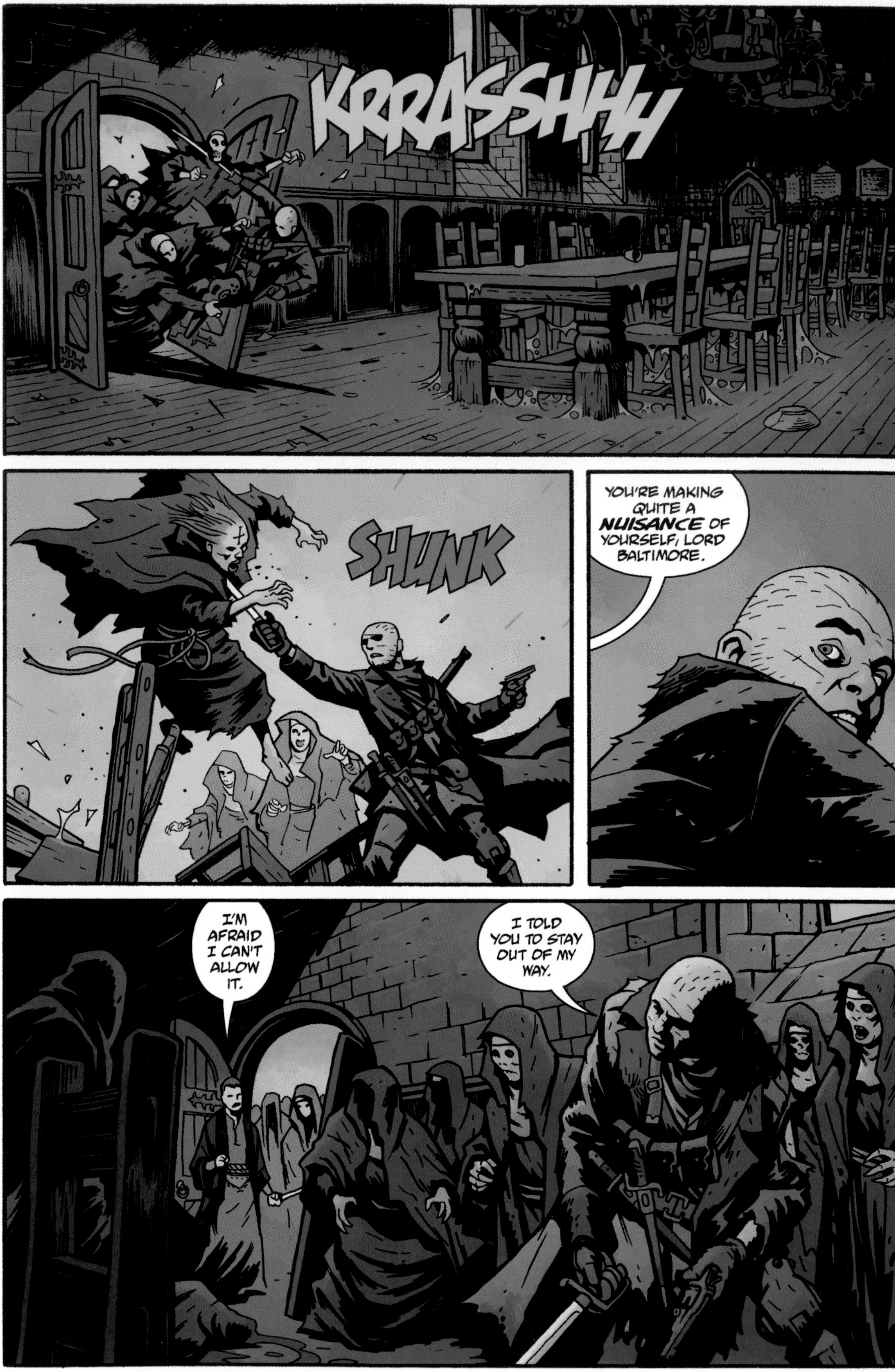
KRRASSHHH
SHUNK
YOU'RE MAKING QUITE A NUISANCE OF YOURSELF, LORD BALTIMORE.
I'M AFRAID I CAN'T ALLOW IT.
I TOLD YOU TO STAY OUT OF MY WAY.

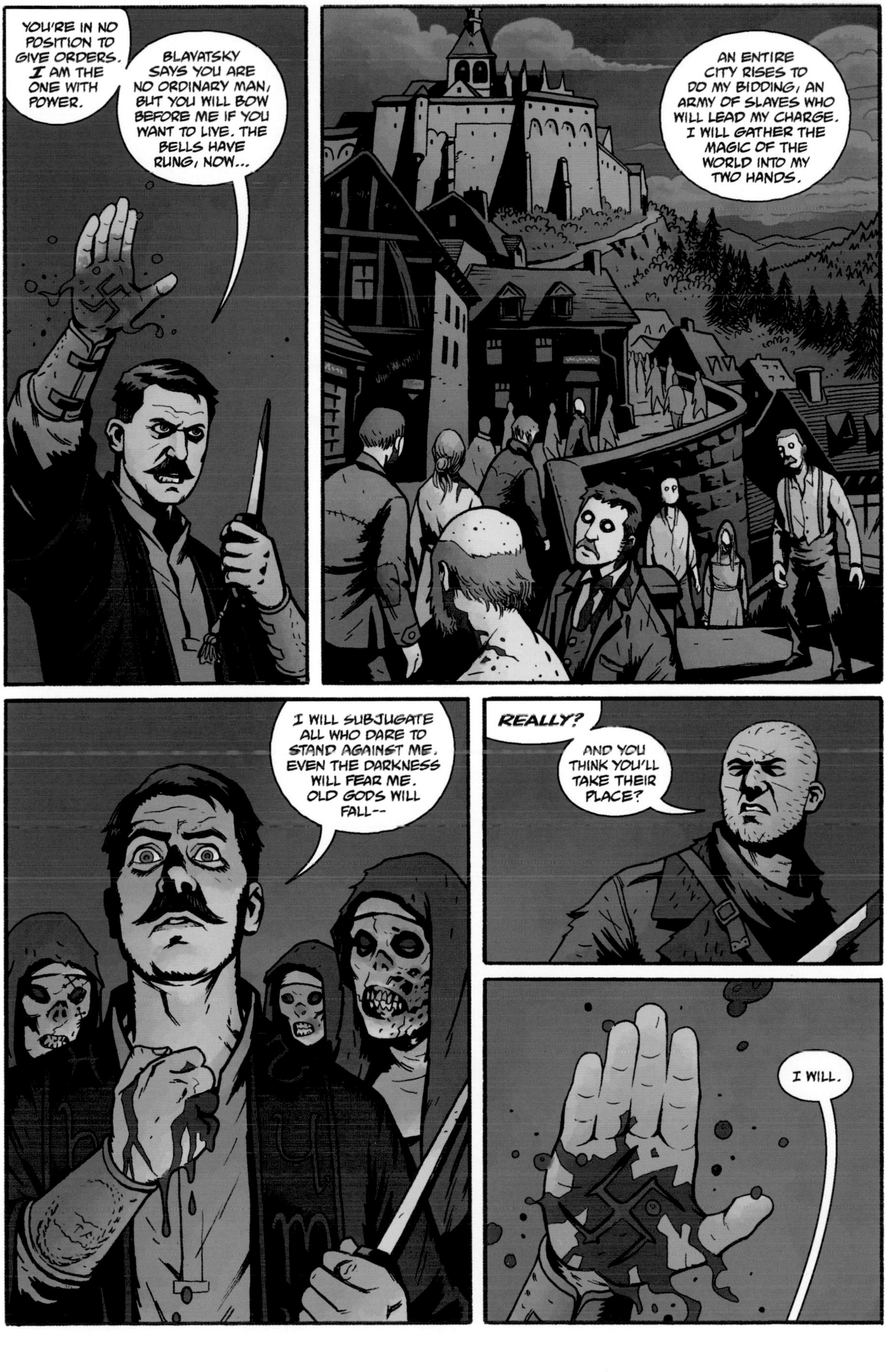
YOU'RE IN NO POSITION TO GIVE ORDERS. I AM THE ONE WITH POWER.
BLAVATSKY SAYS YOU ARE NO ORDINARY MAN, BUT YOU WILL BOW BEFORE ME IF YOU WANT TO LIVE. THE BELLS HAVE RUNG, NOW...
AN ENTIRE CITY RISES TO DO MY BIDDING, AN ARMY OF SLAVES WHO WILL LEAD MY CHARGE. I WILL GATHER THE MAGIC OF THE WORLD INTO MY TWO HANDS.
I WILL SUBJUGATE ALL WHO DARE TO STAND AGAINST ME. EVEN THE DARKNESS WILL FEAR ME. OLD GODS WILL FALL--
REALLY?
AND YOU THINK YOU'LL TAKE THEIR PLACE?
I WILL.

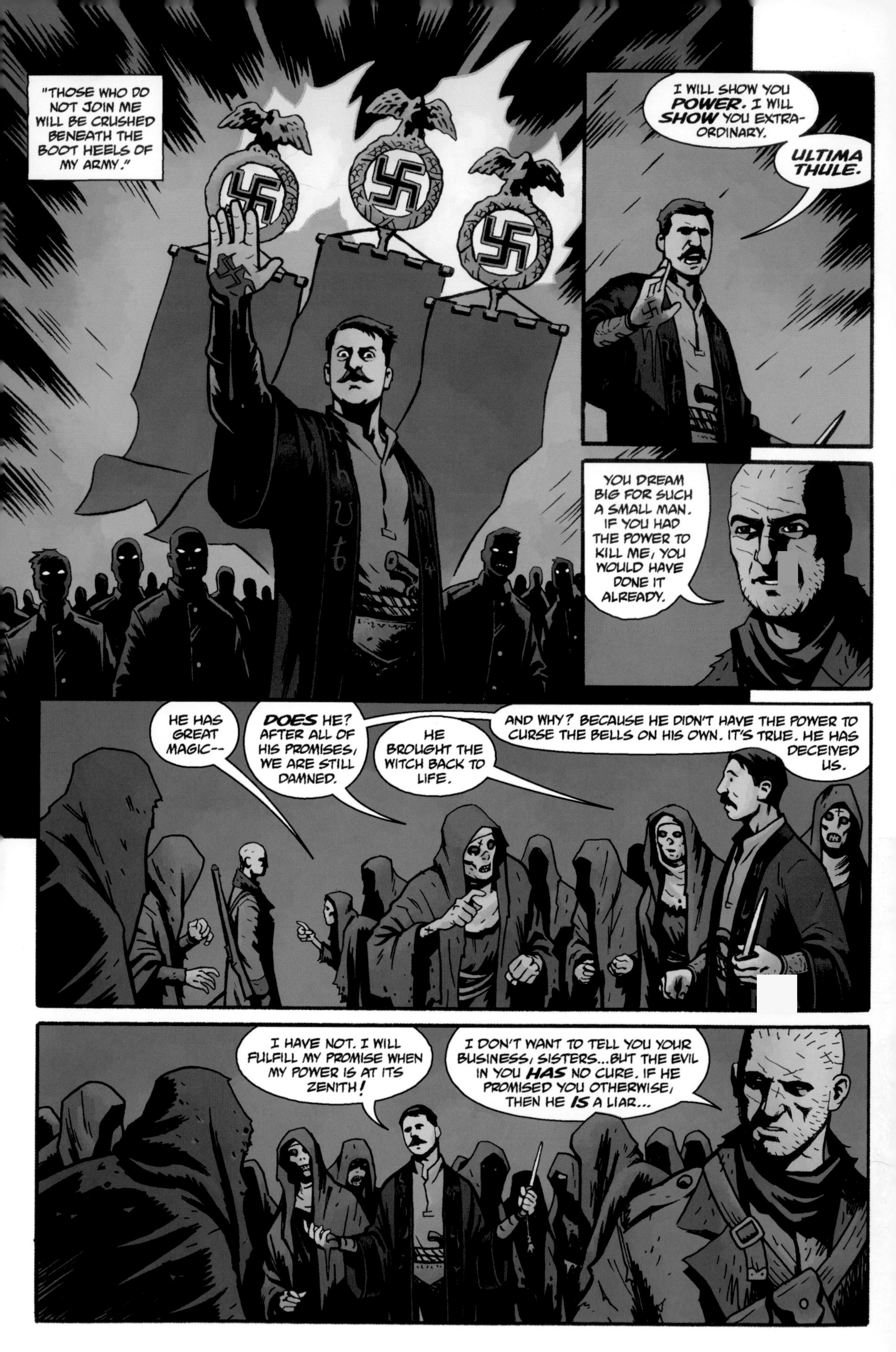
"THOSE WHO DO NOT JOIN ME WILL BE CRUSHED BENEATH THE BOOT HEELS OF MY ARMY."
I WILL SHOW YOU POWER. I WILL SHOW YOU EXTRA-ORDINARY.
ULTIMA THULE.
YOU DREAM BIG FOR SUCH A SMALL MAN. IF YOU HAD THE POWER TO KILL ME, YOU WOULD HAVE DONE IT ALREADY.
HE HAS GREAT MAGIC--
DOES HE? AFTER ALL OF HIS PROMISES, WE ARE STILL DAMNED.
HE BROUGHT THE WITCH BACK TO LIFE.
AND WHY? BECAUSE HE DIDN'T HAVE THE POWER TO CURSE THE BELLS ON HIS OWN. IT'S TRUE. HE HAS DECEIVED US.
I HAVE NOT. I WILL FULFILL MY PROMISE WHEN MY POWER IS AT ITS ZENITH!
I DON'T WANT TO TELL YOU YOUR BUSINESS, SISTERS...BUT THE EVIL IN YOU HAS NO CURE. IF HE PROMISED YOU OTHERWISE, THEN HE IS A LIAR...

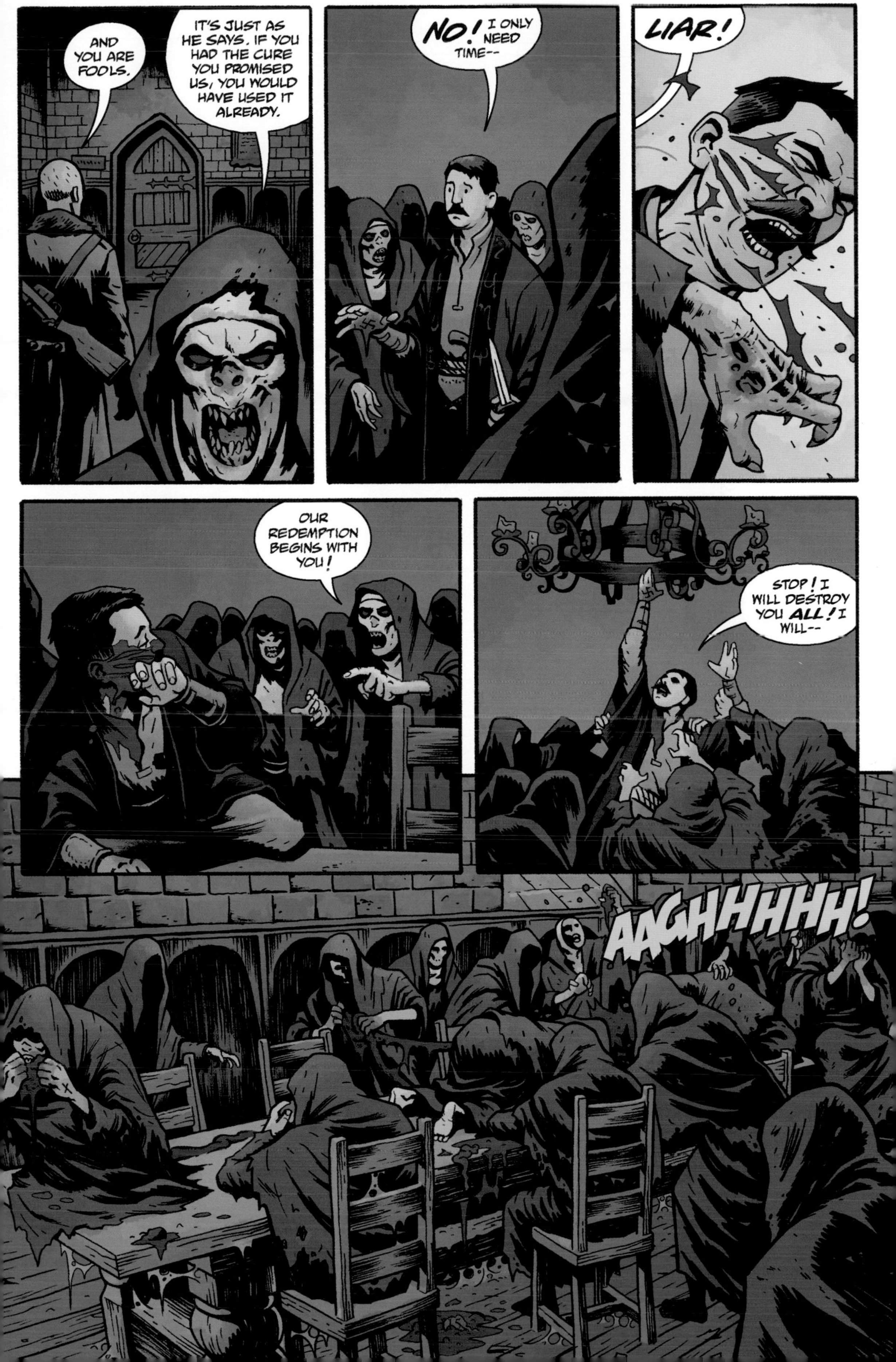
AND YOU ARE FOOLS.
IT'S JUST AS HE SAYS. IF YOU HAD THE CURE YOU PROMISED US, YOU WOULD HAVE USED IT ALREADY.
NO! I ONLY NEED TIME--
LIAR!
OUR REDEMPTION BEGINS WITH YOU!
STOP! I WILL DESTROY YOU ALL! I WILL--
AAGHHHHH!

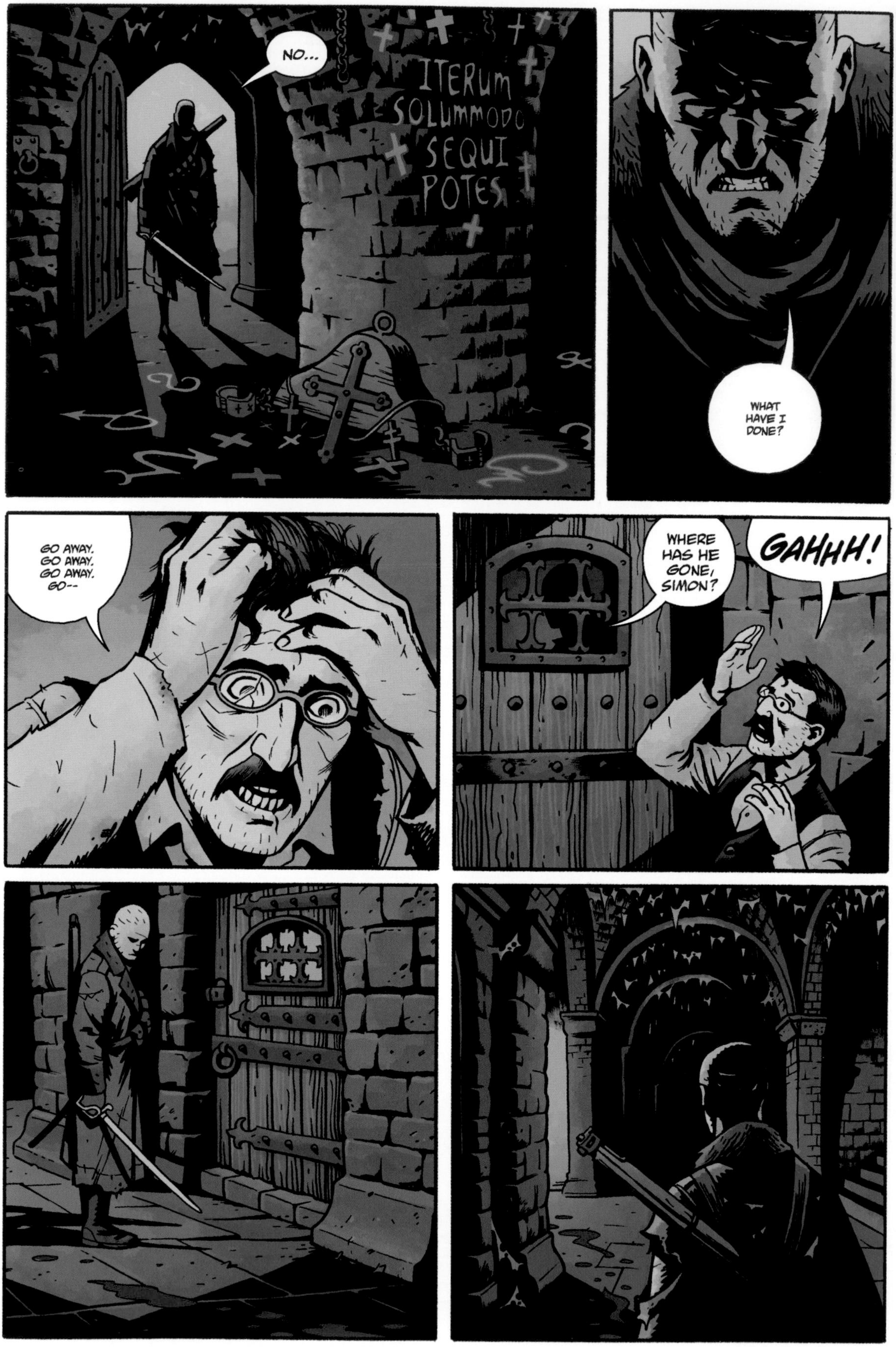
NO...
ITERUM SOLUMMODO SEQUI POTES
WHAT HAVE I DONE?
GO AWAY. GO AWAY. GO AWAY. GO--
WHERE HAS HE GONE, SIMON?
GAHHH!

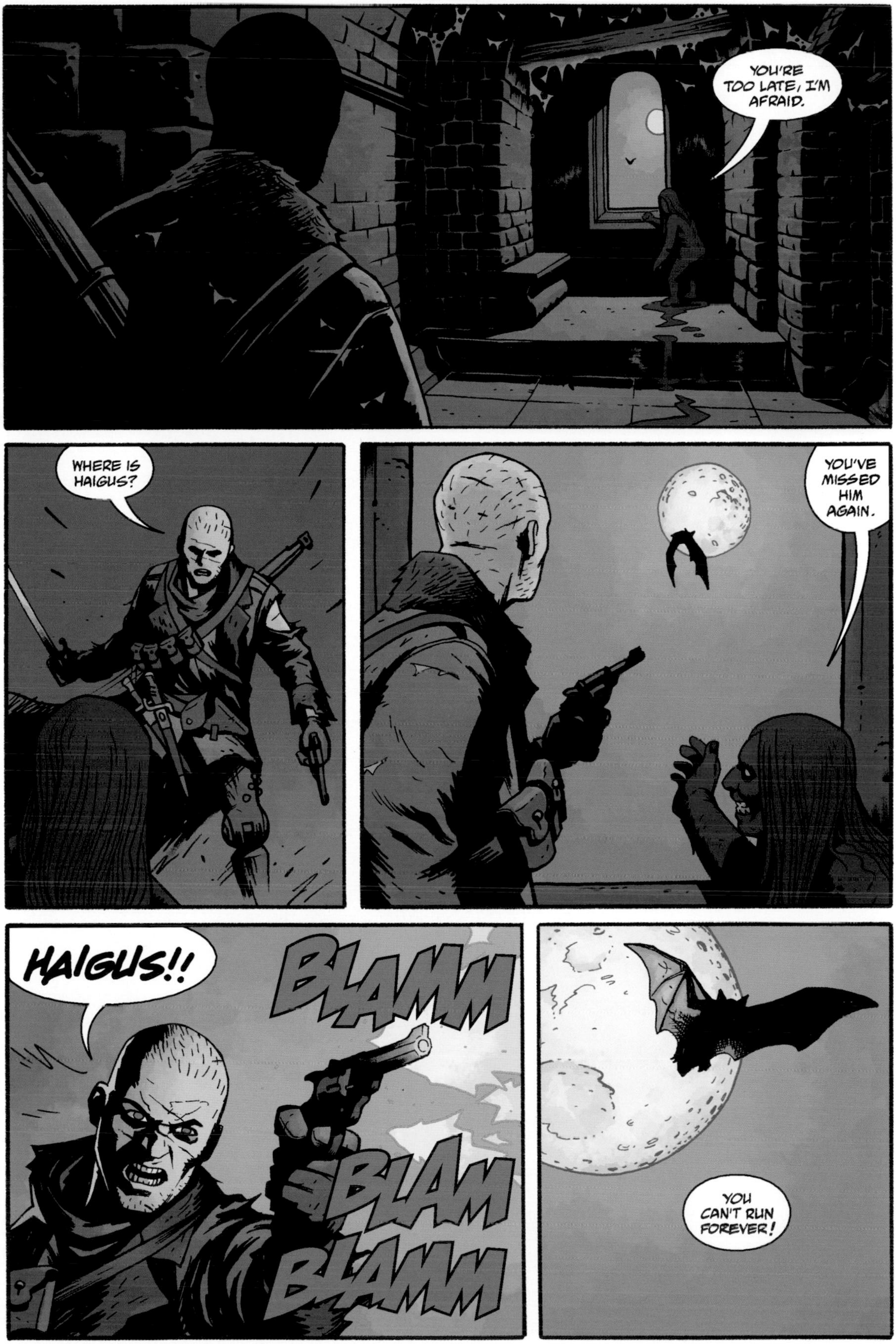
YOU'RE TOO LATE, I'M AFRAID.
WHERE IS HAIGUS?
YOU'VE MISSED HIM AGAIN.
HAIGUS!!
BLAMM
BLAM
BLAMM
YOU CAN'T RUN FOREVER!

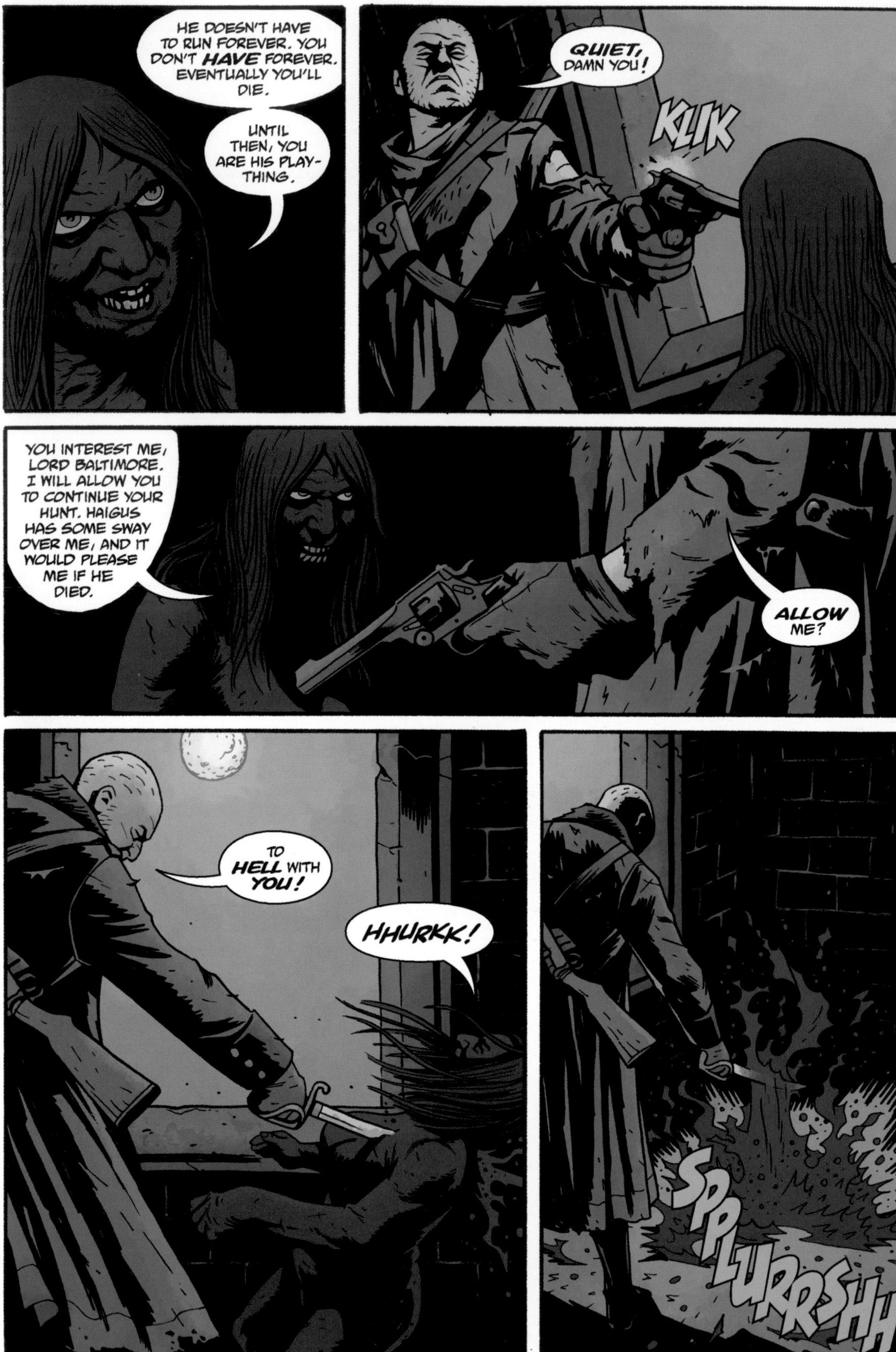
HE DOESN'T HAVE TO RUN FOREVER. YOU DON'T HAVE FOREVER. EVENTUALLY YOU'LL DIE.
UNTIL THEN, YOU ARE HIS PLAYTHING.
QUIET, DAMN YOU!
KLIK
YOU INTEREST ME, LORD BALTIMORE. I WILL ALLOW YOU TO CONTINUE YOUR HUNT. HAIGUS HAS SOME SWAY OVER ME, AND IT WOULD PLEASE ME IF HE DIED.
ALLOW ME?
TO HELL WITH YOU!
HHURKK!
SPPLURRSHH

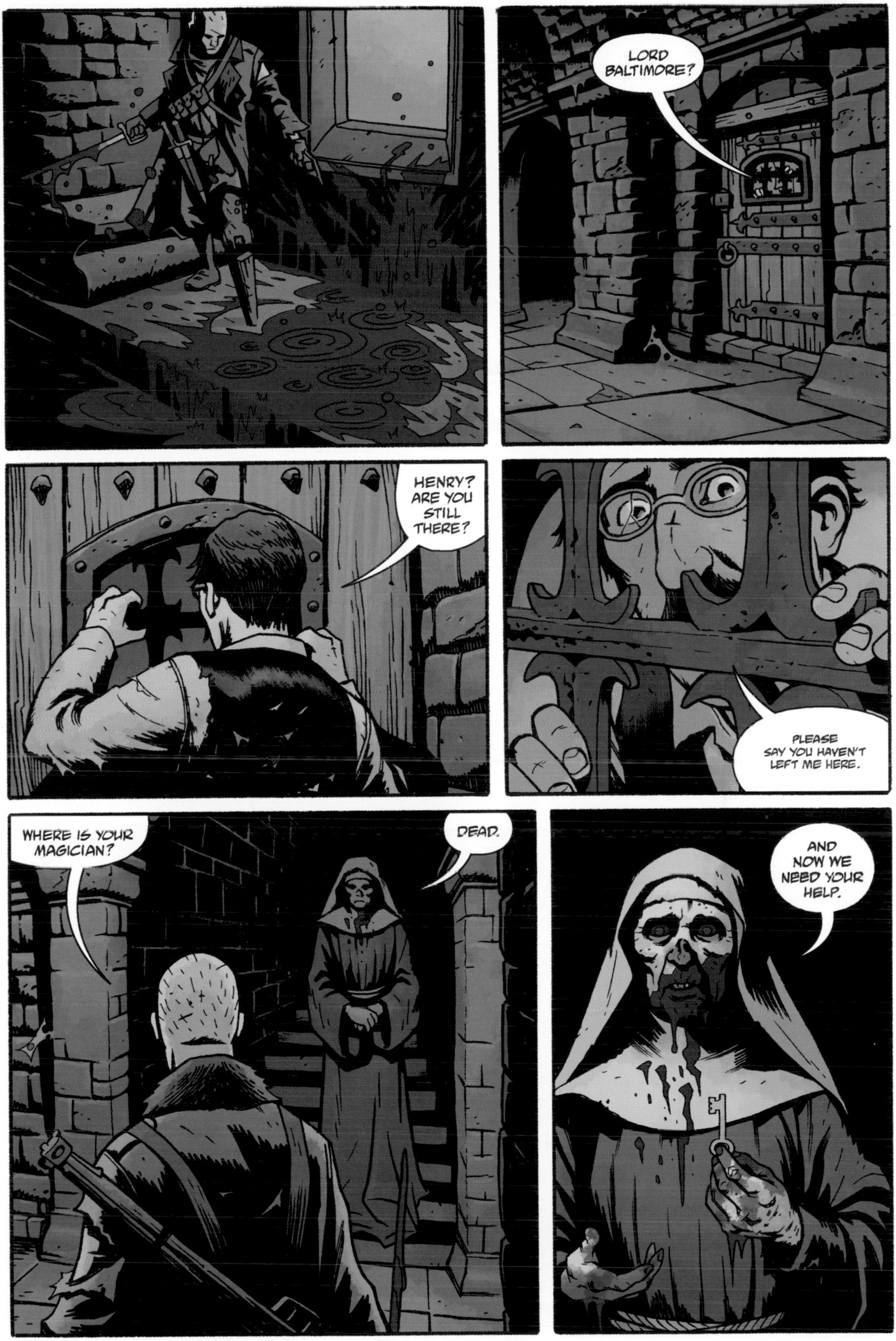
LORD BALTIMORE?
HENRY? ARE YOU STILL THERE?
PLEASE SAY YOU HAVEN'T LEFT ME HERE.
WHERE IS YOUR MAGICIAN?
DEAD.
AND NOW WE NEED YOUR HELP.

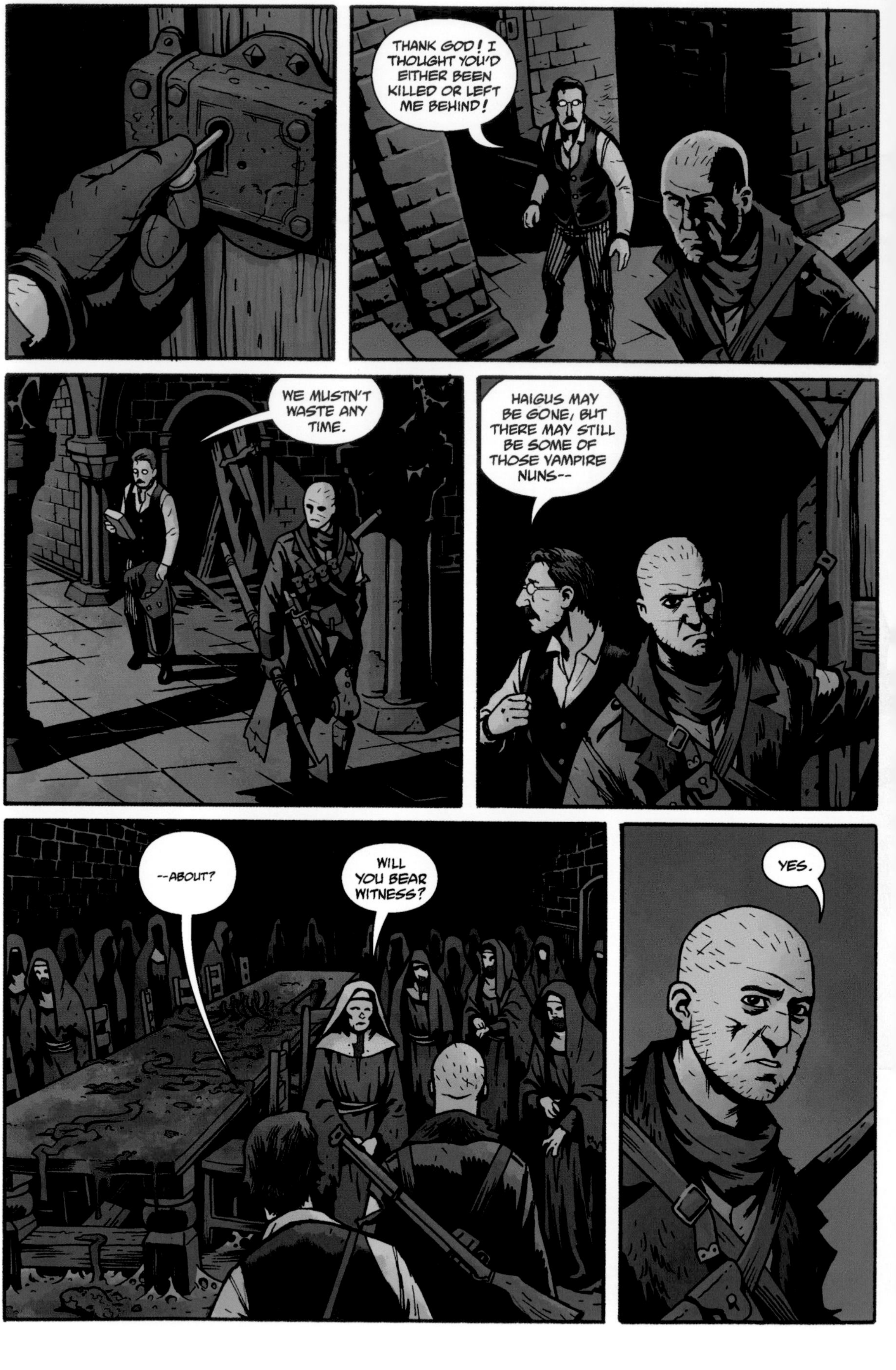
THANK GOD! I THOUGHT YOU'D EITHER BEEN KILLED OR LEFT ME BEHIND!
WE MUSTN'T WASTE ANY TIME.
HAIGUS MAY BE GONE, BUT THERE MAY STILL BE SOME OF THOSE VAMPIRE NUNS--
--ABOUT?
WILL YOU BEAR WITNESS?
YES.

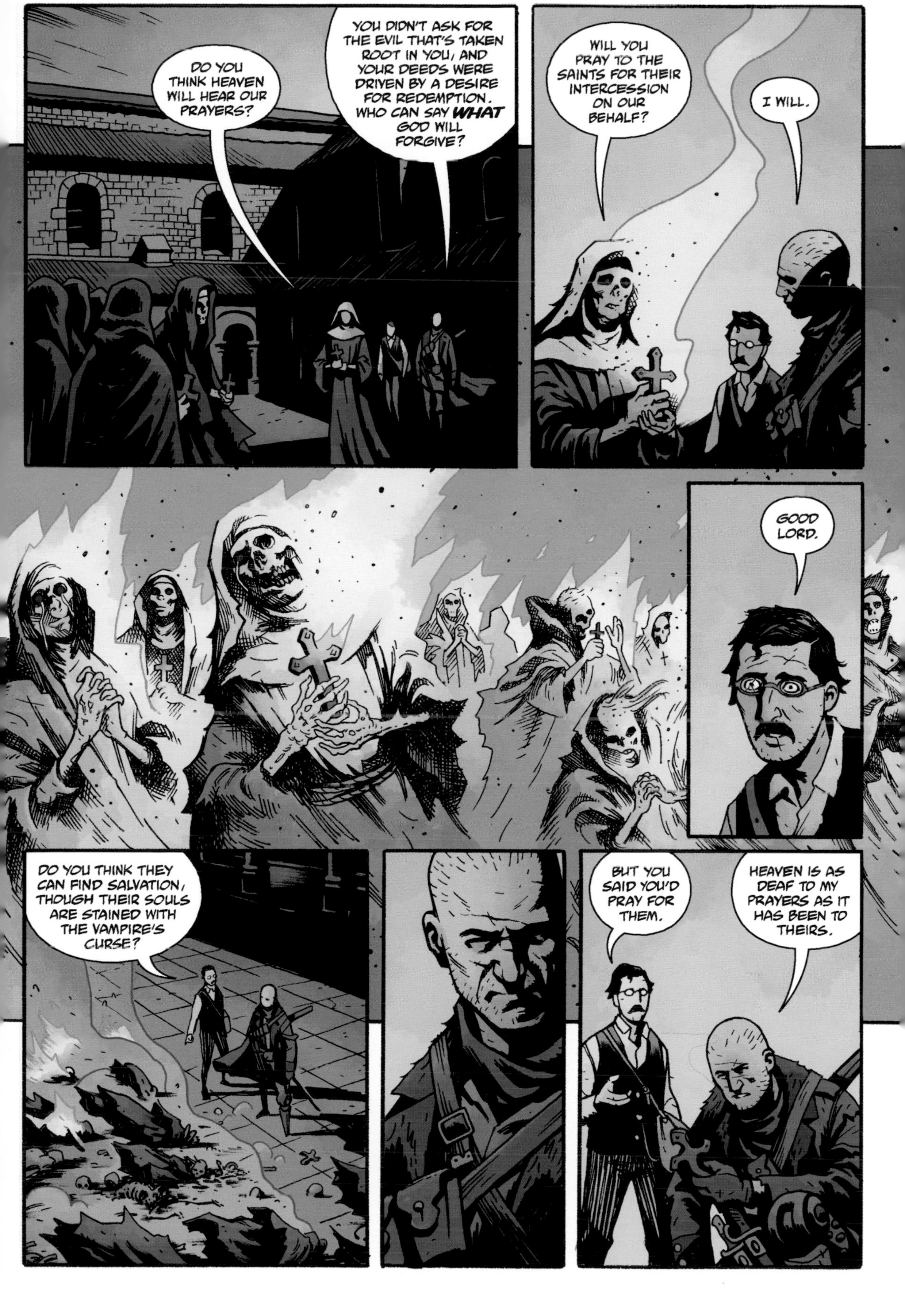
DO YOU THINK HEAVEN WILL HEAR OUR PRAYERS?
YOU DIDN'T ASK FOR THE EVIL THAT'S TAKEN ROOT IN YOU, AND YOUR DEEDS WERE DRIVEN BY A DESIRE FOR REDEMPTION. WHO CAN SAY *WHAT* GOD WILL FORGIVE?
WILL YOU PRAY TO THE SAINTS FOR THEIR INTERCESSION ON OUR BEHALF?
I WILL.
GOOD LORD.
DO YOU THINK THEY CAN FIND SALVATION, THOUGH THEIR SOULS ARE STAINED WITH THE VAMPIRE'S CURSE?
BUT YOU SAID YOU'D PRAY FOR THEM.
HEAVEN IS AS DEAF TO MY PRAYERS AS IT HAS BEEN TO THEIRS.

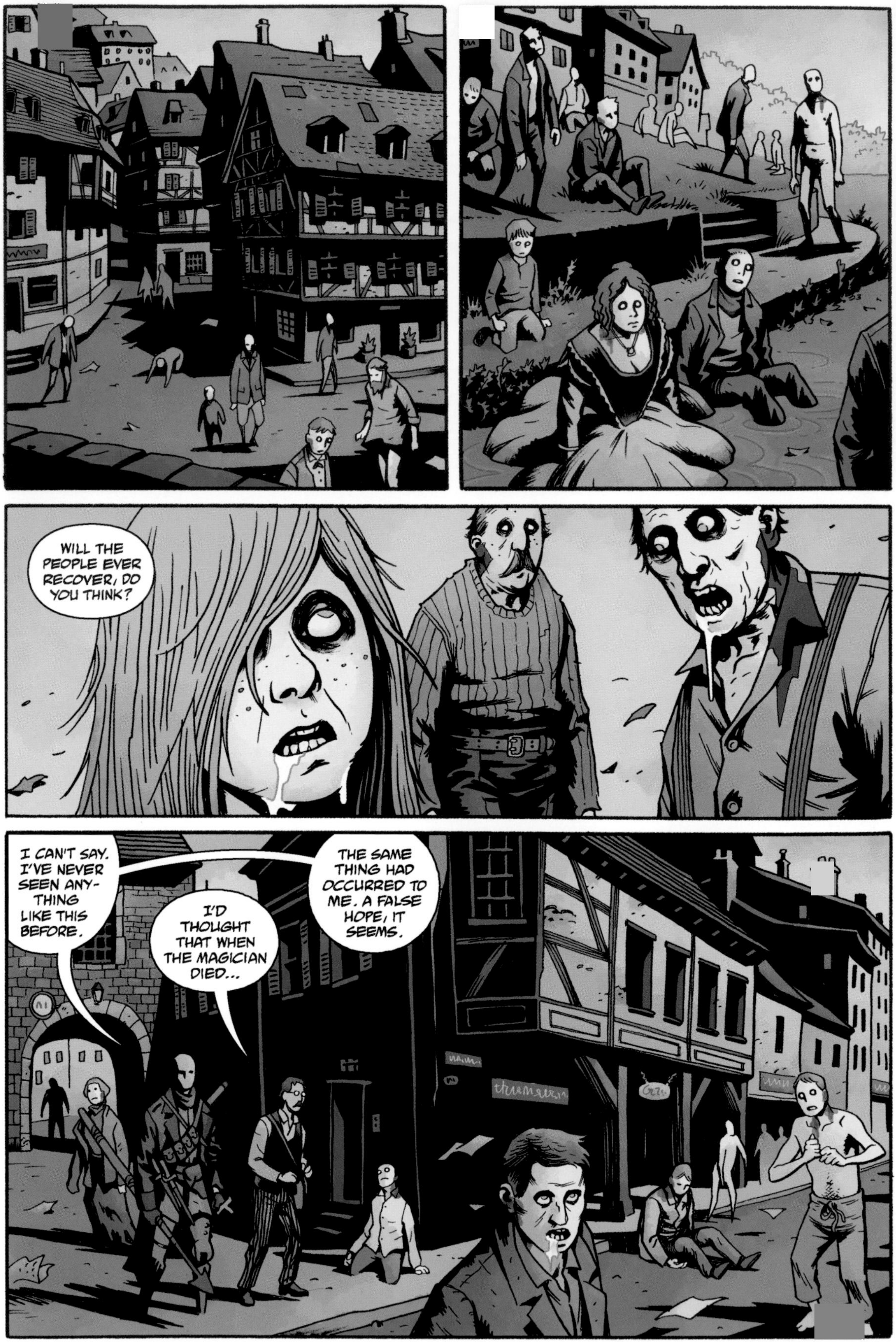
WILL THE PEOPLE EVER RECOVER, DO YOU THINK?
I CAN'T SAY. I'VE NEVER SEEN ANY-THING LIKE THIS BEFORE.
I'D THOUGHT THAT WHEN THE MAGICIAN DIED...
THE SAME THING HAD OCCURRED TO ME. A FALSE HOPE, IT SEEMS.

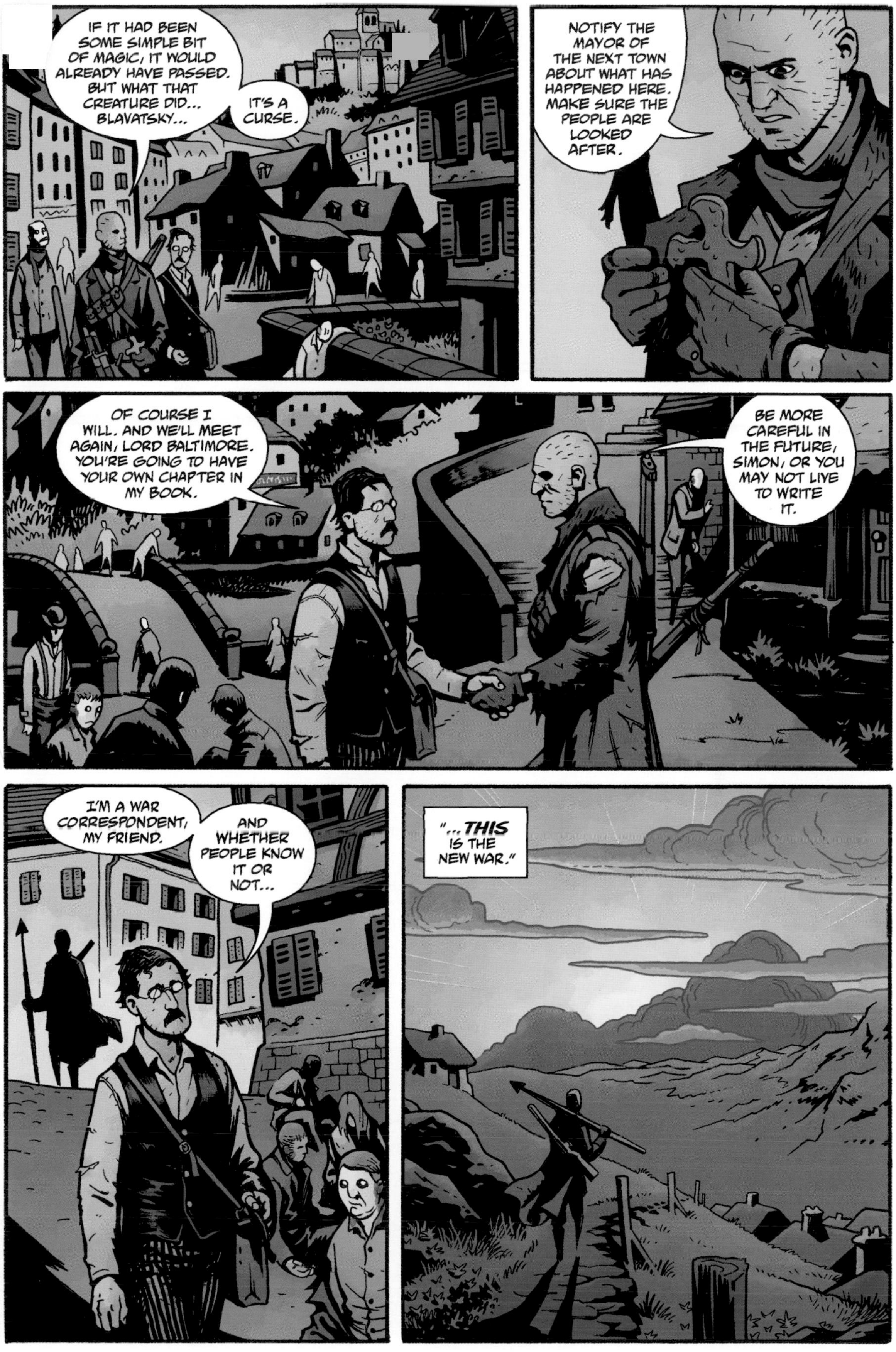
IF IT HAD BEEN SOME SIMPLE BIT OF MAGIC, IT WOULD ALREADY HAVE PASSED. BUT WHAT THAT CREATURE DID... BLAVATSKY...
IT'S A CURSE.
NOTIFY THE MAYOR OF THE NEXT TOWN ABOUT WHAT HAS HAPPENED HERE. MAKE SURE THE PEOPLE ARE LOOKED AFTER.
OF COURSE I WILL. AND WE'LL MEET AGAIN, LORD BALTIMORE. YOU'RE GOING TO HAVE YOUR OWN CHAPTER IN MY BOOK.
BE MORE CAREFUL IN THE FUTURE, SIMON, OR YOU MAY NOT LIVE TO WRITE IT.
I'M A WAR CORRESPONDENT, MY FRIEND.
AND WHETHER PEOPLE KNOW IT OR NOT...
"...THIS IS THE NEW WAR."

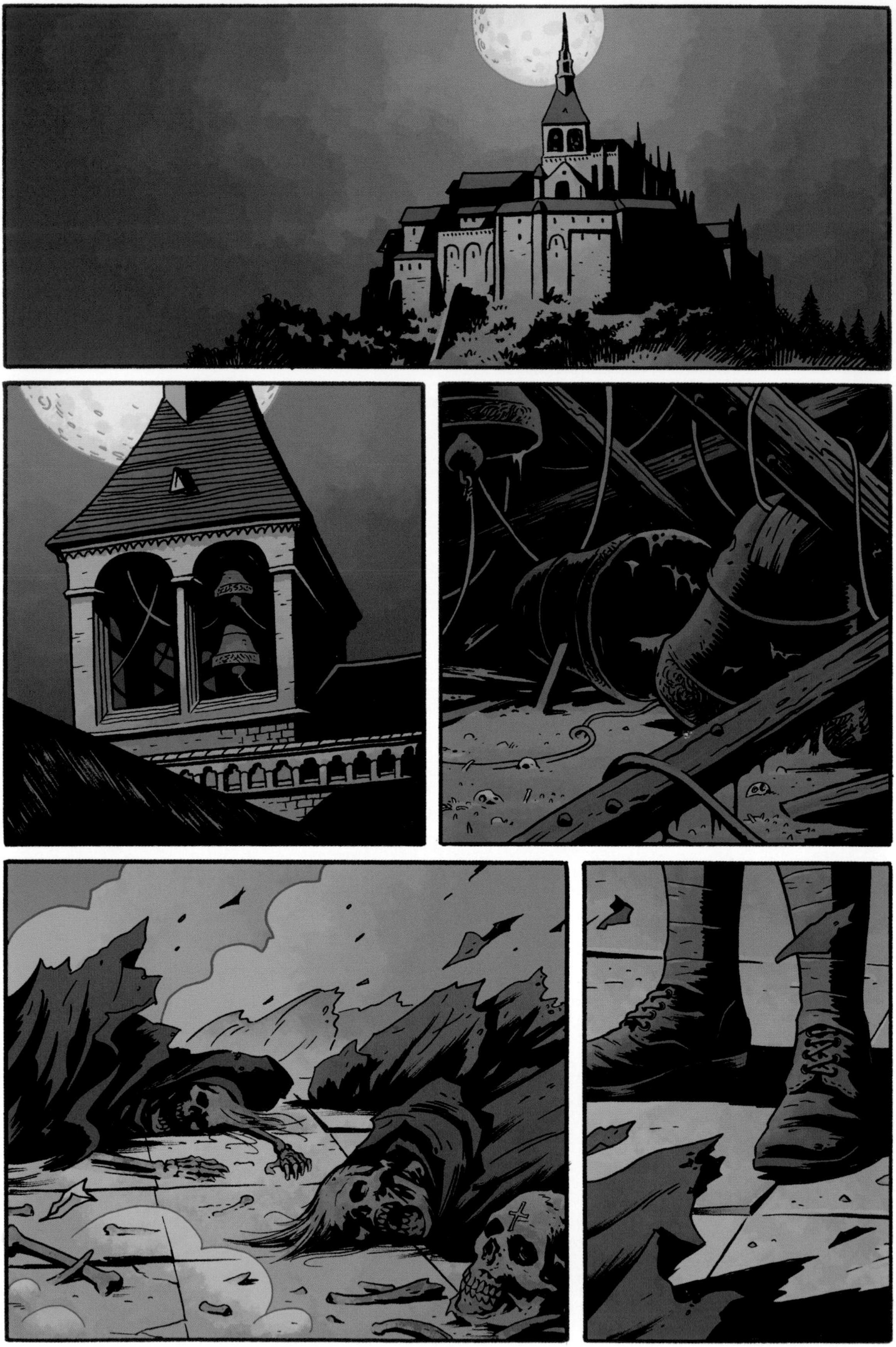

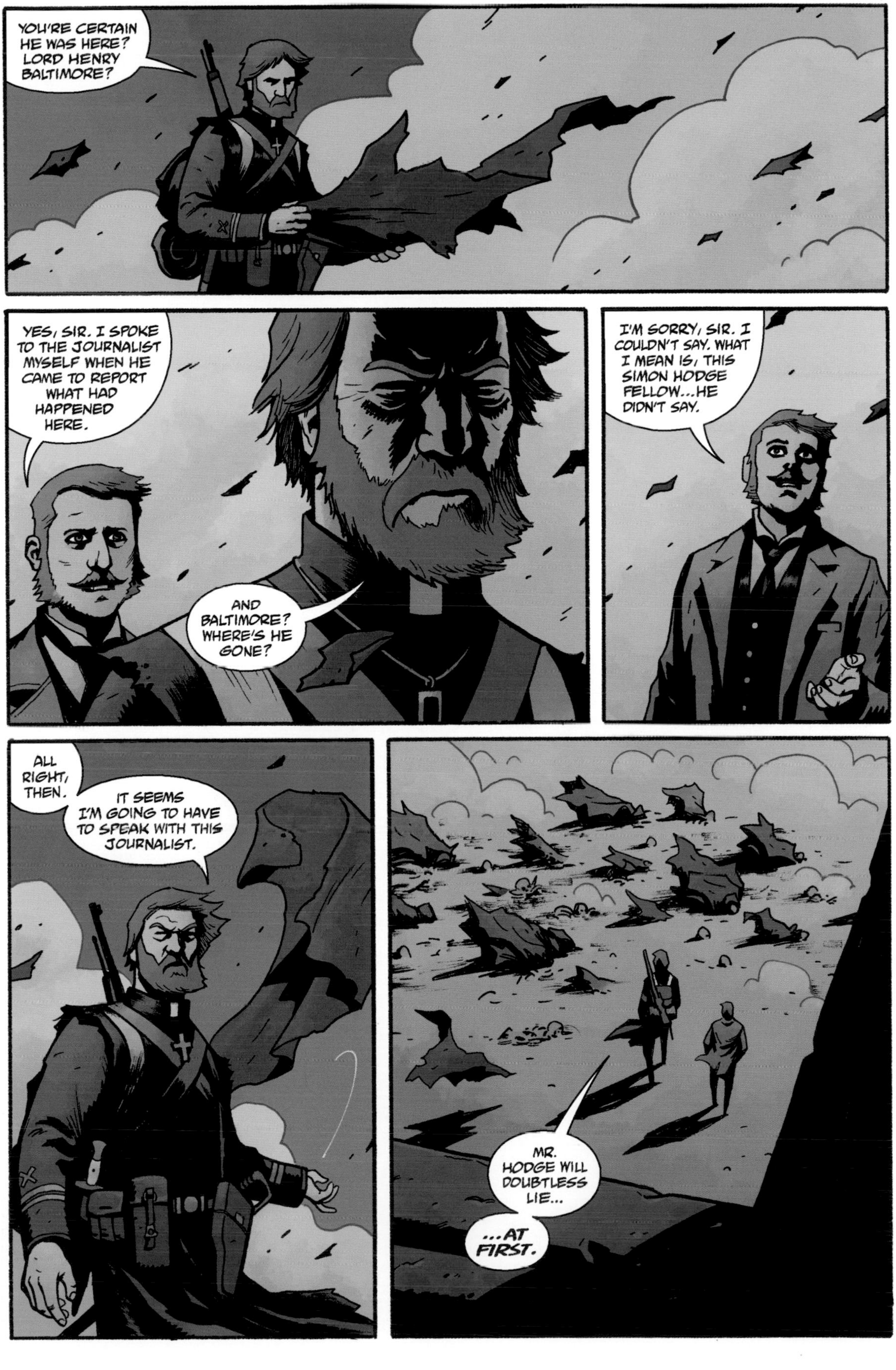
YOU'RE CERTAIN HE WAS HERE? LORD HENRY BALTIMORE?
YES, SIR. I SPOKE TO THE JOURNALIST MYSELF WHEN HE CAME TO REPORT WHAT HAD HAPPENED HERE.
AND BALTIMORE? WHERE'S HE GONE?
I'M SORRY, SIR. I COULDN'T SAY. WHAT I MEAN IS, THIS SIMON HODGE FELLOW...HE DIDN'T SAY.
ALL RIGHT, THEN.
IT SEEMS I'M GOING TO HAVE TO SPEAK WITH THIS JOURNALIST.
MR. HODGE WILL DOUBTLESS LIE...
...AT FIRST.

DING
BONG
DING

DING
BONG
BONG

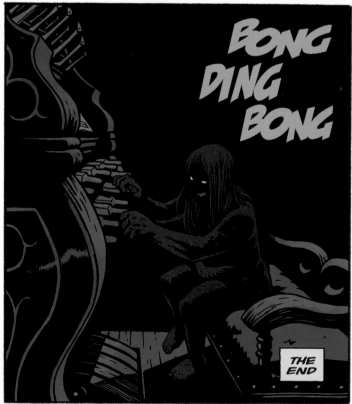

BONG
DING
BONG

THE
END

BALTIMORE™ THE CURSE BELLS

SKETCHBOOK

Notes by Scott Allie

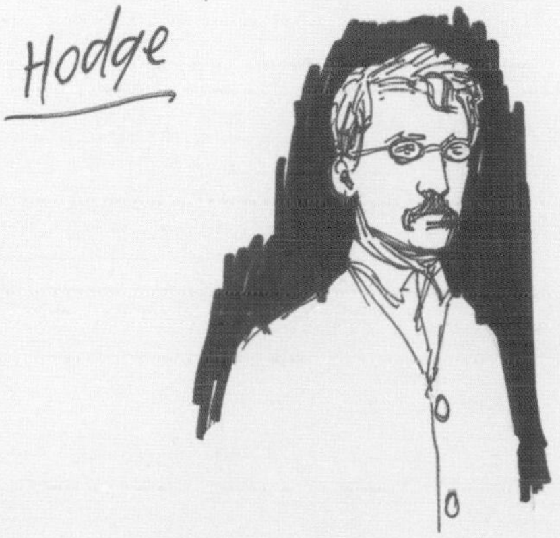
Hodge

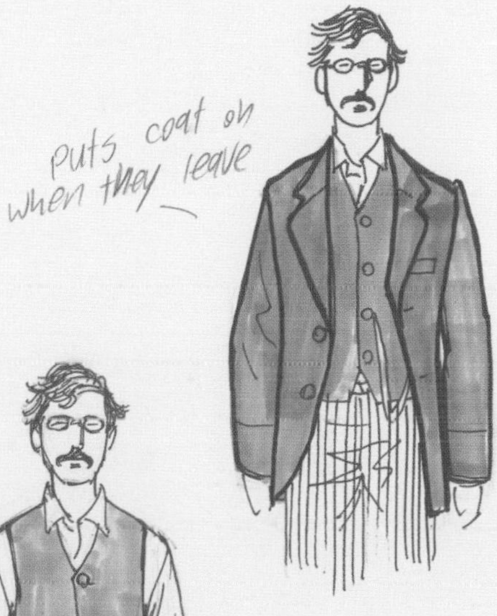
puts coat on
when they leave

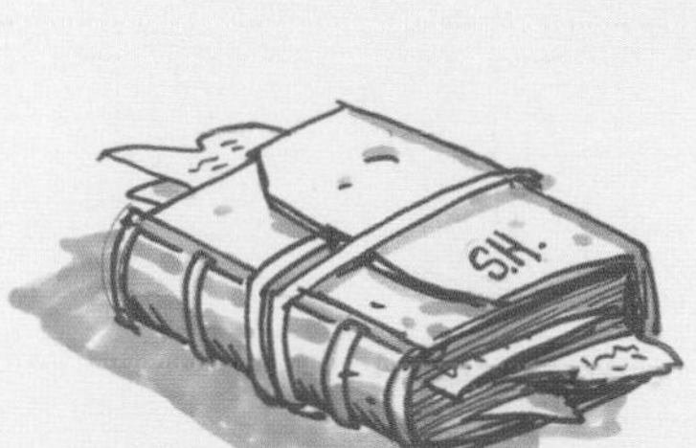
S.H.

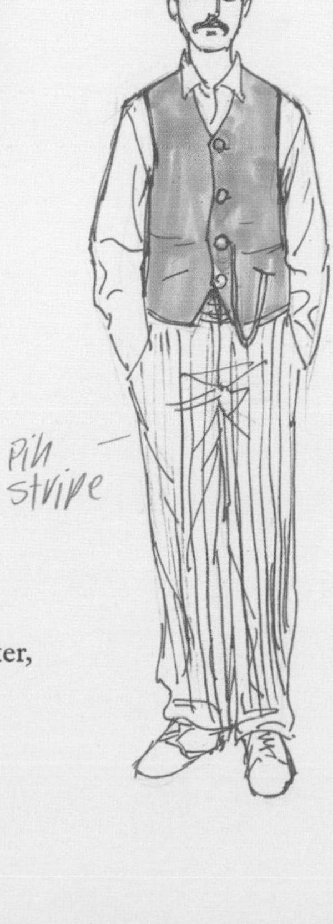
pin
stripe

Ben designs our supporting character, the journalist Hodge.

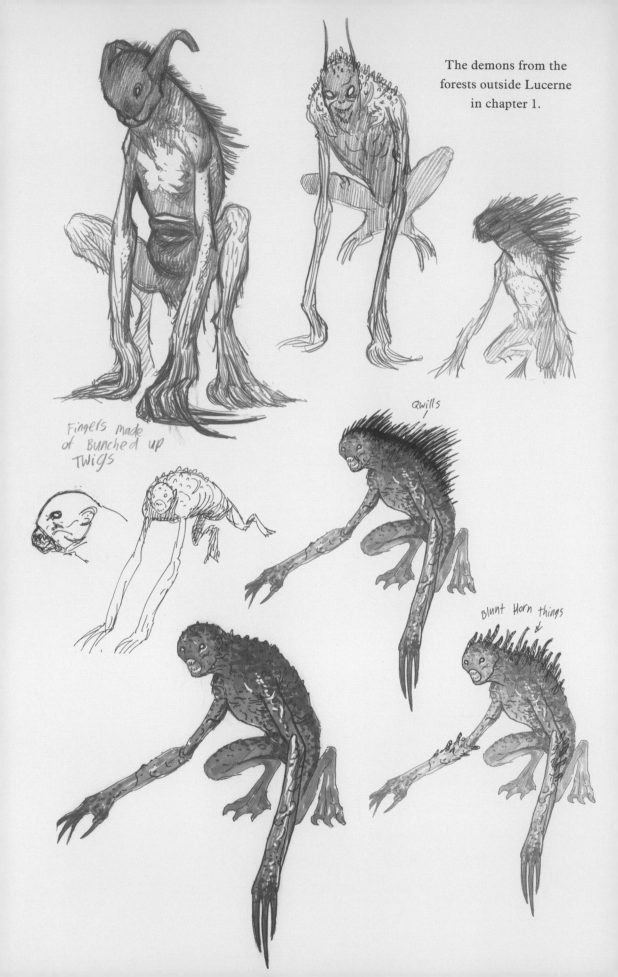

The demons from the forests outside Lucerne in chapter 1.

Qwills

Fingers made of Bunched up Twigs

Blunt Horn things

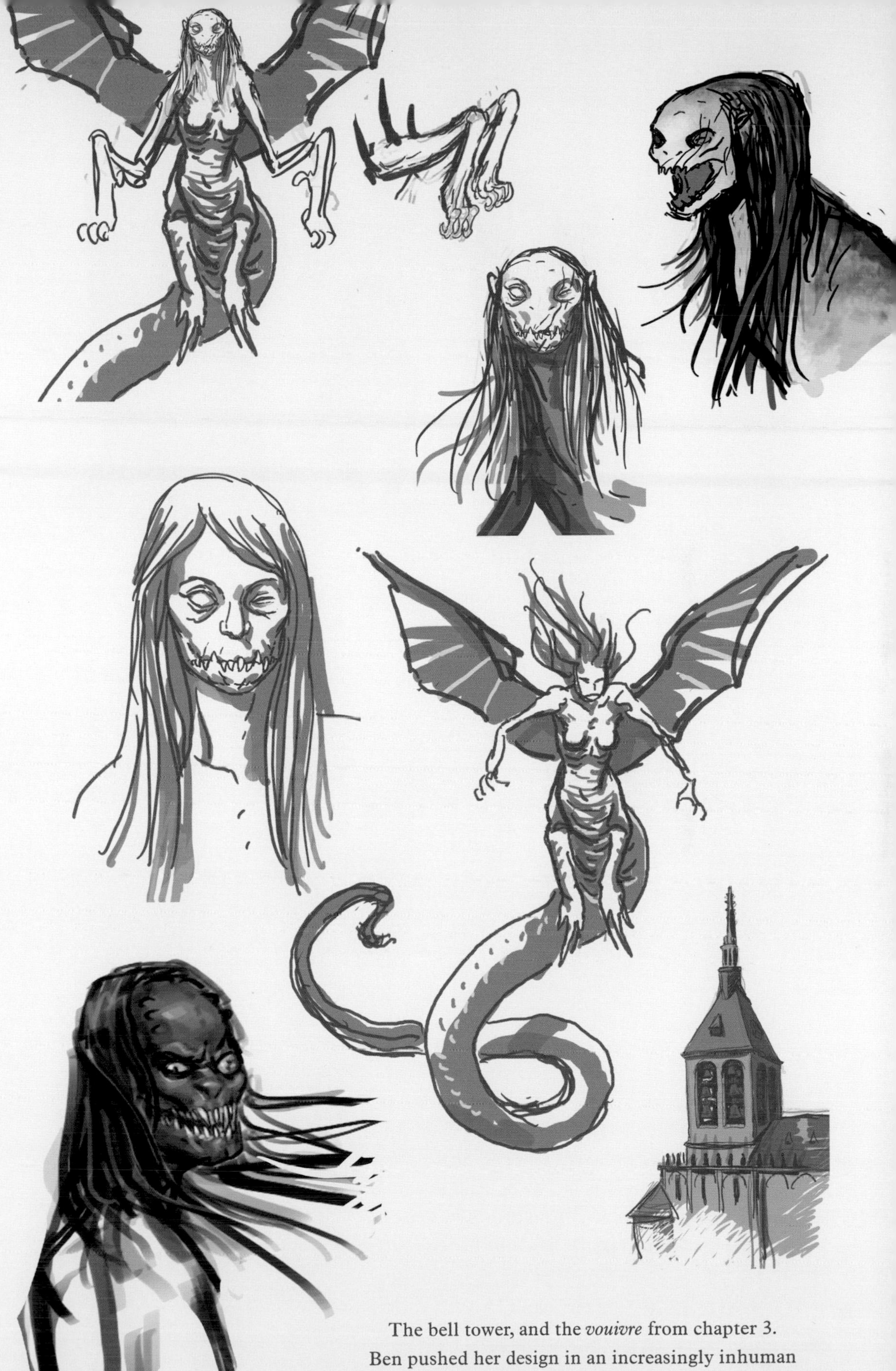

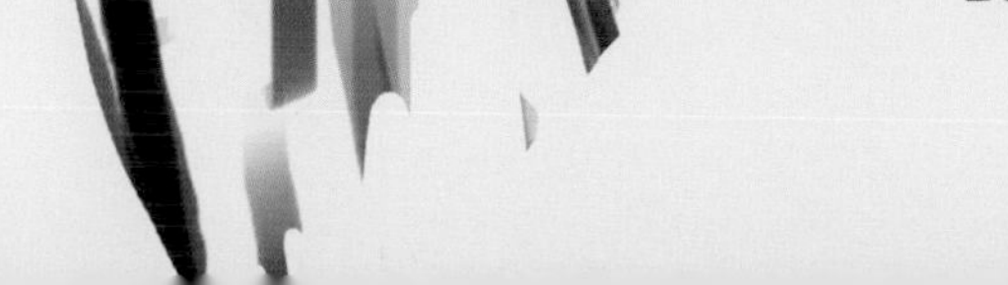

The bell tower, and the *vouivre* from chapter 3. Ben pushed her design in an increasingly inhuman direction, which we loved.

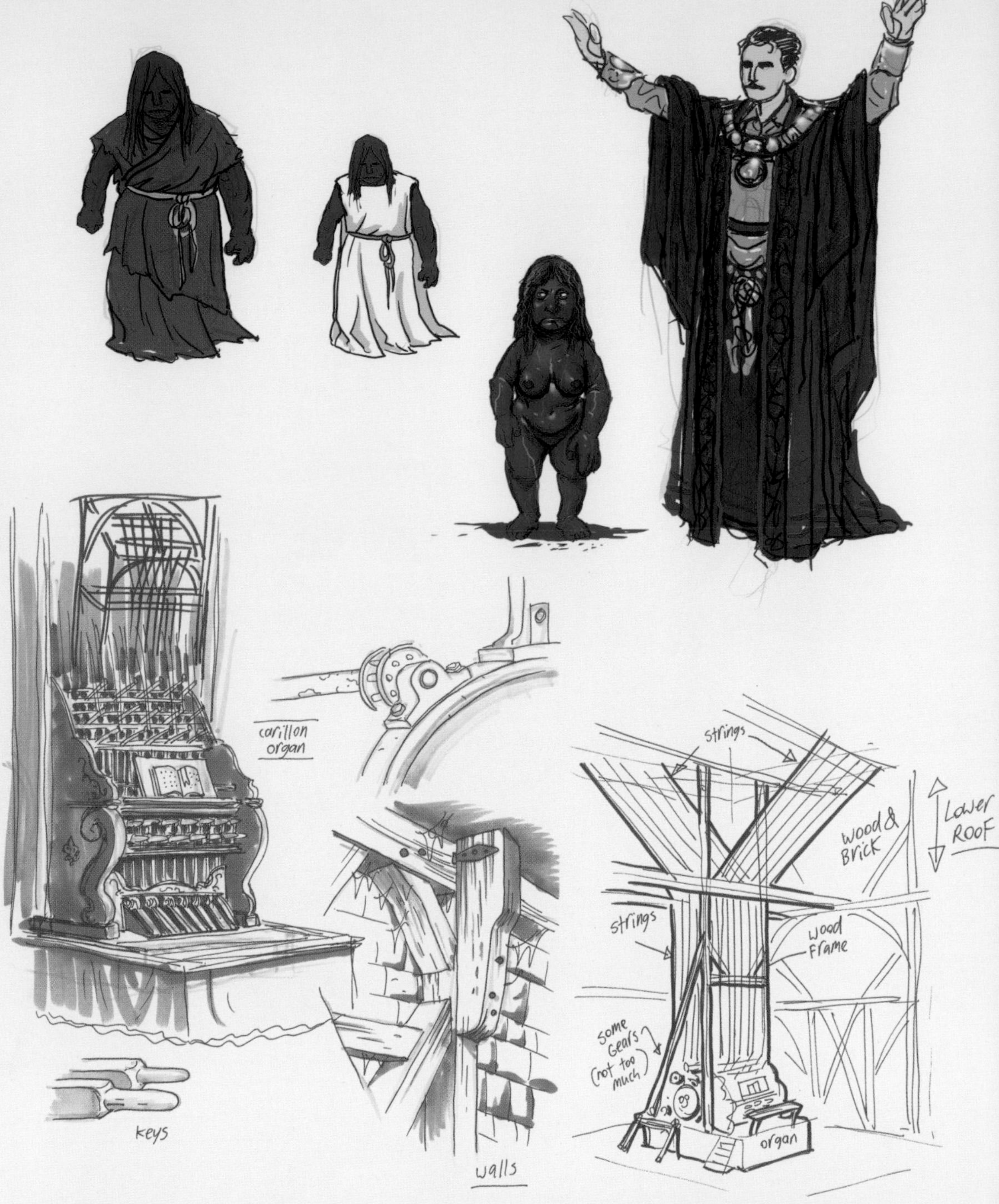
carillon organ
keys
walls
strings
strings
wood & Brick
Lower Roof
wood Frame
some Gears (not too much)
organ

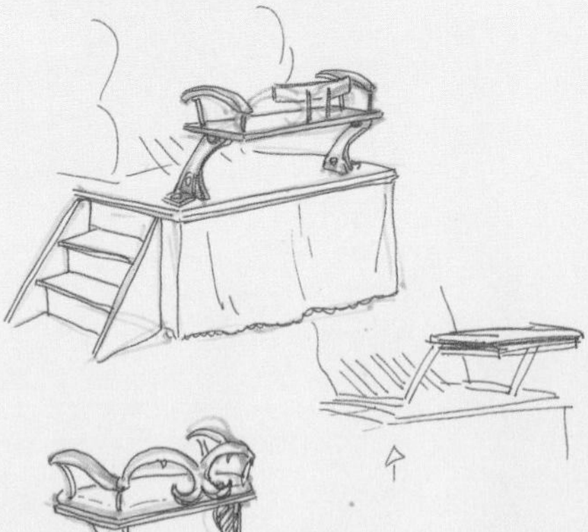

Our main villains: Madame Blavatsky and the madman. We knew that Blavatsky, a historical figure that we were excited to get into a comic, would be difficult to pull off as a naked midget. Ben tried multiple costume options, and we used the bizarre Nicolas Roeg thriller *Don't Look Now* as a point of reference. Adding more shadows to Blavatsky often helped.

Bottom: Ben's designs for the carillon keyboard, the device that controls the bells.

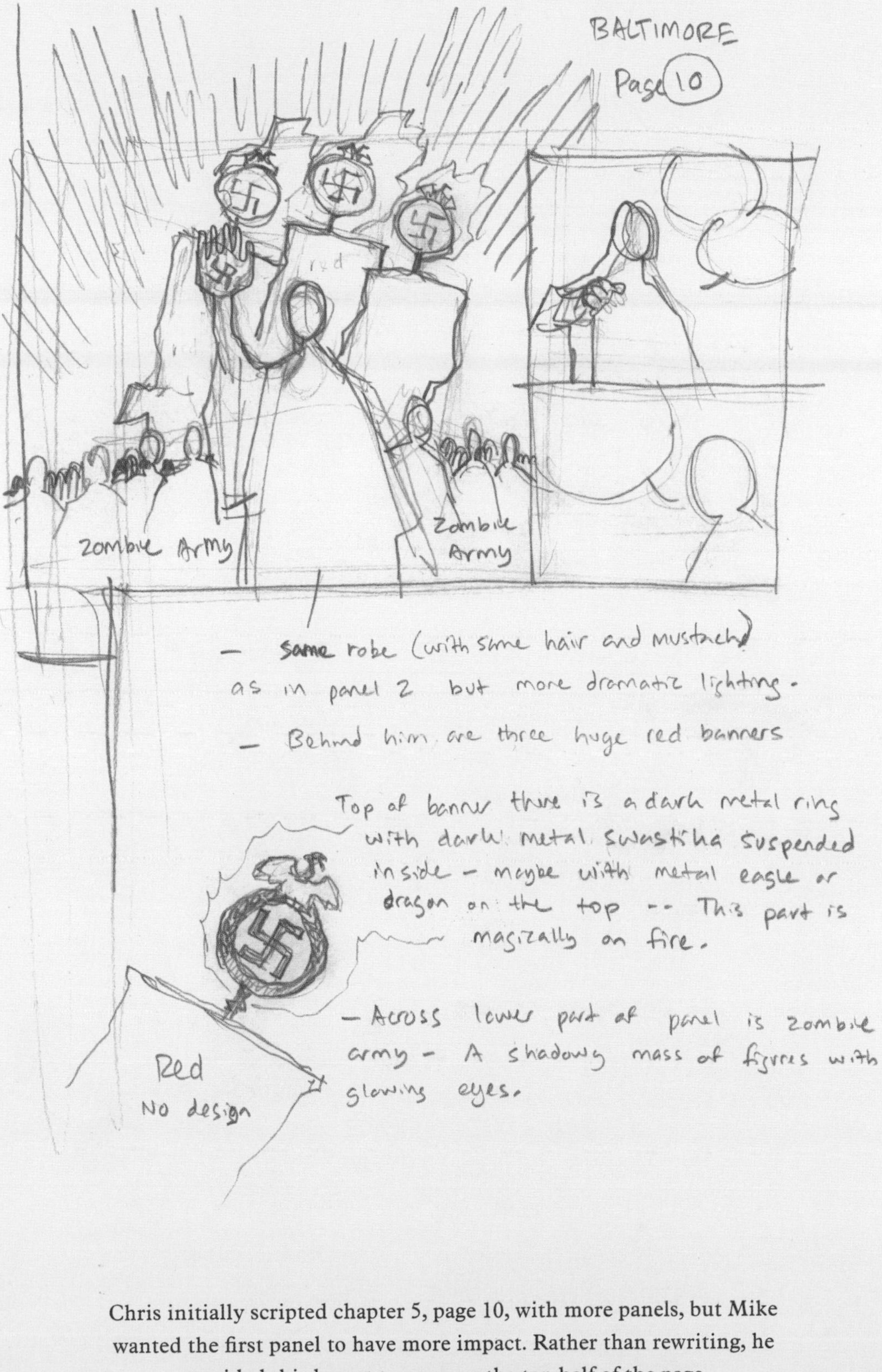
BALTIMORE
Page 10
red
red
Zombie Army
Zombie Army
— same robe (with same hair and mustache
as in panel 2 but more dramatic lighting.
— Behind him are three huge red banners
Top of banner there is a dark metal ring
with dark metal swastika suspended
inside – maybe with metal eagle or
dragon on the top -- This part is
magically on fire.
— Across lower part of panel is zombie
army – A shadowy mass of figures with
glowing eyes.
Red
No design

Chris initially scripted chapter 5, page 10, with more panels, but Mike wanted the first panel to have more impact. Rather than rewriting, he provided this layout to open up the top half of the page.

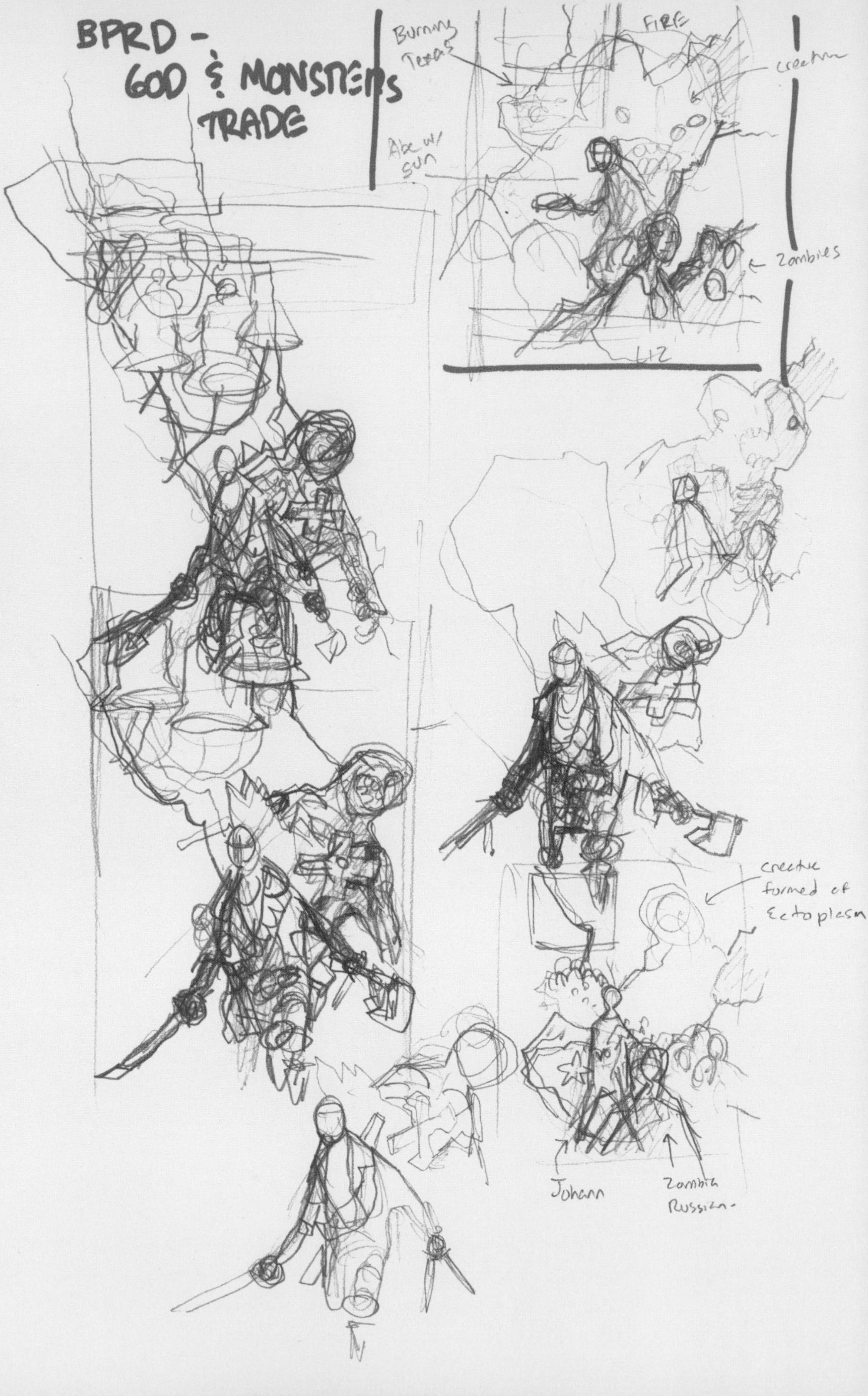
BPRD -
GOD & MONSTERS
TRADE
Burning Texas
FIRE
creature
Abe w/ sun
Zombies
LIZ
creature formed of Ectoplasm
Johann
Zombie Russian

Mike's designs for the *Curse Bells* #1 cover, done on the same sheet as his *B.P.R.D. Hell on Earth: Gods and Monsters* trade cover (facing); his study for Haigus's figure on the *Curse Bells* #2 cover, alongside the variant cover for *Hellboy: The Fury* #3.

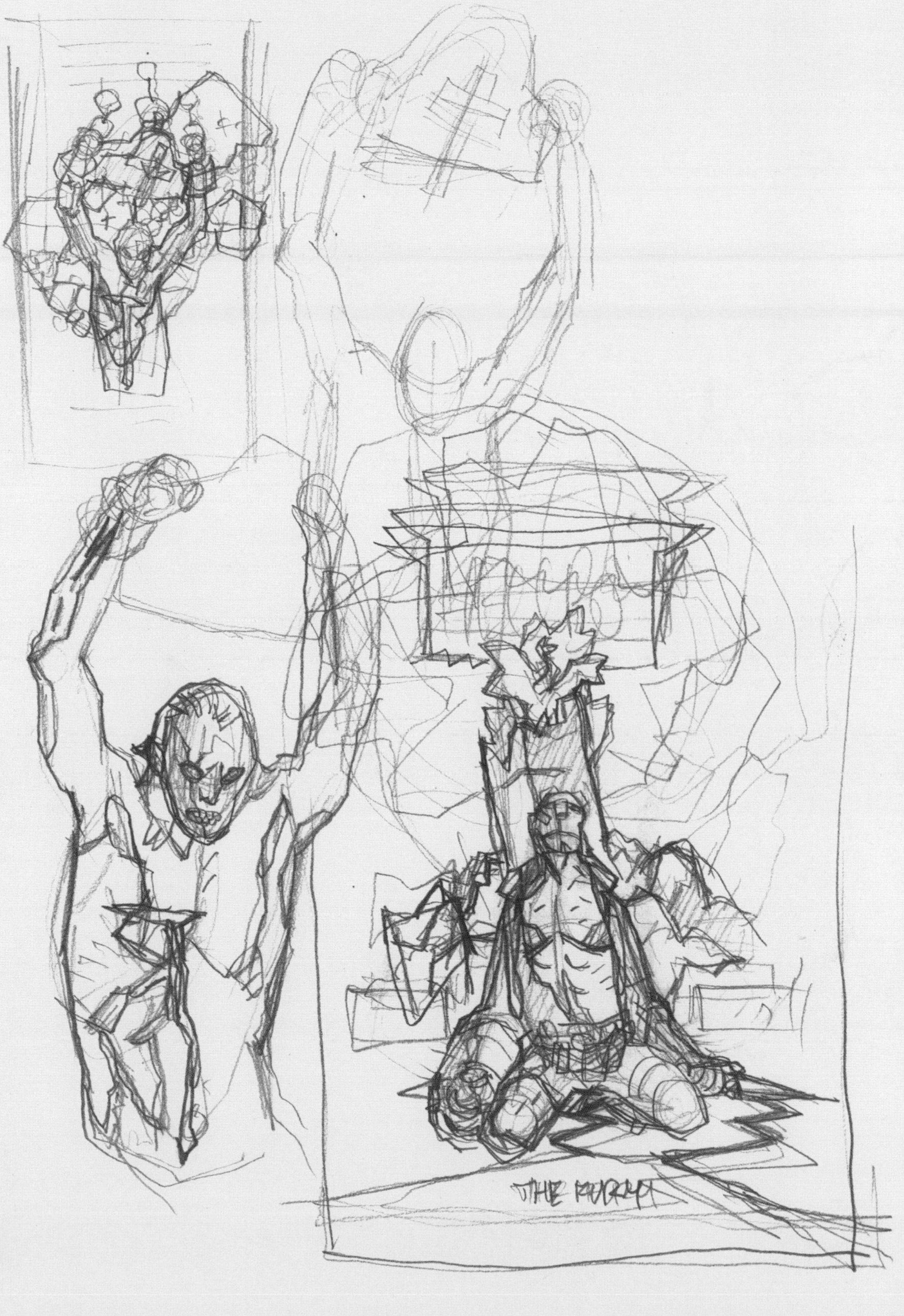
THE FURY

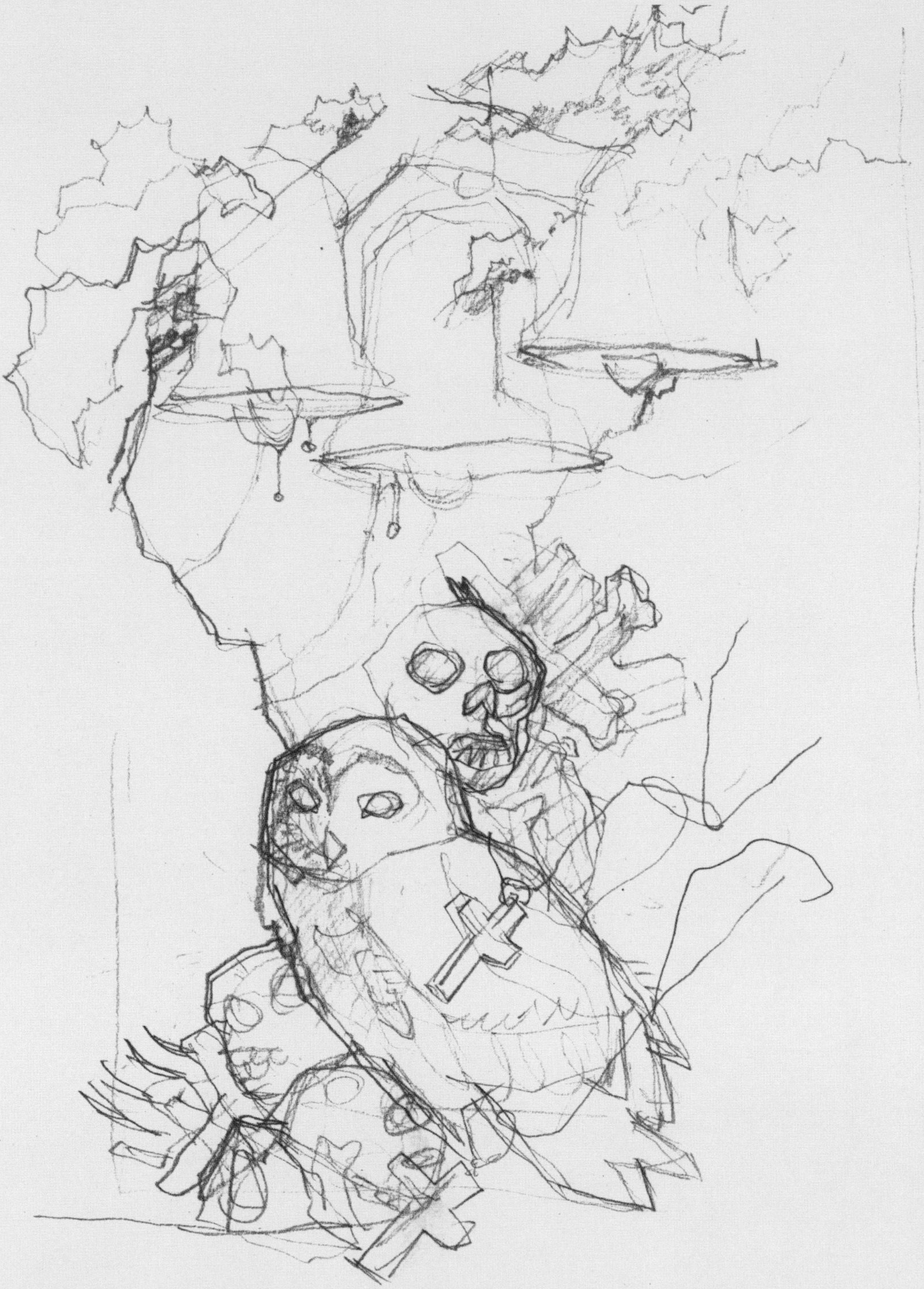

Mike struggled with the *Curse Bells* #5 cover. In his sketchbook he worked out a design featuring an owl (facing), but he couldn't make the owl work, so when he started drawing the cover, he replaced the owl with Baltimore, but abandoned that idea too (below).

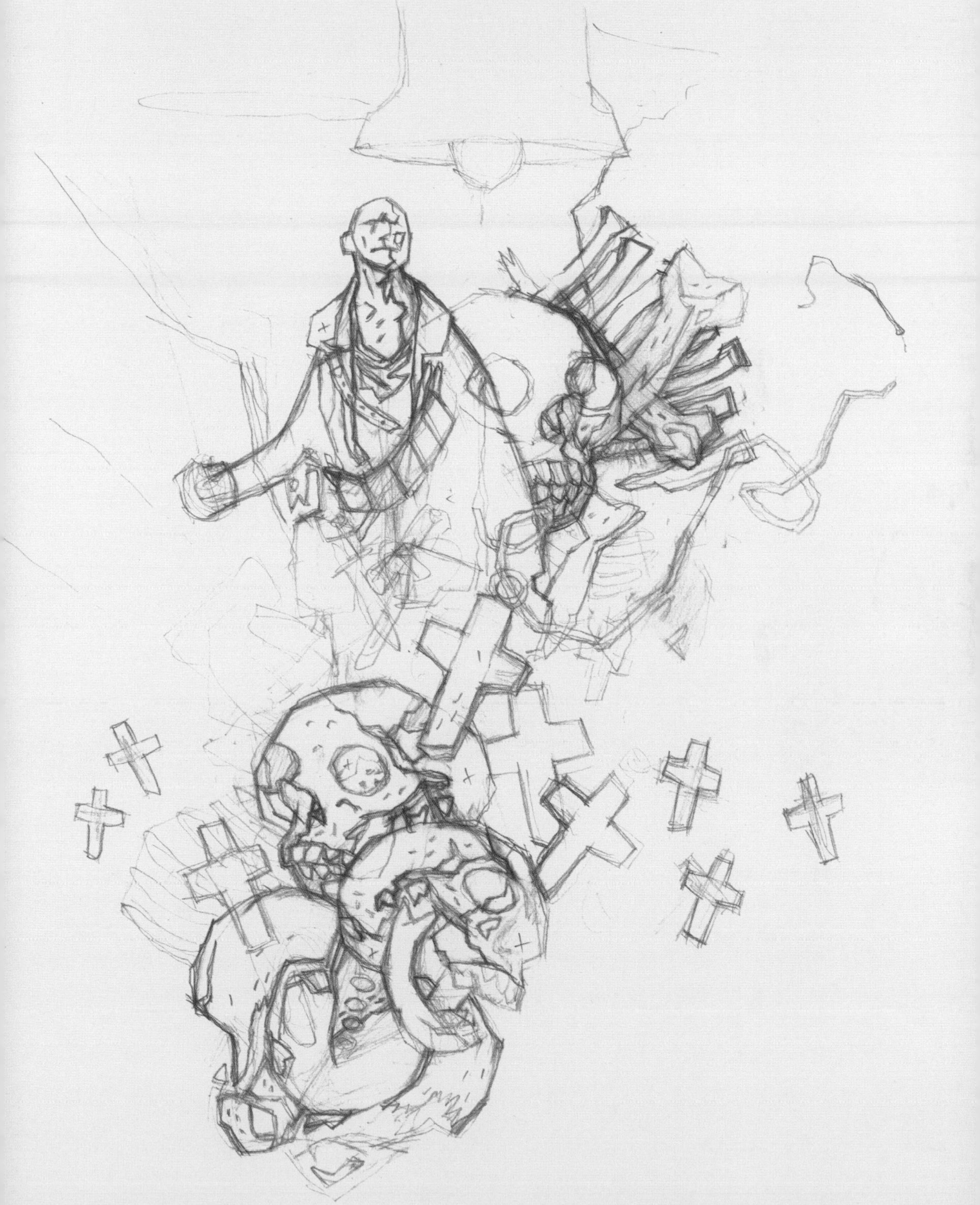

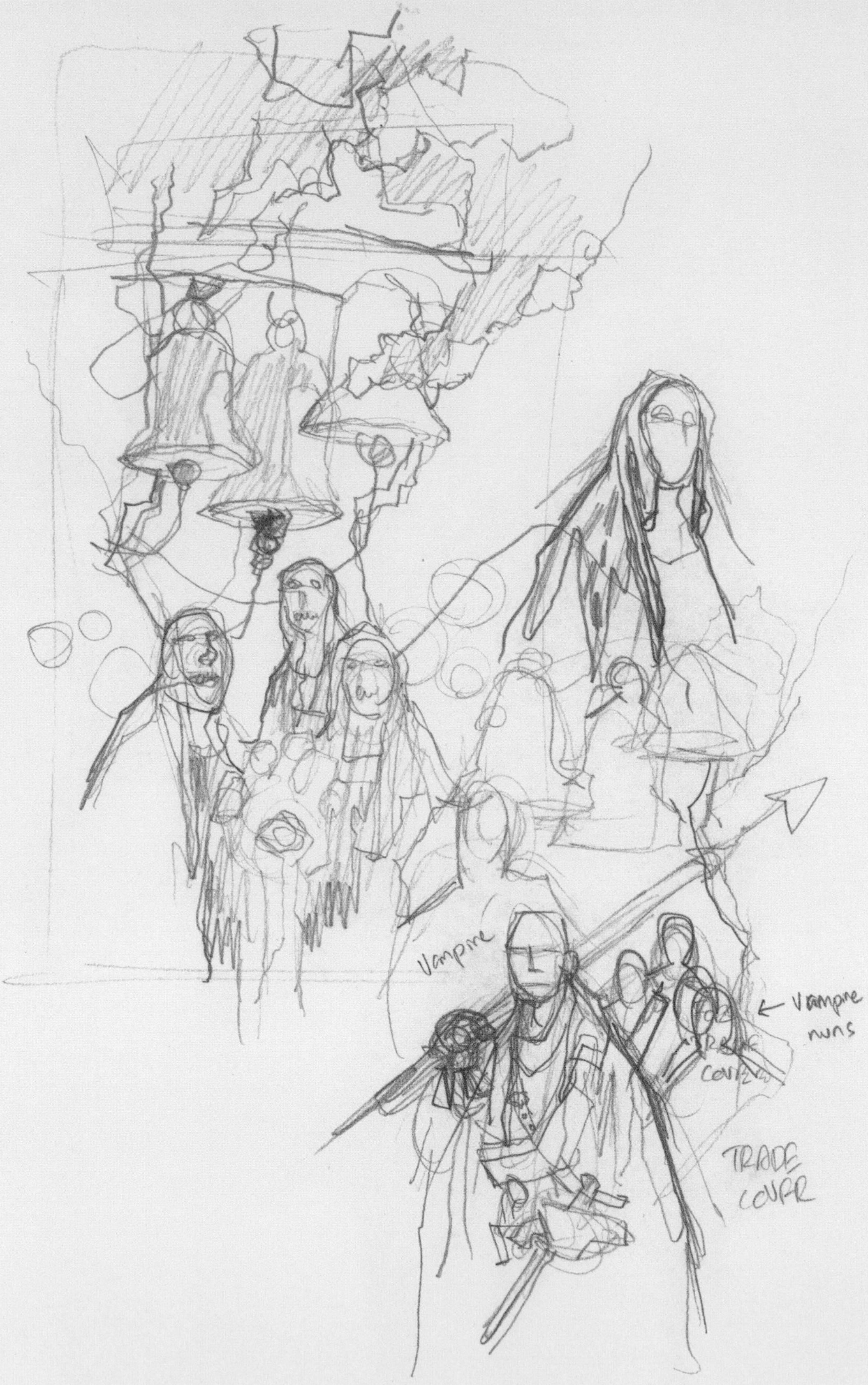
Vampire
Vampire nuns
TRADE COVER

Facing: Mike returned to the sketchbook, replacing Baltimore with the vampire nuns; at the same time that he was working out the *Curse Bells* #5 cover, he started planning the cover for this collection.

With the concept for *The Curse Bells* #5 worked out, he did the small sketch (below) to finalize the composition and some details.

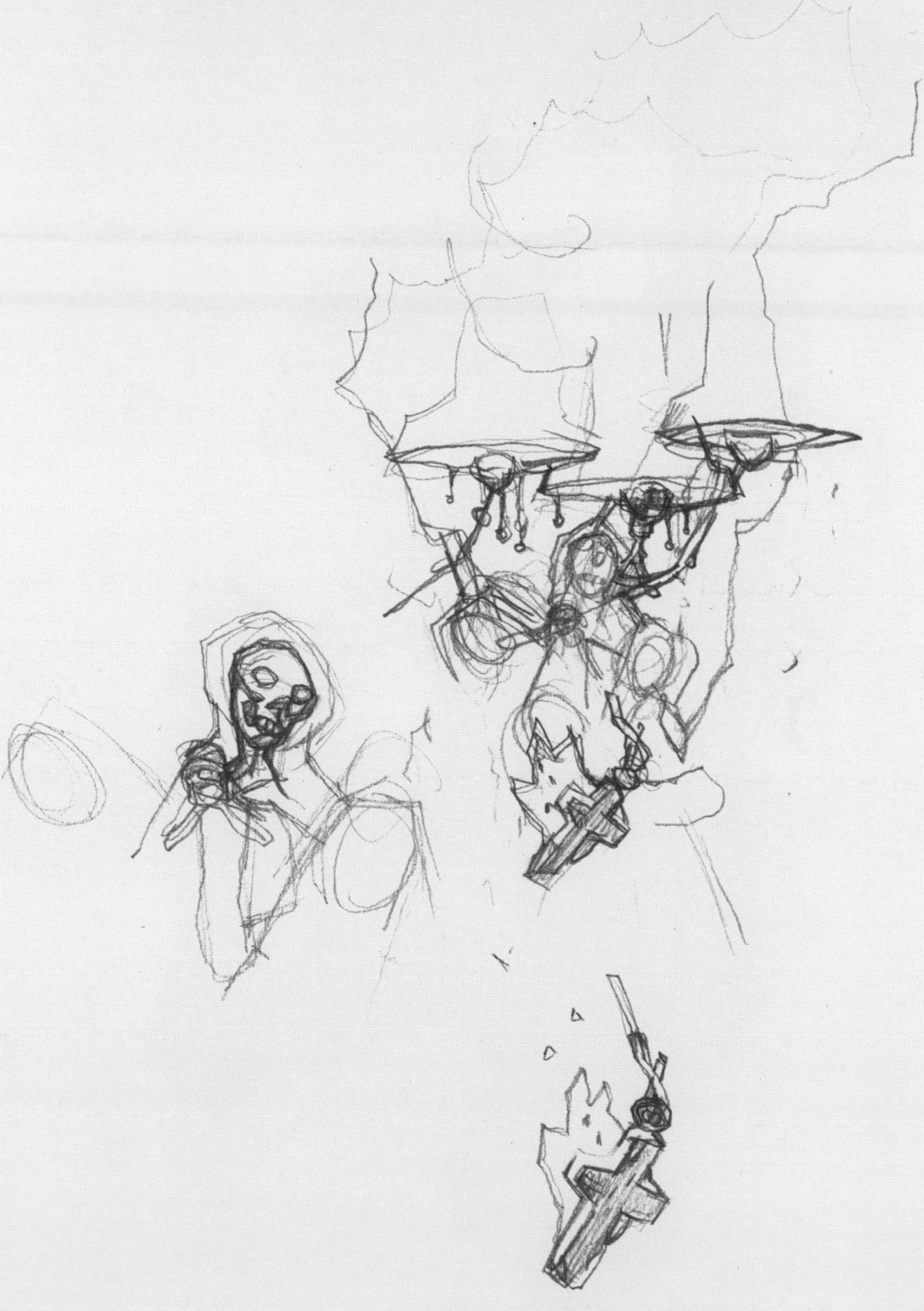

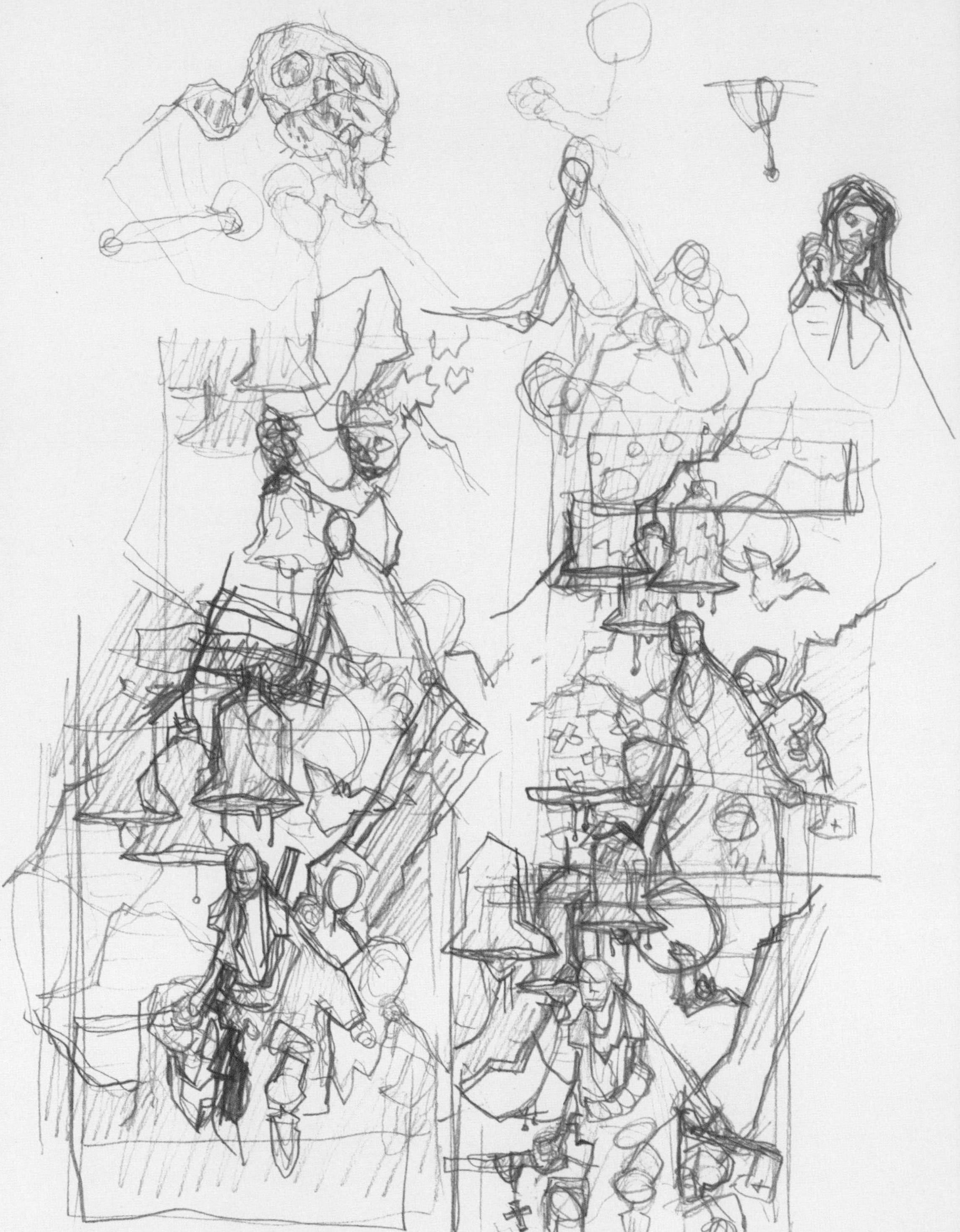

Final sketches for the cover of this volume.

This page: Nearly final pencils for a *Baltimore* cover, although none of us remembers what this was for, or exactly when it was done. It may have been a rejected cover for *The Curse Bells* #1.

Following pages: "I wanted to do some pinups for this book and took the opportunity to do weird horror images that seem like they might belong in Baltimore's world somehow. Also I wanted to draw the *vouivre* again. Cheers!" —Ben Stenbeck

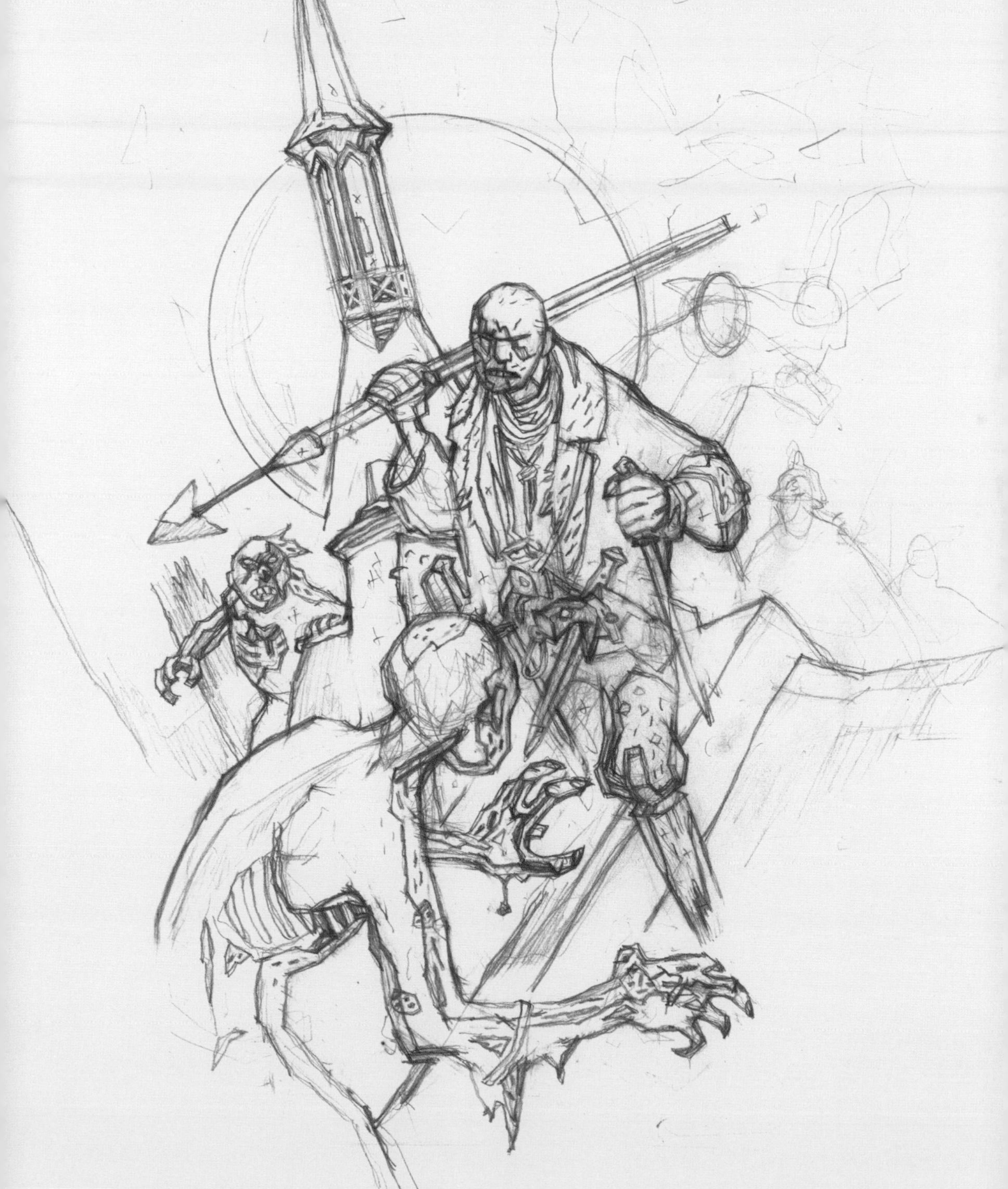

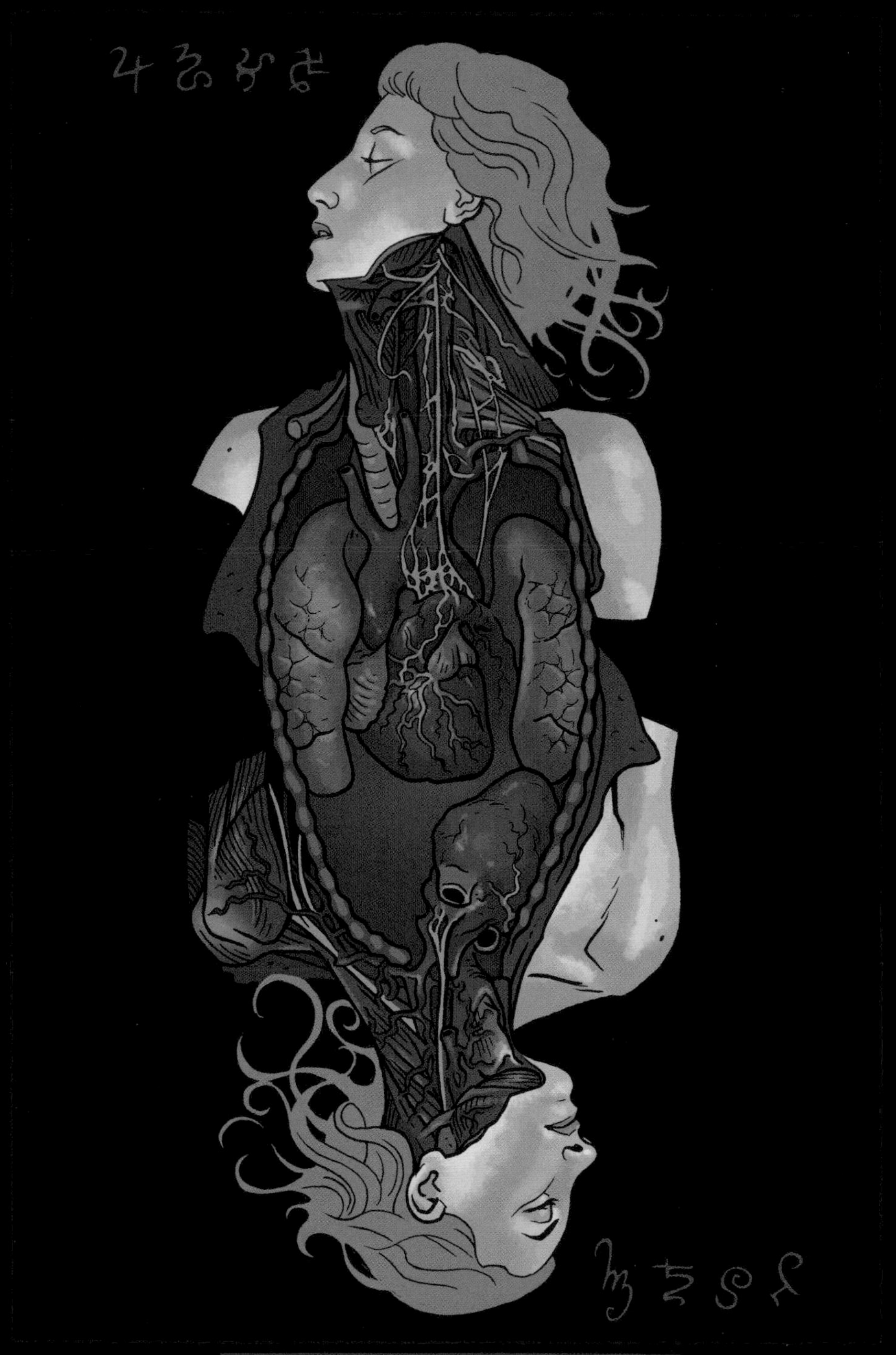

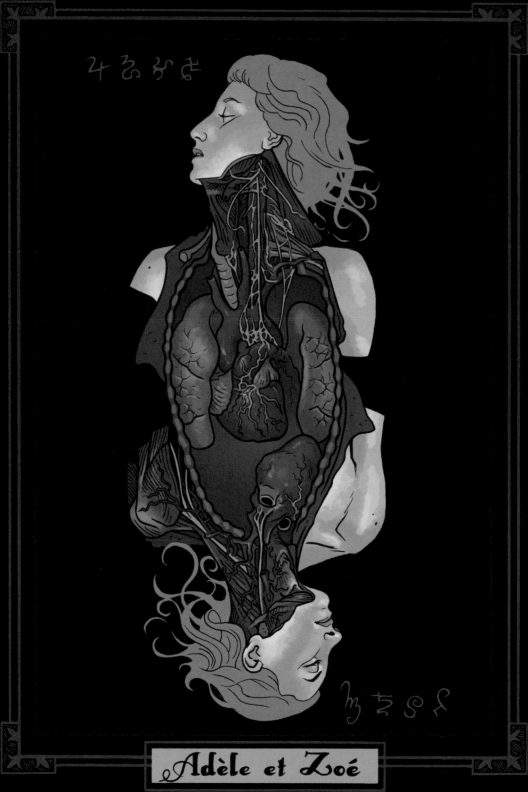

Adèle et Zoé

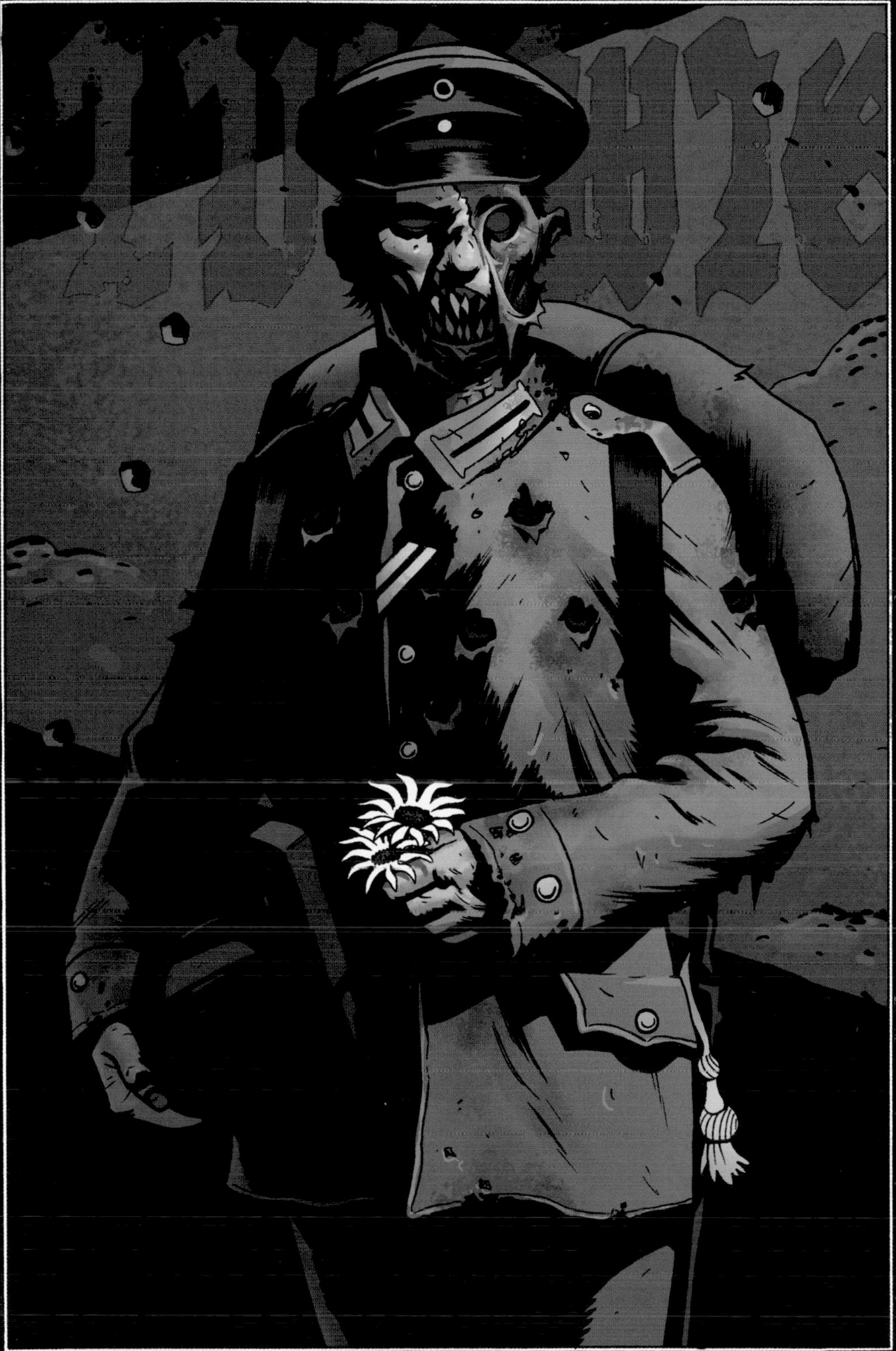

Frederick ~1917~

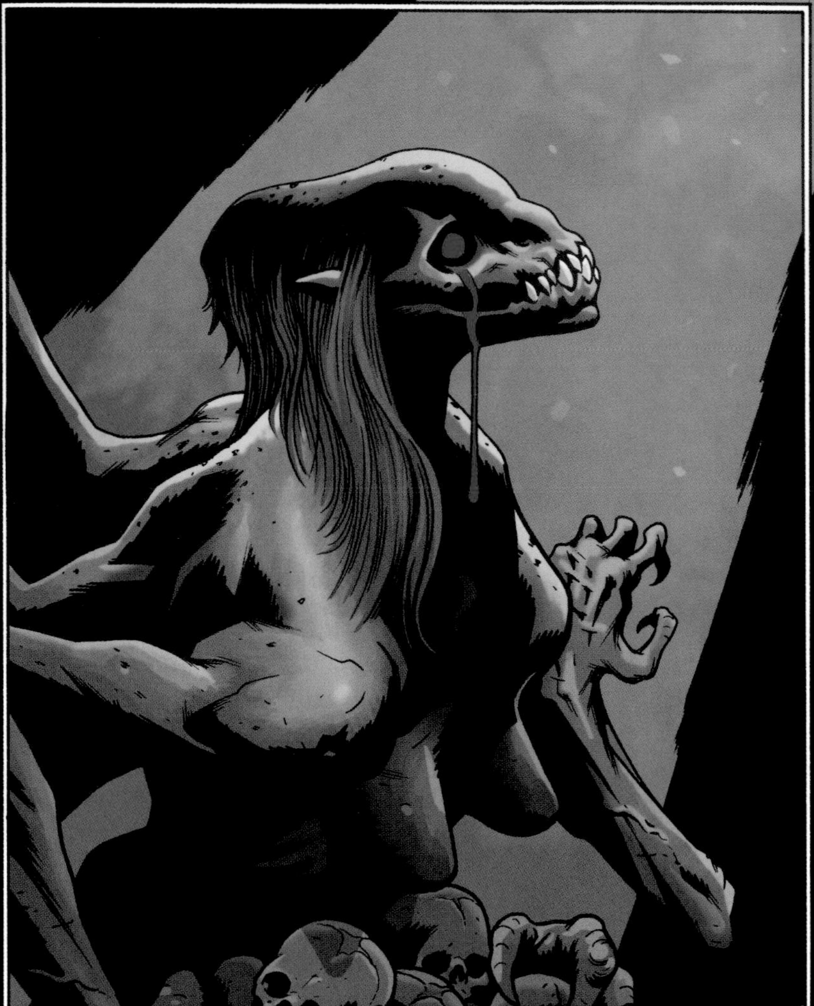

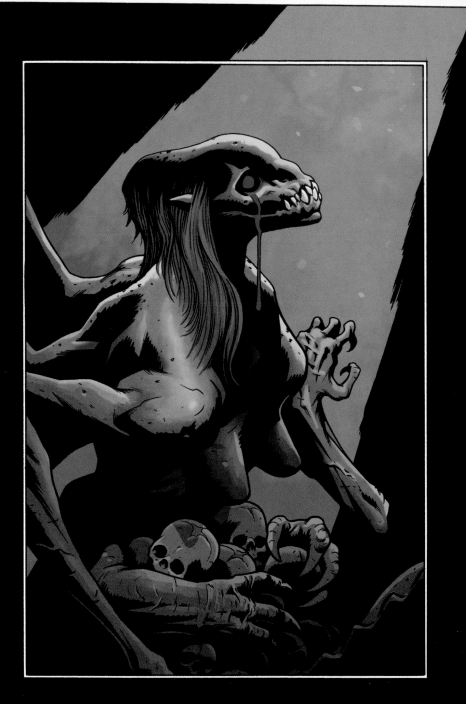

Marta

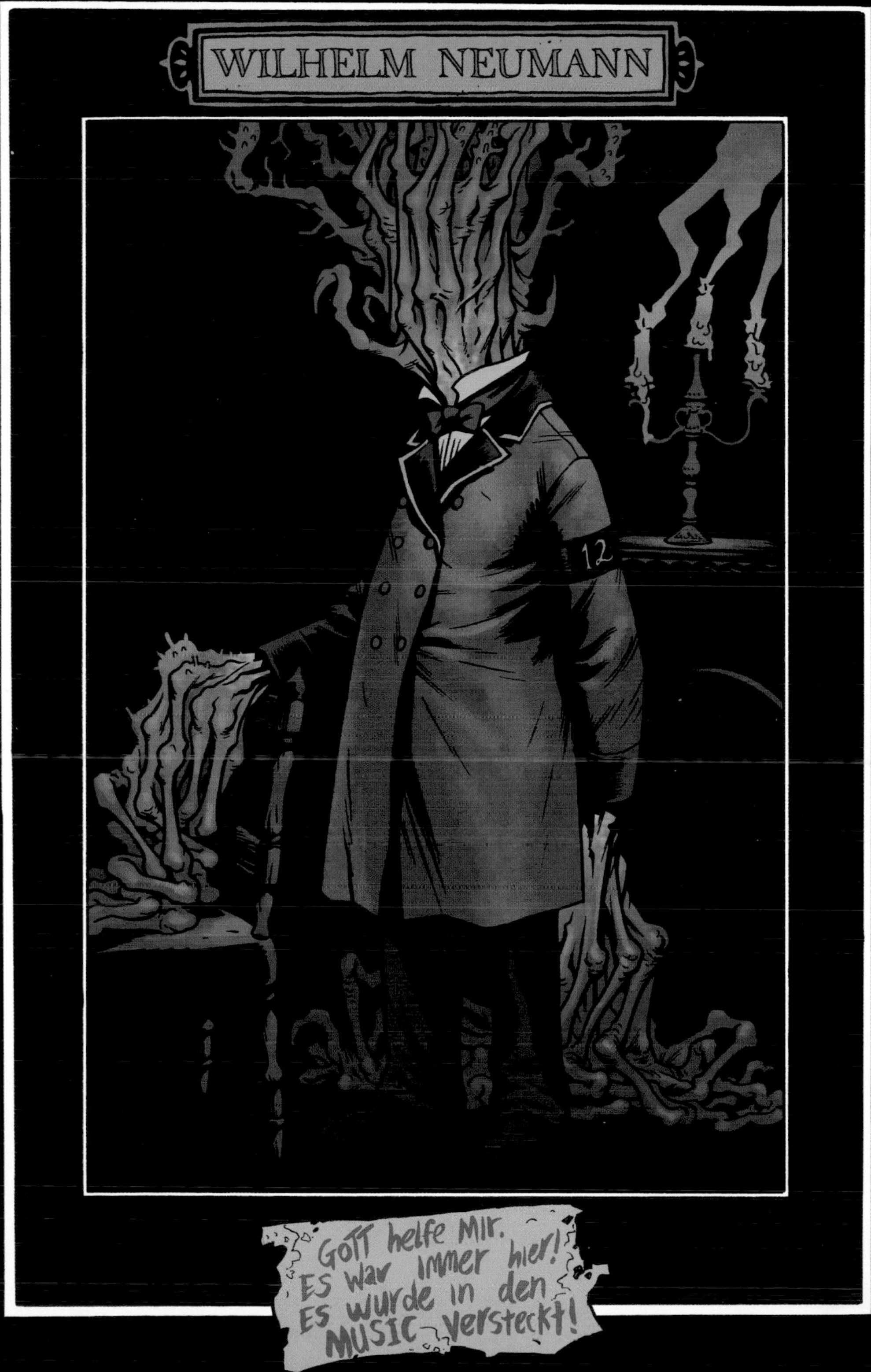
WILHELM NEUMANN
12
GOTT helfe Mir.
Es war immer hier!
Es wurde in den
MUSIC versteckt!

Also by

MIKE MIGNOLA

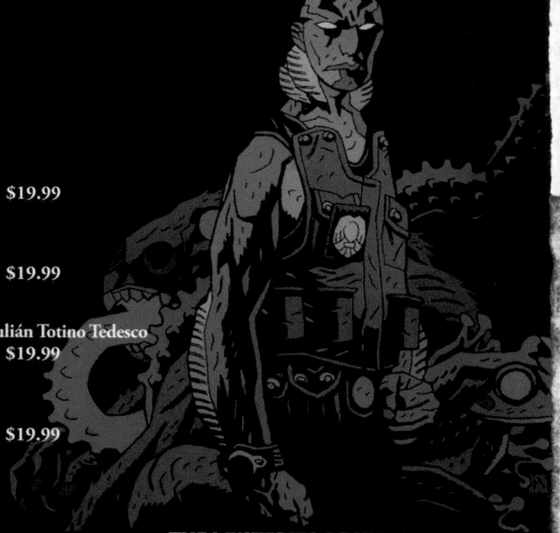

B.P.R.D.

PLAGUE OF FROGS
Volume 1
with Chris Golden, Guy Davis, and others
HC: ISBN 978-1-59582-609-1 | $34.99
TPB: ISBN 978-1-59582-675-6 | $19.99

Volume 2
with John Arcudi, Davis, and others
HC: ISBN 978-1-59582-672-5 | $34.99
TPB: ISBN 978-1-59582-676-3 | $24.99

Volume 3
with Arcudi and Davis
HC: ISBN 978-1-59582-860-6 | $34.99
TPB: ISBN 978-1-61655-622-8 | $24.99

Volume 4
with Arcudi and Davis
HC: ISBN 978-1-59582-974-0 | $34.99
TPB: ISBN 978-1-61655-641-9 | $24.99

1946–1948
with Joshua Dysart, Paul Azaceta, Fábio Moon, Gabriel Bá, Max Fiumara, and Arcudi
ISBN 978-1-61655-646-4 | $34.99

BEING HUMAN
with Scott Allie, Arcudi, Davis, and others
ISBN 978-1-59582-756-2 | $17.99

VAMPIRE
with Moon and Bá
ISBN 978-1-61655-196-4 | $19.99

B.P.R.D. HELL ON EARTH

NEW WORLD
with Arcudi and Davis
ISBN 978-1-59582-707-4 | $19.99

GODS AND MONSTERS
with Arcudi, Davis, and Tyler Crook
ISBN 978-1-59582-822-4 | $19.99

RUSSIA
with Arcudi, Crook, and Duncan Fegredo
ISBN 978-1-59582-946-7 | $19.99

THE DEVIL'S ENGINE AND THE LONG DEATH
with Arcudi, Crook, and James Harren
ISBN 978-1-59582-981-8 | $19.99

THE PICKENS COUNTY HORROR AND OTHERS
with Allie, Jason Latour, Harren, and Max Fiumara
ISBN 978-1-61655-140-7 | $19.99

THE RETURN OF THE MASTER
with Arcudi and Crook
ISBN 978-1-61655-193-3 | $19.99

A COLD DAY IN HELL
with Arcudi, Peter Snejbjerg, and Laurence Campbell
ISBN 978-1-61655-199-5 | $19.99

THE REIGN OF THE BLACK FLAME
with Arcudi and Harren
ISBN 978-1-61655-471-2 | $19.99

THE DEVIL'S WINGS
with Arcudi, Campbell, Joe Querio, and Crook
ISBN 978-1-61655-617-4 | $19.99

LAKE OF FIRE
with Arcudi and Crook
ISBN 978-1-61655-402-6 | $19.99

FLESH AND STONE
with Arcudi and Harren
ISBN 978-1-61655-762-1 | $19.99

METAMORPHOSIS
with Arcudi, Snejbjerg, and Julián Totino Tedesco
ISBN 978-1-61655-794-2 | $19.99

END OF DAYS
with Arcudi and Campbell
ISBN 978-1-61655-910-6 | $19.99

ABE SAPIEN

THE DROWNING
with Jason Shawn Alexander
ISBN 978-1-59582-185-0 | $17.99

THE DEVIL DOES NOT JEST AND OTHER STORIES
with Arcudi, Harren, and others
ISBN 978-1-59582-925-2 | $17.99

DARK AND TERRIBLE AND THE NEW RACE OF MAN
with Allie, Arcudi, Sebastián Fiumara, and Max Fiumara
ISBN 978-1-61655-284-8 | $19.99

THE SHAPE OF THINGS TO COME
with Allie, S. Fiumara, and M. Fiumara
ISBN 978-1-61655-443-9 | $19.99

SACRED PLACES
with Allie, S. Fiumara, and M. Fiumara
ISBN 978-1-61655-515-3 | $19.99

A DARKNESS SO GREAT
with Allie and M. Fiumara
ISBN 978-1-61655-656-3 | $19.99

THE SECRET FIRE
with Allie, S. Fiumara, and M. Fiumara
ISBN 978-1-61655-891-8 | $19.99

LOBSTER JOHNSON

THE IRON PROMETHEUS
with Jason Armstrong
ISBN 978-1-59307-975-8 | $17.99

THE BURNING HAND
with Arcudi and Tonci Zonjic
ISBN 978-1-61655-031-8 | $17.99

SATAN SMELLS A RAT
with Arcudi, Fiumara, Querio, Wilfredo Torres, and Kevin Nowlan
ISBN 978-1-61655-203-9 | $18.99

GET THE LOBSTER
with Arcudi and Zonjic
ISBN 978-1-61655-505-4 | $19.99

WITCHFINDER

IN THE SERVICE OF ANGELS
with Ben Stenbeck
ISBN 978-1-59582-483-7 | $17.99

LOST AND GONE FOREVER
with Arcudi and John Severin
ISBN 978-1-59582-794-4 | $17.99

THE MYSTERIES OF UNLAND
with Kim Newman, Maura McHugh, and Crook
ISBN 978-1-61655-630-3 | $19.99

FRANKENSTEIN UNDERGROUND

with Stenbeck
ISBN 978-1-61655-782-9 | $19.99

THE AMAZING SCREW-ON HEAD AND OTHER CURIOUS OBJECTS

ISBN 978-1-59582-501-8 | $17.99

BALTIMORE

THE PLAGUE SHIPS
with Golden and Stenbeck
ISBN 978-1-59582-677-0 | $24.99

THE CURSE BELLS
with Golden and Stenbeck
ISBN 978-1-59582-674-9 | $24.99

A PASSING STRANGER AND OTHER STORIES
with Golden and Stenbeck
ISBN 978-1-61655-182-7 | $24.99

CHAPEL OF BONES
with Golden and Stenbeck
ISBN 978-1-61655-328-9 | $24.99

THE APOSTLE AND THE WITCH OF HARJU
with Golden, Stenbeck, and Peter Bergting
ISBN 978-1-61655-618-1 | $24.99

THE CULT OF THE RED KING
with Golden and Bergting
ISBN 978-1-61655-821-5 | $24.99

NOVELS

LOBSTER JOHNSON: THE SATAN FACTORY
with Thomas E. Sniegoski
ISBN 978-1-59582-203-1 | $12.95

JOE GOLEM AND THE DROWNING CITY
with Golden
ISBN 978-1-59582-971-9 | $99.99

BALTIMORE; OR, THE STEADFAST TIN SOLDIER & THE VAMPIRE
with Golden and Stenbeck
ISBN 978-1-61655-803-1 | $12.99

AVAILABLE AT YOUR LOCAL COMICS SHOP OR BOOKSTORE! • To find a comics shop in your area, call 1-888-266-4226.
For more information or to order direct visit DarkHorse.com or call 1-800-862-0052 Mon.–Fri. 9 AM to 5 PM Pacific Time.
Prices and availability subject to change without notice.

DARK HORSE BOOKS
DarkHorse.com